People
of the
Nightland

2007

BY W. MICHAEL GEAR AND KATHLEEN O'NEAL GEAR FROM TOM DOHERTY ASSOCIATES

NORTH AMERICA'S FORGOTTEN PAST SERIES

People of the Wolf　　　*People of the Silence*
People of the Fire　　　　*People of the Mist*
People of the Earth　　　*People of the Masks*
People of the River　　　*People of the Owl*
People of the Sea　　　　*People of the Raven*
People of the Lakes　　　*People of the Moon*
People of the Lightning　*People of the Weeping Eye* ★
People of the Nightland

THE ANASAZI MYSTERY SERIES

The Visitant
The Summoning God
Bone Walker

BY KATHLEEN O'NEAL GEAR

Thin Moon and Cold Mist　*It Sleeps in Me*
Sand in the Wind　　　　*It Wakes in Me*
This Widowed Land　　　*It Dreams in Me* ★

BY W. MICHAEL GEAR

Long Ride Home　　　*Coyote Summer*
Big Horn Legacy　　　*Athena Factor*
The Morning River

OTHER TITLES BY KATHLEEN O'NEAL GEAR AND W. MICHAEL GEAR

Dark Inheritance
Raising Abel
To Cast a Pearl ★

★Forthcoming

www.Gear-Gear.com

People
of the
Nightland

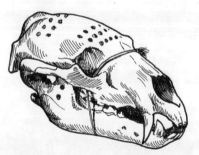

W. Michael Gear
and
Kathleen O'Neal Gear

A Tom Doherty Associates Book
New York

PEOPLE OF THE NIGHTLAND

Copyright © 2007 by W. Michael Gear and Kathleen O'Neal Gear

This book is printed on acid-free paper.

A Forge Book
Published by Tom Doherty Associates, LLC
175 Fifth Avenue
New York, NY 10010

www.tor.com

Forge® is a registered trademark of Tom Doherty Associates, LLC.

Library of Congress Cataloging-in-Publication Data

Gear, W. Michael.
    People of the nightland / W. Michael Gear and Kathleen O'Neal Gear.—1st ed.
        p. cm.
    "A Tom Doherty Associates Book."
    ISBN-13: 978-0-765-31440-6 (alk. paper)
    ISBN-10: 0-765-31440-1 (alk. paper)
    1. Prehistoric peoples—Fiction. 2. Glacial epoch—Fiction. I. Gear, Kathleen O'Neal. II. Title.

PS3557.E19P1937 2007
813'.54—dc22

                                                                        2006051136

First Edition: March 2007

Printed in the United States of America

0 9 8 7 6 5 4 3 2 1

To Pia, Nebi, Keeza, Wyatt, Slipper and Nononi,
Little Snowbear, Golden Boy, Little Blue, and Morgan,
our orphans,
for teaching us that the way to the Great Mystery is not
through singing or dancing, not through reading or praying . . .
it comes from giving life to those who need it.

All of you have given us life in abundance.

Mitakuye oyasin.

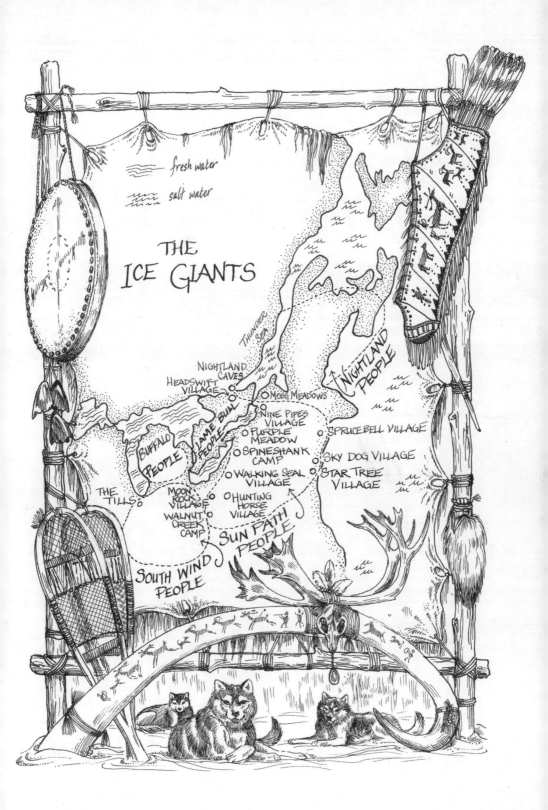

fresh water

salt water

THE
ICE GIANTS

THUNDER SEA

NIGHTLAND CAVES

HEADSWIFT VILLAGE

NIGHTLAND PEOPLE

MOSS MEADOWS

NINE PIPES VILLAGE

SPRUCEBELL VILLAGE

LAME BULL PEOPLE

PURPLE MEADOW

BUFFALO PEOPLE

SPINESHANK CAMP

SKY DOG VILLAGE

WALKING SEAL VILLAGE

STAR TREE VILLAGE

THE TILLS

MOON ROCK VILLAGE

HUNTING HORSE VILLAGE

WALNUT CREEK CAMP

SUN PATH PEOPLE

SOUTH WIND PEOPLE

Foreword

For the most part, global warming is cyclical, as is global cooling. This discovery was first articulated by Serbian mathematician Milutin Milankovitch in 1930 when he published his classic work *Mathematical Climatology and the Astronomical Theory of Climate Change.*

Milankovitch's theory was relatively straightforward. He said that Ice Ages occurred when variations in the Earth's orbit and axis caused the northern hemisphere to receive less sunshine in the summer, and that these short summers failed to melt the snow and ice that had accumulated on the continents during the winter. The result was that the growing white patches on the face of the Earth reflected sunlight away from the planet, causing it to cool, and as the white expanses grew each year, reflecting more and more sunlight, they triggered Ice Ages.

Milankovitch proposed three reasons for this process:

First, he said, every year the Earth's orbit around the sun changed slightly. This cycle took about 100,000 years, but when the Earth was farthest from the sun, the planet naturally grew colder.

Second, he said the angle of the Earth's axis was not constant. The tilt varied between twenty-two and twenty-four degrees. At its maximum tilt, which occurred every 41,000 years, the North Pole received much less sunlight, which led to an accumulation of glacial ice.

Third, he noted that the Earth wobbled on its axis, toward and away from the sun over a span of 19,000 and 23,000 years. These small variations changed how much sunlight each hemisphere received.

As a result, Milankovitch predicted that Ice Ages would peak every 100,000 years and 41,000 years, and that the Earth would undergo small "blips" every 19,000 and 23,000 years.

Today, after countless scientific studies in paleoclimatology, we know that Milankovitch was right.

There *are* slow and regular variations in the Earth's orbit and axis that result in Ice Ages—ten in the last million years.

The Pleistocene Ice Age is divided into three periods, Early, Middle, and Late. The Late Pleistocene began with a global warming episode called the Sangamonian, which lasted from about 135,000 years ago to around 115,000 years ago. That warm period was followed by an episode of glaciation called, in North America, the Wisconsin glaciation.

At the peak of this glacial episode, 20,000 years ago, ice covered most of Canada and extended south into the United States as far as Iowa and central Illinois. The largest glacier, the Laurentide ice sheet, was almost three miles thick over Hudson's Bay. The immense weight of the glacier depressed the Earth's crust more than 3,250 feet below its current elevation.

Glaciers are not static or "dead." Each is a constantly churning ecosystem. The ice is banded with silt, sand, gravel, and rocks that have been scraped up from the Earth. The very weight of the ice makes it plastic, with the lower regions squeezing out at the sides. Water melting at the surface rushes down through fissures, boring a honeycomb of caves. Twenty thousand years ago most of this water flowed directly into the ocean down the Mississippi River drainage. Icebergs also calved into the Atlantic and along an extension of the Gulf of St. Lawrence, called the Champlain Sea by paleoclimatologists (Thunder Sea in *People of the Nightland*). The Champlain Sea, a body of saltwater, extended as far west as modern Hamilton, Ontario. Imagine seeing seals, walrus, and pilot whales in the water off Rochester, New York.

Then another global warming period began. These "interstadials," or periods of ice retreat and rising ocean temperatures, generally occur for the same reasons that global cooling occurs—shifts in the

Earth's orbit and axis. When the Earth moves closest to the sun in its orbit, the planet warms up. When the tilt of the axis reaches its minimum, summers are longer, glaciers melt, and air and ocean temperatures rise. Every system, however, experiences moments of chaos, episodes of "abrupt climate change," that don't obey these rules.

Starting 20,000 years ago, the Earth began to warm and the North American ice sheets began to melt. Everything was proceeding exactly as it should . . . until around 13,000 years ago.

The Younger Dryas Interval, a global cooling period that lasted from about 13,000 years ago to 11,650 years ago, is one of the most dramatic events in prehistory. Within a single decade, the Earth was knocked back into an Ice Age. The North Atlantic Deep Water Current, which warms Europe, stopped running, leaving the continent bitterly cold, and ocean levels rose a stunning eighty feet. The glaciers that had been in retreat for 7,000 years began advancing again.

The cause was simple: Meltwater from the Laurentide Ice Sheet was diverted from its main Mississippi River drainage to the Champlain Sea—today's St. Lawrence River.

What caused this diversion is not so simple. By 13,000 years ago, a gigantic meltwater lake had formed over parts of Manitoba, North Dakota, Minnesota, and Wisconsin. Lake Agassiz, named after nineteenth-century Swiss geologist Louis Agassiz, covered over 80,000 square miles. It held more water than the total contained in all the modern world's lakes. Beaches stretched from North Dakota northward to Manitoba. What is now Winnipeg was under 650 feet of water.

The Younger Dryas was kicked off when the water level in Lake Agassiz suddenly dropped by over 325 feet.

What caused the drop? One of the Earth's greatest cataclysms—which we will discuss further in the Afterword of this book.

For now, let's just say that human beings, people we call Paleo-Indians, witnessed it, and, in a very real sense, it was the end of their world.

Prologue

The site covered a low, rocky hillock overlooking a white frame farmhouse with accompanying silo. Puffy white clouds rose in the Canadian sky.

Two vehicles, a defiant red Dodge 2500 and a white Chevrolet Suburban, were parked beside the white canvas awning that sheltered tables, racks of paper sacks, boxes of ziplocks, and several plastic coolers.

The hilltop had been covered with a grid of yellow strings tied to one-by-two stakes driven into the rocky ground. Little squares had been dug past the black root zone and into rocky soil. In these, young people dressed in T-shirts and jeans shoveled, troweled, and finally screened the dirt they hauled up in buckets.

The door on the Dodge pickup was open, the radio talk show chattering on mindlessly about global warming.

Global warming, Dr. Maureen Cole thought as she stood up and stretched her tired back. For a student of prehistory, it was nothing new.

She studied the jumbled scatter of human bones revealed in the excavation unit at her feet. Six skulls—four male, two female—between the ages of twelve and thirty lay in pieces across the pit floor. Fragments of two femora, one articulated to a tibia, or shinbone, were

mixed in with the skulls. Part of a shattered pelvis was partially uncovered from its bed of sandy gravel.

The eerie thing was that the bone was battered, showing signs of
severe blunt-force trauma. She would have to take specimens back to
the lab to be sure, but to her practiced eye, the injuries appeared to
have been incurred perimortally—or at the time of death—when the
bone was still "green" or living.

As one of the world's leading forensic anthropologists, she had
spent her professional career identifying the dead and determining
the cause of death.

To Maureen, the remains at her feet reminded her of victims recovered from a crashed airplane. But, not having airplanes, how did
prehistoric peoples wind up looking like this?

Part of what she suspected was a human humerus, or arm bone,
was sticking up like a stake, its shaft broken and splintered.

Her mind knotted on the problem, she pulled the canteen from her
belt and took a long drink of water. Though she was thirty-nine, today
she felt twenty. The excitement of the rare archaeological find, and the
constant adrenaline high that accompanied it, had been keeping her
awake for five nights straight. If they kept uncovering more and more
bones, by the end of the week, she'd be stumbling around the excavation, ready to fall flat on her face.

She used her sleeve to mop sweat from her tanned brow. Tall for a
woman, she had traditional Iroquoian features. Her mother, a full-
blooded Seneca, had given her wide cheekbones, dark eyes, and long
jet-black hair. The firm chin and straight nose came from her father.
She wore a tan pair of chinos and a pale yellow T-shirt splotched with
dirt. Moccasins, handmade in the American Southwest, clad her feet.
She had discovered that in her work as a physical anthropologist the
soft leather did less damage to the fragile archaeological sites she was
called in to examine.

Maureen heaved a sigh and looked around at the ten excavation
units filled with archaeologists. A soft murmur filled the air. Every
voice held a reverence, as though they were excavating an ancient
church, rather than a massive bone bed of partially disarticulated human skeletons.

She started walking around the site perimeter, looking into each
unit to see what had been revealed in the past two hours while she'd
been excavating the skulls.

A cool breeze blew through the forest, fluttering the tree leaves and lessening the July heat. She studied the nearby maple, ash, red cedar, and sumac as she walked. The many shades of green looked magical against the cloud-strewn blue sky.

As she approached the ramada they'd set up as a workstation—the place where people labeled and sorted the bags that held bones, artifacts, pollen, and charcoal samples—she saw Dusty Stewart break away from a conversation he'd been having with Jim Miller, the geomorphologist, and hurry toward her.

Tall and blond, with broad shoulders and blue eyes, he had one of those perfect male faces that drew women's gazes from half a block away. But only when he was clean—which he certainly wasn't today. Streaks of dirt and sweat stains mottled his white T-shirt emblazoned with the words, "Eat More Buffalo! Fifty Million Indians Can't Be Wrong!" Blue-tinted sunglasses rode low on his nose.

He strode up to her and blurted, "We just got back the first radiocarbon dates."

Almost breathless, she said, "And?"

A faint smile curled his lips. It must be good. He hesitated just long enough to madden her, before he said, "Eleven thousand two hundred radiocarbon years, plus or minus three hundred."

"My God," she whispered, "that means . . . around thirteen thousand actual years after calibration. Dusty, we're excavating a thirteen-*thousand*-year-old site!"

Most people thought that radiocarbon years—that is, the carbon 14 dates—gave an accurate age for a site. But that wasn't entirely true. Since the amount of carbon 14 that reached the Earth had varied over time, all such dates had to be calibrated, or adjusted to ascertain the actual number of calendar years. So, if the C14 date came back at around 10,000 years before present, the real age of the site was around 11,700 years. If it came back at 11,000 C14 years before present, the site was, in reality, around 13,000 years old.

He nodded, let out a breath, and turned serious eyes on her. "Yeah, interesting, huh?" He scanned the blue shimmering expanse of the Ottawa River to the north. Birds circled over the water's surface.

She gave him her narrow-eyed disdainful glare. "That has to be the understatement of the year. We've uncovered at least twenty-two bodies—so far—and you call it 'interesting'? This is the largest and oldest Paleo burial ground ever found and you—"

"Don't say 'burial ground.'" He waved a dirty finger at her. "We don't have any evidence to suggest these people were buried. I've excavated a lot of burials. These don't look right."

"How's that?"

"The bones are too random."

"Maybe they were processed that way for mortuary reasons?"

He made a face. "Like for secondary bundle burials? There would be cut marks on the bones where the tendons and sinew were severed. And the long bones we've found so far all have lateral and greenstick fractures, like they were snapped and crushed."

"Airplane crash," she muttered under her breath.

Dusty gave her a disgusted look. "Back to why it's not a burial: When you look at the soils around the bone, there's no change in coloration or texture. Burials are generally intrusive. That means you disturb the dirt when you dig a hole, drop in a body, and backfill it."

"Maybe they were just left on the surface?"

He grinned. "You need to spend more time with a trowel, lady." He pointed at a fragment of human rib sticking up from the closest pit. "Burials are orderly affairs. Bodies are laid out with prescribed ritual behaviors. The bone we've found so far is oriented every which way. Up, down, there's no method to it. This just looks . . . well, random."

Maureen blinked. "But artifacts surround the remains. Surely they're grave goods."

Dusty thoughtfully smoothed his blond beard with his hand. "I don't think so."

"Okay. Enlighten me."

"In burials, people tend to keep the same bones with the individual."

"You don't know much about Iroquoian culture do you? We have a rather spectacular ceremonial called the Feast of the Dead."

"And you're saying . . . ?"

She folded her arms and scowled at him. He was an American archaeologist who worked primarily in the Four Corners region of Colorado, Utah, New Mexico, and Arizona. There was no reason he ought to have heard of the Feast of the Dead. It's just that she always expected more of him than she did other archaeologists—most of whom knew a great deal about tiny bits of 10,000-year-old fire-cracked rock, and next to nothing about historical aboriginal cultures.

"All right, listen," she explained. "The Feast of the Dead was by far the most important ceremony for the Huron tribe. At the feast, the bodies of all those who had not died violent deaths were removed from temporary raised tombs and interred in a common grave. The mingling of the bones was believed to release the souls of the dead and allow them to travel westward to the Village of Souls. Basically, Feast of the Dead graves are big bone pits." She extended a hand to their site.

Dusty kept his gaze fixed on her face. "Any evidence of it being practiced prehistorically?"

"Absolutely. At the Fairty ossuary near the Robb site just outside of Toronto, there were five hundred bodies and they . . ." Her voice faded.

He cocked his head, a blond eyebrow rising in amusement. "Have a problem with that, do you?"

"I just remembered that there were almost no artifacts found at the Fairty ossuary. Just one stone scraper and one shell bead, if I recall correctly. Offerings really aren't found in Iroquoian burials until the historic period."

"You lab rats are all alike. If the Huron did it historically, of course it had to be the same thirteen *thousand* years ago. Maureen, we're talking about the end of the Pleistocene! You talk about global warming? Wow! Look around. Everything you see was different. This was the edge of the ice . . . or close to it. These people we're uncovering were hunter-gatherers, not sedentary corn farmers like the Huron. That's like comparing squash and kiwis."

She gave him the disdainful glare again. It was an old competition between them: his expertise and hers.

He frowned out at the site. "Come here. Let me show you something we just uncovered. Maybe you can make sense of it."

She followed him through the patchwork of excavation units to a two-by-two-meter unit and crouched on the lip next to Dusty.

"Hey, guys," Dusty said to the archaeologists, students from McGill University, "why don't you take a break. Maureen and I have some serious confabbing to do."

"Oh, jeez, do we have to?" Brandon O'Neal, an olive-skinned youth with brown hair said. He'd proven to be especially talented at excavation, wielding the trowel like a surgeon's scalpel. Someday, if he stuck with it, he'd make a great archaeologist.

"Yeah," Dusty ordered, "I don't want you to hear Maureen correcting me. Get out of here."

Brandon grinned. He and his friend, Richard, climbed out of the pit and headed for the ramada, where ice chests filled with cold drinks sat in the shade.

Dusty pointed. "Do you see the sediment in the northern half of the unit? That's what we call an unsorted deposit."

Maureen nodded. "When water moves it carries different-sized sand, grit, and stone, based on the hydraulic carrying capacity."

"Right. As the water slows, the heaviest pieces fall out. Floods move boulders; slow-moving water only carries fine silt and clay."

"So, this is a river channel?" She looked around. "Up here on this high spot?"

"Nope. I said this is *unsorted*. Rocks, gravels, and sands are all mixed up. Just like these battered bones. Jim Miller, the geomorphologist, arrived this morning. He said that around 11,000 BC this was the edge of the Laurentide Ice Sheet. It ran right through our site." He pointed at the low hills. "All of this was terminal moraine. You see those giant boulders over by the trees?"

She turned her eyes to huge rounded rocks surrounded by sumac.

"Those," Dusty told her, "were dropped by the ice. The rest of the deposit here is mixed, the soil overlying it was formed over the last thirteen thousand years as weather and plants broke down the rock."

She studied the jumble of sand and gravel. The rounded side of a boulder stuck out of the far corner of the unit. "I don't get it. That means our people were living practically on top of the ice."

He pulled his sunglasses down and stared at her over the rims. "Or maybe *in* the ice."

"What are you talking about?"

He made an airy gesture with his hand. "Well, historically, arctic and subarctic peoples used whatever natural shelter they could find. Keep in mind, thirteen thousand years ago, one lobe of the Champlain Sea came all the way inland to about where Ottawa sits today." He pointed to the east. "Another lobe ran across what is now Lake Ontario all the way to Hamilton, and still a third lobe of the sea ran down to the south of Burlington, Vermont. If you—"

"Get to the point." He had a tendency to be wordy. If she didn't stop him, he'd soon be expounding on the density of the seawater that filled the Champlain Sea at the end of the Pleistocene. "You said they were living *in* the ice."

"Oh, right," he said. "What I meant is that, like all peoples around the globe who live in icy wildernesses, these people may have been living in the natural meltwater caves that dotted the edges of the glacier. It would have been good protection from the wind and weather."

She shivered at the thought. "Give me a tent in the sagebrush any day."

As her eyes scanned the bones in the unit, some oddity struck her. "Dusty, I know we've barely opened this site, but this pit contains only bone fragments and a scatter of broken stone tools."

"Yeah, and a couple of bone awls . . . over there in back." He pointed.

"Maybe not an airplane crash."

She turned around to look at the southern excavation units. An idea was crystallizing in her head, a picture of what might explain the curious distribution of bones and artifacts they were seeing.

"Global warming?" she asked absently as CBC blared out a Tim Horton's commercial.

"Are you going somewhere with this?" He shoved his sunglasses up on his nose again and studied her through the blue-tinted lenses.

"What happens when glaciers melt?" She looked down into the pit in front of them.

His bushy blond brows drew together over his straight nose. He rose to his feet and stared off to the north; then she watched his gaze move methodically from one excavation unit to the next, mentally reviewing what each contained. "In this case, there was a lot of water."

"I've seen this before." She stood beside him. A new adrenaline rush stirred her veins.

He was watching her with that old familiar intensity. "Last time I saw you look like this was when you were trying to convince that Bureau of Reclamation guy in New Mexico that a bunch of skeletons died as a result of starvation."

"I would have been right, too, if I had been allowed to do the research." She nodded soberly, seeing it unfold in her mind.

"Mind telling me what you're thinking?"

"Flood." She nodded, making sense of it all. "A lot of rushing water. Battered bodies"—she glanced at him—"unsorted deposits."

He was grinning at her, a warmth in his eyes that left her off balance. "We're quite the team, you and me."

She felt her heart skip. "How do we prove this?"

"Well, I could buy you dinner tonight. Maybe share a bottle of wine and—"

"The *archaeology,* Stewart. How do we prove that?"

Though his offer had definite attractions, they never could seem to get their relationship off the ground.

He watched her through veiled eyes, as if struggling to say something important. Finally, he shrugged, and said, "Why don't we test your hypothesis by opening a couple of one-by-twos in the middle of the site? What do you think?"

"Go for it. You do the digging, Jim Miller can do the geomorph, and I'll do the bones." Then she grinned. "And, maybe dinner. But no wine. You know I don't drink. And if you empty the bottle, you'll do something dumb again."

"Me? Dumb? When it comes to my favorite beautiful woman?"

"Remember why I left New Mexico last time?" she asked archly.

"Okay, so I shouldn't have called you a pinheaded academic." Dusty turned, cupped a hand to his mouth, and called, "Brandon? Come here. I have a great new project for you."

Maureen was staring at the fragments of bone. They had been people—thinking, feeling human beings like her.

What must it have been like? Where they really living inside *the ice? Then, what let loose the flood? And what would have crushed the bodies so badly?*

One

THE WINTER OF ICEBACKED MAMMOTHS . . .

His name was Ti-Bish. Most people called him "the Idiot." He huddled in the lee of the snowdrift and stared out at the pine and spruce trees that rose like dark spears to threaten the star-glazed night sky. Wind Woman howled over the peaks of the Ice Giants and thrashed the dark forests, whipping branches back and forth. A camp of the Nine Pipes band of Sunpath People—down the hill in front of him— lay quiet and still. The people slept warmly in their conical lodges made from pole frames and covered with hides. Ti-Bish could hear the snoring. Somewhere on the far side of the village, a baby whimpered. He didn't see any dogs. It was cold, very cold. The people must have brought the dogs into their lodges for the night.

"They're asleep," he murmured to himself. "All asleep. No one will see me."

A tall gawky man with a boyish face and two long black braids, he had seen ten and nine summers. He pulled his bearskin cape more tightly around his skinny body, and hunched against the cold. Doing so pulled the straps tight on the floppy hide pack that hung down his back.

On the wind, he heard the rasping sound of feathers shredding air.

A bird? At this time of night? He craned his neck to look up. No great bird darkened the stars, but the constellation known as Horn Spoon Village had climbed high into the sky. At this time of year, it indicated that morning would be several hands of time behind the eastern horizon.

Surely no one would be awake at this time. No one would come outside, even if they heard a slight noise.

He rose and picked his way down the hill, carefully placing his snowshoes. They were made from willow hoops laced with rawhide and bound to his moccasins. If he slipped on the ice beneath the dusting of snow, he would tumble down the hill like a thrown rock. At that commotion, however, the entire village would wake and come looking for the intruder.

He eased into a spruce grove. Amid the dark branches, needles rattled and he could smell human waste. Snow had piled around the trunks. The shadowed hollows of the drifts gleamed dark blue, while the cornices shone purple.

He listened for ten heartbeats, then carefully picked his way down the slope toward the shell midden.

The people of Nine Pipes Village collected freshwater mussels from the nearby lakes and rivers. He lifted his nose and could smell the new shells they'd thrown on the midden.

"No one will care," he whispered. "They've already eaten their fill."

He crept closer and heard something pecking. Talons scratched on shell.

Ti-Bish cocked his head. He had a sudden affinity for the scavenging night bird. "We are all the same when it comes to hunger," he whispered softly, feeling the rightness of it.

He removed his mitten, pulled his pack around, and felt inside. His cold fingers located one of the stones, and he pulled out his bolo, a contraption of three rocks that dangled from thongs. The light of the Blessed Star People reflected from the snow with a faint pale glow. He might be able to see well enough to ensnare an owl. The thought of warm meat made his empty belly moan.

Wings flapped again.

He crept downwind of the shell midden, praying Wind Woman would keep his scent from the owl. When he reached the edge of the midden, the shells glittered faintly in the starlight. He got down and crawled forward with the silence of a dire wolf on a hunt.

A caw erupted, then several more.

Ti-Bish frowned. A raven? Scavenging in the middle of the night? He'd never seen or heard of such a thing. Perhaps the bird, too, was starving?

He fought the urge to rise, to rush around the midden and cast his bolo in one desperate gamble for food. No, way too risky. Ravens were very smart.

Sliding forward on his belly, Ti-Bish could see the bird feasting on the fresh shells at the base of the midden. The raven was big, black as night, with eyes that glowed silver in the star gleam.

Raven stood on a mussel shell, grasping it with his feet, and used his beak to tug out a stubborn bit of meat. Tossing his head back, he gobbled the morsel down, and went back for more.

Ti-Bish took a deep breath, rose on his knees, and judged the distance. He lifted his bolo by the center knot, letting the stones hang.

Raven stopped eating.

Ti-Bish froze.

Raven cocked his head and searched the midden for predators.

Ti-Bish waited, hoping his belly would not moan again and give away his position.

For long moments, he remained still, not even breathing, while Wind Woman battered the forest. Cold began to sting his exposed fingers. Raven's fears eased, and his black beak lowered to flip empty shells this way and that. The clawed feet skittered on the uncertain footing.

With the noise as cover, Ti-Bish drew back and flung his bolo. He put all his strength into the cast, hearing the thongs swish wickedly through the silent air. Raven let out a sharp cry, leaping up as the bolo caught him at midbody, pinning his wings to his sides. He flopped over, and cawed in terror. His frozen puff of breath hung in the air before it was swept away by the wind. Ti-Bish raced forward as Raven clawed to his feet and tried to run.

"Please, my brother, I'm starving!"

He chased Raven over the icy shells, his snowshoe-clad feet slipping and sliding. He made a mad leap, arms out, his body thumping in the snow. He caught a foot, pulled, and got a grip on a partially extended wing.

Raven squawked and pecked at Ti-Bish's fingers when they went tight around his black body.

"Forgive me, Brother," he said as he grasped Raven's neck and twisted, surprised at how strong the creature was. The feathers were warm against his chilled fingers, and for a moment, Ti-Bish marveled at the life pulsing under his grip. Then, with a final wrench, the vertebrae snapped.

Raven's body twitched and jerked, the wings desperate for the air. The feet kicked, and the long black beak clacked woodenly.

Ti-Bish sighed, sinking back on the snow. For a moment, all he could do was stroke the sleek black feathers. Glancing at the village, he half expected to see people ducking out of the lodges, hear dogs barking, and calls on the night.

The world had turned suddenly silent; even Wind Woman held her breath.

Raven is a Spirit Bird!

That memory sent a shiver up his spine. What would come of killing a Spirit animal? He could imagine the look of consternation on the faces of the Elders, see the horror reflected in their eyes.

But they dismissed me long ago. He stared down sadly at the raven, carefully stroking the feathers, marveling at the warmth beneath. He had never liked killing. The destruction of beauty had always upset him.

"Isn't there a better way, Raven? Do we have to kill to live?"

He unwound his bolo, stood, and carried his prize back to the forest. Behind the screen of trees, he nestled in the lee of the snowdrift, partially sheltered from Wind Woman as she resumed her relentless blow.

"I'm sorry I had to kill you, Raven," he whispered as he continued to pet the feathers. "But I'm starving, too. Thank you for your meat."

Drawing a stone knife from his belt pouch, he slit open the bird's belly and cut out the internal organs first. The heart, liver, and kidneys he ate in single gulps.

Ti-Bish drank the blood that had pooled in the stomach cavity and then peeled back the skin—feathers and all—and gently laid it to the side. Using his teeth, he tore the meat from the bones as fast as he could and swallowed it.

When he'd finished, he tucked Raven's bones into the empty skin and carried it to a nearby tree. When he found the right branch, he placed Raven in the crook where the bird's soul could see the sun rise. His people—the People of the Nightland—never left the bones of animals they'd hunted on the ground. To do so was disrespectful. If animals were killed with reverence, the creator, Old Man Above, would send a new body for them, and their Spirits would enter it and fly away again.

"Thank you, Brother," he said softly.

He leaned his forehead against the trunk of the tree and took a deep tired breath. He'd been scavenging this shell midden for several days, but had found little to chase away his hunger.

Yesterday, one of the Sunpath women had brought him food. She'd been kind and beautiful. He'd been hoping she would bring him more today, but she hadn't. He would linger in the area for perhaps another day, then move on.

Lethargic from the feast, he felt too tired to return to the lean-to he'd constructed far back in the forest. A raven had a lot of meat, and his belly was filled to bursting for the first time in several moons. The taste of it lay cloying and musky on the back of his tongue. He placed a hand to his belly as the first pangs lanced through him.

"Shouldn't have eaten so fast."

He walked back into the pines, found a big drift, and began scooping it out to create a snow cave. When he'd finished, he crawled through the narrow doorway and curled on his side. Beyond the entry, snow whirled and gusted across the ground.

He pulled his pack close, wondering what he'd do in case Grandmother Lion or Brother Short-faced Bear also came to scavenge the shell midden. With the strength of Raven's blood warming his belly, he fell into an exhausted sleep.

The Dreaming crept up from the cold ground and twined icy fingers around his body. . . .

In the Dreaming, he and Raven flew side by side over jagged ice peaks that seemed to go on forever. Deep crevasses rent the ice in places, and long cracks zigzagged away from them like dark lightning bolts. Here, in the Dreaming, he was no longer a weak man. He flew behind Raven with his own black glittering wings.

"Look!" Raven said, and tucked his wings, plummeting downward toward a gaping hole in the ice. "Do you see it?"

Ti-Bish dropped toward the cavern and floated beside Raven on the cool currents that blew up from the darkness. The air smelled of moss and algae. Water gushed from the mouth of a tunnel, carrying sand and gravel out in a black stream that ran along a fissure, only to be swallowed by the ice again. Groans and squeals could be heard, as though the Ice Giants were being squeezed and crushed.

Raven tucked his wings yet again and dove. Like a cast dart, he shot through the tunnel mouth into utter darkness.

Frightened, Ti-Bish followed.

Deep in the belly of the Ice Giants, light glowed, pale and flickering. "This is the way," Raven said. "Follow me."

He flapped over a great dark lake streaked with a phosphorescent brilliance, as though the fish themselves left sinuous trails of light through the water.

"Through there," Raven said, and flew up the shore. "Do you see it?"

Raven sailed along the lakeshore, swooping down occasionally to examine the gigantic bones of monsters that eroded from the ice. A trail wove around the ancient skeletons—*a Monster Bone Trail*—and here and there Ti-Bish saw the skeletal bodies of dead humans.

Raven soared to where a wide river spilled out into the fiery lake. For a moment the great bird hovered on the draft. Raven shot a look over his wing, meeting Ti-Bush's surprised gaze; then, with a caw that sounded like laughter, Raven dove into the cavelike opening.

Ti-Bish, squealing in fear, sailed after him.

Only the sound of Raven's flapping wings led him through the blackness. On each side the Ice Giants chittered and cackled. Often their deep groans were loud enough to scare Ti-Bish's Spirit from his body. He flew harder, trying to catch up with the ever-elusive Raven.

For what seemed an eternity they flew through a quaking, moaning world of darkness. The first twinkle of light might have been an illusion, a thing of desperation. No more than a pinprick, it beckoned, luring him forward.

"This is the way," Raven said. "You must be the guide who leads the people this way."

Emerging from the hole, the effect was as if the Ice Giants split wide. They flew out into a dark sky filled with thousands of Star People. Far beneath them, herds of mammoth, long-horned buffalo, and caribou grazed together along the shore of a vast ocean.

"What is this place?"

"This is the land of the Long Dark . . . the place you heard of in stories told by the Elders."

"The land Wolf Dreamer led the people away from so long ago?"

Fear slipped away like elk's winter coat in spring, and Ti-Bish flew wild and free, darting and diving after Raven, who flipped over onto his back and plummeted straight down toward a long-horned buffalo.

Raven alighted on Buffalo's hump. Ti-Bish hesitated, aware of Raven's mocking eye as he backed air, and dropped worriedly onto the buffalo's back. The thick fur compressed under his taloned feet. The animal's massive shoulders rolled up and down as it walked through belly-deep grass.

Raven said, "Buffalo shows you the way. Just as I have. If I'd flown here, to the Long Dark, where there is plenty to eat, I wouldn't have needed to scavenge the shell midden, and you wouldn't have had to kill me. My life is a gift. Use it to grow strong so that you can guide our people back to this paradise."

Ti-Bish burrowed down into Buffalo's thick fur and sighed. Had he ever enjoyed anything so warm and soft? In the distance, he saw mammoth calves running and trumpeting, playing in the starlight. Caribou stood in ponds, moss hanging from their antlers; and high overhead, crimson waves of light rolled across fluttering curtains of green and blue: the brilliant fires of the Monster Children's war that never ceased.

"This was ours once," Raven said. "Before Wolf Dreamer led our people through the ice. But you can lead them back."

"I can?"

"The world is changing. People are turning on each other. Even the Ice Giants moan and wail. You must not fear the conflict, but embrace it, for it will strengthen the people." Raven was watching him with a knowing eye. "It will be difficult, and many will call you a fool."

"They already do." He hated being known as the Idiot.

"You must only believe." Raven paused. "Finally, you must seek out Nashat."

"He hates me. And I've only seen him once since he returned from the south."

"He will lead the Nightland Council soon. He will understand your value. And, finally, you must have him bring the Sunpath woman known as Skimmer to you. Only through you will she believe in me."

"Skimmer?" His heart warmed as he remembered the Nine Pipes woman who had shared her food with him.

"She is my legacy, Ti-Bish. The future of the Dream." The world seemed to shrink, growing ever smaller. "And you must be good to her."

The last thing Ti-Bish remembered was Raven's gleaming eye. The sensation was as if he were falling into it. Dropping into an endless darkness . . .

Two

What is the difference between madness and inspiration? Deputy War Chief Keresa pondered that as she crouched before her group of warriors. She was tall, with long black hair braided behind her head. She clutched a slim atlatl in her right hand; a long war dart was nocked in the throwing stick's hook. Using the stick as a catapult, she could launch the dart with enough force to drive it clear through a man. A thick bearhide vest snugged her chest, its tight fit accenting the swell of her breasts. She wore hunting pants belted at the waist where her war club hung. Tall moccasins rose to her knees.

The trap they were about to spring might be the way to finally break the Sunpath People. She glanced back at the Sunpath traitor, Goodeagle, who had dropped a sudden shining opportunity into their very laps.

She hated the man. The revulsion was instinctual. Something was wrong about him. Perhaps he was just too pretty to measure up to her opinion of what a man should be.

She turned her attention back to Walking Seal Village where it lay in the hollow below them, and wondered again if this was crazy. But many of her notions and actions were considered strange. Not many women dedicated themselves to war, but she had learned early on that her soul was different, perhaps more male than female. She had always preferred the hunt and the arts of war to those of the camp, cooking, and the care of children.

She glanced across at Kakala, high war chief of the Nightland People and her best friend. His body was squat and thickly muscled, the face marred by scars that draped over his round cheeks and flat nose. He had risen from disgrace and despair to become the Nightland People's greatest warrior. Despite being hard-used by life, fate, and the war trail, those piercing brown eyes would soften on those rare occasions when he let his true soul shine through. He was tough, and deadly in war, and the warriors who followed him worshipped the very ground he trod.

Today, even Kakala looked worried as he shot wary sidelong glances at the traitor. Behind him, his warriors seemed to have no such misgivings, but crouched in the snow, atlatls and darts ready. Their wolfish eyes betrayed the lust for battle.

Keresa considered that as she raised her head past the snowcapped ridge and looked at Walking Seal Village. But for the smoke rising from the hide-covered lodges, it might have been abandoned. The winterbare oaks around it lent the place a forlorn look—as if oaks could feel sorrow that Deputy War Chief Karigi and his warriors waited in the great ceremonial lodge.

A poisoned bait in the center of the trap we've laid.

Cocking her head, she could hear voices from below, some shouting happily: noise to make things appear normal. But would canny old Windwolf fall for it? She shot another uneasy glance at the traitor.

Is this really what you wanted, Goodeagle?

The traitor crouched, looking anything but eager. His too-pretty and sensitive face did little to conceal the anxiety plaguing his soul. At the moment, his dark eyes were fixed on the snow before him, pouting lips working. The jaw muscles behind his smooth cheeks kept knotting like frantic mice. Lines of worry incised his normally smooth brow.

Yes, she thought, *you'd better torture yourself over what you've done.*

She glanced back at Walking Seal Village, aware that her own soul was in turmoil. She had always liked Windwolf, enemy that he had become. They had been friendly, if wary, adversaries before the coming of the Guide and the rise of Councilor Nashat.

She glanced down at her slim hand where it clutched the atlatl. In days past—before the Guide—the Nightland, Sunpath, and Lame Bull Peoples had coexisted for the most part. War had been different then, consisting of raids that arose over petty grievances, or boundary disputes. Generally, after each side had proven its valor, peace would be brokered by a third party, Trading would occur, and a mutually satisfactory conclusion would be negotiated between the warring bands.

Then Councilman Nashat had embraced the Guide, and her world had changed. She remembered the laughter and amusement when Nashat first brought the Guide out to address the summer gathering. People snickered and laughed behind their hands, wondering what foolishness the Idiot would spout. He'd been the butt of jokes for years, only to leave, wandering the land like a lost dog, scavenging for scraps left by other peoples.

Then Nashat had brought him back, treating him not only with honor, but insisting that he address the four clans of the Nightland Peoples.

The laughter and jeers had only lasted for moments after Ti-Bish began to speak. Something in his eyes, in the awed pronunciation of his words, had captivated the audience. He had spoken with passion and belief, as he related a vision given to him by the Spirit of Raven Hunter himself.

She had sat amazed, glancing skeptically at the people around her. The Guide's lilting words—delivered with such conviction—had even swayed her soul. She might have believed herself, but for a chance glance in Nashat's direction.

The Councilor had no ears for Ti-Bish or his vision; he had been fixed on the people, his eyes gleaming with a delighted satisfaction, a cagey excitement betrayed by his cunning expression. Nashat kept knotting his fist, almost shaking it victoriously, the way a warrior would after a perfectly executed raid.

Then, at the end, when Ti-Bish finished, and before the people could crowd around, Nashat had bundled the man up, and hurried him away to the ice caves, claiming Ti-Bish needed time to think, to ponder, and commune with Raven Hunter himself.

That evening had changed everything. Four days later, the Council—composed of the four clan Elders, including Nashat—had called for war.

For two moons now, Nightland warriors, fueled by the Power of

Ti-Bish's vision, had waged war on the fiercely territorial bands of Sunpath People. It had been bloody, relentless, and increasingly savage.

And now we are here, about to spring this trap. She felt a wooden dullness around her heart. After this, there would be no going back. This wasn't about valor, or glory, or defense; it was about the cold-blooded murder of a potential adversary.

The oaks surrounding the village hunched like old men under the heavy mantle of snow, their branches drooping as if in defeat. The thin streamers of smoke rising from the lodges seemed tired and resigned.

"I don't like it," she whispered loud enough for Kakala to hear. "Windwolf should have been here by now."

Goodeagle almost winced, pain on his face.

Kakala shot a sidelong glance at Keresa. "He will come. When he does, he will walk right between our jaws."

She was watching Goodeagle as she replied, "Windwolf can smell a trap as well as we can."

Goodeagle stiffened, swallowed hard, and shook his head, as if to will away any misgivings.

Kakala sighed, saying softly, "Karigi's warriors are hidden in the town. There's nothing to give us away. Even if Windwolf suspects . . . he thinks his wife is down there. You know how he feels about Bramble. She is the center of his world. The man we both know will do anything to get her back."

Keresa rolled her lip between her teeth. Could anyone love that much?

She thought about Kakala. He was her best friend. They trusted each other implicitly, and she would do anything to protect him. When he had appointed her his deputy war chief several years back, there had been winks, whispered insinuations, and even ribald jokes—all uttered behind her back, of course. But she and Kakala had never looked at each other with lovers' eyes. The death of Kakala's wife, Hako, stood between them like a great stone.

Is that what really keeps us apart? She frowned, wondering at the odd distance between them. No two people that she knew were as close, sharing fires, jokes, thoughts, and worries; but sexual attraction led her in a different direction. Her relationship with Kakala was more like a sister's with her favorite brother.

Keresa returned her attention to the large lodge that dominated the center of Walking Seal Village. It was a huge thing, covered with mammoth hide. She wondered what Bramble was thinking. By now, Karigi should have had her safely away, guarded for her return to the Nightland caves.

Keresa could imagine the woman, bound, gagged, surrounded by Nightland warriors. She would be shooting frightened glances at her captors, wondering what fate lay in store for her when she faced the Nightland Council. News of her husband's defeat would be like a hollow darkness torn in her soul.

Keresa experienced a moment of regret. She liked Bramble, had admired the woman's good nature, mixed with practical expediency. In all of their dealings prior to the coming of the Guide, Bramble had been poised, responsible, and composed. Keresa had studied the woman on those occasions when they had shared an evening's fire.

I always wanted to be just like her.

But now Bramble was Karigi's prisoner, and that thought sent a shiver down Keresa's back. Bramble, cunning enemy that she might be now, was too good to deserve that.

Keresa fought the urge to lift her lip in disgust as she shot a glance at Goodeagle. But for him—traitor that he was—none of this would be happening. She took a deep breath, stilling her disdain for the man.

It was war. The will of Raven Hunter's vision, granted to the Guide. For whatever reason, Raven Hunter had come to Ti-Bish. His Dream was to return the people to the world beyond the ice. Before the Nightland People could return to that paradise, they had to ensure that no other peoples would follow their path.

Do I believe it? The question nagged at her. For years her people had followed the path of Wolf Dreamer, seeking order and the elusive quest for the One. As did the Sunpath and Lame Bull Peoples.

Now we are different, serving opposing visions of the Spirit World. And given the victories that had been so hard-won over the last two moons, perhaps Power actually did favor them.

Windwolf and Bramble had fought cunningly and well. But for the divisions among their own people, they could have won this thing. The other bands, however, wanted nothing to do with raiding, retaliation, and warfare. Their reluctance had allowed the Nightland warriors to overwhelm and destroy three bands piecemeal. Even the traditionally independent Sunpath would begin to understand. Worse, if Bramble— persuasive orator that she was—could make that clear, the Sunpath might overlook their traditional squabbles to form an alliance capable of withstanding the Nightland onslaught.

To avert disaster, she and Kakala had to eliminate that possibility. Now that they had Bramble, Windwolf was about to pay the ultimate price for his people's refusal to unite.

"Where *is* he?" Kakala muttered.

Young Maga, one of the warriors behind them, said, "If he has discovered that we have taken Bramble, he has turned and run."

"No," Goodeagle said through gritted teeth, "he hasn't."

"Who is his deputy now?" Keresa asked.

"Silt." Goodeagle wiped at perspiration that beaded on his upper lip. "He used to be chief of the Flower band. He called for peace, once. But after you destroyed his village, he bound himself to Windwolf."

"You have said he's capable?" Kakala narrowed his eyes on the trail where Windwolf should have already appeared.

"As capable as I am." Goodeagle swallowed.

"Then," Keresa mused, "he, too, will come over to us?"

Goodeagle lowered his eyes. Kakala was giving her a chastising frown.

At that moment, shouts carried on the air. Not from the Walking Seal ceremonial lodge, but from the trees where the Ash Clan war chief, Hawhak, had hidden his men in ambush.

Keresa tightened her grip on her atlatl as warriors burst from the trees. She lifted her head, recognizing the characteristic dress of Nightland warriors as they paused, casting darts back into the trees. She saw a warrior skewered through the thigh with a dart. Then Hawhak's warriors turned and ran.

"We're discovered!" Kakala muttered. "Forward! The rest of you, cover the retreat! Keresa! Come with me. We've got to pull Karigi out of there!"

Kakala's warriors split off as they crested the low ridge, running to bolster Hawhak's fleeing men.

Keresa caught glimpses of sunlight shining on darts as they lanced down on the fleeing warriors. Then she redoubled her efforts, dashing after Kakala toward the ceremonial lodge. Keresa, always faster than her thick-legged war chief, reached the doorway first.

A fire smoldered in the main room. Hides lay in disarray. Hangings marked the partitions for other rooms off to the sides. The place was empty.

"Goodeagle?" Kakala called as they followed her in. "Which way?"

"The chamber on the right."

Keresa jumped the fire, almost colliding with several of Karigi's warriors as they emerged from the chamber, confusion on their faces. One shot her a dismayed look—one that reeked of guilt.

Guilt?

Kakala ducked into the room.

She heard raucous male laughter mixed with Karigi's shouted orders as he rallied his warriors.

Keresa ducked through behind Kakala, and stared in disbelief. Bloody, her hands bound to one of the lodge poles above her head, Bramble lay naked. The bite marks on her neck, breasts, and belly were red, the smears of semen inside her thighs proof enough of what she'd endured.

The chamber looked like it had been blasted by one of the Meteorite People. Parfleches and broken baskets scattered the floor. The hides under Bramble were twisted and rumpled. She must have fought like a bear when she'd realized the truth.

The plan had been Karigi's: They'd set Bramble up to believe she'd be bargaining, buying him off so he'd let the women and children leave before he attacked. In reality, Karigi was supposed to capture her and drag her off to a safe place before setting his trap.

What's she still doing here?

Keresa took a deep breath, grip tightening on her atlatl with its nocked dart. Karigi, grinning, leaned against the back wall. He reached for his weapons, saying, "On to the next victory."

"Goodeagle!" Bramble sobbed, oblivious. "Goodeagle . . . get out!"

In a tight voice, Goodeagle said, "Kakala, you told me you wouldn't *hurt* her!"

"Goodeagle?" Bramble called, as though he were the last sane thing she could cling to. Then, understanding seemed to dawn. She blinked, and Keresa watched the woman's fear turn to disbelief, and then hatred.

Eyes wide, Goodeagle backed until he hit the wall.

Yes, you see now, don't you? Keresa shot Karigi a thin stare. *I never liked you, animal.*

"War Chief Karigi?" Kakala asked in an unsettlingly calm voice, like the hush that falls before the storm strikes. "Why is she still here?"

Karigi propped his dart over his shoulder and said, "I know you ordered us to—"

"Windwolf is *right behind us!* Get your warriors out there . . . and support Hawhak!"

Karigi blinked. "What? Why? Isn't that Windwolf's destruction we hear?"

"No! We're discovered! Surprised. Do it!"

Karigi took a step back, ordering, "Terengi, take your men and bring me Windwolf's head."

Glancing at each other, the men filed out, striding past Goodeagle.

Kakala stood so still, so quiet, that Keresa saw Karigi fidget nervously.

"War Chief, I intended to bring her to you as soon as my warriors had finished—"

Kakala slammed a fist into Karigi's stomach. When Karigi dropped to his knees, his dart cartwheeled across the floor.

Kakala hissed, "If I didn't need you . . . !"

Karigi staggered to his feet, shaking. "I'm Wolverine Clan! You struck me! When I tell our Elders—"

Kakala grabbed him by the front of his war shirt and threw him brutally against the wall. "You were supposed to be ready to attack Windwolf!"

"But, he was . . . was . . ." Karigi stammered, glaring at Bramble.

"You were so involved with your toy you forgot everything? If you'd prepared your warriors, as we agreed, by now Windwolf would be dead!"

Kakala backhanded Karigi and sent him toppling over a woodpile. Karigi got to his feet, bellowed like an enraged mammoth bull, and rushed. Kakala's kick caught him in the chest.

Keresa's eyes shifted, watching Bramble. She edged a foot toward the dropped dart, toes moving spiderlike toward the shaft. Keresa started forward.

"She's after my dart!" Karigi shouted from where he had sprawled onto the floor. He lunged, grasping the dart before the woman could.

Outside, one of Karigi's warriors shouted, "We're overrun! Run! Windwolf's warriors! There must be ten tens of them!"

Keresa hesitated, looking back at the door.

Bramble screamed.

Keresa spun back as Karigi drove the dart into Bramble's chest.

Karigi's eyes gleamed. "She might have killed someone!" he explained, ignoring Kakala's clenched fists and enraged face. Outside, someone screamed in pain and fear.

"Let's go!" Kakala shouted, glaring his boiling rage at Karigi. "Windwolf's warriors are getting closer!"

Goodeagle stumbled back against the wall. "I didn't know he'd do this, Bramble. I swear."

Faintly, almost inaudibly, she whispered, "Goodeagle?"

Keresa hesitated at the door, hatred brimming as she watched Goodeagle's horror. "You coming? Or staying?"

"Coming." He took a fumbling step toward Bramble, then blindly turned and ran. "This way! We'll go out the back."

She pelted after him, her atlatl at the ready. Where had Kakala and the rest gone?

Feet pounded through the chamber across the lodge, and she heard Windwolf's agonized shout, "Bramble?"

Keresa winced, soul pierced by the fear in the man's voice. By Raven Hunter's breath, if they didn't get away what had happened to Bramble would be child's play compared to what they'd do to her.

The memory of the bite marks and semen on Bramble's body sent a chill through her souls.

Bramble was too good to deserve that!

Then she was out the door, racing Goodeagle for the safety of the forest. As she ran, a voice in her head asked, *What kind of people have we become?*

Three

How did this happen? The Nine Pipes woman known as Skimmer walked with her head bowed. A heavy pack hung from her back, filled with half-cured meat.

She shot a worried look at her daughter, Ashes, who stumbled along the forest trail ahead of her. Ashes, too, carried a pack, smaller, but all that her ten-summers-old body could manage.

They were but part of a line that wound down from the spruce-pine forests above Lake River. The way descended shale slopes, and into a narrow gap that led down to a gravel beach bordered by thick stands of willows.

Skimmer shot a wary glance to the side, seeing Nightland warriors, each carrying weapons, ensuring that none of the women tried to step into the brush, drop their pack, and slip away.

I am a captive! The notion still stunned her. Only days ago, she had been free. *Free! Oh, Hookmaker, why didn't you listen to me?*

But he hadn't. And now, her only memory of him was his broken and bleeding body, lying before the great hearth in the Nine Pipes' winter camp.

She looked out, past the line of sweating women captives bent under their loads, and tried to find Kakala. But he had already disappeared into the willows, probably to scout the river ford.

"Ashes? Are you all right?" she asked as her daughter stumbled over an exposed root and almost fell.

"F-Fine, Mother. I'm tired. That's all."

"It's only a little farther." She glanced up at the low-lying sun in the west. The Nightland always let them camp at night. She tried to measure the angle of the sun. Kakala would push them across the river, though. The Nightland still believed that the Lame Bull lands on the other side offered some protection from the Sunpath warriors who followed Windwolf.

She winced at the man's name. Windwolf, the same warrior who had decimated her people five summers back in a bitter fight over hunting boundaries. Then she had cursed his name. The man had been a menace to her small band, beating them at every turn until Hookmaker had finally sued for peace.

She had hated him with all of her heart. Then, with the coming of the Nightland attacks, Hookmaker had argued for peace, perhaps still stung by the defeat Windwolf and Bramble had handed them.

"It is not our concern," Hookmaker's words echoed in her memory. *"If the Nightland want to war with Windwolf, let them! We've suffered enough at his hands!"*

"How wrong you were, husband." She shook her head, wondering how it had all gone so wrong. Poor Hookmaker, he'd paid for his belief in peace.

When the attack came, it had been without warning, just at the breaking of dawn. She had been stewing dried camel meat in a hide bag when the first whoops brought her upright. She had seen the Nightland warriors emerging from the trees, tens of them, racing through the scattered lodges in her camp.

"Ashes! Run!" she had shouted, and dove inside to find Hookmaker's weapons. Wrapping her fingers around her husband's atlatl and darts, she had emerged and handed them to him, and watched in horror as he fumbled to nock a dart, then cast it. Panic had dulled his reflexes; the dart hissed high over the attacker's heads.

Skimmer had stood rooted, disbelieving as Kakala charged up and knocked Hookmaker down with one blow of his war club.

Husband, you never were a warrior. The thought lay dully in her head as she picked her way down a slope, her back and hips aching under the load.

Oh, she had tried. The memory of the argument she and Hookmaker had had lay like a sour shadow in her soul. In the end, she had even traveled to Headswift Village, pleading with Chief Lookingbill to help her murder Ti-Bish.

And to think I once gave him food. She could still see his hollow face and hunger-filled eyes as she handed him a bowl of hot food.

When was I ever foolish enough to allow pity a place in my soul?

This was how he had paid her back?

Never again. "I will survive," she hissed under her breath. She watched Ashes carefully wind her way through the willows. The winter-bare stems rasped on her clothing and the pack she bore.

As she broke out of the willows, it was to find Goodeagle, the traitor, standing there, watching as each of the women stepped from the trees.

She met his leering eyes, narrowing her own. Each night he picked a woman, ordering her off into the trees for his pleasure. So far, he had taken Kicking Fawn twice, and Blue Wing once.

"Need help with the load?" he asked Ashes.

Her daughter just bowed her head, trudging forward.

"Don't even think it," she barked.

"How about you, Skimmer?" he asked. "Tired of the cold at night?"

"Oh, yes, Goodeagle," she said with cunning. "Pick me tonight. If nothing else, I'll gouge your eyes from that too-pretty head and tear your testicles off your body."

He matched her pace as she followed the line of women down to the first of the shallow channels.

"Do you know why we attacked your little band at the Nine Pipes camp?"

"Guide's orders, I heard."

"He wanted a Nine Pipes woman." Goodeagle sloshed into the shallow water with her. "Maybe he heard that it was you who was plotting to kill the Guide."

"Your Prophet can run his head up his ass and breathe deeply for all I care."

"Such anger, Skimmer."

"You should know. It was you, as Windwolf's deputy, who put it there."

Goodeagle nodded. "You and Hookmaker never did understand war."

"We were hunters, you piece of filth."

"That's what killed the Sunpath People," he said. Then in a lower voice, "That's what killed me. But I understand now."

"I hope the rest of the women here are right, and Windwolf comes to free us. I want to see what he does to you." Skimmer put her concentration into keeping her feet on the slippery round rocks under her feet. The water was cold, with rims of ice on the rocks. She sloshed through, with the current pulling at her thighs.

"You always had to go it alone, didn't you?" Goodeagle asked. Then he paused. "And now you'll do it with Councilor Nashat."

"Is that why you betrayed Bramble? Because she couldn't see it, whatever *it* is?"

He looked away, a spear of guilt on his face.

"Go on," he muttered. "Shiver yourself to sleep tonight. And while you do, imagine what the Nightland are going to do with you." Then he turned. "Blue Wing! When you cross, drop your pack. I think I'll give you the honor of warming my robes tonight."

Skimmer sighed as the man walked back down the line to match his pace with the hapless Blue Wing's. Once she had admired both Blue Wing and Kicking Fawn for their good looks, and the way men watched their bodies as they passed. Now she knew it for the curse it could be.

"Is that true, Mother?" Ashes asked. "Did he really kill Bramble?"

"After a fashion, yes." She took a breath, walking out onto one of the rocky islands, following the wet trail the others had left on the rocks. "But then, maybe we all did."

"Good." Ashes said softly. "Bramble was evil."

"And Windwolf?" she asked.

"I don't know," Ashes said between panting for breath. "People here think he's going to come and rescue us."

She considered that as she followed Ashes into the next ford.

Would Windwolf come to rescue the Nine Pipes? Even after all that we did to ensure that none of the other bands would join him in an alliance?

"We have only poisoned ourselves."

She followed the long line across the narrow channels, through the willows on the far bank, and struggled, her muscles protesting, up into the trees on the first terrace.

"Camp here!" the warriors called as they entered a small clearing in the trees.

Skimmer shrugged out of her pack, looking around at the rest of the captives. These women, people she'd known for years, now appeared as strangers, expressions haunted, faces slack, and eyes dull. Each was living her grief, remembering dead husbands, brothers, and sons left lying, unburied, in the smoking ruins of the Nine Pipes camp. They had become strangers.

As I have become to myself.

"We've been fools, Ashes."

And now it's too late.

Flames danced and flickered as they greedily consumed a collection of broken branches placed on the flames. The fire cast its warmth and light, cheery in the cool night. Keresa sat cross-legged and watched the branches burn, lost in her thoughts. Across from her, Kakala puffed at a stone pipe, blowing out wreaths of blue smoke to rise toward the star-speckled night sky.

She could hear the soft whisper of Lake River, the great braided river that drained from Loon Lake, a great oval-shaped body of fresh water that lay to the west. Technically, Lake River marked the boundary between the Lame Bull and Sunpath territories. Kakala's warriors had forded it earlier in the day, wading through the interwoven channels.

Around them, spruce and hemlock reflected the firelight. Raising her eyes, she could see the five fires the slaves had made in the center of the clearing. The rest of her warriors were spaced around them, most relaxing and talking after having eaten.

Between them and the slaves, stacked bundles of meat and fat had been laid out in a ring. The warriors kept bright fires, a deterrent to hungry bears, wolves, and lions. A stack of branches lay readily at hand in case any of the animals decided to challenge the humans. They would be met by burning brands and sharp darts.

Hunting darts were made with detachable foreshafts that fitted into hollows on the main shaft body. When hunting animals, especially large ones like mammoth and buffalo, the stone-tipped foreshaft was driven deeply into the animal's body, the springy fletched main shaft detaching to bounce back from the animal's side. A hunter could retrieve it, twist another foreshaft onto the dart, and cast again. The embedded foreshafts continued to cut tissue, and allowed the blood to drain from the hole in the animal's side.

In war, her people preferred a solid dart, one that splintered, or broke its point on impact, so that an enemy warrior couldn't pick it up and cast it back again.

Keresa lowered her eyes to the fire.

"You saw the Lame Bull hunters watching us ford the river today?" Kakala asked casually.

"They just watch." She shrugged. "They know we are just passing through."

"So far." Kakala puffed on his pipe before blowing the blue smoke through his puckered lips.

"So far?" She glanced up at him.

"How many of the Sunpath bands are left?" Kakala narrowed an eye as he studied her across the fire.

"Maybe nine. All far to the south and west."

"Nashat is a clever old wolf," Kakala muttered. "He made sure the Lame Bull People knew we just wished to pass in peace. Now we have destroyed most of the Sunpath villages, scattered their people, and left a whole countryside empty." He smiled. "All but a band of Lame Bull People here in the spruce lands. The Lame Bull People have talked themselves into believing our quarrel was with the Sunpath."

She raised her eyes. "You think it is not?"

Kakala chuckled softly to himself. "I think this was most cunningly done. Nashat knew the Sunpath People, understood how independent and disorganized they were. So, what would you do, Keresa? Tackle a large traditionally fragmented enemy? Or take on an easily united, but smaller foe?"

"The Lame Bull People would have been a tougher nut to crack, but they'd have fallen."

Kakala nodded. "And what effect would that have had on the Sunpath People to the south?"

She nodded, already knowing where he was going. "Seeing what we did to the Lame Bull, they'd have overlooked their differences and united with Windwolf to fight us, wishing to avoid the same fate as the Lame Bull."

Kakala gestured with his pipe. "But now they are no threat, and the Lame Bull have come to believe we are invincible. As I said, Nashat is a cunning and devious one."

Keresa rubbed her shins. "So, you think the Lame Bull are next?"

"You know the Guide's words. We are the chosen people. Those who follow the ways of Wolf Dreamer must not follow our path. They are not to bring their pollution into our world."

She glanced out at the slaves, seeing the bowed heads of the women and older children. These had been taken from the Nine Pipes band. For some reason, the Guide had sent them specifically to take the camp. The orders were to bring back *all* of the women. Nashat had insisted that the Guide wanted a *Nine Pipes* woman. Kakala had ensured that they captured every female in the camp.

Normally they only took those who could work.

After a raid, the warriors withdrew with their captives, traveling far enough to ensure that Windwolf's ragged warriors were not in pursuit. Then they went hunting. The slaves carried the kill back to the Nightland caverns along with precious wood.

What had been surprising was the amount of game that had moved into the territories abandoned by the nomadic Sunpath bands. Hunting had definitely improved over the last two winters.

Her people relied on the ice caves. There they carried the summer's catch, placing it on ice to freeze for the winter. Since the beginning of the war, bellies had been full like they'd never been in the past. Back when she was little, summer had been spent hunting the snow geese, ducks, and loons. In hide-covered boats her people netted fish from among the floating bergs in the Thunder Sea. They hunted seals, walrus, and occasional pilot whales and narwhals, rendering the meat and blubber. Throughout the summer, the largess was carried back for freezing in the ice caves, stored for winter. Now her people had grown lazy, letting the slaves carry their burden for them.

"You'd think Raven Hunter really does smile on us." She watched a branch break in the fire.

Kakala was watching her curiously. "What do you really believe? Do you think the Idiot actually had a vision?"

She cocked her head. "Have you looked into his eyes?"

Kakala nodded. "He believes it." He knocked the dottle out of his pipe. "But then, he always believed something. I remember when he was a boy." He studied the end of his pipe. "How does a onetime fool become a sacred Guide?"

"When people believe." She took a deep breath, drawing in the clean scent of the trees. "In answer to your question, I don't know what I believe anymore. I'm lost, Kakala. Nothing has turned out to be what I thought it was."

He grunted. "The Council is swollen with itself. They act like gods themselves."

She raised an eyebrow. "Is that doubt I hear in your voice?"

His great shoulders gave a slight shrug. "I serve my people. No more, no less."

"If you were a Karigi, I would have nothing to do with you."

He barely smiled. "Karigi serves only himself."

"And his passions," she added.

"I noticed he had his eye on you last time we had Council."

"I would rather be Windwolf's prisoner for the rest of my life than Karigi's for a single night." She paused. "He hates you, you know."

"I know." Kakala barely smiled. "It even goes back to before Walking Seal Village. I remember him parading before my cage when I was disgraced. His souls ooze at the notion that I am the high war chief."

"We are Night Clan." She shifted to relieve her cramped legs. "Nashat leads the Council, and you are the clan war chief. There's nothing Karigi can do about it until Wolverine Clan unseats Nashat."

"For that, at least, I can thank Nashat."

She looked up. "But you know that someday, sometime, he's going to repay you for striking him at Walking Seal Village. Karigi doesn't forget."

Kakala was silent for a while. "No, he doesn't."

She frowned, eyes on the fire again as she remembered Walking Seal Village. The look in Bramble's eyes haunted her. She could still hear Windwolf's panicked cry from the other side of the lodge.

"What are you thinking?"

"About Walking Seal Village." She reached for another stick of wood and tossed it onto the flames. "Have you ever thought about how different it would have been if Bramble had lived? If Karigi had sent her out of the village before Windwolf attacked? A living Bramble would never have become the symbol the dead one has become.

With her alive, we could have finally trapped Windwolf. The Sunpath People would have been beaten within six moons. This has dragged on for two solid winters. They fight like madmen."

"Windwolf does," he admitted with grudging respect. "I swear: Wolf Dreamer protects him. How many times has he led desperate charges against us? I've seen an entire war party try and kill him in a fight, but the darts slip harmlessly around him."

She added, "I've seen him stop a panicked flight with a word, turning his warriors, leading them against us when all sense would urge them to run." She gave Kakala a wry smile. "And in the end, it is we who break and flee."

"I liked him," Kakala said sadly. "Back in the old days. He and Bramble both." He stared down at his pipe, words dying in his throat.

"What were you going to say?"

He inspected the stone tube for a moment, then said softly, "That if I could go back, I would change what happened at Walking Seal Village." He sighed. "Even if it meant walking into that room and driving a dart straight through Karigi's midnight heart."

She glanced around. "I wouldn't say that too loudly."

Kakala grunted. "The difference between us is that Karigi does what he does because he likes it. We do it because it is our duty to our people."

"Is that why you have started to warn women and children before our attacks?"

He shot her a questioning look. "Do you disapprove?"

She twisted her thick hair into a rope. "When I disapprove, you will know."

He smiled at that. "I do not know the reasons for this vision of the Guide's. If our people are truly to travel through the ice to a paradise, well and good. But I will not become a monster for him." A pause. "My Dreams are bad enough as it is."

"Nightmares, you mean."

"Oh, yes." He reached for his pack, finding the little pouch of chopped sweet sumac and tamping the leaf into his pipe. "But that is between us."

Soft weeping could be heard on the night. Keresa looked over, seeing a dark shape rise from the darkness just under the trees. Moments later, Goodeagle walked into the firelight, prodding a crying woman before him. Ever since Walking Seal Village, he had been a different man, broken somehow. Not that it ever kept him from taking his pleasure from one of the slave women.

Kakala's eyes narrowed as he watched the wretched woman walk back to a fire. Then Kakala jerked his head toward the warriors' fires. "They don't need to know their war chief has bad Dreams about the things he's done."

Keresa lifted her lip, thinking about the joy it would bring her to split the traitor's head with an ax.

"Or their deputy, either," she added.

Four

Late-afternoon light streamed through the spruce forest, dappling War Chief Windwolf's path like scattered amber shards. The air was heavy with odors of conifer and the scent of damp soil. At times he could hear Silt's soft padding as the deputy followed reluctantly behind him.

Windwolf veered wide around the low-hanging spruce branches. His black hair—cut short in mourning—blew around his oval face, forcing him to squint his brown eyes. Wind Woman's cold breath had begun to eat through his finely tailored buffalo coat and pants, and nibble at his bones. He tugged the laces tighter, shivered, and kept walking.

He carried a pack on his back; long war darts hung from his left hand. A battered war club dangled down his back from a thong, and an atlatl was easily at hand, laced to his belt.

To the north, a full seven-day walk away, the Ice Giants rose like massive snow-covered peaks. He caught periodic glimpses of them as he crested the high places. A windblown haze of white haloed the Giants. Even from this distance he could hear the faint Singing of the supernatural beings. No other sound like it existed in the world.

A rich harmonic of different notes Sung at the same time, it was unearthly, and frighteningly beautiful.

Behind him, his deputy, Silt, said, "Forgive me, War Chief, but this is a bad idea."

Windwolf turned. "Then why have you come this far?"

A medium-sized man with bark-colored eyes and shoulder-length black hair, Silt had a straight nose and full lips. His mammoth-hide cape bore evidence of many campfires. Soot and grease stained the front.

"I'm hoping I can turn you around. We can't afford to be captured by Kakala's Nightland warriors."

"This may be our last chance to save our people, Silt."

Silt gave Windwolf a disbelieving look. "You're on your way to offer yourself up like a sacrificial moose!"

"I don't want you dying with me. You're my best warrior."

Windwolf sucked in a deep breath and let the tangy scents of coming evening, damp earth, and spruce needles soothe his wounded soul. Over the two winters since Bramble's death, he'd watched helplessly as band after band was destroyed. No one had understood until too late. People just didn't think in terms of this kind of warfare. It hadn't been part of their understanding until the Prophet's warriors had made believers of them. By then, it had been too late.

He glanced back at Silt. Silt had been one of the first. A peace chief. He'd insisted that whatever the Prophet's warriors had been incited by, they had nothing against either him or the Flower band of the Sunpath People.

. . . Until Kakala burned his village to the ground, killed the men, and drove off the women and children they hadn't murdered outright.

Silt had miraculously escaped with his life and a handful of warriors. Now they knew. But, by the wind, what a terrible way to learn.

Silt said, "I don't understand why you're doing this. A chief from the Lame Bull People summons you, and you run to meet him? You've lost your wits."

"Maybe."

Silt sounded irritated: "Three moons ago you'd have never taken such chances. You'd have sent in a trusted warrior first, to scout the village, before you—"

"After you turn back, I'll scout the village myself."

"After I turn back? What if it's a trap?"

"I've been in traps before."

"Yes, of course, but you had ten tens of warriors crouching in the forest to get you out. This is different."

"I have to do this, Silt. Alone." *And if the Lame Bull offer is a trap, perhaps I'm better off dead.* He flinched at the pain in his soul. What was the point of living when all a man had to look forward to was the destruction of his world?

Silt made a deep-throated utterance of disgust and bowed his head. "Why? Explain it to me."

Windwolf watched him with numb patience. It got harder every day to teeter around the edges of that chasm that had grown in his soul. Part of him longed to lose itself in that inner pit of darkness. At least then the agony would end. "I've explained it tens of times."

"Do it again."

Windwolf heaved a sigh and stopped short as his keen eyes detected movement. He ducked down, slowly easing under the prickly cover of a spruce. Silent as a ghost, Silt had followed.

Windwolf parted the branches with his hand. A short distance away, a giant sloth, the size of a buffalo cow, snuffled the dirt while it used its huge claws to dig for roots. Covered with coarse, shaggy hair, the slow-moving animal made an easy target for supper.

"I can slip off to the left," Silt barely whispered.

Windwolf considered, then exhaled. "No, let him go. Our packs carry enough for now. Why should we ruin his day, take his life, when all we could carry away is a couple of steaks?" He glanced up. "I'm tired of everything having to do with ravens. And that's who'd have a feast here."

Slowly they backed to the trail. Once again on their way, Silt asked, "Is that what this is all about? You're tired of killing?"

Was it? For two winters now, his rage over Bramble's death had preoccupied him, driven him, and caused him to take reckless risks. Each time, however, Wolf Dreamer seemed to favor him. No matter how audacious his plan, somehow, he had always managed to pull it off.

Have I begun to think I'm invincible?

He said, "Chief Lookingbill asked me to meet with him. I'm fairly certain he understands what our own people did not . . . until it was too late. He's afraid of the Nightland, Silt. He has perhaps three tens of warriors in Headswift Village. Kakala has ten tens. Lookingbill doesn't know if the Lame Bull are next. And he certainly doesn't want word getting back to the Nightland that a group of our warriors was camping with him. That would ensure an immediate Nightland response."

"Let the Lame Bull fend for themselves!" Silt gripped Windwolf's shoulder. "For the sake of the Ancestors, do you think Bramble was the only one who needed you? If old Lookingbill kills you, what will we do? Kakala's warriors have destroyed five bands since last summer! Our women and children spend every day running. If you die, who will lead us?"

"You will, Silt." Windwolf stared into the man's worried eyes. "You, more than anyone, understand what has changed."

Silt stabbed a finger toward the southern pine forests. "There are nine Sunpath bands left—and every one is sick with fear that they will be attacked next." He paused. "Windwolf, you're the only man who has ever been able to create an alliance to protect them. You—"

"You're as good a war chief as I am, Silt. Better, probably."

Silt's gaze turned compassionate. "Bramble's been dead for two winters. You have mourned her enough."

Bramble . . . what did I do to you?

Silt glared at Windwolf through eyes as hard and glittering as stone. "I know you're hurting, Windwolf. Everyone knows it. Time after time, you have tried to get yourself killed. The warriors who serve you believe in one fact: *Power has kept you alive in spite of the risks you take!*"

Windwolf waved it away.

Silt shook his head. "Our alliance is a fragile thing. Without your leadership, the warriors will lose hope, drift away. If that happens, what's left of our people will melt away like a ball of mud dropped into a stream."

Windwolf closed his eyes for a moment and let his soul drift. *Is that why I'm still alive? Power wills it? For what?*

When he opened them again, he found Silt standing with his shoulders squared, as though ready for a fight. The long reddish hair on his mammoth-hide cape glinted in the sunlight.

"Lookingbill is the most respected chief among the Lame Bull People," Windwolf said. "I don't know why he called me, but perhaps he wishes to join us in our fight against the Nightland People. I must find out."

In a low voice, Silt said, "You never answer me honestly. Don't you think I know what this is really about?"

Bramble. It always came back to Bramble. Tiredly, Windwolf said, "Please, Silt. Just . . . let me go."

"Only if I can go with you, to guard your back. You need—"

"No."

Silt stared at him, eyes measuring, worried. "Why don't you let me take you somewhere else? You could rest at Sky Dog Village. It's far to the west, on the border of Southwind lands. They'll never find us there. I'll send a message to Blade that we'll be gone for ten days. She can handle any trouble—"

He shook his head. "No. With me gone, our people need you. That is your responsibility. My duty is to find out what Lookingbill wants, and we both know . . ." He forced himself to continue. "We both know the time away will do me good. I won't have to walk the same trails I walked with Bram . . ." His grief welled, dark and empty.

"The anger has run out, War Chief." Silt reached out, as if to grasp some elusive concept. "And with it, so has hope."

"It's not a matter of hope."

Silt's expression twisted. "All the more reason you need me to go with you. After Goodeagle, you've had enough traitorous—"

"Don't," Windwolf shouted as his inner chasm widened. "I don't want to talk about it, Silt. Leave it *alone!*"

Silt massaged his forehead. "All right." He dropped his voice to a whisper. "Please, I can help you with negotiations with Chief Lookingbill."

Angry despair stirred in Windwolf. "I appreciate your concern. But I must go alone. It's what Lookingbill requested . . . and I've no reason to deny him."

"No reason? The Nightland clan Elders have offered safe haven in return for your dead body! Half the world would turn on their own brothers in return for the promise of safety." Silt paused for effect. "Do you seriously think Lookingbill wouldn't find that a tempting reason to have you come alone?"

Somewhere deep inside, Windwolf couldn't convince himself that it mattered. Death could be lurking around the next turn, and he didn't care. Nothing mattered anymore. Nothing except a fatal mistake he'd made, and the swelling empty grief that hollowed his soul.

He is right. When I ran out of rage, even hope was dead.

"And what about War Chief Kakala?" Silt asked gruffly. "He's out there. If he gets a whiff of where you've gone, he'll be on you like a short-faced bear on a fresh carcass."

A prickle climbed Windwolf's spine. Kakala! Six times since last summer, he'd almost caged Windwolf's ragtag group of warriors. Only desperate acts on Windwolf's part had saved them. But the day was coming, he knew, when without more warriors, Kakala would win. "It'll be harder to find me if I'm alone than if I'm surrounded by tens of warriors."

"Blessed Ancestors, *what* can I say to reach you?" Silt tipped his chin skyward, as though looking to the Spirits for help. Despite the chill wind, sweat glistened on his tanned skin, soaking the ends of hair that stuck to his forehead.

Windwolf exhaled the words, "I'll send a runner if I need you."

"Yes. I know you will. If you can. What happens when we learn Nightland warriors plan to attack another band? Do I leave them defenseless to rescue you?"

Windwolf lifted a hand. "There are always places to hide. I'll—"

"You'll what?" Silt demanded. "Duck into some hole and pray to the Ancestors that when you have to come out to hunt nobody recognizes you? Run for Sky Dog Village where you know you have friends, worried every instant that Nightland spies are going to spot you and you'll endanger everyone there?"

"Why can't you let this go?" He met the hot challenge in Silt's eyes with equanimity, feeling like an observer rather than a participant. It took only moments before Silt's gaze softened, going from fiery to sick worry. He straightened, walked up the trail to a rise, and stared across the Lake River Valley. Beyond the braided channels weaving through the stony riverbed lay the Lame Bull lands. In another four days he would reach Headswift Village where it stood on its high point off to the east.

The Lame Bull village was a natural fortress. As the Ice Giants retreated northward, they had left massive piles of gravel and tumbled boulders behind. The Lame Bull People lived in rockshelters and hollows created by the boulders. Traders who'd visited there said the place was like a rabbit warren, tunnels twisting under the hill like tree roots, going in every direction. Many reputedly ran deep underground.

Windwolf said, "It will be dark soon. I have to cross the Lake River channels while I still have light."

He thought of Headswift Village. Living in such a manner was a strange notion. His Sunpath People preferred hide-covered lodges in open meadows, or along rivers. In their lands, ten days' run to the south, they had oaks, hickory trees, and walnuts. Here, at the edge of the Ice Giants, only pine and spruce seemed to flourish.

Silt said, "I'm fighting a losing battle, aren't I? You're not going to let me stay to guard your back."

They stared at each other a moment, exchanging a silent communication.

Then Silt turned, face somber, and trotted back south, toward his people and a future Windwolf could no longer believe in.

Five

Old Lookingbill, chief of the Lame Bull People, had once been blessed with a tall and robust body. In his old age, the muscle had faded, leaving only large bones and withered skin behind. What little hair he had left had gone silver-white, and his back had developed a slight hunch as the endless seasons wore him down. For this special night he wore a rich beaverhide cape over a beautifully tanned hunting shirt that hung to his knees. His feet were clad in high moccasins, the tops crafted from the neck hide of short-faced bear, tanned with the fur on.

He and his grandson, Silvertip, stood in the crowd that had gathered on one of the lower trails and gazed admiringly at the line of people carrying torches as they wound up the hill. The procession weaved through the boulders like a gleaming snake. On holy days the torches seemed to flare brighter, and the night smelled sweetly of burning spruce sap.

Headswift Village was an anomaly. He knew of no other place like it. In the hilly moraine country south of the Thunder Sea, it rose in a high prominence that gave a stunning vista of the Ice Giants to the north. To the south the braided path of Lake River could be seen, and beyond it, the endless forests of the Sunpath People.

From the time he was a child, he had wandered through the maze of tunnels beneath the village, and wondered at the great rocks. Once he had even tried to make a smaller version of it, piling stones on top of each other and sifting dirt over the whole. The notion had lived with him since those boyhood days that just after the creation, giants had piled these huge rocks in the same fashion, though, as he aged, he'd come to the less-spectacular conclusion that the great pile of stone had been left behind by the retreating Ice Giants. He had seen similar formations melting out of the retreating ice.

For generations his people had lived here, seven days' journey south of the Nightland camps that fringed the westernmost extent of the Thunder Sea. They had hunted and collected in the surrounding forests, bringing their catch, firewood, and other necessities back. Water was obtained from a spring just below the massive pile of rock.

The spring itself was a curious thing. In summer, as Loon Lake to the west rose, the spring's flow increased, only to slow to a dribble by the end of winter. As a result, his people made offerings, dropping sprigs of evergreen into the pool as the flow diminished.

He, too, participated in making his offerings to the water even after he had surmised that it was the lake level rather than their need that determined the flow. Sometimes he wondered if his practical bent lessened the magic that others seemed so intent to enjoy.

"Wind Woman has a bite tonight. Are you warm enough, Silvertip?" He looked down at his grandson. The boy had seen ten and two summers, was slight of build, but tall and straight. Silvertip had always been a bit odd, introspective, and uninterested in the ways of the hunt. Nor had he shown much interest in the games other children played. Sometimes, when the boy was lost in his head, his eyes took on a distant sheen, as if picturing worlds beyond this one. When his aunt Mossy, the Storyteller, related the traditional tales, the boy literally seemed to glow, as if the words lived within his soul.

Silvertip looked up and smiled. "Grandfather, I'm always warm during the holy moon."

A line of torches, carried by the warriors, was weaving through the boulders above them. Around them, people whispered, sharing the enchanting sight of the winding line of torches as they prepared to meet the equinox moon.

Lookingbill smiled. He wished he could be as filled with Power as his grandson. While he believed in the will of Wolf Dreamer, he had always been plagued by the practicality of leadership. "Come. Let us go and see the procession."

They rounded a bend and looked up at the huge cavern formed by tens of toppled boulders. Soft golden light streamed from the entrance, dappling the rocks and throwing patchwork shadows across the landscape.

"Grandfather?"

"What is it, Silvertip?"

"Can I touch the Wolf Bundle?"

Lookingbill was aware of the amused people within earshot. "Someday, when you are a man and it becomes yours, you can touch it. Not yet."

"But I'm almost a man now. Why can't I just—"

"It was the gift of Wolf Dreamer himself to our people. It's too Powerful for a boy to hold. It might kill you."

Silvertip lowered his gaze to stare at the trail passing beneath his feet. "I remember, but—"

"I thought you did."

"The Wolf Bundle is like the trail that leads to the skyworlds, isn't it, Grandfather?"

"It's more like tens of trails," Lookingbill answered. "There are many paths to the One. The Wolf Bundle opens a different one to each person. Some lead to the future, others to the past." He put a hand to his belt, where the bundle rested, warm and comforting in its protective pouch.

As they walked, Sister Moon rose over the ceremonial cave. Her light tarnished the drooping spruce branches and shadowed the trails. On this night, her light would gleam through an opening in the eastern side of their stone fortress and cast a thin white lance across the Council cavern.

So, too, did Father Sun as he pursued his path through the cycle of seasons, traveling north and then south, illuminating different parts of the rock warren.

Silvertip moved closer to Lookingbill, and fingered the worn leather of his sleeve. "Grandfather?"

Silvertip was persistent. Once he asked something, he never let it go. "I'm listening."

"Maybe you could just let me look at it?"

Every face in the crowd was fixed on the rising moon, but Silvertip only had eyes for the Wolf Bundle. "Later, during the Renewal ritual, all right?"

"Maybe now . . . and then I wouldn't have to remember to ask later."

"You think you might forget?"

Silvertip stared up at him, his eyes tight with longing. "Please, Grandfather?"

What is it about him and the Wolf Bundle? The boy is obsessed.

Lookingbill sighed, knelt in the ice-sheathed grass, and untied his belt pouch. As he pulled back the leather to reveal the sacred bundle, Silvertip came forward. The people who'd been walking behind them veered around, smiling. Children pointed and peeked at the bundle for as long as their parents would allow before moving on up the trail.

"Wolf Dreamer made it himself, didn't he?" Silvertip asked.

"Yes, he did, after a fight with Grandfather White Bear."

The bundle had originally been made of Grandfather White Bear's hide and had held his claws. Lookingbill had never dared to open it; he had no idea what the bundle contained—though he frequently heard voices, soft and pleading, coming from within.

He said reverently, "Legends tell us that after Wolf Dreamer led the people up through the dark hole in the ice to this world of light, he placed other things in the bundle: a wolf's tail and teeth, given to him by his Spirit Helper; a lock of hair from a woman he had loved with all his heart; and a stone point crafted by one of his friends. One story even says the bundle contains a fragment of a white mammoth hide—a very rare and precious thing."

Mesmerized, Silvertip unconsciously reached out. Lookingbill grabbed his hand to keep it away. "Careful. You don't want Wolf Dreamer to find you so soon."

"He already knows where I am, Grandfather. You've told me so many times."

"Yes, but he'd want to talk to you if you touched this."

"I want to talk to Wolf Dreamer."

"You just think you do. The things he tells you are not always good." Lookingbill pulled the laces of his belt pouch tight again to hide the bundle. Silvertip watched intently.

"I know how to use the bundle. Did you know that, Grandfather?"

"Do you?"

"Yes," Silvertip blurted excitedly. "You have to hold the Wolf Bundle to your heart and walk up the bright star trail to Wolf Dreamer's Spirit Lodge in the skyworlds."

"Usually, but sometimes Wolf Dreamer reaches out and grabs you by the throat when you least expect it. That's why you can't play with it. The Spirits always think you're serious when you pick up the Wolf Bundle."

Silvertip nodded. "Grandfather, tell me again about how the world used to be filled with sacred bundles? Raven Hunter's bundle, and Dancing Fox's bundle, and Ice Fire's bundle. Tell me about how the Nightland clan Elders stole them all and put them in their ice caves—"

"You have more important stories to think about tonight. Like the fight between Wolf Dreamer and his evil brother Raven Hunter."

Silvertip wet his lips. "Did the other bundles go to the skyworlds, too, Grandfather?"

Lookingbill sighed. "Since we have only the Wolf Bundle, no one knows where the others went. Now, you think about the battle between the Hero Twins."

Silvertip took his hand. "Will you tell me the story?"

"What? Now? You can't wait to hear it from your aunt Mossy?"

"No, please tell me. I want to hear the part about Wolf Dreamer fighting Grandfather White Bear."

He smoothed the boy's black hair and got to his feet with a grunt. His tired old legs ached as they resumed the climb toward the great cavern.

"I'll tell you a little bit. I don't want to spoil the ceremonial for you."

"Thank you, Grandfather." The boy beamed.

Lookingbill took a breath, and his voice grew deeper. "Long, long ago, our people lived on the edge of a great icy sea, a white world of immense beauty and danger. All was darkness. They called it the Long Dark. Then one day—"

"Wolf Dreamer and Raven Hunter were born!"

"I thought you wanted me to tell this story?"

"Don't be difficult, Grandfather." Silvertip mimed his mother's voice, and it made Lookingbill laugh.

His youngest daughter, Dipper, had a gentle hand with children, too gentle perhaps, since Silvertip was growing up much too precocious.

"Grandfather, please, I want you to tell me about Wolf Dreamer. About how he fought the giant bear and rescued our Ancestors from their exile in the dark underworlds, then flew to the Creator, Old Man Above. Old Man Above gave Wolf Dreamer a huge pillar of fire to lead our people through the darkness—"

"I think you know the old stories better than I do. Why don't you tell me what happened?"

"Grandfather," Silvertip pleaded, eyes lingering on the pouch on Lookingbill's belt. "You tell me. Like you do every winter."

"I should be glad you want to know," Lookingbill said half to himself. "Not very many people do anymore."

While he had personal reasons to wish the Nightland Prophet dead, a sad reverie came over him. Since the coming of the Prophet, children were often stolen away. Those who managed to escape after several moons were never the same. While some returned to their beliefs, others who had met the Prophet remained skeptical. Raven Hunter had become their hero, and they longed to find the hole in the ice that led back to the Long Dark.

What Power does the Prophet wield that he can have such an effect on children, even after they have returned to their own? Lookingbill longed to meet the man, to see for himself, but the Nightland People guarded their Prophet jealously. For good reason. Lookingbill, himself, would have loved nothing better than to drive a lance through the man's evil heart. But for eyewitness accounts, Lookingbill could almost believe the alleged "Guide" was an overblown story.

He gazed up past the high boulders at the Blessed Star People. "That's why we live here, isn't it, Silvertip? To protect you."

Before the coming of the Prophet, things had been easier. Now, no one trusted the Nightland People, or their thieving warriors who would pounce on an unattended child. Some had called for war in retribution for the kidnappings, but those cries had grown faint in the wake of Nightland victories among the always-scrappy Sunpath People. Now, for the most part, they waited, unsure of which course to pursue.

"You mean . . ." the boy asked in confusion, "you mean because Raven Hunter tried to kill Wolf Dreamer before he could lead our people up into the light of this world?"

"No, I was thinking something else, but you're right about that."

They rounded a corner, and a deep voice drifted on Wind Woman's breath, rising from the ceremonial cave like the voice of Wolf Dreamer himself.

People milled around outside the small entrance to the chamber, laughing and talking. Lookingbill's heart warmed. During great festivals, Lame Bull villagers came from all over to participate. Every cycle some long-lost relative appeared out of nowhere.

"Father?" Lookingbill's eldest daughter, Mossy, waved as she saw them approaching. She had inherited his height, a stately woman with long black hair and brown eyes. The heavily beaded dress she wore flapped around her legs. He noted her expression: Something was wrong. A tightness around her eyes betrayed it. Her husband, Night Fighter, stood at her side, a hard worry marring his wide face.

"My pride overflows," Lookingbill praised, striding forward to take Mossy's hand. Then he gave her an evaluative look. *What's the trouble?*

She had risen through the ranks to the esteemed position of Storyteller by memorizing the precious ancient stories.

She lovingly kissed his mostly bald head, then extended a hand to an old woman standing slightly behind her. "Father, do you remember Cousin Loon Spot?"

Lookingbill squinted at her. Hunched with age, the woman had her gray hair pulled into a tight bun over her left ear. Her nose stuck out like a sharp dart point. "Scrub's daughter from Purple Meadow Village? I thought you were dead?"

"I tried it. Didn't like it," the old woman muttered.

When Loon Spot scowled, Mossy said, "Father, forgive me for interrupting, but I need to speak you before the ceremonial. Oh, and you must Sing tonight."

"I'm too old to Sing."

"He's too old to do anything," Loon Spot added, and grinned toothlessly when Lookingbill's eyes narrowed.

Mossy said, "Pineleaf is ill. Someone must take his place."

"You have a lovely voice."

"You told me my voice sounded like dogs howling."

"That's because I love you. And the last time you talked me into Singing, half the people mysteriously went home early. I'm not going to embarrass myself—"

"I think I was at that ceremony," Loon Spot interrupted grimly. "That's what convinced me to try being dead for a while. Don't make him Sing."

"I'm not going to Sing!" he declared.

Mossy smiled, but it was a halfhearted expression. "All right, I'll find someone else. Now, please, let's talk, Father."

"Silvertip, wait here for me. I'll be just a moment."

"Yes, Grandfather."

Mossy led him up the trail away from the ceremonial cave. When they reached a dark ledge, she sank down and heaved a sigh.

"What is it, Daughter?"

"One of our hunters just came in. He brought news that another Sunpath camp was attacked: the Nine Pipes band. The hunter said that he saw the slaves carrying more meat north."

Lookingbill felt like a huge hand had reached into his chest and gripped his heart. "What of Skimmer and Chief Hookmaker?"

While Hookmaker had been one of the most strident Sunpath voices calling for peace, Skimmer had come to him less than a moon ago to ask his help in a plot to murder the Nightland People's sacred Guide. Lookingbill had politely declined; his people feared the retribution of the Nightland clan Elders.

Mossy said, "Rumors say that Hookmaker was killed defending the ceremonial lodge. It is said that Kakala himself struck him down."

"So Skimmer may have escaped?"

"Word is that Kakala took all of the women. If she's free, it's a miracle, and Wolf Dreamer himself must have been watching over her."

Mossy studied his expression. "Are you wishing you'd agreed to help them?"

"You and I both know that I argued for it." He glanced out at the night. "It is an unfortunate truth that serving as a leader generally means bowing to the opinion of the people."

Mossy reached out to touch his hand. "Father, we are a different people than the Sunpath, but we also worship Wolf Dreamer. How long do you think we have before the Nightland warriors come for us?"

"Not long," he said softly. "Once they're finished with the Sunpath bands, I've come to believe we'll be next." He looked out at the night. "I was a fool to think they would only war with the Sunpath. Looking back now, I think we have been masterfully outmaneuvered by Nashat and the Prophet. We watched them destroy the Sunpath bands, thankful that they only wished to pass through our lands. Now, however, we must stand alone."

She bowed her head as though suddenly exhausted. "The hunter who brought me the story said that the Nightland warriors have built an enclosure to hold the captive women. He said you can hear their cries from a half day's walk away. They keep pleading for Windwolf to rescue them."

Mossy looked up hopefully at him, and he shook his head. "No, my daughter. He's not here. Perhaps he's afraid to come by himself. We could not have asked him to bring his warriors. The Nightland scouts would have known immediately that we were plotting against them."

"He probably thinks it's a trap. Given the promise of safety from attack that Nashat has made, that's what I would think."

"As would I."

She gestured uncertainly. "Blessed Ancestors, I don't know what to do. Should we leave here? Find a safer place?"

He held her hand tightly. "And go where?"

"South? West? Does it matter? We can find a place far from the Nightland."

"You and I both know that perhaps half, maybe a third, of our people would leave. The rest still cling to the belief that we have done nothing to deserve an attack. Outside of stealing a few children, the Nightland war parties have avoided any confrontation while passing through. They even leave offerings from their hunts in restitution for passing in peace."

"That is only a diversion."

"The rumor is that before the Prophet leads the Nightland People through the ice to the Long Dark, they will destroy anyone who believes in Wolf Dreamer to keep them from following."

She gave him a serious look. "Is that why you've started hiding dried meat and skins of water in the hidden chambers? So that we can hold out here if we have to?"

"Like my daughter, I am no fool." Lookingbill tugged on Mossy's hand to make her rise. "Your mother would be very proud of you."

She hugged him. For several moments they clung to each other, and he knew what she must be thinking. Two winters had done little to ease either of their hearts.

Her mother, his beloved wife, had been murdered by Nightland warriors while visiting Bramble at Walking Seal village. He had gone himself to find his wife's mutilated body lying among the Sunpath dead. Karigi had heaped them out of sight in an abandoned lodge.

He might have meant only to trap Windwolf—but had turned Look-ingbill forever against him in the process.

"There's nothing more we can do tonight, my daughter. Let's go en-joy the Renewal Dance. I'm eager to hear you recite the Old Stories."

They walked up the trail in silence.

When Silvertip saw him coming, he called, "Grandfather!" and ran to meet him. "It's about to start. We have to go in."

Turning back to Mossy, Lookingbill said, "If you can't find anyone else, I'll Sing."

"Thank you, Father." She kissed his cheek. "It will be worth it just to give Loon Spot a reason to be dead again."

The Council cavern was a large, irregular chamber that ran back into the rocks. Silvertip's mouth dropped open. A huge fire had been built of logs in the center of the space. It cast flickering shadows over the rockshelter's high ceiling and the happy faces of the people. Hides had been spread in front of the torch-holding warriors. People sat expectantly; their hushed conversations created a pleasant hum.

Lookingbill guided Silvertip to a woolly buffalo hide in the back. "Can you see?"

The boy nodded. "Yes, this is a good place."

"Wonderful. I want you to remember this day. It has been ten tens times ten summers since Wolf Dreamer fought Grandfather White Bear and found the dark hole in the ice that led to this world. It is a very special day."

Silvertip nodded, and Lookingbill wrapped an arm lovingly over the boy's shoulders and hugged him.

A hush fell as Mossy took her place near the central fire. She had removed her cape and wore a long black-painted dress adorned with mica nuggets; she looked regal. After clearing her throat several times to gain silence, she extended a hand to the worshipers.

"Lame Bull People, we come together this equinox night to cele-brate the freeing of our Ancestors from the terrible Land of the Long Dark."

The crowd responded, "May Wolf Dreamer be blessed forever more."

"We come to praise the name of Grandfather White Bear, who gave his life to keep Wolf Dreamer alive so that he could find the hole in the ice."

"Let the name of Grandfather White Bear be blessed," the people responded.

Mossy raised a fist, and it cast a huge dark shadow against the boulders behind her. "We come to praise the spirit of Wolf, who brought a grand Dream to a boy named Runs-in-Light, a boy who would become the Wolf Dreamer. Old Man Above sent Wolf Dreamer to teach us the way to the One. It is through the One that we conquer his wicked brother, Raven Hunter. It is through the One that we find peace and harmony."

People called, "Let the name of Wolf be blessed forever more."

A shiver played along Lookingbill's spine—one spurred by memories of ancient stories and a longing that this feeling of community might last forever. He stole glances at the people around him. Their faces gleamed with faith and reverence, particularly Silvertip's face.

"He who seeks light in the dark places, may he seek light for us and for all of the Lame Bull People."

Mossy walked straight across the cavern and out the front entrance, to prepare for the telling of the great story. The young Storyteller-in-the-making, Ringing Shield, a youth of six and ten summers, took her place. He began a recitation of all the sacred names of Wolf Dreamer and Raven Hunter.

At the mention of Raven Hunter's name, Silvertip's breathing quickened. Lookingbill patted him gently on the back. Leaning down, he asked, "What's wrong?"

"Raven Hunter is evil."

"It is said that he tried to deceive and destroy our people."

Silvertip stared into Lookingbill's eyes. "He isn't gone, Grandfather. He's come back."

"Our prophecies tell us that if that ever happens the Last Mammoth will trumpet Raven Hunter's arrival, and Wolf Dreamer will send a new Dreamer to save us."

"But what if the new Dreamer—whoever he is—fails? Would Raven Hunter lead the Nightland People against us and kill us all?"

The boy's words wrung a pang from his heart. "Don't think such things, Silvertip. Wolf Dreamer would not punish us so."

Silvertip dropped his gaze. In a panicked whisper, he said, "I had a Dream last night, Grandfather. In it Raven Hunter swooped down, and his black wings sound like a huge wind—"

At that moment a white-haired man stepped into the cavern. The shell beads stitched on his long cape reflected the light, making it glisten as if it were sprinkled with filaments of fire. The stranger's eyes searched the temple, going over each firelit face, fixing on Lookingbill's and nodding.

"Forgive me, Grandson," he said. "I must go, but I'll return soon."

As Lookingbill walked through the crowd, people's gazes followed him.

"Trembler?" he called when he reached the mouth of the rockshelter. "Old friend, what have you learned?"

"He's here."

A curious mixture of relief and anxiety flooded Lookingbill's veins. "Where?"

"We're hiding him in a rockshelter at the foot of the hill. War Chief Fish Hawk and six warriors are guarding him."

Lookingbill followed the old man down the hillside trail. Above the cliff, Sister Moon wavered through a layer of mist, casting a milky light on the towering spruce trees.

A raven cawed in the forest—unusual for the middle of the night—and a sudden shiver climbed Lookingbill's spine. He looked toward the distant trees and could feel a presence out there, a looming darkness that peered wide-eyed at him, like a huge predator about to pounce.

He's come! Silvertip's words haunted his soul. *Let's hope the Last Mammoth isn't about to trumpet.*

He'd felt such Power before, many times, usually when he picked up the Wolf Bundle.

He put his hand on his belt pouch and hurried toward the group of warriors who guarded the rockshelter.

Six

Nashat disliked the cold. His thoughts dwelled on that inescapable fact as he strode down the cavernous dark tunnel. Around him, the ice groaned and creaked. He could hear the constant harmonic of wind as it blew through the tunnels that honeycombed the ice. Once he had thought it familiar and comforting, but that had been his childhood ignorance. Only after he had left, traveled, and finally returned did the place give him shivers.

Tunnels and caverns were formed by meltwater. The constant warm winds blowing up from the south melted the upper ice, creating pools in hollows. The gravel, sand, and dust that settled in the pool bottoms caught sunlight, warming the water even more. When a shift in the ice created a crack, warm water trickled down. The action bored tunnels, passageways, and hollows into the depths. When the pools drained, they drew warm air after them, cooling it, causing it to sink, and sucking more warm air behind it, all of which caused even more melting, enlarging the passageway.

At such times, the sound of rushing and falling water added a roar to the moaning winds, the creaking ice, and the clatter of gravel and stone borne by the deep-ice streams.

Living inside such a mass of unstable ice now seemed lunacy, especially since cave-ins, collapses, and sudden quakes could crush a person under slabs of rock-encrusted ice. Some, who ventured far back into the tunnels, could be isolated when the ice shifted, blocking a tunnel and leaving them to die alone in the darkness.

Floods during summer and early fall were another hazard. A collapse somewhere deep in the ice could block a passage, backing the water until it roared into a different fissure, only to flood down a long-dry tunnel.

For generations, the dead had been carried back into the ice, left in orderly ranks, and allowed to freeze. Then, when he was a child, the ice had shifted in midsummer, and a sudden flood of meltwater had been diverted through the burial chamber. The icy, gravel-filled water had washed the corpses out into the Thunder Sea, where they bobbed and floated, fouling the shores and terrifying the people for months until the bodies finally sank into the depths—or washed up on the shores to feed the birds, foxes, wolves, and bears.

That would have been a warning for anyone with sense to leave this place!

But his people hadn't. They'd been living inside and around the ice for so long they could imagine no other existence.

But I can. Nashat made a sour face as he followed the deep-ice passage. He knew the way by heart. The Council liked to hold their meetings where people couldn't listen in. Nashat lifted the little bark lamp he carried before him. The pale flicker illuminated water-sculpted walls. Dirt-encrusted ice was layered with crystalline streaks of bluish white. Fog froze from his breath, wavering. His feet crunched on the gravel that had settled on the floor.

He alone, of his people, had seen the south. As a young man he had traveled, following the highland trails down to the south. There, at long last, he had stood at the edge of the crystalline turquoise waters of the gulf and stared out at the sunlight glinting on white beaches.

Along the way, he had visited with many of the forest peoples, those who hunted mastodon, forest buffalo, and the giant tortoises that lumbered along chewing on lush green vegetation.

I must have been out of my mind to come back. He fondly remembered the woman he'd lived with down there. The weather was so warm that clothing was optional.

But a longing for family, friends, and clan had stubbornly uprooted him, bringing his wandering feet back. Sometime in the five winters he had been in the south, he had changed. The homecoming he had longed for had turned hollow on the first day. People had marveled at his stories, and then dismissed them as the ravings of a fertile and overblown imagination.

But I know the truth!

He still did. Once he had managed to stifle his disgust at his own narrow-minded people, he had considered the things he knew. That he had traveled so widely had exposed him to different ideas, different ways of dealing with problems. After the first six months, he had begun to speak up at Council, to offer new ways to deal with hide-bound traditional problems.

The fact was, he was no longer blinded by old teachings and beliefs. His Nightland People addressed problems the way they always had, as their Ancestors had before them. "But that's *not* how we do things!" The tired old refrain had irritated him endlessly.

"Well," he had countered, "try it my way for once."

Grudgingly at first, they had adopted some of his suggestions, and when they worked, they had paid heed to his opinions.

Over the years, Nashat had risen to become the youngest Elder on the Council.

He smiled at that. All he had to do was make his wishes known, and the Council just nodded, as if he, and he alone, had the ear of wisdom.

Then Ti-Bish had come to him. The Idiot had looked up with his glassy eyes, awe filling his thin, half-starved face. The Idiot literally gushed about Raven Hunter's Dream.

Nashat chuckled. "And you gave me everything."

He had taken a calculating gamble by asking the Council to let the Idiot address the summer festival. But no more than a finger's time later, the entire crowd was enthralled, eyes widening, mouths forming little circles of wonder.

From that moment on, the four Nightland clans had surrendered themselves to the Idiot's Dream. Fueled by Ti-Bish's glowing promises, they were a people possessed; and he, Nashat, possessed the sacred Guide.

He puffed out a breath, shaking his head. Everything had gone right. Well, but for a couple of bumps like the mess Karigi had made of the Walking Seal Village trap. Nashat would have been much better served with Bramble here, under his thumb, than a dead symbol of resistance.

In time, however, even that pesky Windwolf would be dealt with.

He caught the faint flicker of light ahead and walked across the crunching gravel into a small cavern in the ice.

His three counterparts—Ta'Hona of the Loon Clan, Satah of the Wolverine Clan, and Khepa of the Ash Clan—were already seated on folded sections of mammoth hide to keep their old butts from freezing.

"We almost gave up," Satah muttered. "How long did you expect to keep us waiting?"

Nashat stepped into the room and lowered himself on the thick folds of hide. He carefully placed the lamp on the woolly hair and crossed his legs.

Satah, ancient and white-haired, studied him through dim eyes, mostly clouded with white. He was an emaciated wreck of a man, but his clan still doted on every word the old fool uttered.

"Something came up. The prisoners from Nine Pipes Village were brought in by Kakala. The Guide had a special interest in this raid."

"And what was that?" Ta'Hona asked, his bright eyes gleaming in the flickering lamplight. "You never tell us these things!"

Nashat waved it away. "The Guide doesn't elaborate on all of his wishes." He narrowed his eyes, glaring at old Ta'Hona. The man's face was deeply scarred, and his right arm didn't work—results of a mammoth hunt gone wrong when he was young.

"What of the Lame Bull People?" Khepa asked. "Is it time to turn on them now?"

"Perhaps." Nashat placed his fingertips together. "I wasn't ready—"

"Perhaps?" Khepa's expression turned sour. "I'm starting to believe I'll never live long enough to see the Long Dark! I didn't think this would take so long. I was ready to follow the Guide through the hole in the ice the day after he delivered Raven Hunter's Dream."

Grunts of assent came from around the room.

Nashat spread his arms wide. "As am I. But you heard the Guide. He said that none of the old believers must follow us. Or do you want their heresy in the Long Dark with us?"

"No," Khepa snorted, "I do not. My sons were both killed long ago in raids against the Sunpath People. I'm sick enough of the problems they cause as it is. But for them, we would have been gone from this place long ago."

Nashat nodded, fingering the fine buffalo-calf hunting shirt he wore. No one tanned hides like the Sunpath People; this fine shirt with its fringed shoulders had been brought to him as a gift from Kakala, who had taken it as plunder from a destroyed village. In fact, none of his people complained about the fine things the warriors brought home from the raids.

"Think back," Nashat said. "Before the Guide's vision, we lived hand to mouth." He gestured around. "These caverns in the Ice Giants have protected our people for generations. The Thunder Sea draws waterfowl by the tens of tens every summer. It provides us with fish, seals, walrus, and whale meat. On the tundra, mammoth, musk ox, caribou, and elk feed. Every summer, we have hunted the bounty, carrying it into the caves to freeze for winter. The fat we render from the seals and walrus, as well as the other game, provides us with fuel for our lamps and cooking."

He glanced around. "Yes, it's cold here in the summer when the air drains off the ice, but it's comparatively warm in the winter when we're out of the wind. Over the years, our clans have flourished, supplying us with warriors. Perhaps that is why Raven Hunter came to the Guide when he did. We were finally ready—not only to hear his words, but we had the strength to drive off those who still cling to the old ways."

"And the heart to really wage war," Ta'Hona reminded. "That is our strength in this world, as Raven Hunter is among the Spirits."

"That, too." Nashat didn't remind them that it had been *his* idea to abandon the old ritual of petty raiding parties and send the warriors out in strength. Or that attacking the Sunpath People first had been his emphatic demand prior to dispatching Kakala on the first massive raids.

"How many of the Sunpath bands remain?" Satah asked. "How soon before we unleash ourselves on the Lame Bull People and their pollution?" He looked around. "This is the very night that they consecrate their arrival in this world. It is an affront to Raven Hunter and his Guide."

"They will get their due . . . soon," Nashat promised. "Kakala reported that at least one Sunpath band has pulled down their lodges, heading west. According to the story, they are leaving for good. If the others follow, we can turn our full attention on the Lame Bull People. Then, as soon as they are broken, dead, or dispersed, we will be prepared to leave."

"And the Guide?" Khepa fingered his snowy hair. His hand trembled as he did. "Is he ready?"

Nashat managed to avoid making a face. "He muttered something about finding a woman first."

"I thought he didn't lie with women!" Ta'Hona declared hotly. "Isn't he the one who claims that coupling masks the path to the Spirit World?"

Satah chimed in, "If he takes a woman, will he still keep Raven Hunter's favor? Can he show us the way?"

Nashat waved them down. "It's not about a warmer for his bed! He was in one of those states . . . carrying on about a sacred bundle."

Satah's white eyes swam in his head, as if searching for something. "I thought we had all of the bundles. That was the point of the first raids. To obtain them."

"All but the Wolf Bundle," Ta'Hona growled. "The Lame Bull have that one. But why Wolf Dreamer's bundle should travel with us to the Long Dark is beyond me."

"Leave it to Power," Nashat urged. "If the Guide desires it, we will obtain it for him. Who knows, maybe that is the last sacrifice we must make before leaving?"

A tremor rumbled through the ice. All eyes went to the curved ceiling, where gravel and bands of white ice glistened in the flickering light.

Recovering, Nashat added, "If we burn the Wolf Bundle as a last act in this world, so be it."

"What of Windwolf?" Khepa asked. "Did Kakala report anything about him?"

"He did." Nashat studied his hand as he clenched and opened his fingers. "One of his warriors overheard a conversation among the captives. Something about a meeting with Chief Lookingbill. I have already dispatched Kakala and his warriors to investigate. It may be that Windwolf will fall into our hands, at the same time giving us reason to turn on the Lame Bull. True or not, Windwolf will be a minor irritation."

"Not if he keeps killing our young men the way he has been. I'd give almost anything to put him in a cage for a while and watch him bleed."

"Blame that on Karigi," Ta'Hona replied.

"Leave my war chief out of this!" Satah pointed a hard finger. "No one ever had to put him in a cage for incompetence."

Nashat raised his hands to placate. "We have enough to worry about without turning on ourselves. Our war chiefs have done all that was expected of them." And, after all, Karigi had his uses. Kakala, however, had started to worry Nashat. Rumors were that he had taken to warning camps before he destroyed them.

The last thing I need is a war chief with a conscience.

Which brings us to . . . "We have another problem."

All eyes turned to Nashat.

"The slaves are eating more than they are producing. We have too many. Especially with this last bunch the Guide had us bring in."

"We can't just turn them loose," Ta'Hona replied, a frown lining his scarred old face.

"No." Nashat narrowed his eyes. "They are dangerous. The fools still cry out to Wolf Dreamer, asking his blessing and help. Others sing the praises of Windwolf. I would hate to see this get out of hand. The accursed man causes us enough problems without some slave getting the idea he might come in some silly attempt at rescue."

"Then deal with it." Khepa waved a thick-veined hand in dismissal.

"That is the will of the Council?" Nashat asked.

Three heads bobbed.

"Then deal with it, I shall." He smiled. "As a token of the respect I have for the Wolverine Clan war chief, Satah, I shall let Karigi attend to it."

Satah grinned, exposing his toothless pink gums.

"I still don't see what the Guide wants with this woman," Ta'Hona growled.

Nashat could care less what Ti-Bish wanted with a woman. His concern was Windwolf—and the Lame Bull People.

Seven

Lookingbill followed Trembler down the night-dark trail. War Chief Fish Hawk—big and raw-boned—stood before the rockshelter with his war club gripped in a tight fist. Six more warriors could be seen around the slope, their gazes trained on the darkness.

Lookingbill walked up to Fish Hawk and said, "I want you to move far enough away that your warriors can't overhear. There are enough stories spread as it is."

"Is that a good idea? This is Windwolf we're talking about."

"By coming alone, Windwolf has shown his trustworthiness."

Fish Hawk gave him a long, penetrating look, then lifted a hand and called, "Warriors, spread out. Let's not get caught by surprise."

Lookingbill turned to Trembler. "If you would move up the trail a ways, you could ensure that we are not interrupted by anyone coming to look for me."

"I'll make some fitting excuse, old friend." Trembler laid a hand on his shoulder. "Perhaps something about a problem with your bowels."

He sighed. "Oh, and they'd love to believe that!"

Lookingbill ducked into the cramped space, and the small oil lamp in the middle of the floor flickered. The hole consisted of three boulders slanted against each other. Lookingbill sniffed, smelling dry, cold rock; but there was something else, a hint of human sweat, the faintest odor of old campfires.

"War Chief Windwolf?" he asked the form huddled back in the shadows.

"Lookingbill?" Windwolf straightened. He was a tall man, broad-shouldered, with hard eyes. His black hair had been cut short in mourning. Two winters, and he still hadn't healed from Bramble's death? Though his darts and an atlatl stood against the wall by his side, he had a knife and war club tied to his belt.

"I am glad that you have come," Lookingbill said. "Given the promise of safety made by the Nightland, I wasn't sure that you would."

"I am ready to grasp at the faintest thread." But he made no effort to step away from his atlatl and war darts.

Lookingbill hobbled toward the lamp and slumped to the floor. Even this trace of warmth was welcome.

Windwolf studied him for a moment, then asked, "Why did you ask to meet with me?"

Lookingbill gestured to the floor on the opposite side of the lamp. "Come, sit. Let us talk as friends."

Windwolf hesitated, glanced at the mouth of the rockshelter, then picked up his darts and atlatl. He walked around to kneel just to the left of the entrance. He rested a long dart across his knees. "The Lame Bull People have rarely been our friends."

"Perhaps it's time that changed."

"A great many lives would have been saved if it had changed two summers ago."

Lookingbill nodded. "Oh, yes, War Chief. My people, however—like yours in the beginning—prefer to delude themselves."

Windwolf glanced out the entrance at the positions of the warriors, then turned back. "I'm listening."

Lookingbill exhaled. "Do you know much about Ti-Bish?"

"Some. Not much."

"Apparently he is very charismatic. Many of my own people have been fooled by him."

"Among my people, also."

"There are witnesses who claim that an evil Spirit appeared beside his cradleboard the day he was born. It wrapped Ti-Bish in a white mammoth hide and fed him lightning bolts."

Windwolf's face showed no emotion. "Dreamers arise constantly, Chief, like wolves among mice. He's no different."

"People say he is."

Windwolf didn't respond.

Lookingbill smiled faintly. "Are you aware that many women from Foxfire's line have been killed recently? Most have died under suspicious circumstances. No one claims the responsibility."

Windwolf's brows drew down over his pointed nose. "Foxfire? Wolf Dreamer's half brother? The son of Ice Fire and Dancing Fox?"

"Yes." Lookingbill's gaze fixed on the lamp's tiny flame. As Wind Woman sneaked into the rockshelter and sniffed around the walls, it fluttered, on the verge of going out.

Windwolf said, "Why is that important?"

"Because prophecies tell us that in the last days, just before the destruction of the world, a new Dreamer will be born. He will lead his people to safety . . . and he will come from the Foxfire clan."

Silence filled the chamber.

When Lookingbill said no more, Windwolf asked, "How many women from Foxfire's line are left?"

"My daughters, Dipper and Mossy, and a cousin, Loon Spot; but she's too old to bear children. She would be no threat to Ti-Bish."

"Do you think he's deliberately trying to kill off your family? To make sure the prophecies are never fulfilled?"

Lookingbill stared out into the night. He felt it again, that looming presence, as though the darkness itself had ears. "It's possible. Ti-Bish is a curious character. He claims that Raven Hunter came to him and gave him a Vision."

"You tell me old news. That's when he began preaching that Wolf Dreamer was wicked and Raven Hunter was good. He says the two are locked in a constant battle over the fate of our world."

"He also believes that anyone who worships Wolf Dreamer is evil. That's why he has targeted your Sunpath People."

Windwolf's bushy black brows drew together. He stared at the sputtering oil lamp for several heartbeats before asking, "Both the Southwind and Lame Bull People worship Wolf Dreamer. You and I know it's more than that. The Nightland People are using the Prophet's religion as an excuse to take our lands. It's only recently that Ti-Bish has gained any followers." He paused. "Even his own people called him the Idiot."

"But all that changed two summers ago when Nashat found him."

"Yes." Windwolf exhaled the word. "Nashat plucked Ti-Bish from the forests, cleaned him up, and started announcing the arrival of the Blessed Guide promised in the Old Stories."

"Selling him?"

"Clearly. We had no problems with Ti-Bish until he began preaching that anyone who worshipped Wolf Dreamer was evil." Windwolf tilted his head and appeared to be listening to the night sounds outside. Softly, he continued, "Since the attacks began, many would like nothing better than to kill him . . . and Nashat wouldn't like that."

Lookingbill nodded in understanding. "You've been on the trail for many days. Have you heard that the Nine Pipes band was attacked and destroyed?"

Windwolf's face slackened. "Were there survivors?"

"Kakala took all the women. I was told earlier that Nashat has ordered them held in some sort of pen and was waiting for Ti-Bish to decide their fates."

Windwolf massaged his brow. "His soul must be loose."

"Sometimes it seems so. The servants in the Nightland caves say that after Raven Hunter talks with Ti-Bish, he wanders the ice labyrinth for days, mumbling to himself, waving his arms like a madman, trying to find the hole in the ice to lead his people back to the time of the Long Dark."

Windwolf's eyes glowed as though from an inner fire. "Let us get to the point. Why did you ask me to come here?"

Lookingbill held that intense gaze and saw something frail behind it, as though the man was trying very hard to cover a soul-deep pain.

"You're here because I want to help you find a way to kill the Nightland Prophet."

Eight

In a world gone mad, Skimmer shivered and struggled unsuccessfully to find some faint thread to cling to. She huddled in the darkness, clinging to her daughter, Ashes, for what little warmth they could share.

She had stared in disbelief when Kakala's warriors had herded them into the pen. The walls were a curious construction of spruce poles carried up from the Lame Bull lands, sections of whale, mammoth, and other ribs, all lashed together. It was the sort of thing her people built to trap animals in.

Who could have thought up such a thing? And what was its purpose?

Then Nashat had walked out, peered through the bars, pointed to high-breasted young Blue Wing, and ordered her removed. Skimmer and the rest of the women had watched silently as pretty Blue Wing stepped out, endured Nashat's rude assessment of her slim body, and then was ordered to be taken and delivered to the Guide.

Skimmer had silently thanked Wolf Dreamer that it wasn't her. Now, after four days, she wasn't so sure. Blue Wing might have to endure Ti-Bish pumping himself between her legs, but she probably had food and drink.

Skimmer swallowed down her dry throat. *Is that what I have become? An animal willing to let a twisted beast use my body in return for a drink and something to eat?*

And what of Ashes? She considered at her daughter, safely nestled at her feet.

Skimmer shivered, and looked up at the moonlit night. Only the wind from the south gave them hope. When it faded, the terrible cold came rolling down from the Ice Giants. She could see them above the line of poles, rising white and misty in the moonlight.

Skimmer had never been this close to the huge mountains of ice, had never imagined that they could be so big. They filled the northern horizon, rising in oddly shaped peaks that rose to twisted points. Here and there, she could see where some had slid down, the ice cracked and broken. The whole of it was riddled with dark holes that ran down to where?

The very thought of it sent shivers through her bones that not even her chilled flesh could mock.

What brought me here? Her reeling soul couldn't quite grasp her situation. It was like living a disjointed Dream, some impossible twist of imagined horror.

Oh, Hookmaker, how did this happen to us? But her husband was gone. The time to plead with ghosts was over. The fate they had feared had come to collect them. Hookmaker was dead. She'd stood behind his body, had stared in disbelief that the man she loved and argued with lay bleeding and dying before her. In that shocked moment, some voice within had urged her to run; but she had remained rooted, eyes fixed on her husband as he groaned and blood ran out of his head. She'd barely noticed the warriors who surrounded her, lifted her, and carried her away. She had turned, staring in horror at Hookmaker's body until it was out of sight.

"Mother, I'm scared. Where's Father?" Ashes' pleading voice interrupted her misery.

"Don't cry, Ashes," Skimmer whispered. "Hallowed Ancestors, please don't cry."

She glanced up at the pole palisade that surrounded the cramped captives. Like wicked black fangs it rose against the moonlit night. She turned her head away, trying to send her souls back to a place where Hookmaker lived, where the stench of human feces, urine, and fear didn't clog her nose.

"Are they going to kill us?" Ashes whispered fearfully. "The Nightland warriors?"

"No. We're going to escape. I promise you."

Ashes clutched Skimmer's leg. Her young lips had swollen and cracked until she could barely speak. Skimmer stroked her matted hair, wondering how much longer Ti-Bish would force them to suffer.

Tens of people, survivors of the attacks, packed the small log enclosure, standing shoulder to shoulder. Children cried everywhere, mothers impotent to heal the wounds of thirst or hunger. And many of the women were injured. Bloody bandages wrapped arms, legs, and skulls. And these had been the strong ones: the women and children who could carry heavy packs back to the Nightland villages.

They'd been waiting for days, tortured by thirst, the icy wind tearing at their flesh. Several women had gone mad, screaming and lashing out at anyone who unknowingly pressed against them, trying to maintain their slim boundary of space. The sick and weak, too feeble to stand, took turns sitting, heads braced on drawn-up knees. Some were already dead, their bodies hauled to a stinking pile against the back wall. Every time the cold wind changed direction it brought her the scent of rotting corpses. Bile would rise in her throat, and she had to drape her sleeve over her nose.

We live a nightmare. Wolf Dreamer? What have we done to anger you so?

To keep herself standing, Skimmer concentrated on hate. Hatred of all the Nightland People—but especially Ti-Bish and the Nightland clan Elders. She *had* been plotting the Prophet's murder. It was not an easy task. Nashat rarely allowed the Prophet to appear in public, and then only when thoroughly protected by guards. And always, always, with Nashat at his side. But she'd find him vulnerable someday.

"Where's Windwolf?" Kicking Fawn moaned. "Has anyone heard? Where's War Chief Windwolf?"

Hunched and haunted, Kicking Fawn stood only a few hands away from Skimmer, her eyes fixed intently on the ground. Matted hair—spruce needles still visible—hung down over her ears. Several times on the journey north, the traitor, Goodeagle, had taken her off in the trees. Each time she had come back with an ever-greater distance in her eyes.

Skimmer tried to pry her eyes away, but couldn't. Kicking Fawn had been vivacious and beautiful. Could this empty-eyed woman be the same quick-witted, smiling Kicking Fawn? Her daughter, Swan, a girl of nine, stood beside her. She patted her mother's hand. "He's coming, Mother. I know he is. He'll be here soon."

"He's coming?" Kicking Fawn's eyes lit with hope. "Someone told you?"

"Yes," Swan said, but she was obviously lying. "I heard it only moments ago. He's coming."

"Windwolf is coming," Kicking Fawn sighed. "He'll save us. He'll kill these Nightland dogs."

"Yes, now, don't worry. Why don't you try to sit down?"

By midnight, Kicking Fawn's soul had drifted loose. She screamed, "Sunpath People, I see a giant wave rolling down over us! It's huge! Don't you see it?"

Kicking Fawn pointed toward the Ice Giants. "Oh, Spirits, we can't escape!"

Worried mutterings erupted as the packed women staggered, pushing each other, straining to see where Kicking Fawn pointed. When they discovered only blue-white mountains of ice, they turned sharply, staring.

"Can't you see it? What's the matter with you?" Kicking Fawn shoved Swan away and fell to the ground. She covered her head and writhed as though in the throes of a fit.

Swan stared fearfully down at her mother.

At first people only stood quietly, riveted by terror, but as the woman's wailing grew to hideous shrieks, someone shouted, "Stop her! I can't stand it!"

"Bright glittering water, it fills the whole sky!"

Swan stroked her hair tenderly, "Mother, please, it's all right. There's no water. You're just tired and thirsty. We—"

"Oh, Blessed Ancestors have pity. Have pity!"

"She'll drive us all mad!" Mole, a woman from the Black Elk band, wailed. "Someone shut her up!"

Swan tried to calm her mother. "Stop this, Mother. You'll use up your strength. You have to save your strength or you'll die like grandmother. You—"

"Can't you see it?" Kicking Fawn asked in an agonized whisper.

"The sky is empty, Mother. Just a few Cloud People, that's all."

Kicking Fawn suddenly sat up and screamed, "What's the matter with you all? The wave comes from the caves of the Nightland. They've sent it to destroy us!"

"I don't care if you have to kill her," a dirty-haired woman named Kite shouted. "Keep her quiet!"

Swan looked up, eyes wide, moonlit tears glistening on her cheeks.

Some woman Skimmer didn't know hauled back and kicked Kicking Fawn in the mouth.

Swan gathered her mother in her arms protectively, sobbing, "Don't hurt her! The warriors killed the rest of our family. She's crazy from the pain!"

White Bat, once a good friend, thrust a finger into Skimmer's face, saying, "You're a chief's wife. Make her stop!"

"Stop her yourself," Skimmer whispered, and looked away. "Where were you when we tried to rally our people to fight the Nightland?"

"Listening to your husband," White Bat answered acidly. "It was Hookmaker who counseled for peace and restraint."

Skimmer glanced around the enclosure. Terror shone from every face, madness about to burst the very walls enclosing them. Trembling from fatigue and panic, soon they'd all be crazy enough to kill for a breath of silence, or a place to lie down.

"Our souls are loose," Young Elk said. "It . . . it must be the cold."

"Yes, the cold."

As the night dragged on, fights broke out when women struggled to find sleeping positions. Skimmer remained standing, letting Ashes sleep between her spread feet. In the distance, the towering bulk of the Ice Giants gleamed with an unnatural blue fire. Legends said that a vast ocean of fresh water spread beneath them. She dreamed of dipping her hands in it, and drinking endlessly.

Then, in the middle of the night, when the Blessed Star People gleamed like frost crystals cast across the heavens, a wrenching scream sent a jolt through her. In the dim star glow, she saw Kicking Fawn stand up and stretch her arm toward the Ice Giants. Her hair jutted out at odd angles, making her look like an evil Spirit straight from the underworlds.

"Look! The wave! It swallows our children! Oh, Spirits above, what have we done to deserve such punishment?"

Skimmer stared up at the Blessed Star People, trying to force her thoughts from the horrifying prediction. A meaty slap sounded in the darkness, followed by another and another. Three women shoved the crying Swan away and grabbed Kicking Fawn. They pressed her to the ground, each kicking the woman.

Kicking Fawn cried, "Why can't you see it? It's so close! Can't you—"

"Hallowed Ancestors, shut her up!" a hoarse voice called. "We have to get some sleep!"

Grunts sounded, and Skimmer turned to see one of the women drive an elbow into Swan's face as she tried to interfere. Another woman jammed a hide knot into Kicking Fawn's mouth. She struggled pitifully, choking. Swan huddled to the side, dark blood dripping from her nose.

Skimmer squeezed her eyes closed. Would the night never end?

Quietly she prayed, "Wolf Dreamer, why won't you help us?"

She put a hand over her mouth as silent, dry sobs choked her.

"M-Mother," Ashes said, patting her mother's leg soothingly. "Don't cry."

Skimmer sat down, squeezing tightly between two women, to hug her daughter.

"Get up!" an older woman yelled. "There's no room!"

The woman cursed and pounded her back, but she huddled against the beating, refusing to rise. Her trembling legs refused to hold her.

"Don't hit my mother!" Ashes shrieked, using her tiny fists to weakly flail at the woman's leg.

In a cold voice, Skimmer said, "If you touch me again, I will get up and *choke the air out of your throat!*"

In defeat, the woman lifted her hands, muttering, "All right. For now."

Ashes crawled into Skimmer's lap. "Don't cry, Mother." Her daughter extended a tired, dirty hand to pat her back.

Skimmer stroked Ashes' hair. "You're the one who must sleep. Tomorrow might be worse. We have to save our strength."

"But you have to sleep, too."

"All right, I'll try. Close your eyes now."

Ashes relaxed in Skimmer's arms.

She turned to glance through the mass at Kicking Fawn. The woman was staring across the enclosure with still black eyes.

Two guards had climbed up to sit on top of the logs. In the silver wash of starlight, their faces shone a ghostly gray.

Nine

War Chief Kakala was an unhappy man. He peered through a tangle of rosebushes and counted the Lame Bull warriors. His black-painted beaverhide shirt and pants—the hair turned in for warmth—blended perfectly with the darkness. Seven guards stood in front of the cave. Worse, tens of villagers moved up and down the trails. They wore their finest capes. For them—as it had been for him in his youth—this was a holy day. But that had been before the coming of the Guide.

Jewelry flashed, catching the moonlight as the Lame Bull People passed up and down the trails that laced their rocky warren together. He could hear the pleasant clicking of shell bracelets and anklets, and see the sparkle of buffalo-horn earpins, and mammoth-ivory pendants.

"You will take your warriors and run south to Headswift Village." Nashat's order still rang in his ears. *"Rumors among the Sunpath say that Windwolf is headed there. No matter what, War Chief, you find him. Either bring me Windwolf, or bring me his head."*

Kakala had stared in disbelief, pointing at his exhausted warriors, explaining how half had already gone to their families' lodges.

"Take what you have. And go now!" The order had been explicit.

So here he was, with a handful of exhausted warriors, staring at a bristling village.

"Keresa?" he called softly. "How long has he been in there?"

She sprawled on a boulder to his left, having a better view of the warriors who guarded the hole where the man they thought was Windwolf had gone to ground.

Her soft voice was little more than a whisper. "It's been a hand of time since Maga and Goodeagle saw him enter. Chief Lookingbill just came down to meet him."

"Maga?" he called softly.

"Over here, War Chief." The youth lifted his head.

"Keep an eye on him." Kakala wriggled back through the prickly roses, trying to keep the thorns from rasping on his clothing. He caught Keresa's eye and motioned her back.

Together they crouched, winding down through the boulders to where the rest of their warriors waited in the bottom of a spruce-lined gully. Exhausted, they had gratefully accepted the opportunity to throw themselves on the rocky bottom of the drainage. Most, he noted, were already fast asleep, heedless of the uncomfortable rocks they lay on. That they could sleep so, and just out of dart range of an enemy village, was proof enough of their fatigue.

"What do you think?" Keresa asked as they crouched in the darkness.

"I think I don't like it," Kakala muttered. He tensed his muscles, rolling his shoulders, fighting the lethargy that sucked at his very bones. "Nashat was out of his mind to send us. We were tired before we were ordered on this raid. We've covered a seven-day trip in four."

Keresa gave him a weary smile. "Would you rather he'd sent Karigi?"

"I remember the last time Karigi tried to trap Windwolf. No, but he could have sent either Blackta or Hawhak."

"They weren't there. We were." Keresa glanced back in the direction where the man they thought was Windwolf had hidden in the rocks.

"And it was just luck we arrived when we did," Kakala muttered. "If that's Windwolf, and he's talking to Lookingbill, it doesn't bode well for us."

"Neither does attacking the Lame Bull with a small party of warriors who are asleep on their feet!" she reminded. "Goodeagle swears it was Windwolf. I could hear the truth of it in his voice."

"Yes, I know." Goodeagle had sounded like a man condemned when he confirmed the stranger's identity.

She was watching him with concerned eyes. "Nashat meant it when he said, 'Don't fail me, War Chief.' If this doesn't happen just right, he's more than capable of putting you in a cage again."

Kakala swallowed hard, nodding. His people could inflict no greater punishment. The miscreant was locked into a small wooden cage and left there for a moon or two. During that time, he was the object of derision and insults, and was often pelted with feces, urine, and trash. Kakala's back and pride had ached for moons after his eventual release. Overcoming the stigma had taken half his life.

"I would really like to believe that Lookingbill has concocted some sort of trap. That he believes Nashat's offer of protection for anyone who surrenders Windwolf to him."

Keresa grunted.

"What? You don't believe our clan leader, either?"

Keresa glanced at the sleeping warriors. Caution still guarded her tongue. "You know what I think of Nashat."

Kakala couldn't help but grin, weary as he was. "It's not too late. You could still accept his offer." He yawned. "Who knows? Sharing his blanket might not be that bad. You wouldn't have to run yourself sick with fatigue. No one would drive a dart through your guts in some raid, and, well, given the number of women Nashat takes to his bed, he must have developed some little skill at pleasuring a woman."

Her disgusted glare should have been answer enough, but she added, "The women who have been in Nashat's bed say that the only pleasure is Nashat's." She shivered at the thought. "I'll take a dart through the guts any day."

They had watched too many of their warriors die that way for Keresa to have said such a thing in jest. She really hated the man.

He said, "It boils down to this: That's probably Windwolf hiding in that hole. Nashat said to take him, no matter what. He's there, guarded by seven Lame Bull warriors. We'll never get a chance like this again."

Keresa studied the sleeping warriors. "If we attack, it means war with the Lame Bull. There will be no going back."

He nodded, a sick sensation in his guts. Nashat hadn't told him to incite hostilities with the Lame Bull. If he did, and it went wrong, he'd be back in the cage. "As I see it, we have three choices. First, we could go back and say that we couldn't be sure Windwolf was here. The problem is that neither Maga nor Goodeagle would keep silent about it. Second, we can pull back, wait, see if Windwolf leaves alone."

"Assuming we see him leave," she countered. "But all bets are off if Windwolf's warriors are out there in the trees somewhere, waiting on word from their war chief. We could find ourselves caught between two forces." She looked at the sleeping warriors. "And in our condition, even if we fought our way out, they could run us down."

"The third option is to take him now, tonight, and hope the Lame Bull don't follow and kill us."

She nodded, drawing a weary breath. "I know." She hung her head. "We need a diversion. Something to draw off the Lame Bull. No matter what, we have to distract them long enough to kill Windwolf, cut off his head for proof. . . ."

He raised an eyebrow at the reluctance in her voice. "Yes?"

She shook her head. "Nothing."

He sighed, staring up at the full moon. "I know. We should hate him for the pain he's caused us. But by Raven Hunter's black cloak, he's fought brilliantly and bravely."

She stiffened, giving him a stony gaze. "Let's be about it. The sooner we're back home, the sooner we can sleep for a week."

Kakala drew a line in the air with his finger. "You and I will take three warriors and capture Windwolf. I want Maga and the remaining ten warriors to make a feint at the main village. His job is to keep them occupied. We will rush that hole, kill as many of the guards as possible, and chase the rest off. After Windwolf is dispatched, you hold off the Lame Bull until I cut his head—"

"War Chief?" Maga hissed from above.

He and Keresa scuttled up the slope, slipping around the patch of forlorn roses to the boulder Maga hid behind. Keeping low, they peered over the rock.

"What?"

"There." Maga pointed.

Kakala's eyes narrowed as a white-haired elder trotted down the trail and ducked into the rockshelter. "Blessed Spirits, who is he?"

"Just another old man," Maga decided. "Doesn't matter."

Keresa muttered a curse. "Killing Lame Bull elders will add to their wrath."

"Impress on the warriors that this is a raid to get Windwolf," Kakala added. "Remind them that the fewer Lame Bull People we kill, the less likely the others will be to pursue us."

Keresa shot him a glance from the corner of her eye. "Aren't you the one who insists that accidents happen when darts fly?"

He whispered, "Don't remind me, remind the warriors. If we can just get Windwolf, nothing else matters."

Ten

Windwolf watched the single flame on the oil lamp flicker. "Chief Lookingbill, I have to ask: I know that you turned down Skimmer's request for an alliance. Why now?"

Lookingbill spread his old hands wide. "Because for the first time, my people will agree. Like yours, they firmly believed that the Prophet had no reason to attack them. This idea of raid after raid, in endless succession, was beyond their comprehension."

"But not beyond yours?" Windwolf asked.

"In the beginning, yes." Lookingbill stared sadly at the lamp. "But Ti-Bish has changed the world. The miracle is that it worked. We have acted as if the old ways would eventually be respected. That everything would return to the way it was."

"I understand." Windwolf sighed. "Like you, I have finally come to the realization that our world is dying, Chief." He lifted his eyes. "Take a close look when you leave here tonight. Enjoy the rest of the full-moon ceremony. You, and your people, will never see another."

Lookingbill's eyes widened. "You mean that, don't you?"

Windwolf nodded. "For two years my people have fought the Night-land warriors. Among their ranks, I have even seen Sunpath warriors.

Like Goodeagle, they have come to believe Raven Hunter's Dream, and have willingly joined to fight beside Kakala, Karigi, and the rest. They believe the Prophet is going to lead them to the paradise of the Long Dark."

Lookingbill sat silently, his dark eyes fixed on a distance within. Then he asked, "What do you think, War Chief?"

Windwolf ran his fingers down the smooth shaft of his war dart. "I think Raven Hunter is back."

"Then were we wrong all these years?"

Windwolf shook his head. "Only half right." He shifted. "Remember the stories. In the beginning, before Wolf Dreamer led the people through the hole in the ice, he and Raven Hunter battled for the souls of the people. Wolf Dreamer won. Ever since, our Dreamers have sought the One. Going off, secreting themselves, fasting, sweating, purifying their souls to escape to the Dream.

"In the process, we have forgotten that the Dark Twin has his own Power." Windwolf met Lookingbill's eyes. "Now I wonder if Raven Hunter hasn't been biding his time, waiting for us to grow weak. I recall my grandfather telling me how in his grandfather's time, everyone sought Wolf Dreamer's vision. But today? How many of your people dedicate themselves to finding the One?"

Lookingbill nodded. "I can think of a handful." He smiled slightly. "Like my grandson."

"Silvertip?"

"You've heard of him?"

"The rumor is that he will find Power."

"If it doesn't kill him first. He's obsessed with the Wolf Bundle." Lookingbill patted the large pouch at his belt. Then he looked up. "We have forgotten that we are all One. Instead we are Sunpath, Lame Bull, Southwind, Nightland, and so many others. The Prophet is now making us pay for forgetting that single truth."

"Or Nashat is."

Lookingbill studied him. "But Nashat only follows the Prophet's orders."

Windwolf shrugged. "You haven't crept up close to Nightland warriors in their camps. They may say they follow the Guide's orders, but listen through their words and it is Nashat who directs them. When you piece together different conversations, you learn that Nashat may have given an order in the Prophet's name but a few days past, while others insist the Prophet has been in the caves for over a moon." A pause. "To me, this does not make sense."

Lookingbill leaned back, a frown on his face. "Then perhaps it is Nashat that we should kill."

Windwolf shook his head. "Nashat may be the cunning soul behind the war, but his authority derives from Ti-Bish. If we chop off the lion's head, the rest of the beast will cease to claw at us."

"And how do we chop off the beast's head?"

"A massed attack." Windwolf leaned forward. "Part of the brilliance of this war against us is the quickness with which it moves. We are forever disorganized, fighting defensively while four different war parties attack in different directions."

"Which means?"

"Who defends the Nightland villages?"

Lookingbill frowned. "But to strip warriors from protecting our villages is to leave them defenseless."

"I never promised that doing this thing would be without risk." Windwolf leaned back. "If I join my warriors with yours, it must be done quickly, and with as much strength as we can muster. So, you must ask yourself: Is it worth the risk to strike at the heart of the Nightland? Is it worth the destruction of your home and family to kill the Prophet?"

Lookingbill sighed, his shoulders slumping. "That I do not know. Are you sure there isn't another way?"

"Name it, and I will consider anything."

"Chief?" old Trembler called from outside.

"Enter," Lookingbill called.

The old man ducked inside, bowed to Windwolf, and glanced at Lookingbill. His white hair gleamed in the faint lamplight.

"Forgive me," he said. "Dipper wanted me to tell you that the ceremonial is over and the feast has begun."

Lookingbill nodded. "Tell Dipper I will be there shortly."

"I should be going, too," Windwolf said as he rose and checked his weapons. "Should you decide to do this, I need to send word to my warriors."

Lookingbill grunted as he got to his feet. The lamp cast his shadow on the rear wall like a black ghost. "You should stay for the night. I have many extra hides in my chamber. You are welcome to—"

"No, Chief, though I appreciate your generosity. My presence here only endangers you and your people. I must go."

Trembler said, "Please, come to my chamber first. I will fill your pack with food for the trip back."

"That's not necessary, but I thank you."

Trembler shrugged, stepped out into the darkness, and Windwolf heard the old man's steps move away up the trail.

Lookingbill walked out after him.

Windwolf stood at the opening for a few moments, listening to the sounds of the village. Many voices carried on the night; most were light and happy. One woman laughed. How long had it been since he had heard such carefree sounds?

Lookingbill turned back. "Is everything all right?" His deeply wrinkled face had turned somber.

"I was only remembering what peace sounded like."

War Chief Fish Hawk and his warriors formed a crescent around the shelter entrance, dark forms in the gleaming moonlight.

Windwolf looked beyond them, to the shadows, and a shiver played along his spine.

Lookingbill noticed. "Don't tell me you feel it too?"

"Feel what?"

"I don't know." He frowned out at the night. "It's a—a darkness that watches . . . listens." He frowned. "Something is wrong here."

Shadows played over the trees at the base of the boulders. Windwolf caught movement. A hint of buckskin where there should have been only black tree trunks. He reached down and nocked a dart in his atlatl. Very quietly, he said, "War Chief Fish Hawk, we are about to be attacked. Chief Lookingbill, do whatever it takes to protect yourself."

Lookingbill's eyes widened, and he swung around to peer at the trees.

"Someone's out there? Are you sure?" Fish Hawk asked uncertainly.

Lookingbill sternly added, "Whatever you do, War Chief, ensure that Windwolf is safe! I want it made perfectly clear that—"

Windwolf lifted his atlatl to cast. "Lookingbill, *run! Now!*"

War cries split the night as warriors burst from the darkness. Windwolf knew that dark form: Kakala! The big man ran out front, his muscular legs pumping.

Windwolf whipped his arm back, cast at the elusive shadow, and saw Kakala stumble. A hit? His heart soared. Before he could determine Lookingbill jumped in front of him and shouted, "Go to the ceremonial cave! Tell my daughter Dipper to take you to the Deep Cave. She'll know—"

A dart drove half its length through the old man's shoulder. Lookingbill staggered at the impact. He gave Windwolf a terrified glance and shouted, "Save yourselves!"

Fish Hawk's warriors cast at the charging forms.

Windwolf hesitated only long enough to snap the dart in two and shove Lookingbill into the hole behind him. "Stay there!" He turned. "Fish Hawk! The rest of you! Stop standing like stupid ground sloths! Fall back to the rocks! Take defensive positions! *Move!*"

A voice from the village cried, "We are attacked!"

As Fish Hawk's warriors sprinted up the trail, Windwolf nocked his atlatl and drove a dart through a charging warrior. He could hear shouts, whoops, and screams from the slopes below Headswift Village.

Through instinct, Windwolf ducked a whistling dart. Then he turned and ran, pounding along behind Fish Hawk's dark figure.

Kakala! Where is Kakala?

Eleven

The insane night attack had broken up almost as quickly as it began. Once the Headswift villagers had retreated to their rocky warrens, the prowling Nightland warriors had backed off, lurking in the shadows, calling insults.

Windwolf had stopped Fish Hawk's warriors when they reached a narrow rocky defile. With their few remaining darts, they had discouraged any further pursuit by Kakala's raiders. Now they waited, hidden in the shadows of the rocks, ready to ambush any incursion by Nightland warriors.

Fish Hawk shot a look at Windwolf. "You saved our lives back there, War Chief."

"I just hope Lookingbill is all right."

"You saw the wound. Was it mortal?"

"Only if it becomes infected. The dart was high in the shoulder. Someone is going to have to get him out of that hole. And soon."

Windwolf took a deep breath, leaning out to inspect the moon-bathed trails. If he ran, it wouldn't take but a—

Fish Hawk clamped a hand on his arm. "I know what you're thinking, but no. You have done enough this night. I don't know what happened in that Council you just had, but my chief gave orders. You are to be kept safe."

"Fish Hawk, had I not been here, none of this might have happened."

The war chief shrugged. "Perhaps not tonight, but eventually." He gave Windwolf a sad grin. "We are allies now. What damage is done, is done. In the meantime, you will serve my people better by living than dying in an attempt to save my chief." He raised his voice. "Dipper! My chief has ordered that this man be taken to a place where the stinking Nightland cannot find him. Take him to the Deep Cave."

Seeing the insistence in Fish Hawk's eyes, Windwolf surrendered, and followed his guides through a hole down into the rocks.

Windwolf had to bend low to follow Trembler and Dipper through the narrow passage that led into the depths of Headswift Village. The little bark lamp Dipper carried flickered on the rough-sided boulders. The tunnels were often so narrow that the shoulders of his buffalo coat scraped roughly against the stone. In the dry coolness, the smell of the fresh-roasted elk tongue Dipper carried in her belt pouch sent growls of anticipation through his stomach.

Now Trembler stopped and blinked at another of the many smaller tunnels that jutted off from the main one they followed. "Dipper? This is the turn, isn't it? I thought I remembered—"

"No." She shook her head, and long black hair fell over the front of her cape. A pudgy woman with a face too round and eyes too large, she reminded Windwolf of a timid owl.

"No, it's farther." Her voice cracked.

"My place is with the warriors," Windwolf insisted.

"Father said to keep you safe!" she cried, almost to the point of tears.

Windwolf closed his eyes. The chasm of dread in his chest yawned until it seemed a somber, frightening darkness pervaded everything.

"What made these caves?" he asked, thinking to distract them, and himself.

"Ice." Trembler swallowed hard. "In some of the lower ones, the ice is still there. It melts back a little each year. The big rocks settle some with each summer."

Dipper seemed to have collected her wits. "It's this way. Trust me."

She started forward. Finally Dipper led the way into a small rounded chamber. Windwolf ducked his head and followed.

In feeble lamplight, the cavern spread five body lengths across and about seven tall. Calling it a cave was a curious word. Actually, it was a pile of boulders and dirt that had, at some time in the past, been hollowed out by water. A stack of dusty, rolled hides rested against the rear wall. Gourds and hide bags filled the crevices in the walls. Food and water? Or ceremonial objects?

"What is this place?" Windwolf asked, dusting off his shoulders.

Dipper said, "Father calls it the Deep Cave. He comes here to Dream and pray. It's the only place he feels truly s-safe." Her voice broke, and she put a trembling hand to her mouth.

"Dipper," Trembler whispered. "Why don't you go back up to see what's happening? I can care for—"

"Soon. Not yet." She walked over to the stack of hides and began rolling them out. "The insides shouldn't be too dusty."

Windwolf spread out his hide and sat down.

Dipper untied her belt pouch and handed it to him. "You must be hungry. I grabbed this for you. Please, eat. I'll fetch water." She went to one of the wall niches and pulled down a gourd, which she set beside Windwolf.

"You have my thanks, Dipper."

Dipper spread her hide and sat down across from Windwolf, but Trembler paced nervously.

Windwolf pulled out a thick slice of elk tongue and took a bite. It tasted wonderful and tender. He forced himself to eat slowly, to savor it.

Trembler sighed. "War Chief, I assume Lookingbill told you that we have to kill the Prophet."

Windwolf swallowed his food and looked up. His gaze went first to Trembler, then to Dipper. "He did. We can only hope the Nightland haven't altered it."

Trembler and Dipper exchanged solemn looks.

Windwolf took a long drink from the water gourd and wiped his mouth on his sleeve.

Trembler turned away, and seemed to be staring at the small gourds that filled one of the wall niches. Lamp oil, perhaps? He said only, "You'll need to stay here, until Kakala leaves."

Dipper added, "I pray there's something left alive after Kakala finishes with us."

Windwolf looked down at his atlatl. It would be too good to be true, but maybe he'd gotten lucky with that first cast. Maybe Kakala was lying in the moonlight, coughing blood out with his last breath.

Darkness

*P*eople often ask me where I live in the Nightland Caves, mostly because they hope to find me. But I am never quite able to answer that question. You see, my home is not a place; it is a black womb that floats somewhere between the brilliant Star People and the dark hole in the ice, a womb that never stops giving birth to me.

By day the darkness empties my soul of its own petty worries and self-ishness. By night it Sings to me until the Dreaming comes . . . and I begin the search for a legend.

I have heard holy people say that darkness is evil.

I've never understood their words. For me darkness is light. Light is darkness. That is the hoop of life. That is goodness. Evil arises only when the hoop is broken into two parts; then both light and darkness wound.

Like the Hero Twins.

Wolf Dreamer and Raven Hunter were once One. But the instant they became two, evil entered the world. . . .

It is the Dream Rift.

The instant of becoming homeless.

I must return to that instant before the Rift became.

Twelve

Skimmer watched a great gray owl soar through the darkness over-head. Beneath her drawn-up knees, Ashes lay in a deep sleep. Skim-mer let her leaden arm drop to gently stroke the little girl's exposed toes. The freezing temperatures had sapped what little strength she and Ashes had left.

Wind Woman whipped across the walls, peppering the crowd with sand, but no one moaned; no one moved. A deadly hush had fallen over the enclosure, as though every prisoner held her breath. When would War Chief Windwolf come? When?

As dawn neared, a deep blue halo arced over the eastern horizon, and she heard the monotonous drone of voices outside, people speak-ing with Sunpath accents. This was the most holy night of their lives, and they were not in their own villages at the ceremonial celebrations.

"Do you think they know we're here?" old Yellow Woman asked in surprise.

Her gray hair had turned dark from the dirt and blowing dust. She looked at Skimmer through sleepless eyes. Beside her, her niece—a girl named Mink—stood numbly. Skimmer hadn't heard her murmur a single word in two days. Her hope seemed as dead as the pile of corpses in the rear.

"Of course they know," Skimmer answered. "They have given up on their people and joined the Nightland to follow the Prophet's Dream."

She rubbed her gritty eyes. *And perhaps I should, too.*

Yellow Woman rubbed a grimy hand over her face. "I can't believe I'm awake. How can our own people allow us to be tortured this way?"

"As long as they can turn their heads, they don't care."

She thought of the Lame Bull People and Lookingbill, and wondered what he would think when the Nightland warriors came for his loved ones. A flicker of anger burned through her.

But for you, none of this would have happened. But then, even now, she understood the hesitation. She'd seen it enough among her own people back in the beginning. It was someone else's problem. Why twist the lion's tail?

Yellow Woman shook her head. "For three summers we've been fighting to keep the old ways . . . the ways of kindness. And now no one cares what happens to us? Those are our relatives out there!"

As if to reinforce her words, echoes of laughter carried on the night wind.

"Are they?" Skimmer asked.

Yellow Woman's eyes roamed the foreboding pole walls around them. "How can you ask such a thing? Of course they are. All Sunpath People are brothers and sisters."

"The world has changed since the coming of the Prophet. The word 'family' now only applies to those who follow him. Today, even cousins turn their heads."

A mammoth trumpeted from somewhere in the distance, and every head turned to listen to the sacred animal. Whispers broke out. It was so rare to hear them these days. In her mind, Skimmer pictured the animal standing in the starlight with its trunk up.

A bitter voice within asked, *How did it get so close? It is a sign of Nightland arrogance that even a mammoth can wander in without discovery.*

The mammoth trumpeted again, and its lilting cry penetrated clear to her soul.

Is it the Last Mammoth signaling Raven Hunter's return?

"Our people are bewitched," Yellow Woman said softly. "It's the

Prophet's work. He steals their souls. He has some kind of magic that—"

"He's *not* a witch," Skimmer insisted. "People flock to him because he promises he'll lead them back down into the paradise of the Long Dark, where Raven Hunter is waiting to embrace them. Few believe in Wolf Dreamer any longer. He's abandoned us too many times."

"That makes me sad. The only thing we have left is Wolf Dreamer and Old Man Above."

"You still believe? After this?"

"Of course. Don't you see? Wolf Dreamer and Old Man Above must know we have faith in them. This is a test. We've no right to hate Old Man Above or Wolf Dreamer. Like a father punishing his child, every instant of pain has a reason, to teach us something. It's a sign of love. It hurts Wolf Dreamer as much as it does us."

"Wolf Dreamer is *dead*!" she shouted bitterly. "He died here, this very day! If he *ever* existed." Her heart was pounding. Did she believe that? Was her faith one more thing to add to the growing pile of dead in the back corner?

Tears welled in the old woman's eyes. "Do you know that this torture isn't the greatest horror to the old people?" She waved a hand at the death-scented enclosure. "This passes. The greatest horror is that Wolf Dreamer no longer lives in the souls of the young. I can endure. But you losing your faith . . . that leaves my soul weeping in despair."

Skimmer didn't answer. Five body lengths away, a young girl, perhaps ten, gripped the feet of her dead sister, trying to drag the corpse to the pile.

"Move?" the girl begged a cluster of people blocking the way. "Please! I'm not very strong, and I have to—"

"Go the other way round. We're too tired to move." A young woman just glared. "Or leave her there. We're all dead anyway."

The girl struggled to comply, dragging her sister three paces in the opposite direction. But the women there refused to move. All paths were closed. Finally, in defeat, she dropped back to the ground and buried her face in her sister's dirty shirt to muffle her sobs.

Softly, Skimmer began the First Song:

Flight of the bird, so big so loud,
calls the thunder from the cloud,
Sun children kill each other,

Long way south for the death of a brother,
Hot, dry, war is nigh,
War is nigh . . .

Legends said that Wolf Dreamer's first teacher had been an old woman named Heron, and that she'd died with those words on her lips.

Yellow Woman bowed her head. Tears dripped from her long nose and landed glistening on her filthy sleeve.

Skimmer stared. How could she have so much water left after so many days of thirst? It didn't seem possible. Her own tears had dried up long ago.

"They're going to slaughter us," she wept. "You know it too, don't you?"

"Everyone knows it."

"We must do something. We can't just let them kill us. What can we do?"

"Fight. We can band together and fight."

"Are you mad? Do you want to try and climb the walls? In our weakened condition—and against armed warriors who can dart us all in a few heartbeats?"

"I won't just sit here and let them kill my daughter."

Skimmer rose to her feet, aware of Ashes' frightened look.

A din of voices erupted outside. People were calling, *"The Guide! It's the Guide! Look!"*

"Do you think he's really out there?" Yellow Woman asked. "The Guide. Do you—"

"Guide? Prophet? What does it matter?"

"Maybe he thinks we've suffered enough and will let us go. Maybe he's come to—"

Skimmer laughed. "Do you think Wolf Dreamer has sent him to save us?"

"Yes . . . yes, that's it. Wolf Dreamer has finally seen our agony and—"

"Even Wolf Dreamer turns his head tonight, Yellow Woman. All the Spirits have."

"It's not true!" she shouted angrily. "We're his relatives. He loves us!"

Skimmer studied the guards. They'd changed positions. Instead of walking along the log walls, they stood massed before the gate. Receiving orders to do what?

"We're not going to die," Yellow Woman said. "You'll see. He's come to forgive us."

"Sunpath People!" a voice boomed through the gate. "Greetings from the Guide."

"Hallowed Spirits, let us go!" Yellow Woman shrieked.

Cries rose across the enclosure, people screaming for mercy, striking those next to them to drive them far enough away that the Guide could see their waving arms and repentant faces.

Skimmer cocked her head. That wasn't Ti-Bish's voice. This was Elder Nashat.

More guards climbed onto the log walls. They had their atlatls nocked with beautifully fletched darts.

"I believe!" a young woman screamed. "I believe in the Guide's Dream!"

"I've seen the Truth! I know the Guide is the promised Dreamer!"

People wept and promised allegiance to Ti-Bish, if only he would let their children live.

Skimmer gazed down at the soft outline of Ashes' legs beneath the hem of her cape. Was her daughter dead? Is that why she didn't move even though a cacophony of shrieks and shouts filled the air?

Gratitude overwhelmed her. For days she'd been girding herself to kill her girl before the Nightland warriors could get their filthy hands on her. Perhaps Wolf Dreamer did exist and had spared her?

"No," Yellow Woman insisted, eyes glistening with tears of hope. "He's going to save us. I feel it. Don't you feel it? Wolf Dreamer has sent him to release—"

"Witness," Nashat called through the gate, "the power of the Guide you all conspired to murder."

The gate was pulled open, and Karigi strode in at the head of a party of warriors. Each held a stone-headed hammer.

Skimmer blinked, reading the dark expressions on their faces. They had their jaws clamped, as if resolute to do something terrible. In that instant, Skimmer reached down, jerking Ashes to her feet.

Women surged forward, reaching out. They had no chance. Cries of hope became shrieks of pain, and the hammers swung crashing down.

Skimmer broke free from the press, looking around, seeing the pile of corpses in the rear. Screams and pleas couldn't hide the smacking sounds of stone on flesh.

"Mother?" Ashes asked in disbelieving fear.

"This way."

Women panicked and tried to run, pushing Skimmer ahead of them. She dragged Ashes toward the pile of dead.

Despite the press of bodies, she shoved Ashes down, shouting, "Don't move! Don't speak." Powered by fear, she reached up, grabbed a cold limp ankle, and pulled. She threw herself on top of Ashes as the pile shifted and cold dead corpses slid down on top of her.

Ashes moaned, "Mother?"

"*Quiet!* Lie still!"

She hunched her spine, trying to protect Ashes as someone scrambled across her back, climbing the collapsed pile of corpses. A heavy foot drove her flat as a man chased the fleeing woman up. Skimmer winced as the hammer thumped into flesh. The woman screamed. A second whistling impact brought silence. Then she felt yet another corpse toppled onto those that covered her.

For long moments, the hammers could be heard, men grunting with the effort.

"Thirsty . . . Mother," Ashes whispered.

"Shhh!"

The weight of the bodies piled on top of her was almost unbearable. Something wet and cold was leaking down, dripping onto her cheek. She clamped her eyes shut, thinking, *I am dead. Just another of the dead.*

"War Chief Karigi?" Nashat asked. "Are you sure that's all of them?"

"Yes, Elder." Then, "You men, turn each one over. Make sure."

"Even the dead ones in the pile?"

"Are you an idiot, or just a fool?"

Occasional snapping smacks carried in the suddenly still air. Skimmer ground her jaw, dry sobs racking her chest. She knotted her fists. *How can such a thing happen?*

A man's whispered voice nearby said, "If I was an idiot at least I could become a Guide someday."

Someone else snickered.

Ti-Bish! Skimmer remembered the half-starved creature she had once given food to. *Why didn't I drive a dart through your foul heart when I had the chance?*

Because back then she had still believed.

But now, on Hookmaker's blood, I swear I'll repay you for this!

She tensed as a voice above said, "Come morning, have some of the other slaves carry this mess out."

"Yes, War Chief. What do you want done with the bodies?"

"Drag them out to the tundra." Karigi laughed. "Maybe the wolves will take them back to Wolf Dreamer. Me, I'm going after that mammoth. While the wolves eat, so will we."

Voices grew fainter, and for long moments she lay, barely daring to breathe, her heart pounding in her chest.

The corpses seemed to grow heavier. She struggled to wrench her head around so she could gaze upward through the tangled mass of limbs to the sky.

Blessed Star People glimmered through the blanket of the heavens. Ancestors floating in a vast cold sea.

Ashes, moaning, brought Skimmer awake. She started as memories came flooding back.

She began shoving at the dead bodies. Her muscles trembled, weak from starvation and thirst. The glacier-scented winds carried the pungency of blood. Raising her head, she looked around. Nothing moved among the sprawled corpses. The gate, so long closed and guarded, gaped wide.

She shook her daughter. "Ashes? Wake up."

"I'm awake," Ashes said groggily. "Thirsty."

"We have to go. There will be water soon."

And then, Ti-Bish, I'm coming for you.

Thirteen

Windwolf slept, his right arm stretched out, the darkness draping him like a blanket. The Dream slipped over his soul like a soft mist. . . .

Bramble stood on a high promontory. Wind tossed her long black hair, sunlight playing down the sleek strands. She wore a formfitting elkhide dress that accented her thin waist and full bust. He could see elk ivories glinting from the yoke and sleeves.

She turned to him, her knowing eyes gleaming with sadness. The light seemed to play with the smooth lines of her face, and a wistful smile saddened her full lips.

"Bramble?" he asked, struggling desperately to climb up the rocky slope to her.

She shook her head sadly, and looked down to her side.

Windwolf caught movement, slowing in his mad scramble to reach her.

A great black wolf stepped out beside Bramble, leaning against her thigh, staring at him with gleaming yellow eyes. Bramble lowered her hand, letting it trace along the black wolf's head in a caress.

"Bramble?" Windwolf cried. "I'm coming!"

He resumed his desperate climb, but the soil slipped under his war moccasins, and the harder he clawed and climbed, the more the loose earth rolled beneath his feet.

He was panting now, feet sliding with each powerful attempt to lever himself up the loose scree.

He screamed as Bramble shot him one last smile. Then she turned and slowly walked away. For a moment, the great wolf watched him with its burning eyes before it, too, turned, and with a flip of its bushy tail, disappeared.

Screaming his rage, Windwolf attacked the slope, fighting his way bit by bit to the top. There he leapt to the peak and stood, breath tearing at his throat.

The high peak gave a view of the west. To the northwest, he recognized Loon Lake shining in the sunlight. The sounds of war, men shouting, screaming, and the clacking of war clubs drew his attention to the north. There, at the foot of the Nightland Caves, he watched his warriors running through the Nightland camps. As they ran, women and children fled before them. Even across the distance he could hear war clubs smashing heads. Children screamed as they were run down and murdered. He watched in mute horror.

Bramble? Where is Bramble?

Turning, he looked west. And there, far out over the forest, he could see Bramble, the wolf at her side, marching off like some distant giant toward the low hills on the western horizon.

"Bramble!" he screamed, falling to his knees.

She looked back across the distance, the wind still teasing her long hair. He thought she smiled, and then pointed toward the distant hills. After a final knowing glance she turned and continued on her way.

The wolf hesitated for a moment, staring at him through those odd yellow eyes before it trotted off in Bramble's tracks, the tail waving until both were lost against the distant hills his people called the Tills.

"She's gone to the Tills," Windwolf whispered to himself.

He rose to follow. Setting his steps toward the west. But with each step he took, the ground seemed to slide beneath his feet, leaving him stuck in place. All the while, behind him, he could hear Nightland women and children screaming, pleading, and dying under the weapons of his warriors.

"Bramble?" he asked weakly. "Come back to me."

But the distant Tills remained empty, almost shimmering in the eerie light.

"Bramble . . . ?"

"**W**ar Chief? Wake up!"

Windwolf blinked, started, and sat up to stare stupidly around a rocky enclosure. It took a moment for him to remember the old white-haired man who held a small bark lamp in his hand.

Trembler looked down with kindly eyes, saying, "You were Dreaming, War Chief. I hated to wake you, but it's morning. The Nightland have left. You are needed."

Windwolf rubbed his face, shaking off the last fragments of the Dream.

He nodded, collected his few belongings, and followed Trembler back along the tortuous route they'd taken the night before. Today, he could see the splinters of dull light that penetrated between many of the boulders. They dappled his path with a cold white gleam.

"Lookingbill is alive, but he's weak," Trembler said. "He ordered me to bring you to him."

"I understand. What about the village?"

"Oddly, Kakala did but little damage. He spared the women and children when he could have killed them. Most of the elders survived. But . . ." He exhaled hard. "The Chief's daughter, Mossy, was killed in the fighting."

He forced himself to think, the image of the Tills still lingering in his soul's eye. "What about your warriors? How many survived?"

"We lost ten, War Chief. It could have been much worse." He glanced back. "Kakala turned several of his captives loose. He said that he was only after you. That if we would turn you over, he would simply leave."

"How kind of him."

They stepped out into the gray morning and took the trail that led to the enormous ceremonial cavern. Just outside, fifteen dead bodies were laid out in rows. They'd all been freshly bathed and dressed in clean hides.

As they passed, Trembler said, "Fish Hawk saw only ten and six warriors with Kakala, thank the Ancestors. Five of those will not be returning home with him."

"Kakala was outnumbered. He'll be back with five tens."

Windwolf shivered slightly as he stepped to the mouth of the cave. Though most of the sky was clear, snowflakes fell from the drifting Cloud People, lighting as softly as feathers on the ground and frosting the boulders. The sharp fragrance of wet spruce needles and damp earth rode the breeze.

Images from the Dream kept spinning behind his eyes: Bramble, striding westward over the forest, the wolf by her side. All the while, he could hear the piteous cries of the Nightland women and children as his warriors struck them down.

The black wolf's eyes seemed to burn inside him.

His dread had lifted, replaced by a terrible weariness that made all things seem blessedly unreal. He'd been living out a precarious charade, laying battle plans for his warriors, speaking to people only when absolutely necessary, retreating to his hides at night, knowing he'd Dream. And finally he would jerk awake in the darkness, sweat pouring from his body. Images of Bramble, blood welling from her mouth, would linger.

Thank the Spirits that his warriors knew him well enough to leave him alone when those moods were upon him.

So, what am I going to do?

On impulse, he said, "I need to send a runner to my warriors as soon as possible, Trembler."

"I know just the person. I'll arrange it."

"Good. Oh, and if you could put a pack together, something with food for a fast-traveling man, I would appreciate it."

"But," Trembler said in surprise, "if you're sending a runner to your warriors, where are you going? How will we contact—"

"It's better if you don't know. When my warriors are in place, I'll send a runner to you with the time and place to meet us."

Trembler shifted his gaze to the snow falling through the evergreen branches. "I will need to discuss this with Chief Lookingbill and the other Elders, but I suspect we will do as you say."

"Good."

"Maybe you should consider resting here for just a day or two, then—"

"Trembler, think about it. The sooner I'm gone, the safer you will be. I'd appreciate it if you would find that runner for me immediately."

Trembler hesitated as though he wanted to say something else. Instead, he said, "Lookingbill is waiting for you in his personal chamber. Just walk up this trail. Fish Hawk is guarding him. He'll take you to Lookingbill."

"You have my heartfelt thanks."

Trembler bowed and walked away down the slope toward the base of the cliff.

Windwolf clenched his hands into fists. How long could he keep this up? When would his body and soul finally let him down?

Bramble, I need you.

For ten and three summers she'd been the thin, shining blade that had flashed between him and the world. She'd been the other half of his life, the part that balanced his foibles, sharpened his ideas, and kept him from blunders. Memories of her laughter haunted him. The sound rose so clearly in his mind he thought he'd heard it. He started to turn before he physically stopped himself.

Dead. She's dead. He remembered her sad smile in the Dream.

He shook off the image.

War Chief Fish Hawk, with four warriors, stood in a group before one of the higher entrances into the rocks. Windwolf picked up a snapped dart, seeing Nightland colors on the shaft. He pitched it off to the side.

As he climbed, the Thunder Sea came into view across the distant tops of the spruce forest. The silver water was dotted with shining icebergs. Father Sun's light turned them into white spears. The icebergs, children of the Ice Giants, played constantly, rolling over and over in water, Singing in sweet clear voices.

Behind them, almost lost in the low clouds, he could make out the jagged line of the Ice Giants themselves. Their cold seemed to seep into his very bones.

What terrible things do you hide in your dark depths?

Fish Hawk called, "Our chief is waiting for you, Windwolf."

Windwolf picked up his pace. "It's good to see you alive, Fish Hawk."

"And you also, War Chief. But for you, it would have gone far worse for us." He turned to the cave entrance and called, "Chief Lookingbill? Windwolf would see you."

"Have him enter."

Windwolf ducked beneath the leather curtain and was surprised to see the mostly bald elder sitting up, his back leaned against a roll of hides. His deeply wrinkled face had lost a good deal of color, but he looked better than Windwolf had imagined he would. His arm was in a sling, and a thick bandage covered his left shoulder.

Windwolf said, "You're tougher than I thought."

"Kakala's dart glanced off my collarbone. It only hurts when I turn my head or try and move my arm. It bled cleanly. I'll be all right." He paused. "Do you know how often a man turns his head and tries to lift his arm?"

"I can imagine."

Windwolf's gaze swept the chamber. The place was four paces across, and extended perhaps three body lengths. Five massive slabs, of rocks had sagged against each other to create the space. No sunlight penetrated between the slabs, which meant it must be a warm, dry haven. The fire that burned in the middle of the chamber cast a ruddy hue over the walls.

"I was sorry to hear about the death of your daughter, Chief."

Lookingbill's old jaw quaked as he said, "She was our Storyteller. As well as she knew the oral traditions of our people, she was also an expert with the atlatl. She killed one of Kakala's warriors before he darted her."

"I'm doubly sorry to lose her."

Within Lookingbill's reach, a variety of weapons rested: six darts and an atlatl, plus a buffalohide shield painted with blue images of falcons and yellow doves.

Windwolf walked forward and gestured to the weapons. "When I met you last night, I was surprised that you did not come armed. What if I'd meant you harm?"

Lookingbill winced and shifted his back, trying to ease the pain in his wounded shoulder. "You do not have the reputation of killing unarmed men who ask to counsel with you."

"Then, perhaps we can only hope the Prophet will seek a meeting?"

Lookingbill laughed, and winced at the pain.

Windwolf knelt beside the fire and extended his hands to the flames. "I asked Trembler to find a runner for me. After I dispatch him, I'll be on my way. If I'm gone when Kakala returns, he might leave you in peace."

"I think it more likely that he will punish us for having sheltered you to start with. Which means I want you to come back soon—and with your warriors. Why do you wish a runner?"

The memory of screaming women and children haunted him. "To send a message to Deputy Silt."

Lookingbill frowned. "But . . . where are you going?"

Windwolf looked back at the doorway, lowering his voice. "To scout the Nightland villages myself." He waved down Lookingbill's look of protest. "No one can evaluate an enemy better than I can, Chief. Alone I can cover the same ground in four days that a war party can in seven."

"And if you're captured?" Lookingbill asked softly.

"I won't be." He chuckled. "I'll move by darkness. I don't need to take risks."

"And where will we meet your warriors?"

How do I tell him? "That will depend on where the Nightland warriors are." He paused. "And it would be a dead giveaway if Nashat learned that my warriors were assembling here with yours."

Lookingbill nodded. "Of course." He paused. "You should know that a survivor from the Nine Pipes band came through this morning. He said he thought Skimmer and her daughter were alive. Their bodies were not among the dead in the camp."

Alive? What implications did that have?

"War Chief, they may have been taken captive."

"In which case they're already among the Nightland." He glanced up. "Is there any reason she might come here?"

"To ask once again for my help?" He winced as he slowly shook his head. "I turned her down once. Why should she?" He glanced up. "Do you have a reason for asking?"

"I would like to hear this plan of hers. She may have information about the Nightland Caves that we can use."

Lookingbill smiled faintly. "Should she show up, I'll make apologies and tell her how foolish my people and I have been."

Voices rose outside, and Trembler called, "War Chief Windwolf, I found a runner for you."

Windwolf turned to Lookingbill; the old man pointed a stern finger at him and said, "You stay alive, too. Or I fear we'll all be dead soon."

Fourteen

The sacred caves formed an intricate labyrinth through the Ice Giants. Many of the passageways wound for several days' walk through utter darkness. In the blackest depths, there were chambers known only to a precious few: the holiest Elders of the Nightland People . . . and Ti-Bish.

We live like a nest of rats.

Nashat frowned at his chamber. Nine paces across, it was larger than most, but the ice walls had been melting away. They'd become thin. It annoyed him that today he could hear children laughing.

He paced his chamber, wide awake, sipping warm seal broth—thick with fat—from a wooden cup. The warming fire—resting on a bed of gravel—cast his shadow over the pale blue walls like a leaping giant.

"May I go now, Elder?" Blue Wing glanced longingly at the leather door curtain.

A beautiful woman, she had broad cheekbones and an aquiline nose. Her thin lips were pursed, a simmering panic behind her eyes. She should be afraid of him. As should all Sunpath People. He had dressed her in a fine elkhide smock that hung down to her knees. The moment he'd heard the Guide had set her free, he'd had two warriors fetch her back. With a body like hers, she was much too enchanting a woman to waste.

"No, let's talk for a time."

"What about?"

The fear-spawned hatred in her eyes fascinated him. He smiled, finding it both enticing and amusing. "You told me that even against overwhelming numbers, the Sunpath People would fight back. How did you know?"

"They're desperate."

"Then perhaps they should stop plotting to kill Ti-Bish."

"You can't expect them to abandon beliefs as old as the world."

He smiled. "Not only do I expect it, I demand it."

The ceiling had a shiny gleam. Every night when the slaves brought in a fresh supply of wood, it melted, but refroze while he slept.

"And what does the Guide demand?" she asked.

Nashat's eyes narrowed. Discussing Ti-Bish gave him a stomach-ache. "He demands whatever I tell him to."

"Where is he? He set me free!"

"Does it matter? He's an idiot, Blue Wing. I assure you Ti-Bish could care less what orders I give War Chief Kakala. Did you hope Ti-Bish might order me to stop attacking your relatives?"

"I just hadn't seen him in a few days, and I wondered where he was. That's all." She stared at the floor, her hopes dashed.

"Ti-Bish went to his Dreaming Cave. Raven Hunter called him suddenly." He sighed. He couldn't help it; it was so ridiculous.

"You demean your Guide and his Spirit Helper?"

"Demean? No. I take Spirits very seriously. A wise Elder can build an empire on the back of a Spirit."

"You don't believe in Raven Hunter?"

"I believe in Raven Hunter's Power. And I appreciate what he's done for me." He motioned to the magnificent chamber with its wealth of hides. Precious shells from the far oceans, and bits of painted hides and bark collected from Sunpath ceremonial lodges were stacked here and there. Painted mammoth-hide shields sat on tripods around the chamber—more loot taken from Sunpath chiefs who no longer needed them.

She said, "The Guide is Powerful. He'll hear what you've done to me."

"Powerful? The Sunpath People are crying out for him to save them, but has he answered them? No. He's locked away in his Dreaming Cave, talking to the great and mighty Raven Hunter."

At that moment, young Cedar called from beyond the room hanging. "Elder? I have news. The Guide wishes to see you."

Blue Wing took that opportunity to stalk past him.

He waited until she'd ducked beneath the curtain before he called, "I'll just have the guards bring you back. Shall I offer them a reward for your return? Perhaps a few hands of time with you?"

Her steps went quiet in the tunnel. It took several heartbeats before she returned. The look of total defeat on her face delighted him.

He said, "Life comes at a price, Blue Wing. Never forget that. Be grateful for what you have. Meanwhile, I want you to stay here until I return."

He set his tea cup down and walked out into the ice tunnel where two guards stood. "Blue Wing is spending the night in my chamber. See to it."

"Yes, Elder," the young warrior, Cedar, said.

Nashat lifted one of the little oil lamps from its hole in the wall and strode through the magnificent arching tunnels. He followed an old tunnel, traveling deeper and deeper into the Guide's personal labyrinth—a strange series of interconnected ice caves that led into the very bowels of the Ice Giants. No one would live down here but Ti-Bish. The groans and squeals of the Giants were often so loud even he wanted to run, screaming.

It is only for a while longer.

He lifted his flickering lamp high, and it illuminated the arches and rounded domes. If he were not a wiser man, he, too, might fear coming around a bend and suddenly standing face-to-face with the legendary Raven Hunter.

As he walked around a curve in the tunnel, he saw two slave girls dressed in grimy hides. An oil lamp with a hide wick burned on the floor at their feet.

"Little Deer? Pipe? What are you doing? You're supposed to carry food to the Guide."

The girls looked up, suddenly wary. Little Deer said, "That crack has been growing wider over the past moon."

Pipe said, "The Guide says that in the deep tunnels tens of tens have appeared."

"Have you seen them?"

Fear glittered in her eyes. "I don't go there. That would scare me. There are ancient monsters that live down there."

"Where did you hear that?"

"The Guide told us," Pipe said. She had a round face with wide dark eyes.

Nashat gave her a mean look. He'd never liked her.

But she would learn. Both girls were young. Little Deer had seen ten and one summers. Pipe had seen ten. Their breasts had not even begun to bud. Perhaps that's why Ti-Bish kept them close. They would not distract him from his holy mission.

Nashat patted Little Deer on the head as he passed. "You're a good girl, Little Deer. Someday I'm going to reward you handsomely for your loyalty. Perhaps I'll give you a buffalo hide."

Her mouth dropped open at the thought of such wealth. "Thank you, Elder. I wish you a pleasant morning."

"And you as well."

The cracks are widening. How long before it all falls down on my head?

The leather door curtain that covered the mouth of Ti-Bish's cave hung in tatters. The Guide said he liked it that way, so Nashat had left it alone. No one came down here anyway. Just Nashat and a handful of slaves.

Nashat called, "Ti-Bish? I received a message that you wished to see me." He pressed his ear close to the curtain. No sounds came from within. "Ti-Bish?"

"What?" a soft confused voice answered. "Nashat?"

"Yes. You sent a runner for me. What did you want?" Nashat massaged the tight muscles at the back of his neck.

"I did?"

"You did. May I enter?"

"Yes, of course."

Nashat ducked beneath the curtain. The high ceiling arched five body lengths above him, its heights lost in the darkness. He scanned the chamber. A crackling fire atop a flat stone burned brightly. Several heating stones were glowing in the coals. The stone perched on a rack of whalebone in the middle of the floor to allow air to circulate below it in an effort to keep the floor from melting. The raised hearth was surrounded by thick buffalo hides. Beside the fire, a tea bag hung from a tripod. Several wooden cups and a pair of mammoth ivory tongs lay at hand near the bag.

As Nashat walked toward Ti-Bish, he grimaced. Because of the heat, the ice walls had begun to melt and shone with an unnatural brilliance. Pale blue shadows scalloped up toward the dark ceiling. Ti-Bish had few belongings: A pile of bedding hides lay rolled to the right, along with three mammoth-hide parfleches filled—Nashat presumed—with personal items. Beside the parfleches, he could see several split-tree-root baskets and a bladder of water.

Nashat waved a hand at the fire. "Do you think this is wise? Every day the Ice Giants roar and more caves collapse." As if to accent his words, a droplet of water spattered onto the floor beside him.

Ti-Bish stared at him. "I . . . I called for you?"

He wore his hair in two long frizzy braids that clearly hadn't been washed in days. His long bearhide cape, painted with tiny black ravens, looked as though he'd been sleeping in it. Ti-Bish always looked worn when he finished "talking" with Raven Hunter, but this time he looked worse than usual.

"Yes, Ti-Bish, you called for me," Nashat sighed. "And I was glad to hear it. I feared you were still wandering the tunnels beneath the caves looking for the hole in the ice. If you're not careful, someday you'll get lost down there, and we'll never find you."

Ti-Bish gave him a vague look. "There's a—a lake of fire down there. I see things in the flames."

"A fiery lake? No wonder the Ice Giants are melting." Nashat barely hid his annoyance. Ti-Bish always told wild stories when he returned from his vision quests.

Nashat put a hand on Ti-Bish's shoulder and pushed him toward the buffalo hides spread out around the fire. "Sit down, Ti-Bish. I'll warm you some tea."

Ti-Bish sat cross-legged and gazed up at Nashat as though waiting for further instructions.

Nashat used the mammoth ivory tongs to pull a hot river cobble from the fire and dropped it into the tea bag. Steam exploded, filling the chamber with the fragrance of dried tundra wildflowers.

He dipped one of the cups into the tea bag and handed it to Ti-Bish. "Drink this; you'll feel better."

Ti-Bish took the cup and smelled it, but did not sip.

"How is Raven Hunter?" Nashat asked as he dipped a cupful of tea for himself and sank to the warm buffalo hides.

"He's worried."

"Is he? About what? Something we've done?" Nashat smelled the tangy fragrance of the tea before he drank. He took small sips. Little Deer had added a few lumps of pine sap brought up from the Sunpath lands to sweeten it.

"It's not us," Ti-Bish said. "It's the Sunpath People. Wolf Dreamer is watching them. They're Singing their souls up to him."

"Indeed? I assume that's bad?" *Blessed Spirits, spare me from having to hear more of this.*

"Yes. I think so."

"Why does Raven Hunter care? If they Sing all their souls out of their bodies, we won't have to fight them any longer. They'll all be dead."

Ti-Bish blinked owlishly. "They are dead."

Nashat studied him over the rim of his tea cup. Ti-Bish knew nothing about his attacks on the Sunpath villages. Or did he? Perhaps Little Deer or Pipe had heard some bit of gossip and repeated it. The last thing he needed was Ti-Bish wandering out and stopping his war.

Nashat said, "The Nightland clan Elders have been concerned about you. Raven Hunter kept you for ten and two days. Do you realize that?"

Ti-Bish's brow furrowed. He swirled his tea in his cup. "He needed to speak with me. An angry Sunpath war chief is going to scout the entrances to our caves to see if we can be attacked."

Nashat's cup froze halfway to his mouth. Not that he believed it, but on occasion Ti-Bish's prophecies had proven correct. "When? Did he tell you?"

Ti-Bish tilted his head uncertainly. "He just said we have to double the number of guards around the Nightland Caves' entrances. We have to be prepared."

Nashat nodded. "I'll take care of it immediately."

Ti-Bish's eyes went wide and empty. "Raven Hunter also said you must stop punishing our warriors for losing battles, Nashat. If you don't, some of our warriors will turn against us."

"Raven Hunter said that?" He drummed his fingers on his leg.

"Yes. Every warrior whispers the name of Brookwood Village when they're about to go on a raid."

Nashat just stared at him. Ten and two summers ago, the Council of Elders had ordered War Chief Gowinn to attack a Lame Bull village and steal children to serve as slaves. He had failed miserably—lost half his warriors—and the rest had run like scared dogs. In punishment, the Council had ordered the survivors locked in pine pole cages for moons. Many had died, including then–Deputy Kakala's wife, Hako. Since that day, their warriors, especially Kakala, had lost few battles.

Nashat looked around. "What did you do with the woman I sent you?"

"Woman?"

"You asked me to get a woman for you. One from the Nine Pipes band." Nashat frowned, feigning ignorance. "What was her name? Blue Fern, Blue . . ."

"Blue Wing!"

"Yes."

"I sent her home."

"I don't suppose you could tell me why?"

"She was the wrong woman."

Nashat stared in disbelief. "The *wrong* one?"

"Raven Hunter says it doesn't matter anymore. The right one will come to me."

How do I explain that *to Kakala?*

Ti-Bish abruptly leaped to his feet, cocked his head as though listening to someone, and ran across the chamber for his mittens. As he slipped them on, he said, "Forgive me, I must go meet with the Elders."

"About what?"

Ti-Bush's gaze darted around the walls as though to check on the darker patches of ice. "I have to tell them about punishing warriors, and the Sunpath souls."

Gulping the rest of his tea, Nashat said, "This must be done now?"

Ti-Bish nodded. "Kakala has to be in the right place at the right time." He shot a suddenly worried look at Nashat. "If they put him in a cage, nothing will work right."

Nashat stifled his desire to wince. "You have told me, Guide. That is enough. The Council does as I wish. No need for you to go." *The last thing I need is you inciting panic.* "Leave it to me."

"You'll see to it?"

"Of course."

Fifteen

By the Guide's sacred eyebrows, I'm sick of all this. Kakala filled his lungs, expecting sweet night air. Instead, he drew in the stink of Maga's rotting guts.

He made a face, turning his head away. To his right, Maga groaned, his right leg stiffening, the heel digging a groove out of the spruce needles.

Kakala stared up through the branches, seeing slivers of a partly cloudy night sky. The waning moon had already lost part of its western curve.

Three of his remaining warriors huddled around a low fire, its glow hidden by the rounded piles of rock surrounding it. The others lay out around the periphery of the spruce-clad ridge, keeping watch for any pursuit.

Maga drew a series of fast breaths, his mouth wide.

Kakala reached down, laying his cold hand on Maga's sweat-hot forehead. "Easy."

"S-Sorry, War Chief." Maga swallowed hard. "More water?"

"Of course." Kakala reached for the bladder, untied the neck, and dribbled the cold fluid into Maga's mouth. The man swallowed wrong, coughing and crying out as his punctured guts spasmed.

"Sorry," Kakala soothed. "My fault."

"No, War Chief. Mine."

Kakala ground his teeth, his fist tightening on the neck of the bladder. Maga had taken a dart low, just above the bony ridge of the hip. The keen stone point had cut straight through, Maga's abdomen scarcely slowing the long dart.

Five dead. And Maga. He glanced up at the spruce, thinking how nice it would be to be a tree instead of a man. As a tree, he could just live, his roots deep in the soil, his branches extended to the sun.

But it all has gone wrong. He couldn't help but glance back to the north. If he were to walk down the slope, peer past the trees, he could see the distant Nightland villages, their fires winking far across the narrow band of tundra.

When I return, it will mean disgrace. The cage. He could almost wish he were Maga. Even dying of a pus-fouled gut would be better.

"War Chief?" Maga asked.

"Yes."

"I am going to die."

Kakala smiled down in the darkness. "I wouldn't think that. You know old Gataka, don't you? He was gutted worse than you, and still lived. No, Maga, you're as tough an old crow as the next man. Tougher. You'll make it."

"Lying has never served you well. You're not good at it."

Kakala smiled. "This time, I'm telling the truth."

"You're better than the rest of them."

"Better than who?"

"Nashat, Karigi, Hawhak. All of them."

"Thank you."

Maga swallowed hard, panting to cool his burning body. "I would ask a favor of you."

"Anything."

"Bring me the medicine bag."

Kakala's heart skipped. "I don't think it's—"

"I have watched too many men die from wounds like mine. I will not go the same way."

Kakala bowed his head, his heart beating slowly in his chest.

"War Chief? Did you hear?"

"I did." He rose to a crouch and ducked through the low-hanging branches. When he walked down to the fire and lifted the hide bag with an image of Raven drawn on the side, the three warriors watched with wary eyes.

No one spoke as he walked back, ducked under the branches, and carefully removed the herbal teas, the poultices, and wrappings they used for bandages.

"Are you sure, Maga?"

The man laughed weakly. "I can already feel my soul floating in and out of my body, War Chief." A pause. "I have no fear of death . . . only the manner of it."

"I know."

"Tie it tightly, War Chief. I don't want to draw this out."

"I will." He paused. "If you change your mind, just call out. I'll hear you and remove the bag."

"I know, War Chief. My decision is final."

Kakala steeled himself, slipping the thick leather bag over Maga's head. The greased leather had been double stitched, waterproof, and had served this purpose too many times for a sane man to remember. Kakala settled the leather around Maga's neck, folding it, and then drew the cord tight, knotting it snuggly.

Kakala waited. He was still waiting, even after Maga's heaving lungs stilled and the body began to cool.

Skimmer peered between the boulders, searching the moonlit forest for Nightland warriors. Since their escape from the Nightland villages, she had run like a worried hare. Mostly they traveled by night, keeping to the low spots, holing up in the morning.

How long had it been? Time no longer had meaning. More than once, she had noticed that her hands shook. And she dared not let her soul drift, or she was back in the pen, the corpses of the dead piled atop her, and even the fall of a spruce cone sounded like a heavy stone mallet crushing a woman's skull.

To her surprise, more than once, she had wilted to the stony ground and burst into uncontrollable sobs.

"Mother?" Ashes asked. "What do you see? Are they coming after us?"

"Not yet. They probably think we all died." Her hands were shaking again. She stuffed them into the front of her dress, knotting her fists.

The stink of the dead still clung to the dress, impregnated in the stains left by whatever had been leaking out of the corpses.

My world is death. It hovers around me like a mist.

In the distance, the Ice Giants swelled like a vast white mountain range that went on forever. Their groans and rumbles carried on the cold air.

"Where are we going, Mother? The Nightland warriors burned our village."

"I'm not sure. Once I know we're not being followed, I'll make a decision."

Ashes toyed with the fringes on her cape, twisting them around her fingers. "The Guide is going to send his warriors after us, isn't he? No matter where we go?"

Skimmer didn't have the strength to lie to her. "Probably."

"Can't we go away and hide along the lakeshore?"

Skimmer knelt and reached for her daughter's hand. "Ashes, I want you to do something for me. Can you try?"

"What is it?"

"Remember your grandmother's clan?"

Ashes frowned. "Of course. She was Trickster Clan."

Skimmer took a deep breath of the icy air and squeezed Ashes' fingers. "If anything happens, and we're separated, I want you to—"

"But we *won't* get separated, Mother," she whispered in panic. "You won't leave me *alone!*"

"No, I won't. Not unless I have to. But if the Guide captures me, or I'm killed, I want you to run to the closest Sunpath village and tell the people you're Ashes from the Trickster Clan. Can you remember not to say the Redtailed Hawk Clan?"

Tears glimmered in her daughter's eyes, and her mouth trembled. "Mother, I don't—"

"Do you understand?"

"Yes." Ashes put both hands over her mouth and started to cry, the soft sobs like a mewing lion cub. "Mother?" she asked in a choking voice. "Where's Father? Is he dead?"

Skimmer couldn't answer. Somewhere in the past few days her own unbearable anguish had faded. How did one find the energy to mourn after what they'd just survived? She'd forgotten whatever tale she'd told Ashes when she found her among the Nightland captives. But even if she'd remembered, there'd been no time to discuss Hookmaker's death.

"I think he . . . he may be."

Tears filled Ashes' eyes. In a choking voice, she said, "Are you sure? You said he got away."

Skimmer gathered her daughter in her arms and held her tightly. "Let's go hide. The spruce boughs hang low to the ground. Then we'll try to make our way through the moraines to Headswift Village. Lookingbill may turn us down again, but maybe we can get food there . . . clean clothes. Lookingbill will have news, and then we can decide where to go."

And what if Lookingbill won't even give us that?

Sixteen

Ti-Bish pulled his hood down over his face to block the wind, and gazed out at the open treeless landscape that bordered the ice. Most of it consisted of jumbled piles of rock and gravel, and travel through the rubble left by the retreating Ice Giants was hazardous unless a person stuck to the established trails that wound through the boulder fields. The Ice Giants had been melting since the beginning of the world. In their wake, they left boulders, gravel, and filthy islands of ice behind.

Beyond the rock belt, the tundra stretched southward until it connected with spruce forests, then to a lush world of pines, oaks, hickory, and walnut trees that lay another ten days' travel beyond that.

As he walked, he examined the ugly shore of the Thunder Sea as it stretched off to the east. A low fog hung perpetually over the lake, cold air draining off the glaciers reacting to the warmer waters. He could see patches of cracked ice, the summer melt beginning. Locked among them were bergs that had broken off. Even as he watched, one tilted and flipped over, breaking the thin lake ice. He could see waves buckling the rotten ice around it.

Equinox was but days past. Summer was coming.

He tipped his face up and sighed at the feel of Father Sun's light. He had not been out of the caves in a moon. Though it hurt his eyes, the bright gleam felt wonderful.

Early this morning, he'd taken a lamp and walked down to the deep ice tunnels. He knew the ones that led to the surface. He'd sneaked out of the caves without anyone noticing.

A cold northerly wind blew, flapping the hem of the grimy cape he wore. Nashat always insisted that he be dressed regally when he left the caves, but Ti-Bish hated painted shirts and jewelry.

On the shore ahead, several women had gathered to wash clothing. They dipped the hides into a meltwater lake, then pounded them with rocks to loosen the soil, and dipped them again. Upon finishing they would carry the clothing home and place it on racks near their small fires to dry.

For as far as he could see, hide lodges curved around the lakeshore. Bull boats—made from moose hide—rocked on the water. He could hear the fishermen calling to each other.

The Nightland People moved back and forth across the tundra six or seven times a summer. Each time they would bring fish, meat, birds, and berries to place in the caves to freeze for winter. In early fall, the villages began packing up to move here for the winter. Through the winter they ate from the foodstocks until spring brought the migratory fowl back. Hardy souls would walk out onto the winter-frozen Thunder Sea, and chop holes to fish through.

Then as the plants greened, they moved southward again, into the spruce forests that bordered the Sunpath nation. That was the problem. The Sunpath nation held the vast nut forests of walnuts, oaks, and hickory trees. The Nightland People's numbers were growing. They needed those forests. It had begun to create problems many summers ago.

A shout rode the wind.

Ti-Bish turned to gaze at the ice maw that led into the Nightland Caves. For generations his people had retreated to those shelters. Living in a cave in the ice was preferable to being out here, at the mercy of the deep cold and terrible winter winds.

The Thunder Sea, however, was a dangerous place in warm weather. The tides that rose and fell were tricky enough, but even more nerve-racking, occasional chunks of ice split off, splashing down and sending fierce waves that washed away everything in their path. For the most part, that happened later in the summer, after the warm winds blew hot from the south.

Other frightening things had been happening. Several times last winter Father Sun had risen as red as blood and had no light.

Omens. Signs and portents. He'd asked Raven Hunter what they meant. His eerie answer: *"The end of the world is almost upon you. . . ."*

Ti-Bish walked around the curve of the Thunder Sea and saw four women kneeling around a crying infant. The boy seemed to be sick. One woman was holding his head up, letting him drink from a shell cup, while the others Sang and fanned him with eagle feathers.

Ti-Bish walked forward. The boy's soul was hovering above his body. As Ti-Bish approached, one of the women looked up, worry bright in her eyes. It took a moment before she recognized him. She gasped, slapped one of the other women on the shoulder, and said, "It's him. It's the Guide!"

All four women jerked around to look with startled eyes.

"A pleasant morning to you," Ti-Bish said as he knelt beside the boy. "How old is he?"

The woman who held the boy's head, replied, "Two moons, Blessed Guide."

"How long has he been ill?"

"Since the day he was born." She looked up at Ti-Bish with moist eyes. The young woman was pretty, perhaps ten and five summers, with long black hair. "I've tried everything to Heal him, Blessed Guide. Nothing has worked. Every day his fever gets higher."

Ti-Bish reached out. He touched the pale blue soul hovering just above the small body. Slowly, carefully, he pressed the soul down until he could feel it enter the infant's body.

"There, little one. That's your home now."

The baby's cries stopped, and he blinked his eyes open, brown and soft. A drooly smile curled his tiny pink lips.

The women watched in stunned silence.

Ti-Bish said, "The child's soul is invisibly linked to an object in the Spirit World. I must cut the cord that connects him to it." He closed his eyes and concentrated on the silver filament that stretched up from the child's blue soul. He could sense it, long and thin before it disappeared high in the air. He used both hands to tug it apart.

The boy let out a sharp cry, then blinked and peered up at Ti-Bish with wide eyes.

Ti-Bish smiled and rose to his feet. "He'll be all right now. But for four days you must Sing frog songs over him. Frogs travel through the Spirit worlds all the time. If you pray to them they will send his soul home the next time they see it hovering over his body."

The young mother blinked, tears of relief welling in her eyes. "Thank you, Blessed Guide."

Cries erupted when the women washing clothes realized who he was. In mere heartbeats the shore came alive with running people. A man shouted, "He's Healing!" and people dropped what they'd been doing to hurry toward him.

A weeping woman in a torn, bloodstained cape grabbed his hand. "Guide, I beg you! My husband was wounded in the fighting. Come and Heal him. Be merciful. Heal him. Please! He fought for you."

"Bring him to my chamber tonight at sunset. I will tell the guards to let you in."

She dropped to her knees and kissed his moccasins. "Thank you! Thank you!"

From behind, an old man jerked the hem of Ti-Bish's robe so forcefully, he stumbled backward.

"Guide!" the man cried. "My daughter was drowned out on the water. Bring her back to life. I can't live without her!"

"I can't make the dead live again. Forgive me."

"But people have seen you do it! Why can't you do it for me?"

The crowd kept growing. There were so many. He staggered, helpless and frail beneath the weight of their needs.

"Raven Hunter?" he called over their heads. "Raven Hunter, I beg you: Help these people."

"Guide!" a filthy woman in ragged hides shrieked, shoving against him. She fairly threw her child into his arms. "Guide, cure my little girl next. Please, she's—"

"No, my son is sicker!" A dark-haired crone crowded into the circle.

From every corner, every lodge, they came, shouting, pleading, shoving him.

He looked down at the girl. Her battered head lolled limply. "What happened to her?"

"She was climbing the rocks this morning and fell. She hit her head many times."

Ti-Bish brushed her dark hair away from her face. "Raven Hunter? Heal this child?"

Behind him, a clamor of voices rose, fiery and indignant. He didn't understand the sudden enmity until he heard Nashat's voice ordering, "Get back! *Back away!*"

The woman shouted, "No, don't take him from us!"

Nashat strode up surrounded by guards, grabbed the girl from Ti-Bish's arms, and thrust her at her mother. "Take her home. The Blessed Guide has done all he can."

"But . . . but . . ." Ti-Bish stammered.

The woman clutched the little girl to her breast, pleading eyes on Ti-Bish. He started to reach out for her, only to have Nashat pull him back.

"Surround him," Nashat ordered the guards, and the men started hitting people with their war clubs, knocking them back to form a ring around Ti-Bish.

"But . . ." Ti-Bish reached out, desperate to reach the injured girl.

"Guide, we love you," a one-legged man propped on a walking stick implored. "We need you! When are we returning to the Long Dark?"

Nashat waved to the guards, and—tugging insistently on Ti-Bish—started back for the mouth of the big cave that led into the ice tunnels.

Nashat said, "Were you trying to get yourself *killed*? Tell me the next time you wish to go out Healing, so that I can make sure you're safe."

Ti-Bish wet his lips and nodded. "They *need* me!"

"We *all* need you."

He stared at Nashat, longing to tell him that he wanted to go out alone. But he couldn't. The words just stuck in his throat. *Can't I just have peace and tranquility around me?*

Finally, he managed to bravely say, "I *wanted* to be with them, Nashat."

"Well, you mustn't do this again. I know you trust everyone, but not everyone deserves your trust. The Sunpath People have assassins everywhere."

"I—I looked for you this morning. I couldn't find you."

"I apologize. We captured one of the Sunpath conspirators, and I had to question the—"

"Skimmer?" Ti-Bish took a step toward Nashat. "She's here?"

"Skimmer? Who is Skimmer?"

"The Nine Pipes woman. I asked you to bring her to me."

Nashat gave him that old familiar look of irritation. "You said to bring you *a woman* from Nine Pipes Village. You didn't say which one!"

Ti-Bish frowned, his thoughts reeling. "But I must have Skimmer."

"She plotted your murder with Lookingbill."

He smiled. "But she's *necessary!*"

Nashat glanced sidelong at an empty square of tall posts. He shook his head, thinking, then said, "Well, we'll look for her." But Nashat hid something behind his words.

Ti-Bish sagged in Nashat's grip. He remembered Skimmer. She was very beautiful. And she'd given him food when no one else would.

"I need to speak with her." Then he remembered. "But you needn't worry after all." He smiled. "She'll come to me."

Nashat gave him a hooded, amused look, as if somehow that was very funny.

"I'm sure she will." Nashat put a hand on Ti-Bish's back and shoved him through the entrance before turning to the guards. "Don't let anyone in until I have the Guide back in his personal chambers."

"Yes, Elder."

To Ti-Bish he said, "You always get carried away. Try thinking without your heart. Those people out there could kill you just by trying to touch you all at once; then they'd panic and trample each other. They're like a frightened herd of mammoths."

"I—I'll ask Raven Hunter to keep me safe."

"Ti-Bish, really. Raven Hunter has other things to do than hear our petty cries every day. We need to handle this ourselves."

"Are you saying that you don't believe Raven Hunter will protect me?"

"No, no, of course not. It's just that I don't want to burden the Spirits with things we can take care of ourselves. Too many requests over insignificant—"

"He's never come to you! That's why you doubt."

"Of course I believe, Ti-Bish. Don't get upset."

You don't! Ti-Bish started to tremble, and a need to weep filled his chest. He said, "I'll be . . . be in my Dreaming Cave."

"Again?" Nashat called in exasperation.

Seventeen

Ti-Bish veered sharply right at the next tunnel, leaving Nashat behind. His heart hammered frantically; he could barely breathe. He broke into a headlong run, plunging into the bowels of the Ice Giants. He knew the tunnels as no one else did, but soon found himself panting in a pool of darkness. Why hadn't he thought to grab a lamp? Tendrils of cold breathed from the stone-impregnated ice. The darkness was complete.

"Raven Hunter," he called, feeling his way along the walls. "It's me. I need you."

It took perhaps a full hand of time to work his way through the darkness. The deeper he went toward the lake of fire, the colder the air grew.

"Raven Hunter, your people need you." His voice echoed in the stillness. "Please, come to me."

After another hand of time, he grew too tired to travel and sank to the floor. Pulling his cape tightly around his body, he closed his eyes. No one would miss him. Not for many days. And he would be able to think and pray.

Sleep came quickly. . . .

*F*araway thunder—like giants walking—awakens me. I listen to the black-ness. As the thunder rumbles closer, the Ice Giants shriek and groan. I try not to tremble.

I have found strange animals and plants in these tunnels. Once I tripped over the bones of a huge buffalo, twice the size of those outside, with horns more than two body lengths long. Supernatural buffalo, buffalo that have not existed in our world for many many summers—if they ever did. The shore of the fiery lake has even more peculiar things. A moon ago, I watched glowing fish swim through the gigantic spine of a monster that stretched for twenty body lengths.

I rise from the floor and feel my way farther down the tunnel.

When I notice that the darkness is not quite black, but has a faint glow, I know the sacred lake is ahead. The pastel luminescence increases until I can make out the shape of the ice tunnel. A little taller than my head, it has narrowed to barely the width of my shoulders.

As I round the curve, the tunnel opens to my Dreaming Cave. The ceil-ing soars into sheer blackness above me. I have been here tens of times since I was a boy. I know every sculpted curve and undulation in the floor. This is my secret place. No other human comes here, or ever has that I can—

A dark form passes to my left. The faint glow ripples.

I spin around, breathless.

He always startles me, frightens me.

A Spirit in the shape of a man, his black body has a shimmer, as though his jet feathers catch the light.

"I knew you'd come."

"You're never alone," the Spirit says in a voice that sounds like the soft beating of wings. "I'll always be here when you truly need me."

"Since that night above the Nine Pipes camp when you first came to me, I've known you watch over me."

"Why have you called?"

"Nashat tells me that Sunpath warriors have destroyed several of our villages. Tens of tens are homeless and hungry. Even now, they cry for food out in the forests. I—"

"Don't concern yourself, Ti-Bish. They will have food. I will make sure of it."

Gratitude floods my fevered body like cool water. "I thank you."

"I sense there's more."

My eyes trace the shape of the lighter darkness around Raven Hunter. Though I've never seen the Spirit's face, I know he is very beautiful.

"We can't find Skimmer. Nashat brought the wrong woman. I know if I could only talk with her, pray with her for a few days, she'd understand you."

"You want to pray with her after she plotted to kill you?"

"Yes, she's a good woman. She gave me food once. I can do this for her . . . bring her to you."

Raven Hunter's soft laughter sounds like rustling wings. "And what would you tell her?"

The darkness shifts as though being blown about by Wind Woman. I can't see Raven Hunter as clearly now.

"I'd tell her of your goodness and Power. I'd explain to her the wickedness of Wolf Dreamer. I'd show her—"

"She won't believe you."

"But why?"

"Old ways die hard. Especially old Spirits. But we will win this battle in the end."

The blackness flutters closer, and I feel a light touch on my face. The warmth sends a tingle through me, making me feel better.

"Kakala's warriors will finally bring her to you."

"They will?" I say in surprise, and steel myself. I feel a strange attraction toward the woman. Just thinking about her sends a flush through me, even though a part of me also hates her for the suffering she has caused.

"I want you to give her something. Hold out your hands."

I extend my hands, and he places a small leather bundle in them. "What is this?"

"You must never open it. Do you understand?"

"Yes."

I feel it with my fingers. "What's it for?"

"It's a bundle for Skimmer."

"But I don't under—"

"For her and no one else. A gift."

The bag feels light. "When will Kakala bring her to me?"

The dark air pulses again, as though touched by fluttering wings.

"Soon. If you can keep Nashat from putting him in a pole cage. It's very important that you follow my instructions exactly."

"You know I will. Please tell me what I must do?"

"Skimmer is the source. When she arrives, you must listen to her very carefully. She will say things you don't want to hear."

"I'll listen," I answer breathlessly, my heart starting to pound. I long to have her close where I could teach her . . . and just talk to her.

I can feel his eyes on mine. "You love her."

"With all my heart."

"You know what happens when a Dreamer lies with a woman?"

"It could cost me my life."

"Would you pay that price?"

"I . . . I . . ." Blinking, I shake my head. "It's not that way."

He watches me, and the silence stretches. Fear grows inside me.

"Raven Hunter?" I call in a voice smaller than I intend. "I try so hard to please you, but sometimes I feel stupid and inadequate."

"You are all I expected you to be, Ti-Bish."

His voice comes from farther and farther away, as though he is soaring down the tunnel toward the fiery lake. "Never forget that truth shines through the hurt eyes of everyone around you. Love everyone . . . teach everyone."

"And you'll take care of us?"

A spiraling black hole appears down the throat of the tunnel. . . .

Ti-Bish woke with a start, panting, soaked in sweat. His cape had become twisted and tangled with his long legs. He kicked them free and sat up.

"Spirit Dream," he whispered.

When he started to stand, something tumbled onto the floor. He felt for it. As his fingers slipped across the soft leather, he knew what it was.

The bundle for Skimmer.

He clutched it to his heart, braced one hand against the wall, and rose.

The ice tunnel had a strange scent now, like falling rain. He breathed deeply, a gentle smile on his lips.

Eighteen

Supper consisted of the hind leg of a caribou that Bishka had managed to dart while scouting. The roasting meat was a welcome addition to Kakala's dwindling supplies.

No one had spoken much during the meal. Too many times, Kakala caught his warriors glancing uneasily to the north. Thoughts of Brookwood Village lay heavily on all of their minds.

All but Goodeagle, of course. He had walked in, cut off a slice of meat, and stepped out beyond the boundary of the fire. Kakala could see him, a dark shadow perched on a partially exposed boulder. What would it be like to be that lonely and despised?

But then, he knew. He'd been in the cage, suffered the heaped insults. He'd watched his wife die, and had finally crawled out, back bent and aching—the hurt in his body no match for the pain in his soul, or the staggering sense of loss. Some said he'd been half-mad for years.

Kakala, belly full, extended his hands to the fire and looked up at the stars.

"I'm worried about Keresa," Rana said. "She's been gone too long."

"Trust her," Kakala replied, hiding his own concern. "She's the best. No one else among us could sneak in so close to Headswift Village. If Windwolf is there, she'll find him."

"And then we go back?" Corre asked, glancing uneasily toward the spruce tree where Maga's body lay.

"I'll take the chance," Bishka said before biting off another strip of steaming meat. He chewed, swallowed, and gestured with greasy fingers. "Handing over Windwolf's head keeps us out of the cages."

"I still don't understand." Rana shook his head. "It was as if Windwolf *knew* we were there. By the Guide's balls, I'd swear the man can see in the dark."

Kakala chuckled.

"You find that funny?" Rana gave him a flat stare.

"First, you should be careful how you speak of the Guide. What is said here will go no further, but should you slip before Karigi, or, Raven forbid, Nashat, the cages will look like a blessing compared to what they will do to you." He paused. "Windwolf, however, does not see in the dark. No more than I do. He's just a man."

"Sometimes, I wonder," Bishka muttered, ripping off another chunk of meat.

Movement at the corner of his eye sent Kakala scrambling for his weapons, only to relax as Keresa—wearing a Sunpath woman's dress—stepped into the firelight.

"About time," Kakala muttered, sighing with relief as he replaced his war club by his side.

Keresa dropped a rolled pack containing her war clothes to the ground. It landed with a thud. She grinned as she seated herself next to him. "My stomach is an open hole. That meat smells better than anything I've ever known."

Kakala watched her fumble into the rolled pack to retrieve a hafted stone knife. Her nimble fingers quickly sliced a long strip from the thinning haunch.

"Well?" he asked.

She sank her teeth into the meat, making happy sounds as she chewed. Then, wiping her sleeve across her mouth, swallowed. "Windwolf is gone. I overheard that much."

"Where?"

"No one knows." She took another bite, wolfing the hot meat. Mouth full, she said, "Lookingbill has sent runners out, offering sanctuary to any Sunpath People who need it." She met Kakala's eyes.

"We've stirred up a hornet's nest. The woman who drove a dart into Maga was Mossy, their Storyteller."

"Lookingbill's daughter." Kakala's heart sank. Raven take him, the old chief would never forgive them.

"How's Maga?" she asked.

"He has sent his soul to Raven."

She nodded. No one survived a gut wound like that.

"Anything else?" Kakala asked.

"Some sort of alliance was brokered between Windwolf and Lookingbill. I managed to slip close to several fires last night. People are talking about it, but no one seems to know the details." She gave him a horrified look. "Perhaps the chiefs don't trust us with such knowledge?"

Kakala sighed, shoulders sagging. "Then there is nothing else for us to do but return . . . and face the consequences."

All eyes lowered, fixed on the fire.

Keresa continued to eat, no doubt thinking she'd need to stock up before a couple of moons in the cages. Then she looked up. "Well, we could always run off and join Windwolf. He doesn't punish good warriors."

Kakala arched his back. "This is all my fault." He looked around, meeting the eyes of his warriors. "I think the rest of you should stay out here. Under Keresa's command, you should keep looking for Windwolf."

The warriors looked back and forth at each other.

It was Keresa who said, ". . . And you will go in and take all the blame?"

Kakala nodded. "I survived the cages once. I can do it again."

He could see confused relief mixed with sudden guilt on his warriors' faces.

"No!" Keresa said adamantly. "We did just as we were *ordered*. Nashat himself sent us out as a small party to capture *one* man. Had Nashat allowed us to take all of our warriors—as we thought prudent—the outcome would have been very different."

Kakala arched an eyebrow. "Let me get this straight. You want to walk in, heads held high, and tell Nashat and the Council it was *their* mistake?"

She narrowed an eye. "Why not?"

"They'll order Karigi to kill us all."

"Let him try." Keresa didn't budge.

Corre asked, "Are we talking about fighting with our own people?"

"No," Kakala muttered. But he had to admit the idea of driving a dart into Karigi had a certain appeal. "We do it my way. I'll go in. The rest of you continue the search for Windwolf. He's probably headed back to find his warriors. No matter what happens to me, I want you to locate Windwolf, keep an eye on his warriors, and report back. If they are joining up with Lookingbill, we need to know. That's more important than any of us." He met their eyes, one by one. "That's an order from your war chief."

Keresa gave him a sour look. "Sometimes I wonder who the enemy really is."

An avalanche of boulders littered the slope that Skimmer and Ashes climbed. Frosted by starlight, the boulders resembled monstrous wind-sculpted statues.

It looks like a broken garden of the Spirits. She blinked, fighting the sudden tremble in her hands. *Like the ruins of my own soul.*

Her daughter trudged up the slope behind her. "It's scary here. I don't like it."

"No. Me either.

Many of the boulders looked like upraised fists, others like angry faces, their raging expressions long ago quieted by the storms. She shook herself, trying to rid the images of dead women in the moonlight, their crushed faces staring. . . .

"Mother, could we rest for a while?"

"Just a little farther; then we'll rest."

Ashes suddenly gasped, and high overhead one of the Meteor People streaked across the night sky, leaving a luminous trail.

"He's headed toward the Ice Giants," Ashes breathed in awe.

Let him. Skimmer watched until he'd sailed out of sight, then continued the climb. When she reached a fallen log near the crest, she sat down. Her blood-soaked cape hung stiffly, and her waist-length hair fell over her shoulders in gore-matted tangles.

Ashes wiped a sleeve under her running nose and sat down hard beside her. In the starlight, her eyes shone gray-blue.

"Where's Headswift Village?" she asked.

Skimmer pointed. "We'll be there tomorrow night."

"I wish we were there now. I'm hungry."

Wind Woman whistled up the path, and Skimmer closed her eyes against the sting of wind-whipped sand. *Yes, pelt me, make me hurt. At least with pain, I can feel something.*

"Hungry? There's no time to hunt, Ashes. I'm sorry."

"It's all right. It's not your fault."

My fault? Everything is my fault.

Faintly, she heard the whoosh of wings in the darkness, and looked up.

Fear choked her. She reached out a quaking hand to gently touch her daughter.

Ashes looked around. "Is it time to—"

"Shh!" Skimmer pointed.

Ashes turned and saw the two warriors standing on the boulders up the trail. Silhouetted against the Blessed Star People, they looked tall and dark.

"We still have a chance," Skimmer whispered. "Do you remember the pile of rocks we passed on the way up? I want you to slide off this boulder very slowly, and sneak down the trail. Hide in those rocks until I come for you. If they catch me, do you remember what I told you?"

In a tight voice, Ashes whispered, "Yes."

Gravel scritched as Ashes slipped off the boulder and sneaked down the trail.

Skimmer sat perfectly still, giving Ashes time to conceal herself before she followed. If they spotted her, and she could draw them far enough away, Ashes might escape.

Just as she was preparing to run, a rock flew out of nowhere to clatter off a boulder beyond the warriors. The men flinched, clutched their weapons, trotted away to investigate.

From no more than three paces behind her, a deep masculine voice softly ordered, "Hurry. Follow my voice. There's a hole here."

"Who—"

"Do it!"

She slid to the ground, ducked low, and scurried toward the voice.

She found the shelter—little more than a crawl space beneath a toppled slab—and slithered under it on her stomach. Scents of dried grass, human sweat, and rodent dung stung her nostrils. Packrat middens of twigs, dried berries, and oddly shaped rocks lay at the bases of the boulders. Eyes glinted in the very back, a body's length away.

She whispered, "Who are you?"

As her eyes adjusted, she could tell he held a war club in his fist.

"Quiet."

Feet pounded on the trail, heading down the slope. She couldn't make out the words, but she heard the warriors whispering to each other. They stopped three times—looked around—and continued on.

The man whispered, "Those are Kakala's warriors. He's camped up in the spruce. Your daughter won't try to run, will she?"

Skimmer shook her head—and prayed she was right.

They stared at each other. He was tall and heavily muscled, with a straight nose and short black hair—hair recently cut in mourning. As hers would soon be, when she had the luxury of grieving for Hook-maker.

He whispered, "Who are you?"

"Skimmer, of . . . once of the Nine Pipes band."

He studied her with dark, unblinking eyes. "Stay here until I tell you to follow me."

He crawled out and studied the rocky slope. After several moments, he called, "Come. Quietly. Let's go find your daughter."

"Who are you?" she whispered as she crawled cautiously from under the rock.

"I am Windwolf . . . your new friend."

Nineteen

Kakala and Keresa stood at the edge of the spruce belt, their eyes fixed on the fantastic shapes of the Ice Giants filling the northern horizon. Father Sun had just risen above the gleaming surface of the Thunder Sea like a bloody ball. He shot a gaudy red light across the ice floes, like liquid fire. The bergs jutted up, casting long shadows over the water.

The crimson light bathed the high spikes of the Ice Giants, contrasting with black shadows and thick fog that glowed with a dark pink.

Keresa shivered at the sight. The sky had taken on such odd colors of late. Was it a sign that their world was about to die, as some rumormongers insisted?

She glanced at Kakala. "I wish you would not do this thing. There is no reason we can't all continue in our search for Windwolf."

Kakala looked down at his darts. The long shafts hung from his left hand, slim and deadly, their stone points catching the weird red of the morning sun.

He sighed wearily and said, "The Council must know of this new alliance between the Lame Bull and Sunpath. No matter what the consequences, we still serve our people."

"But," she wondered, "do they still serve us?"

He shot her a warning look.

"I'm serious." She narrowed her eyes, staring out at the purple tundra that separated them from the Nightland villages. "We owe our loyalty to our people. We accept their orders, and die—like Maga—trying to the best of our ability to fulfill them. You have won victory after victory, broken the will and spirit of the Sunpath People. And now, because you do not bring Windwolf's head, they will punish you?" She shook her head. "This is not right."

"We don't know that they will punish me." He gave her his reasonable look. "I will explain the situation to them."

"They will say that you do not serve the Guide's Dream. That Power has forsaken you. Somehow, the blame will be placed on your head."

He raised his right hand in a calming gesture. "Perhaps they are right."

She gave him a wide-eyed stare of disbelief. "That is absurd!"

"Karigi has already told them that we have begun warning villages, allowing time for the women and children to escape. That does not sit well with Nashat."

"We already have too many slaves to feed as it is."

He gave her a warm smile. "When Karigi is made the high war chief, do not use that tone of voice with him."

She glowered at him.

In reply, he said mildly, "Keresa, all we can do is see this thing through. We each have our responsibilities."

"I will *not* serve Karigi."

He shook his head. "I don't understand. Having won everything, I have a feeling, deep in my gut, that we are about to lose it all."

"We *won* everything because of *your* leadership, War Chief. *You* were the man who planned it all; it was your skill and courage that led the way for our warriors to destroy the Sunpath People. If the Guide's prophecy comes true, it is because you cleared the way."

He smiled, reaching up, running his fingers down the side of her cheek. "You have been a good friend to me, Keresa. I did nothing. It was us. Together. The warriors know the truth. They take your orders because they know without you, none of this would have happened."

Words choked in her throat. She looked away, watching the strange red light play across the Ice Giants. The fog had turned orange now.

"If they put you in a cage . . ." She swallowed hard. "Well, it won't be long."

"And why is that?"

"Because I'm coming after you."

Skimmer followed Windwolf as he wound his way through the brooding spruce trees that rose like spears above the old moraine. In the hollows, willows lined the now-dry pools, snow clinging to the shadows. Brown grass lay flat on the ground, waiting to send the first shoots up from the soil. Patches of roses, and old wilted stems, rasped on their moccasins.

Through the trees she could see the odd red morning light. Exhaustion lay like stone in her muscles. Her mind wandered, replaying bits and pieces of her life, all disjointed and fleeting.

Windwolf! How did I happen to find him, of all people?

She glanced at his broad back, the leather of his war shirt tight around his muscular shoulders, bunched where his belt snugged it around his slim waist. His long darts hung ready in his left hand, his atlatl in his right.

She had been a young bride, just married to Hookmaker, when the Nine Pipes band went to war with Windwolf and Bramble. They had fought bitterly over a border dispute—and lost.

Mine was one of the most strident voices speaking against an alliance when Windwolf and Bramble first proposed it.

Now she shook her head. How petty it had all been. Her people had defeated themselves long before the first Nightland war party came slipping down from the north.

The irony of it wasn't lost on her. It had only taken the death of her husband and the corpses of the dead women in the pen to make her understand.

They walked in silence for another two hands of time. Then Ashes started to stumble from exhaustion.

Skimmer said, "We need to stop for a while. My daughter has to rest."

Windwolf's gaze went to Ashes, and he seemed to be examining her, judging her level of exhaustion, probably trying to determine how much farther he could push her.

He said, "All right. You two sleep. I'll keep watch."

Ashes glanced uncertainly at the tall man. "Can we trust him, Mother? He's Windwolf!"

She whispered back, "This time he fights the same enemy we do. Let's try to sleep."

Skimmer thankfully lowered herself to the ground. Ashes curled up with her head in Skimmer's lap. In moments her daughter's breathing changed to the deep rhythms of sleep. Exhausted herself, she leaned her head back against the gritty rock and studied her old nemesis.

"Are we safe?" she whispered.

Without turning, he said, "You sleep, too."

Skimmer glared. "Can you speak without giving orders?"

He turned to look at her, hesitated, then said, "Not very well. Forgive me. Let me try again. We're not safe. Not for an instant, but I'd rather not tell you that. I'd rather have you get as much sleep as you can so that when the time comes, you can both run."

She let out a breath. "I understand. I'm grateful for your help."

He pointed at Ashes, who shifted in Skimmer's lap. "What's her name?"

"Ashes."

"Quite a little girl. She bit me when I tried to drag her out of the rocks last night." He pulled up his sleeve, showing a red crescent of tooth marks.

"She didn't mean it. She was just—"

"Oh, yes, she did. You didn't see the satisfied gleam in her eyes at the sight of my blood."

"She was frightened."

"So was I." He spread his feet and propped his darts close at hand. "Are you thirsty?"

"Yes."

He untied a gut water bag from his belt and handed it to her.

In a sleepy voice, Ashes said, "I don't like him, Mother. He killed our people."

"Sleep, Ashes. We might have to run again soon. Do you want a drink?"

Ashes gave the man a distinctly unflattering look, then buried her face in Skimmer's cape, said, "No," and closed her eyes.

The corners of his mouth tucked in a suppressed smile. "She's perceptive."

Skimmer closed her eyes, fighting exhaustion. Images flashed, and for one terrible moment she was back in the pen, hearing the snapping sounds of stone against skulls.

She jerked her eyes open, but couldn't find her voice. Then croaked, "No! Please! I . . ." She shivered, hands shaking. Saw movement, and tensed. Only to recognize him. And remember. "Windwolf!"

His bushy brows lifted. "The last time a woman said my name like that, I had to dive for cover. And I hate running battles."

She tried to lift the bag for a drink, but her hands were shaking and she sloshed the liquid over her sleeve before it could touch her lips. She kept hearing the people in the enclosure screaming his name. Gripping the bag in both hands, she lowered it to the ground. "What are you doing here? You should be out protecting one of our villages."

"I was returning from scouting the Nightland villages. I thought maybe I could get past the guards and kill the Guide. They had too many warriors at the cave mouths, so I gave it up. Then, heading back, I stumbled onto Kakala's warriors. I was actually hoping for a chance to drive a dart into Kakala's back when he finally got around to presenting it to me," he said sternly. "But in the process I happened to find you."

"Me?"

"Or was that someone else I found last night trying to stumble into Kakala's camp?"

As his words sank in, she felt light-headed. She lifted the gut bag again and drank several swallows. When she handed it back to him, she asked, "How did you manage to find Kakala?"

"I followed his trail after he attacked Headswift Village. It seems the Lame Bull People have finally caught the Nightland's attention." He studied her carefully, taking in the gore that matted her hair, eyes lingering on the bloodstains. And, by the Wolf Dream, he couldn't have missed the stench of death that clung to her like sap.

"Then Lookingbill is finally going to fight on our side?"

"He's going to try."

Tears suddenly burned her eyes. She turned away so he couldn't see her face.

In a gentle voice, he said, "I pray Wolf Dreamer helps him. He's going to need it."

"Don't talk to *me* of prayers," she hissed with more violence than she'd intended. "Tell me where your warriors are. They're the only thing that can help us."

His eyes narrowed. "I thought you were a believer?"

"Only a fool would believe in Wolf Dreamer after what I . . . The things . . ." A pause. "Fools . . . we've been fools." She blinked away tears, aware her hands were shaking again.

Spirits, please! Not now! Come on, Skimmer, keep yourself together. She knotted her fists, clenched her jaw, muscles rigid.

He watched her with knowing eyes, and then looked northward toward the glittering bulk of the Ice Giants. Red light burned in the high jagged ice peaks. "Yes, but I like fools. On the other hand, I agree with you. The only reliable shields our people have are their weapons, the strength of their bodies, and the skill of their hands."

"And the hatred that keeps us going."

His tall body was silhouetted against the red sky's gleam. The crimson light framed his oval face and made his eyes look like black empty sockets.

He didn't say anything for a time; then he came down the slope and knelt in front of her. "Lookingbill's daughter was recently murdered. I don't know how well he will be when we arrive. He—"

"Murdered, by whom? Nightland warriors?" Her tumbling soul fixed on that, desperate to concentrate on anything that didn't remind her of horror.

"Lookingbill told me that his family is cursed. Apparently many of the women in his family have been murdered. Keep that in your heart when you speak with him. He's worried sick about his last daughter, Dipper."

What is one more dead woman? But she said, "I will."

A gust of wind flapped the hem of his war shirt. "Lookingbill also told me that you had a plan to kill the Guide. Is it true?"

"Oh, yes." Here finally was something to live for.

"How did you plan to do this?"

Do I trust him? She rubbed the back of her neck. "I'm too tired to think. I'll tell you when we reach Headswift Village."

He ground his teeth in frustration. "All right then, at least tell me why the Guide is so obsessed with you."

"I was plotting to kill him. Isn't that enough of a reason?"

"No," he said softly. "Many of our people have tried to assassinate him. I just gave it up as a bad idea for a lone man. Outside of me, you're the only one who is still alive. I find that interesting."

Her laughter exploded from within, shaking her, maniacal. Peals of it rolled out of her chest, waking Ashes, who stared up at her in dismay.

Skimmer couldn't stop. She laughed, and laughed some more, until the laughter mixed with tears, and tears into sobs that wrung her soul dry.

She was vaguely aware of Windwolf and Ashes. Their gazes locked and held, sharing some terrible communication.

Images flashed across her soul . . . the enclosure, the stone mauls sailing down from on high, the screams . . . the little girl dragging her sister . . .

In the end, she lay slumped wearily against the stone, her body trembling, chin on her filthy chest. Within her, only emptiness remained. Fear, hatred, horror—all of it had drained away, as exhausted as her cold flesh.

His gaze softened. "I would hear your story."

"Kakala's warriors came with the morning," she began. She told the whole story: Words, with all the feeling of stone, seemed to tumble from her mouth. As if from a distance, she heard herself, wondering how she could tell it so flatly, without inflection or passion. But in the end, they were only words, fleeting things that died on the cold air.

Through blurred eyes she saw he sat stone still, hatred and grief flickering over his handsome face.

He took several long drinks from his water bag, but gripped it tightly, as though to wring the life from it. Ashes blinked, nodding on occasion. Sometimes she'd watch Skimmer, other times, Windwolf, perhaps to see if he understood.

When Skimmer had finished, the long silence was broken only by the red squirrels chattering and the wind in the trees.

Windwolf finally said, "We'll kill him for what he did."

Somehow she mustered the words: "Don't make promises you can't keep. I've been trying for three summers to kill him and haven't—"

"We *will* get him."

She turned dull eyes on his. "We?"

"You haven't lost your fervor for battle, have you?"

"Fervor? What is fervor?"

She contemplated the dark circles beneath his eyes, the deep lines etching his forehead. What was he doing out here alone? Didn't he know the Nightland clan Elders had offered safety in return for his dead body?

Windwolf said, "You don't want to join the fight?"

Ti-Bish's mad eyes stared out from the fabric of her soul. "I want a place where my little girl and I can live without worrying about being killed in our sleep."

He rose to his feet again and frowned at the trail. "There is a price for such freedom."

"I've already paid it." A sob rose in her throat again. Her shoulders heaved, but she didn't make a sound.

"Obviously you didn't plan to kill the Guide by yourself. Did you have an organized group?"

She mustered enough strength to nod.

"How many?"

"Two tens."

"How many of those were warriors?"

"They're all dead. It doesn't matter."

"Did you see them killed, or is there a chance the warriors might have escaped? Can you send a runner to—"

"*Stop it!*" she cried. "Can't you see how . . . how tired and . . . *I want to be left alone!*"

"We all do." He studied her for several moments before asking, "Think you could sleep?"

She wiped her wet face on her sleeve. "Yes."

"Good."

Skimmer watched him nock a dart in his atlatl and prop it on his shoulder. She leaned her head back against the rock and stared up at the vast reddish orange heavens.

Even the sky is bleeding.

She closed her eyes, thinking to only nap.

Twenty

Windwolf eased through the trees, sticking to cover as he made a careful scout of their surroundings. The spot where Skimmer and Ashes slept wasn't the best hiding place they could have picked, but he hadn't the heart to wake them.

Such compassion could get us all killed.

He growled at himself, irritated more with his own fatigue and depressed spirits.

Nashat and Karigi waded in and murdered over two tens of women and girls! Just like they were cracking nuts! He winced, hatred and loathing rising like bile into his throat.

He backed away, having searched the approaches to the best of his ability. Stepping around the tree, he cocked his head, studying Skimmer and the sleeping girl. Despite their awkward postures where they were propped on the rock, neither had moved. He raised the flat of his hand to the sky, measuring six hands up from the horizon to the sun. To have slept that long, in such an uncomfortable pose, told him just how exhausted they were.

He hunched down, reaching for a slab of dried meat in his pack.

Clamping the hard stuff with his teeth, he twisted a piece off, chewing. Food would buy him some time before he, too, collapsed.

Skimmer lives. He glanced back toward Headswift Village. *But what does that mean for us?*

He studied her slack expression, partially hidden by her gore-matted stringy hair. The odor of death clung thickly to her clothes. It took no stretch of belief to imagine her secreting herself beneath a pile of the dead.

Would I have had that kind of desperate courage?

When he and Bramble had fought the Nine Pipes band so many years ago, he hadn't had a very high opinion of Hookmaker. Brave and brash, the young war chief had led his warriors straight into Windwolf's ambushes three times. In each, the Nine Pipes warriors had fought bravely, standing and casting while Windwolf's warriors shot them down one by one from concealment. Each time they had finally broken and fled. When the Nine Pipes had finally offered a settlement, it had to have stung.

Yes, Skimmer had stood against him and Bramble when they tried to forge an alliance. Why wouldn't they? But now, with those events so distant in the past, neither he nor Skimmer were the same people they had once been.

So, Skimmer, have they finally broken you? She reminded him of an eggshell, fragile, so easily shattered. He had seen the terror bright in her eyes, watched her shake uncontrollably as she relived the memories of those last days in the pen.

He shook his head. *What little push would it take to crack what remains of your shell, Skimmer?*

"Not much," he whispered to himself, and sighed.

He started to rise, figuring to make another scout of the surroundings. In the split instant before he could comprehend, the world seemed to tense. Then the jolt shivered earth and air. A soft boom followed by a faint rumble accompanied the quake. Squirrels chattered; birds cried and flew.

Windwolf felt it through his feet, into his very bones. Such things were commonplace, but they always left his soul tingling.

It was a measure of Skimmer's and Ashes' exhaustion that they slept right through it, only shifting to new positions as the stone and ground they rested on quivered.

He looked out to the north. "Too bad it didn't bring your rotted ice caves crashing down on your heads!"

The dream began as it always did . . . Windwolf was running, running hard. . . .

Ahead of him, just over the hill, he could see the roof of the ceremonial lodge where Bramble should be waiting. He charged head-long for it. As he crested the hill, Walking Seal Village filled the hollow. Hawhak's Nightland warriors fled in panic before them, some turning, casting wild darts that hissed as they cut the air, then clattered and snapped as they hit the hard earth.

"Windwolf! This is madness!" Silt yelled behind him.

The village was in chaos. Fleeing Nightland warriors reminded him of hares on the run.

My people! Where are my people?

"Continue the attack, Silt!" Windwolf commanded. Heedless of danger, he ran with all his might, heading straight for the center of the village and the large, round-topped lodge. He caught a glimpse of several Nightland warriors sprinting from the opposite stand of trees. Kakala, Keresa, and . . . and *Goodeagle?*

No, it couldn't be! He'd just had a glimpse.

How could this have happened? What had he missed? But for the chance encounter of a fleeing woman, he'd have walked right into the trap. What had gone wrong? Something . . . something critical. Bramble had sent word that she was meeting to talk peace with Deputy Karigi.

Peace?

He heard Silt's feet hammering the ground behind him. "Windwolf, the villagers need us," Silt panted. "We have to press the attack on the Nightland warriors! If they regroup, it will go badly for us!"

"Do it!" he ordered.

Windwolf passed the first of the lodges, leaping over the body of a Nightland warrior who stared terrified at the dart point protruding from the middle of his chest.

Breath tearing at his throat, Windwolf raced past the first lodge, instinctively shooting a glance inside. The blurred image had to be fantasy. Those couldn't be people piled in there!

He raced full-out for the ceremonial lodge. A Nightland warrior burst from behind the next lodge, paused long enough to cast a wild dart, and ran for all he was worth. The whistling dart passed off to the left. Silt, on the run, grunted as he cast his own dart. It sliced the air past Windwolf's head, arced out, the shaft gleaming in sunlight as it pierced the fleeing warrior's right buttock. The man tripped, landing hard on his chest and screaming.

Silt cried, "Bramble knew what she was doing! She bought us time. We have to go. Now! Do you hear me?"

"I told you to press the attack!"

Windwolf leapt the fallen warrior, who was reaching behind himself, fingers slipping along Silt's shaft.

Kakala's inside. With how many more?

Heedless of the danger, Windwolf rounded the side of the great lodge and charged full tilt through the doorway. He heard Silt shout, "Hurry! I'll cover the door, but they're coming fast!"

Windwolf's heart hammered against his ribs as he burst into the main room. Panting, he raised his atlatl, ready to drive the first shaft into Kakala's breast. The room was empty, the great fire in the center smoking.

"Bramble?" he bellowed.

He threw back the first door curtain and leaped inside, crying, "Bramble?" The clan room was empty, parfleches, packs, and sacred bundles spilled out on the floor as if by angry children.

He bolted for the next chamber, shouting, "Bramble! Where are you?" He dove through the door curtain, ready to kill.

The sacred shields had been smeared with blood and excrement to kill their Spirits, and left on the floor. Overturned parfleches, wooden dishes, wadded-up hides, and Clan Matron Agate's gutted body lay before him.

The only sounds were the horrified shrieks of the warriors outside, fighting for their lives.

"Bramble!"

He searched the piles of bloody hides. A fierce battle had taken place here. Had she . . . had she made it out? Was she even now waiting for him in the forest beyond the village?

Hope leapt within.

He rushed to the next chamber.

She lay naked, sprawled across a sacred mammoth hide, her hands bound to a pole. A tall war dart had been driven deep into her chest. Blood leaked red and slick from her mouth and nose. The fluid smearing the insides of her thighs was proof of what they'd done before they'd killed her.

He cast his darts aside, cut her hands loose, and knelt, gently lifting her head. His eyes fixed with disbelief on the dart shaft sticking out between her breasts. Blood pumped out around it, but she was still breathing.

He snapped off the dart and murmured, "Bramble, hold on. I have to get you out of here."

As he slid his arms beneath her to lift her, she groaned. Her dark eyes flickered, and a faint smile touched her lips. Barely audible she whispered, "Foolish. You shouldn't . . . have come."

"Save your strength, we've—"

"No." She shook her head weakly. Blood-matted locks of long black hair fell over his arm. "Listen . . ." She twined weak fingers in his hide sleeve and seemed to be mustering her failing strength. "Goodeagle . . . betrayed . . . us. Goodeagle was . . . was here. Karigi . . . he . . ."

She gasped, and her body convulsed.

"Windwolf?" Silt yelled. "Windwolf, *it's now or never!*"

Feet came pounding through the lodge. Silt threw back the curtain, and came to a sudden halt when he saw Bramble slumped on the floor, her beautiful face slack with death.

Windwolf gathered her in his arms and pulled her tightly against him, murmuring, "No."

Silt gave him five heartbeats to mourn, then gripped his sleeve and roughly dragged him to his feet. "She's *dead!* We have to hurry!"

Together they ran back to the village and straight into a barrage of darts. . . .

W indwolf?" a woman's voice called.

"Bramble?"

"Windwolf!" she hissed. "Hurry. Get up!"

A hard kick in the side brought him wide awake, lunging for his weapons. Before he'd even made it to his feet, he had a dart nocked in his atlatl. "What is it? What's wrong?"

He was in the spruce lands, trees bathed in faint reddish gray light. Instead of Bramble's blood, he smelled sweet air scented with spruce.

Skimmer was giving him a wild look, her fragile eyes wide.

Skimmer! Bramble's dead. He pinched his eyes shut, shaking off the last of the Dream.

Fearfully, Ashes asked, "Mother?" and scrambled to her knees.

"Quiet!"

Skimmer pointed. The gray rays of false dawn filtered through the trees to the east, but between the dark trunks warriors moved. They were working their way down the slope, taking their time, being thorough. In the front, he recognized Keresa.

Windwolf grabbed Ashes and pulled her to the ground behind one of the boulders. Skimmer ducked down beside them.

"Have they seen us?" Windwolf asked, trying to clear the fragments of the Dream.

"I don't think so, but they may not be the only scouting party out looking for you."

He spun around and scanned the slopes below them. "Let's go."

Doubled over, keeping to cover, he hurried down the trail. Behind him, he heard Skimmer and Ashes stumbling, their moccasins sliding on the gravel.

Ashes whimpered, and in a cold voice that brooked no disobedience, Skimmer hissed, "Stop it!"

Ashes went silent.

Windwolf made it to the base of the slope; the trail forked. He surveyed the forest. The spruce boughs swayed in the wind, their needles glimmering.

When Skimmer and Ashes came to a halt beside him, Skimmer asked, "Do you know these trails?"

Windwolf pointed. "This leads back to Headswift Village."

"Won't they be waiting for us there?"

"Almost certainly."

"Then why—"

"Not now!"

He led them on a roundabout path through the spruce, then charged straight south across a patch of snow shadowed by the trees.

"We're leaving tracks!" Skimmer's voice carried the seeds of panic.

"Headed straight south," he added. "When we reach the other side, we continue south; but just long enough to let our moccasins dry. Then, at the first outcrop of stone, we turn back toward Headswift Village."

"Do you think it will work?"

"No, but it will take them a while to figure it out."

Skimmer and Ashes followed him, stepping into his tracks as they left the snow. A finger of time later, Windwolf found what he was looking for. Stepping from stone to stone, they left the trail. Then, well wide of their old route, he led them back north, then after crossing another couple of boulder patches, turned toward Headswift Village.

"Now we run."

Twenty-one

Young Horehound stopped at the edge of a thick patch of trees. He'd seen smoke rising from the other side with the last light of sunset, and hoped that today he would find Deputy Silt.

Horehound rolled his shoulders and flexed his weary legs. A tall, thin youth, he had seen ten and seven summers. When Chief Lookingbill and Windwolf had picked him for this task, he hadn't any idea it would turn into such an epic of cross-country travel.

He'd been dogging Silt's tracks for days, but always seemed to arrive late. Deputy Silt never remained for long in any one place. Not only that, but only yesterday, Horehound had almost stumbled headlong into one of War Chief Hawhak's Nightland war parties.

His only warning had been the sudden cry of a man in pain. Horehound had dived headfirst into a patch of sumac, and huddled among the stems as Hawhak's warriors topped the crest of a low hill and filed past. Five of the twenty-some warriors had been limping, the others looking surly.

Horehound had overheard mutters of "ambush" and "stinking Sunpath cowards."

Only after they were long gone had he crawled out of the sumac and grinned.

He'd had enough of walking through the blackened frames of lodges, kicking at smoking debris, and shaking his head. These people might have been Sunpath, but after the attack on Headswift Village, they were now allies.

He resumed his pace, trotting through a patch of mixed oak and pine. His wary eyes constantly swept the forest, alert for the first sign of movement. Then he caught the faint scent: smoke on the wind.

He pulled up at the edge of the trees, looking out at yet another ruined village.

Warriors walked through burned lodges . . . probably searching for bodies. They were obviously Sunpath, because a short distance from the village, three tens of Sunpath villagers had gathered. Not only that, none of the warriors wore Nightland garb that sported ravens, black circles, or the other symbols they had adopted after the coming of the Prophet.

Still.

As his gaze took in the clearing, searching for threats, he adjusted the twisted rabbit-fur mantle that draped his shoulders. In the distance he could count four fires that continued to smolder, and though he did not know these Sunpath lands well, he assumed they marked recently destroyed villages. He'd met several groups of refugees on the trails. All were headed north to Headswift Village.

The only thing Horehound knew for certain was that Headswift Village could neither protect nor feed them all. Worse, as more and more refugees flooded in, Headswift Village would become an increasingly alluring target for Nightland warriors.

As if we wouldn't have been anyway, once the Prophet's warriors finished with the Sunpath.

He trotted out from under the trees. When the men saw him, a shout of alarm went up and four warriors sprinted toward him with their nocked atlatls up and ready to cast.

Horehound spread his arms wide, showing that all of his weapons were tied to his belt, and called, "I have a message for Deputy Silt from War Chief Windwolf! Is Deputy Silt here?"

A big ugly man with shoulders as wide a buffalo's trotted up, eyed Horehound's weapons belt, and kept his arm back, ready to drive the wicked-looking dart into Horehound's chest.

Horehound sighed and repeated, "Is Deputy Silt here? I carry a message for him from War Chief Windwolf."

One of the other warriors said, "He must be telling the truth, Bot. No man would just run in here like that unless he thought he was safe."

Bot gave Horehound a murderous look, but said, "What is your name, warrior?"

"I am Horehound, from Headswift Village. War Chief Windwolf sent me to find you. I have been on the trail many days. Mostly because you never stay in one place!"

Bot scowled. "If we did, the Nightland warriors would find us, instead of us finding them. Were that the case you'd be talking to little bits of my liver right now. Which wouldn't do you much good, would it?"

Horehound shook his head. He didn't want to mention that standing here talking to Bot's face wasn't doing him much good either. "Is Deputy Silt here? The message I carry is urgent."

Without taking his eyes from Horehound, the big man said, "Dogwood, fetch Silt."

The warrior ran off down the trail. A short time later, he trotted back accompanied by a medium-sized man with shoulder-length black hair and dressed in a soot-stained mammoth-hide cape.

"I am Deputy Silt." The man eyed Horehound severely. "What is this message you claim to carry?"

"Deputy, I am to tell you that Kakala has attacked Headswift Village. The attack may have been meant to kill Windwolf, but many of our people died, including our Sacred Storyteller, Mossy. You are to know that Lookingbill considers this but the first attack to be made on our people. The Lame Bull People welcome the Sunpath People as allies in our mutual war against the Nightland warriors and their accursed Prophet."

Shouts went up. Some of the warriors actually Danced.

"And Windwolf?" Silt asked, grinning. "Is he well?"

"Yes, Deputy. Well, and beloved by our people. It was he who spoiled the Nightland attack on Headswift Village. At no small risk to himself, he saved Chief Lookingbill's life, and probably that of our war chief, Fish Hawk, and many others as well."

His statement was met with grins.

Silt was beaming. He clapped a hand to Horehound's shoulder. "You bring good news, Horehound. News beyond our hopes."

A feeling of delight shot through his breast. "That pleases me,

Deputy. Also, you should know that Headswift Village is currently sheltering refugees. Though I do not know how long our food will hold out."

"How are things in the north?"

Horehound spread his hands wide. "I have passed through nothing but burned camps and fleeing people. Most of the country is empty." He took a breath. "And only yesterday I hid from a party of North-land warriors."

"Headed which way? How many?" Bot demanded.

"Perhaps twenty, and five were badly wounded."

Another of the warriors nodded. "We ambushed them here." He gestured at the people beyond the village. "They were to be the slaves to carry loot and food north."

"Twenty?" Silt mused. "Hawhak started this raid with more than fifty. Somehow, I don't think Councilor Khepa is going to be pleased when his war chief returns home."

"We could follow," Bot suggested. "Hit them again. They won't be expecting us to be so hot on their trail."

Silt considered. "But we have no idea where Blackta, Kakala, and Karigi might be."

Horehound interrupted. "Deputy, there is more."

"Yes?"

"War Chief Windwolf told me this message was for your ears alone."

Bot made a growling sound. "That doesn't sound like Windwolf. He would never—"

"He might," Silt corrected, "if he feared that the news would get around too quickly."

Silt motioned for Horehound to follow him as he walked ten paces back up the trail. When Horehound glanced over his shoulder, he noticed that the warriors kept their atlatls nocked and aimed at his back. Even a poor warrior could hit such a big target from ten paces. His skin crawled.

Silt said, "What is this message?"

"Windwolf sends his regards, and an order that he wishes you to follow, though he knows you will not wish to."

Silt spread his feet. "Why am I not surprised?"

"He orders you to gather as many Sunpath people as you can and head west to the Tills in the lands of the Southwind People. He said he will be sending more warriors to you."

"What are you talking about? We're not running!"

The deputy had raised his voice loud enough that his warriors could hear.

Horehound deliberately kept his words low. "He said he knew you would not wish to obey him—"

"I have *never* disobeyed one of his orders," Silt said through gritted teeth. "But . . . but this . . . It makes no *sense*! Why would he give such an order? Did he explain?"

Horehound spread his arms. "He said you would ask. His answer to you is that the Tills are easily defensible. The rolling forested Sun-path lands are not. He asks that when you arrive, you make a study of the high points, figure out the best way to defend them so as to kill as many attackers as possible."

"We're going to defend the Tills? When our own lands are here?"

Horehound nodded. "Those who are not laying traps for pursuing Nightland warriors are to hunt, but in small parties. Windwolf wants you to rest, fill your bellies and packs, and be ready when he sends for you."

"Ah!" Silt's smile returned. "He is planning something?"

"He is. And, no, he did not tell me what. But he did say to tell you that trying it with exhausted, half-starved warriors . . . as he put it 'would not be wise.'"

Silt was frowning. "And the Lame Bull People?"

Horehound took a deep breath. "Some of our warriors will be sent to join yours in the Tills. Others will come at the last moment, meeting at a place Windwolf determines."

Silt looked at him from lowered eyes. "I'm just supposed to trust him?"

"He said I should tell you these words. He made me memorize them: 'Tell Silt that Walking Seal Village taught me he is the only man I can trust. Tell him that I beg him to trust me in return.'"

Silt's grave expression slackened. He looked away and his gaze drifted over the forest. Wind Woman's touch was calm and cool today, barely stroking the pine boughs.

Finally, Silt asked, "Where is he? Still at Headswift Village?"

"He was when I left."

Silt walked a short distance away and, more to himself than to Horehound, whispered, "The Tills lie ten *hard* days' run to the west. Why not someplace closer?"

Since Horehound didn't figure that question had been aimed at him, he kept silent.

Silt's head swiveled, and the look he gave Horehound cut like a stiletto to the heart. "I have a message for Windwolf."

"What is it?"

"Tell him I will meet him at the Tills, but if he is not there in two moons, I'll come looking for him."

Horehound nodded. "I'll tell him."

Silt gestured to the north. "We may know that Hawhak is scurrying home with his tail between his legs, but Kakala, Blackta, and Karigi are still out there somewhere. If you fall into their hands, and they make you talk . . . Well, it wouldn't be pleasant."

"War Chief Silt, by nature I'm a cowardly man. You can bet I'll take special measures to keep my hide in one piece."

Twenty-two

The magnificent Nightland Council chamber had a spongelike quality. The walls were as porous as a wasp's nest. Some of the cavities twisted back into the ice like wormholes, going in every direction and disappearing into blackness. And it was huge. It arched ten body lengths over Nashat's head and spread fifty paces across.

Two of the precious pine torches, carried all the way up from the Sunpath lands, burned in the center of the chamber. The pale yellow gleam danced across the high ceiling and glittered on the black wolf hides that covered the thick gravel floor.

Nashat pulled the sleeves of his heavily painted buckskin shirt straight and glanced at Ti-Bish. The Guide stood on the far side of the Council chamber, watching War Chief Kakala from the corner of his eye. The war chief was a big, heavy-boned man who wore his long black hair in a single braid. The bloodstains on his gray bearhide cape had turned brown from age, and almost looked like painted symbols. He had a raw strength about him that women reputedly found irresistible. Nashat wondered how they got over his scarred, ugly face.

Nashat said to Ti-Bish, "Blessed Guide, Kakala has not been able to capture War Chief Windwolf. I know this will disappoint you."

Kakala merely exhaled and shifted his gaze to Ti-Bish.

Barely audible, Ti-Bish said, "But I—I need to pray with Skimmer."

Nashat said, "You have failed your people, War Chief. You have failed our Blessed Guide."

Kakala's dark eyes returned to Nashat. "Elder, your orders prevented me from finding Windwolf. And, as to Skimmer—"

"You mean, *the Guide's orders!*" Nashat interrupted quickly, shooting him a warning look.

Kakala lifted a shoulder. "The *Guide's* orders sent me south with sixteen warriors. Windwolf was in Headswift Village. I split my force, sending Maga with ten to feint at the rocky warrens while I took four and tried to kill Windwolf as he met with Lookingbill. I had no leverage to force them to turn him over. If I'd been allowed to take the Elders captive, I—"

"Who is Windwolf?" Ti-Bish asked.

Kakala's brows raised enquiringly.

"A Sunpath war chief," Nashat answered. "I *told* you about him. A very evil man. He's killed many of our warriors."

Kakala said, "I wouldn't call him evil, Elder. He's a brilliant warrior. He's fighting for his people; he just—"

"It's just that some of his people have been trying to *kill* our Blessed Guide." Nashat gave Kakala a warning look and extended a hand toward Ti-Bish.

Kakala turned confused eyes on Ti-Bish, and seemed to be scrutinizing him with a new understanding.

As though he sensed the war chief's revelation, Ti-Bish said, "The blessings of Raven Hunter be with you, War Chief," and swiftly headed for the exit.

Nashat reached out and grabbed hold of his cape to stop him. "I realize it's your prayer time, Guide, but please, just a little longer."

Ti-Bish swallowed hard, gave Kakala an askance look and murmured, "All right. A little longer."

"As to Skimmer . . ." Kakala began.

"You, *War Chief,* have failed me for the last time." He gestured to one of the warriors standing by the entrance. "Take him to his justly earned punishment. He can contemplate his failures there. When Karigi returns, have him come to my chambers. I would speak to him about the position of high war chief."

Kakala swallowed hard, seemed to sway, and stood as the guard stepped close, his hand on a war club.

"You won't need that," Kakala said through a strangled voice. He walked proudly from the chamber, head high, the muscles in his back stretching the travel-worn cape over his shoulders.

Nashat paced in front of Ti-Bish. "He's a warrior. He doesn't understand. The Nightland clan Elders made the decision to find Windwolf, capture him if possible, and if not, kill him." He looked into Ti-Bish's wide eyes. "You do understand, don't you, Guide? There are people out there who would kill you before they would allow Wolf Dreamer's heresy to be supplanted."

"But, I—"

"There are no *but*s, Guide. Your responsibility to the people is to lead them to the hole in the ice when the time comes. Mine is to ensure you live long enough to ensure our return to the paradise of the Long Dark."

Ti-Bish nodded, his eyes dropping.

Nashat said, "You can go and pray now."

Keresa didn't look back as she trotted out onto the tundra. Moss and sedges padded her steps as she led the line of her remaining warriors. She could hear Goodeagle's thudding moccasins behind her. That he was second in line irritated her.

I'd prefer that he ran last. Maybe he'd do us all the pleasure of simply fading away.

No, not Goodeagle. For better or worse, he'd committed himself to them.

She shook her head, worry about Kakala spinning through her soul. They had followed his orders. They'd looked for Windwolf, had even tracked some elusive fugitives, but lost their trail. A man, woman, and child, from the tracks in the snow. A fleeing family, not a hunted war chief.

To her delight, not a single warrior had looked askance at her when she'd made the decision to head back. Each and every one of them understood what Kakala had done for them.

Odd, isn't it? Their loyalty is to Kakala, and not the Council. How did this happen to us? What have we become that our hearts beat for each other, and not the will of our people?

But then, if they found Kakala in a cage—given everything he had sacrificed for his people—the Council would have crossed some line that even she barely understood.

And if he's in a cage, Keresa, what will you do? She wondered. Were she to cut the bindings and free him, what then?

"It doesn't matter," she muttered under her breath. "We'll deal with that future when it confronts us."

But the deep-seated worry gnawed at her. How did nine warriors and a Sunpath traitor defy the Council and remain alive?

As they wound through the willows that lined Moose Creek, the sunset sky turned a livid shade of red. The bellies of the drifting Cloud People looked bloody.

Windwolf shielded his eyes to scan the heavens. "I've never seen the sky turn that color after Father Sun descends into the underworlds for the night. Have you?"

Skimmer shook her head. "No. But many strange things have happened since last summer."

"I remember the day Morning Star never went to sleep," Ashes said.

"As do I." Windwolf lowered his hand and let his gaze drift over the massive boulders that mounded the hills. Scrubby spruce trees sprouted from the crevices.

If they'd been on the main trails, they would be less than one hand of time from Headswift Village. Slogging through the muskeg in drainage bottoms took longer, but was much safer.

Somewhere out there, Kakala had an ambush set up for him.

Skimmer came up beside him. "You look worried. Why? Do you see something?" Long strands of black hair blew around her angular face. They had finally stopped long enough for her to wash most of the matted gore away.

"I was just thinking that if I were Kakala, I'd cover every trail that led to Headswift Village, and post lookouts on all the high points for a day's walk." He pointed to a mountainous pile of huge boulders. "Like that one."

Skimmer stared at it for a long time. "I don't see anyone there."

"No, but he might be looking straight at us. We need to keep to the low places: meltwater channels, creeks, gullies."

Ashes sank down on a rock and smiled. "Look," she said and pointed to the north. "There's a giant beaver."

The beautiful animal, as big as a black bear, swam in a pool of water that had collected to the side of Moose Creek.

Skimmer took a few blessed moments to enjoy the sight. Over the beaver's back, on the hills in the distance, a small herd of caribou could be seen. They resembled gray dots moving against a bloody background.

"Windwolf, before we go after Ti-Bish, there are some things I must tell you about him."

"We?"

She rubbed her cold arms. "That was yesterday."

Windwolf waited for her to say more. The glassy look of fear lay bright between her eyes. She reminded him of a chert nodule, ready to shatter into angular fragments at the slightest blow.

She clenched a fist and glared at the dusky heavens, the glitter of panic growing brighter.

He said, "You have done enough."

"I'm not thinking of myself."

Both of them looked at Ashes. The girl yawned and pulled her cape more tightly around her waist. In a few moments, she'd doze off.

Windwolf said, "I, too, have lived the pain of losing someone I loved. I'm not sure I'd take the risk either."

She gestured to his short-shorn hair. "Who do you mourn? May I ask?"

That tender place inside him, the chasm left by Bramble, ached. "My wife. We'd been together for three and ten summers."

"Bramble died long ago, Windwolf."

"To me, it will always be yesterday."

Their gazes held, his guarded, hers uncomfortably vulnerable.

Softly, she asked, "Why do you blame yourself?"

He squinted against the memories. "A runner came in. He told us that Karigi wanted to negotiate. We set up a meeting at Walking Seal

Village. Bramble went to speak with him." He exhaled hard. "It was a trap. A friend betrayed us."

"I've heard. You seem so . . . whole . . . I wouldn't have guessed."

"That's good to know." Too bad she couldn't see beneath his skin.

Ashes curled between two rocks and closed her eyes.

Skimmer mouthed the words, "Should I wake her?"

Windwolf shook his head. "Let her nap for a few heartbeats."

Skimmer sank back against the ledge and followed his gaze to the herd of distant caribou. They looked like they were playing, running and bucking. As dusk turned to evening, the bloody sky faded to deep purple.

"I heard you tried to rescue Bramble," she said cautiously.

"I was too late."

Skimmer closed her eyes and let Wind Woman's chill breath blow across her face. "I—I couldn't. Go back. For my husband."

"Captives don't have that luxury."

Skimmer tightened her arms across her chest, barricading her heart. "No. They don't."

Windwolf stared at her for a long time. "Why don't you believe it?"

"I just stood there, staring, unable to believe. I could have run. Could have—"

"No, you couldn't. I've seen that look many times on the faces of warriors . . . watched them stare in shock at their friends on the battlefield. Even though there was nothing they could have done, they always believed if they'd just said something, called out, they could have saved them."

She swallowed the lump in her throat. "Tell me something: After fighting tens of battles, do you ever stop being afraid?"

"Only if you want to die." He smiled grimly. "Somehow, Kakala's warriors have proved incredibly inept."

She smiled for the first time.

Windwolf looked up at the sky. "May I ask you a question?"

He saw the sudden trepidation, but she said, "Yes."

"Have you truly lost your faith in Wolf Dreamer?"

She nodded. "There—there was a woman in the enclosure. She told me it was a test—that Wolf Dreamer and Old Man Above had to know we had faith in them. That it was like a father punishing his child: Every instant of pain had a reason. That our pain . . ." She choked on the word, and had to swallow hard before she could continue. "Our pain hurt Wolf Dreamer as much as it did us."

He remained silent, listening.

When her hands started to shake, she knotted them and stuffed them under her armpits.

Windwolf asked, "What did you say?"

"That Wolf Dreamer was dead."

He shifted against the ledge, and his cape made a soft scraping sound. "Do you believe that deep down in your soul?"

Her eyes narrowed. "If Wolf Dreamer has to murder my family to test my faith, he's a monster. I prefer to believe he never existed."

His gaze rested on her face for a moment, then moved away, back to the star-spotted sky.

What do I believe? He puzzled for the answer, and it eluded him.

After a long silence, he murmured, "You said there were things you needed to tell me about the Prophet? What things?"

She clumsily fumbled with the laces on her cape, pulling them tighter. "I met him once."

Windwolf jerked around to look at her. "Where?"

"Outside of a Nine Pipes village. Ashes had just been born. She was sick. I had seen six and ten summers. I'd gone out at dusk to carry a bowl of mussel shells to the trash midden and found him there. He looked like a frightened animal. He was huddling over the midden using his teeth to scrape tiny bits of meat from old shells. When he saw me, he let out a whimper like a terrified dog—one that's been kicked too often. He tried to scuttle away. I called to him, but he disappeared into the forest." She rubbed her arms again. As night deepened, the air turned bitterly cold. "I went back into our lodge and filled a bowl with the last of the warm snowshoe hare we'd had for supper. We'd been very careful, eating just enough to keep us alive. I was supposed to save the rest for breakfast."

"But you didn't?"

"No. When I went outside again, he was back at the midden, working on the mussel shells again. I crept up very carefully and handed him the bowl."

"How did he react?"

She tilted her head, remembering the expression on his face. "He looked as though I'd just given him enough buffalo hides to ransom a village. As though to thank me, he handed me a raven feather."

Windwolf leaned against the ledge beside her. "When did you see him again?"

"I never did. He was around—people would see his tracks. I heard hunters say that they'd seen him at this village, or that, but he never returned to Nine Pipes territory."

Windwolf grunted thoughtfully, but didn't say anything.

Somewhere out in the darkness a wolf yipped. Then a whole pack began serenading the night. Their lilting howls echoed across the hills.

"Do you think that's why he's so interested in you? You helped him once?" Windwolf asked.

"Maybe. I think his soul is loose. He needs to be Healed by a Soul Flyer, someone powerful enough to find his lost soul and fix it to his body again."

Windwolf ran his hand over the carved wood of his atlatl. It was such a soft, loving gesture, it reminded her of the way a man would touch a woman's skin. "I hope you won't allow your pity for him to cloud your thoughts when the time comes to kill him."

Memories flashed across her soul: Ti-Bish hungrily gobbling down the warm meat with tears in his eyes . . . Hookmaker shouting at her to run . . . the screaming women in the enclosure. . . .

"No." She shook her head. "It won't."

An owl flapped over the creek on silent wings. They watched it soar just above the water before it vanished into the darkness.

A queer uneasiness taunted her. She said, "And what about you? Do you believe in the Blessed Wolf Dreamer?"

He bowed his head, and nodded. "Oh, yes, very much."

He wondered why he'd just said that, when, in truth, he really didn't know.

"Then you're a fool."

"I suspect so." She didn't catch the irony in his voice.

He shoved away from the ledge and gazed up at the night sky. "The Blessed Star People have begun to open their eyes. We should go. Given the trails we have to follow, we have a way to travel before we reach Headswift Village."

She woke Ashes, and they walked quietly in the deep blue shadows of the boulders, stopping frequently to listen for the sound of footsteps on the path behind them.

Twenty-three

Kakala turned his head away as someone threw a cupful of something liquid at him. The cold stuff spattered on the cage bars, and on his crouched body. His nose immediately detected the cloying scent of urine.

He closed his eyes, breathing deeply. The cage was a wooden box, constructed of spruce poles carried in from the distant groves where they extended in small patches into the tundra. The poles had been hacked into lengths, the corners bound together with wet sinew and allowed to dry snug and tight.

He had room only to crouch in the waist-high box. Food and water were brought daily—the former consisting of scraps collected from the camps, bits of gristle, previously gnawed bones—anything thought unfit for the evening fire.

Other people don't do this. The notion seemed stuck in his head. No people he'd ever heard of treated their miscreants this way. Among the Sunpath, traveling from camp to camp with the seasons, a family was responsible for its own. A man who compulsively stole, or acted violently or dangerously, was simply smacked in the back of his head when he wasn't looking. It was a way of recognizing that something was wrong, that some evil had taken possession of his soul.

Why are we so different?

He shifted, feeling the muscles in his back, thighs, and calves cramp. And this was just the end of the second day.

He clamped his eyes tight, grinding his jaw.

At least it is only me this time.

Each heartbeat that he spent bent double and aching was one that Keresa, Bishka, and the rest did not. He was here for them, enduring for them.

Not like last time. That had been true horror. He had watched his beautiful wife wilt, her soul ebbing in futility, as she crouched two cages down from him. At first they had called reassurances back and forth. But as the days passed, she had grown reticent, and then, finally, ceased to answer his pleas completely.

He liked to believe that she died the night of the storm, that it was the cold wind, blowing snow, and fog that had killed her. Not a loss of will.

He needed but look back to see her long dark hair, the sparkle in her eyes. Oh, how she'd laughed, her white teeth shining behind full lips. Had any woman ever lived to match her?

Their life together had been special. She, like Keresa, had been born to the hunt, to the trail, and adventure.

Perhaps it is time for me to die, as well. Nothing is left.

With Nashat's order, he had felt everything slip away. All of the long hard years it had taken to rebuild his life and reputation had vanished in an instant. Nashat had taken it all with a snapping voice, disdain in the man's eyes.

"Why?" he whispered. "What have our people become?"

Opening his eyes, he looked up past the polished spruce poles to see the Star People, so many of them, on the clear black night. They packed so closely together they made the sky seem small.

Like me. I am small. And getting smaller.

Exile

The Sunpath People call the time before Wolf Dreamer led humans through the hole in the ice the Exile. They believe it was a period of eternal darkness and cold, a lonely time when the gods had abandoned them.

How strange that they do not realize Exile requires solitude and abandonment in order to reveal its truths. It is only when the gods desert us that we dare to look deep inside and ask why. . . .

Ti-Bish tried his best to be invisible as he took step after careful step up the irregular course of the ice tunnel. In the sacred stories, it was told that great shamans, witches, and Powerful Spirit Beings could wish themselves invisible.

But I am not one. I am not that worthy of Power's gifts. The knowledge pained him, but could not be helped. For him, it was enough to just try with all the longing in his heart to fulfill the terrifying destiny Raven Hunter had chosen for him.

He stopped short, seeing the standing figure in the half-light. The man was illuminated by a thin streamer of light slipping past the hanging in the great Council chamber.

How can I pass him? Ti-Bish swallowed hard, fear rising in his bony chest. The man was obviously a warrior, for he held a thick wooden club, and stared watchfully up the tunnel toward the exit.

Frozen in indecision, Ti-Bish raised a foot, only to cringe when the guard looked his way, squinting in the faint light.

Ti-Bish fought the urge to flee, then sighed. He was caught. Wearily he walked up to the man, seeing reserve melt into recognition.

Now I am in real trouble.

To his surprise, instead of calling out to Nashat, the guard dropped to his knees. He wore a caribouhide hunting shirt with hair out around the shoulders. The man's long black hair was pulled back in a braid. Looking up with reverential eyes, he whispered, "Guide!"

"I don't mean to bother you."

The man slowly shook his head, eyes oddly gleaming. "No bother, Guide. Do you wish to summon the Councilor?"

"No, I—"

"*Unacceptable!*" Nashat's harsh voice boomed from behind the curtain. "You left here with fifty warriors, Hawhak! *Fifty!* And all you had to do was destroy a couple of villages, and return with a handful of captives!"

"Councilor, we were ambushed! Silt came out of nowhere, with *all* of his warriors! Not even Kakala—"

"Kakala's in a *cage*! Which may be where *you* belong!"

Ti-Bish winced at the violence in Nashat's voice. He glanced at the guard, only to find the man's attention fixed entirely on him.

"Kakala's really in a cage?"

The guard nodded, expression still awed. "The Councilor ordered him there two days ago. He failed to kill Windwolf."

Ti-Bish frowned. "I don't understand." He flinched at each explosive outburst from beyond the curtain.

"The Councilor ordered it in your name. You must be enraged at the war chief's failure."

Ti-Bish opened his mouth, closed it, then shook his head. "I *need* Kakala. He's going to bring Skimmer to me."

"But, I . . ." The guard shrugged helplessly, then licked his lips, as if daring to say something.

"Yes?" Ti-Bish prompted, hoping to hear more about Kakala.

"My child, Guide. My wife told me how you fixed my little baby . . . how you fixed his soul. I thank you, Guide. With all my heart, I just wanted you to know."

Ti-Bish smiled. "Yes, I remember. The child is doing well?"

"Oh, yes, Guide. Smiling, eating, it's . . . it's a miracle." The man's face beamed with worship.

"I am glad."

From behind the curtain, Nashat bellowed, "You will wait until Karigi's return, and then, before the entire Council, you will tell us just *why you failed*!"

Ti-Bish glanced furtively back the way he'd come. Then, to the warrior, he said, "I must do something. Please, do not tell Nashat that I was here." He clasped his hands, hoping desperately that the man wouldn't order him back down the tunnel.

To his amazement, the man nodded, "Of course not, Guide. Do you have any other orders for me?"

"I . . . well, no. Only that I urge you to keep your faith. It won't be long now."

The man nodded, hanging on every word. "Thank you, Guide. Thank you so much."

Ti-Bish gave him a weak smile, and hurried on.

Kakala is in a cage? This is terrible!

Twenty-four

Windwolf followed Dipper up the dark starlit trail that led through the rocky warrens of Headswift Village. Skimmer and Ashes followed behind him, though he could hear the little girl's dragging steps. The miracle was that she'd made it this far after days of hiding, running, little food, and the terror she'd survived.

Skimmer was another matter. Every time he turned, he caught sight of her brittle eyes, scrutinizing the whispering villagers who lined the trail.

Windwolf said, "Many of these are Sunpath People. Where—"

"Survivors," Dipper said. "They have heard we offer protection." Then she added, "My father has been praying for two hands of time that you would return soon. He ordered me to bring you to him as soon as you arrived. He doesn't know what to do with all of the Sunpath People. And there's . . . something else. . . ."

"What else?" Windwolf asked.

"My father will tell you."

Skimmer frowned at Dipper's back. "How did your father know we were coming?"

"He didn't. He's just been begging Wolf Dreamer to bring you here."

From the corner of his eye, Windwolf caught Skimmer's roll of the eyes. Indeed, she no longer believed. He considered that. But then, after what the woman had been through, how could he blame her?

Dipper hurried up the slope with her mourning-short black hair flopping about her ears.

When they entered the ceremonial chamber, Windwolf slowed. The place was dark—not at all like the last time he'd been here for the Renewal Ritual. A tiny bubble of light gleamed in the rear. Dipper led them toward it.

The huge boulders leaned over them like monsters hunching to listen to their conversation.

"Father," Dipper called, "Windwolf just arrived." She paused for effect. "He has found Skimmer!"

"Skimmer? It is too good to be true! Come, my friends. We must talk."

Windwolf could make out Lookingbill and his grandson sitting behind a small lamp. The distinctive scent of burning oil grew stronger as they approached. In the pale gleam, Lookingbill's fleshy nose seemed larger, his wrinkles more deeply cut. The few strands of hair that clung to his head were silver in the light.

"Thank Wolf Dreamer that you're here," Lookingbill said, and gestured to the hides spread on the floor. "Please, sit. Can I get you anything? Food? Water?"

"I will see to it," Dipper said as she turned and walked out.

Skimmer and Ashes settled themselves on the hides, but Windwolf remained standing. He noticed that Lookingbill's grandson, Silvertip, knelt beside a Spirit bundle painted with white wolves. The boy kept sneaking glances at the bundle, and wiping his palms on his pants, as though he longed to touch it.

"What is it, Chief?" Windwolf asked.

"A runner came in two hands of time ago. One of our spies in the Nightland Caves sends word that Nashat is talking about attacking us. He is waiting only for Kakala's return."

"Word must have gotten back that you have allied with us." Windwolf clenched his fists.

"Perhaps. It was inevitable."

Windwolf slowly nodded. Kakala was a pragmatist, a very effective one, but he wasn't creative.

Windwolf said, "I suggested this once before. Now I urge you to pack up your village and move. Immediately."

"As soon as we heard about the attack, we convened the village Elders to discuss it. We have many children and elders, not to mention the Sunpath People who have come seeking safety. We cannot move swiftly. And, War Chief, what's to say that Kakala wouldn't follow and slaughter us? We'd be out in the open. It would be much easier to ambush us on the trails." He looked up. "Our people voted to stay."

"I have to admit, if we're going to fight, it would be better to do it here. If we can hand Kakala a stinging defeat, he will withdraw, lick his wounds before trying it again. That would be the time to leave."

"Fish Hawk hoped that you might have a plan?"

Windwolf chuckled. "When it comes to war, I always have a plan." He considered a wild idea that had filled his thoughts on the trail. Something Kakala would never suspect. "Tonight someone must show me every tunnel here."

"Yes, of course, Fish Hawk will do that. In preparation we've already carried basket-loads of food and gourds of water to the most remote tunnels." The old man ran a hand over his balding head and heaved a sigh. The scents of the night—the smoke of campfires and roasting meat—drifted into the chamber, along with threads of conversation from the people who had collected on the trail outside.

Lookingbill raised his eyes. "How many warriors will they be sending? Can you guess?"

"That will depend on how many of their warriors are close."

"Then you will be happy to hear that Horehound has just returned. Your deputy Silt dealt Hawhak a severe blow. Karigi and Blackta are both south, seeking to find more of your villages and camps."

"Horehound delivered my message?"

"He did. Silt will obey your orders. Horehound said that he didn't like it, and wants you to know that after two moons, he's coming looking for you."

"After two moons, Chief, we will either have won this thing, or we'll be dead."

Neither Lookingbill nor Skimmer showed any change of expression.

"So, with the war parties out, Kakala won't have a large force to work with. . . ." The twists and turns were coalescing into a plan, and becoming a good deal more frightening. Without even realizing he'd spoken, he whispered, "That's the last thing Kakala would suspect." He knelt on the hides beside Skimmer.

Chief Lookingbill inhaled a shaky breath and sat back on his hide. He gazed at Windwolf with watery brown eyes. "Go on."

"Skimmer," he said, and turned to her. She straightened beneath his gaze. "Tell me in the fewest words possible how you plan to kill the Prophet."

She closed her eyes, and took a deep breath. "I must do it."

"You?" He remembered the brittle cracks in her soul, the way her hands shook, the desperation in her eyes over the last few days.

"Ti-Bish wants me."

Lookingbill's gaze narrowed. "He wants you?"

Silvertip extended his hand to touch the bundle, and Lookingbill ordered, "No, Grandson. We've discussed this. Leave it alone."

The youth drew his hand back, but his breathing had gone shallow. He cocked his head as though listening to something no one else could hear. Ashes had fixed her eyes on the boy, wide, fascinated.

Skimmer said, "I have heard that Kakala took all of the Nine Pipes women because the Prophet wanted one." She swallowed hard. "I think it was me. But somehow, Nashat didn't understand."

Lookingbill shook his head. "You were plotting his murder."

Ashes twined her fingers in Skimmer's sleeve and gazed at her in terror. "Mother? I don't want you to go."

"We'll talk about it later," she said, and smoothed Ashes' hair.

Windwolf cracked his knuckles. "He won't believe it if you just walk into his arms. He'll know it's a ruse. And even if he doesn't, Nashat will. He sees plots everywhere."

Skimmer bowed her head and seemed to be examining the fine black bear hides that glittered in the lamplight. "I just need to see Ti-Bish. I think I can convince him."

Taken aback, Windwolf crossed his arms over his chest.

She craned her neck to meet his disapproving stare. "He *will* protect me. I can't tell you how I know. It was something in his eyes that long-ago night."

"Some . . . communication," he said skeptically. "You're speaking like a Soul Flyer, which means you're making no sense at all."

From the corner of his eye, he saw Silvertip wet his lips and look frantically at Lookingbill.

"Grandfather?" the boy said in a shaking voice. "I—"

"Not now, Silvertip." Lookingbill's gaze was fixed on Skimmer. "Let's say you're right. Ti-Bish lets you in and he protects you from the Nightland clan Elders. What then?"

Her expression went hard, unyielding. "When the time is right, I'll kill him."

"You?" Windwolf and Lookingbill asked at that same time.

Skimmer held up a hand and raised her voice. "I don't know how yet, but I will."

The burning wick sputtered, and gigantic shadows leaped over the boulders. The only one who seemed to notice was young Silvertip. He watched them with wide eyes, as though he expected them to soar down and grab him by the throat.

Windwolf said, "If you did kill him, it would throw the Nightland People into chaos. Once his warriors know he's dead, they'll fall apart like a lump of dirt in water."

Lookingbill added, "A dead Prophet is a false Guide."

"It may take me a few days," Skimmer said. "I suspect I'll have to convince him I mean him no harm before he'll let me get close enough to kill him."

Windwolf nodded. "I think we can give you perhaps a quarter moon." He turned to Lookingbill. "We will have to keep Kakala's forces busy here for that amount of time. Do your people have the heart for such a fight?"

"They'll fight for as long as they are breathing."

He turned attention to Skimmer. *You are the weak link? What if your soul seizes at the last moment? What if you break?*

Did he dare send a fragile woman like Skimmer into a position even more dangerous than the one Bramble had faced? Bramble had been an experienced, shrewd warrior. Skimmer had never had a man's blood on her hands. She'd barely kept from collapsing into a quivering mass on the trail.

He said, "Forgive me, Lookingbill. But Skimmer is not the right person to perform this duty."

"What?" she asked in surprise.

"I mean we can't chance that you will lose your nerve at the last instant."

With softness as excruciating as a mother's last good-bye, she murmured, "I can do it."

The lamp threw a pale glittering shawl over the stone walls, and turned people's unblinking eyes into mirrors.

Windwolf clamped his jaw.

Lookingbill asked, "If not her, who?"

Dipper entered, a wooden plate in her hands. She stopped short at the tension in the very air and settled onto her knees, the food forgotten in her hands.

Windwolf kept his eyes on Skimmer when he said, "My life depends on my ability to judge people and their abilities. In the end, she won't be able to kill Ti-Bish."

What he would never admit was that the last time his instincts had screamed at him this way, a trusted friend had betrayed him.

Skimmer turned to Lookingbill, fire in her eyes as she said, "Chief, I am the *only* one who can do this. Who will take care of my daughter while I am gone?"

"I will," Dipper said without hesitation. "I think Ashes and Silvertip will get along well."

At the mention of his name, Silvertip wrenched his gaze from the bundle. "What? Did you call me?"

As though the discussion were over, Skimmer rose to her feet, grabbed Ashes' hand, and said, "Where will we sleep tonight?"

"In my chamber," Dipper told her. "I've prepared places for the three of you."

As Skimmer walked by him, Windwolf grabbed her arm. Despite her brave words, she trembled in his grip.

In a voice only he could hear, she murmured, "I won't fail."

"If you do, many innocent people will die."

Lookingbill gasped suddenly, and shouted, "Grandson!"

Windwolf released her, grabbed for his war club, and spun, expecting to see Kakala himself striding into the chamber.

Silvertip's fingers were a hair's breadth from grasping the bundle.

"Silvertip, I told you not to touch it!" Lookingbill chastised.

Silvertip wet his lips. "But Grandfather, there's a man's voice in there. He keeps ordering me to pick it up."

Lookingbill got to his feet, hobbled over, and grasped the bundle. As he clutched it to his chest, he stared down into his Silvertip's eyes. His anger quickly turned to fear, then reverence.

He put a hand on the boy's shoulder and guided him across the chamber to speak with him privately, but Windwolf heard Lookingbill say, "What did he tell you?"

While the two of them whispered, Windwolf asked, "What is that?"

"It's the Wolf Bundle," Dipper whispered, her gaze on her son.

"The Wolf Bundle?" Windwolf frowned. "Wolf Dreamer's own Spirit bundle? The one he made after he fought Grandfather White Bear?"

"It's been passed down through our family for tens of generations."

Ashes glanced up at Skimmer, then Windwolf, and finally her gaze went to Silvertip. She seemed to be watching his tormented expression. She asked, "Why would Wolf Dreamer want to talk to that boy?"

In a clipped voice, Skimmer said, "Wolf Dreamer is dead, Ashes, and has been since the beginning of the world."

Ashes' brows drew together.

When Lookingbill placed the bundle in his grandson's hands, Dipper let out a small cry and put a hand to her mouth. "Not my son," she whispered. "Blessed Ancestors, please. *Not my son!*"

Twenty-five

The voices had begun to whisper in Kakala's ears on the fourth day. He no longer saw the people who came to stare, call taunts, and toss their refuse at him.

The world had collapsed, fallen in, compressed to the cramped square of wood that confined his doubled body. For the most part, Kakala huddled, eyes closed. Behind the tightly pressed lids, he ran in green fields, his hand in Hako's. He watched the sunlight gleaming in her blue-black hair, watched her slim body as she sprinted beside him.

"I love you so much."

In answer, Hako twisted her head, hair flying, partially obscuring the radiant smile she flashed his way.

"*You are going to die here,*" a voice whispered into his ear.

He had started, blinking, shooting frightened glances to the side—and found nothing but the heartless wood.

"Go away," he whispered.

"*We have come to watch,*" another voice mocked from above his head. But when he'd looked up, only the hazy sky arched over the confining bars.

"I did nothing wrong."

"Oh, yes, you did."

"I served my people."

"And this is what service has brought you to!"

The voice chuckled, the rasping sound of it unnerving.

"I am nothing." He stared down at his scarred hands where they rested between his bent knees. The feeling was gone from his legs, drowned by an endless aching pain.

The world is pain.

He blinked again, aware only of the beating of his heart, the air that he drew into his lungs.

"No different than an animal. This is the great Kakala!"

"Stop it." But the hard bark of his voice, used to command, made only a weak rasp.

He clamped his eyes shut, clapping hands against his ears to block the voices that chattered and whispered.

Nothing. I am nothing.

Desperately he searched the darkness for another vision of Hako. But she, too, now eluded him.

"War Chief?"

He barely heard the voice, muffled through his hands.

"War Chief Kakala?"

He laughed, the sound maniacal as if rattled around inside his empty soul. "No, I'm not playing that game. You have tormented me enough."

"This is a mistake," the muffled voice pleaded. "We must let you out."

"Oh, yes. Out to what? Out like Hako?"

"Who?"

"My wife. But I'll fool you. When my soul's finally free of the pain, it will find her."

"I didn't know you had a wife."

"I didn't. Not after Brookwood Village. They killed her here. In the cages. Where they'll finally kill me."

He felt the cage shake, and blinked his rheumy eyes.

The images eluded him for a moment: Night. The star-shot sky overhead. When had the sun set? How had he missed it?

A thin shape hunched as it fingered the thick knots that imprisoned him.

Kakala blinked. "What are you, phantom? Can't you get inside to whisper to me?"

"These knots . . . they're difficult."

"They're tied with wet sinew . . . so that it dries hard. They wouldn't want me to pick them apart."

"I have to get you out, War Chief. You have to find Skimmer for me."

Kakala made a face, shook his head, shifted, and cried out at the pain of movement. He drew a deep breath of the cold night air. As it escaped from his lungs he saw it fog in the starlight.

Kakala reached out, feeling the cold reality of the bars as his fingers wrapped around them. The thin phantom hadn't vanished as he'd expected, but continued to worry the knots.

No, this was real: an actual human being plucking ineffectively at the sinew.

"I don't know who you are, but if some warrior comes along, they'll put you in with me because of what you're doing."

"I don't think so," the soft voice said. "He wouldn't let it happen."

"He?"

"Raven Hunter."

"Of course." He slowly tried to straighten his back. "Raven Hunter talks to you, does he?"

"Not as much as I'd like."

"Me, either," he added dryly. "Look, friend. I was serious. If they catch you trying to let me out, they'll make you wish you'd never been born."

The dark form hesitated, and Kakala could see the shadowy face staring in at him. The gentle voice said, "I've wished that before. Back before Raven Hunter came to me. I didn't understand. All of those terrible things, they were necessary. I had to know hunger, loneliness, and despair before I could understand that they were distractions. Raven Hunter didn't come to me until I had lost all of myself."

"Guide?" Kakala whispered incredulously. "Is that you?"

"I'm sorry, War Chief. I just learned about what happened to you. I came as quickly as I could."

"Why are you doing this?"

"Because we need you."

"We?"

"You have to bring Skimmer to me."

"I already did. She was among the captives I took from the Nine Pipes band. Just as you ordered. I turned her and the rest of the women over to Nashat."

The Guide stopped short. "Nashat never brought her to me. He brought a woman called Blue Wing. I never could understand why."

Kakala cursed under his breath. "I remember Blue Wing. Tall, attractive, with long hair. Goodeagle couldn't get enough of her on the trail."

"He never listens to me."

"You talk to Goodeagle?" Kakala made a face. "Why?"

"I don't know Goodeagle."

"Lucky you."

"I meant Nashat. He never listens."

"Noticed that, have you?"

The Guide sighed, pulling his hands back from the knots. "I have to go and find something to cut this."

A familiar voice from the darkness said, "No, you don't."

"Keresa?" Kakala's heart leapt. He watched as her dark form emerged from the shadows; behind her, other men slipped through the night to stare warily around.

"War Chief," she said severely. "It figures I'd find you in a mess like this."

"And what were you going to do?"

"Chop you out of there," she said firmly, shooting the Guide wary looks.

The Guide asked fearfully, "You can free him, Deputy Keresa?"

"Of course, Guide." Keresa stepped forward.

Kakala heard the whistle, followed by a snap, and the cage shivered under the impact. She took three more whacks at the bottom binding, and then turned her attention to the top. Finished, she laid a woodworking adz to the side. Keresa's strong hands wrapped around the bars, tugged, and one side came free.

Helping hands reached in to pull Kakala from the cage. He groaned, toppling onto his side, legs like fire as he extended them.

Keresa bent over him, her hands running down his spine. "It's going to hurt for a while."

Kakala laughed, panic barely masked. "I'll bear it."

He saw Keresa straighten. "Guide, what are you doing here?"

"I came to free the war chief."

She studied the thin man in the starlight. "Nashat isn't going to like that."

"I know," came the weak reply.

Windwolf sat with his back to the stone, elbows on his knees, wrists loose. He had watched the fire burn down to coals, casting periodic glances at Skimmer's form where she slept with her daughter in the rear.

Dipper and Silvertip lay side by side; the boy whispered, the words mostly incoherent. But on occasion, the boy would say, "Wolf Dreamer?" with enough anguish to send shivers down Windwolf's spine.

Is the boy really a Dreamer?

He leaned his head back against the stone and wondered. To do so was a diversion that kept him from pondering his own mad plan. What had seemed inspired took on the cloak of the ludicrous. His plan now seemed little more than the ravings of desperation.

Since they'd arrived, he'd secretly endured the same fear that lined the faces of those closest to him: wondering how they'd survive Kakala's next attack. But it angered him to be reminded of it every moment by their eyes—eyes reverent with faith in him. They believed he could protect them, and of all the things that could be said about him, how could a man who had lost his wife, who had watched his people destroyed and dispersed, save this vulnerable band of Lame Bull People?

He sat, back against the resisting stone, and put his hands on either side of his head, pressing hard, trying to force some sense into his worry-laced soul.

"Come on, Goodeagle," he said, barely audible. "Don't let me down. Tell Kakala exactly what you think I'll do."

But in the heat of battle, he knew he wouldn't have time to second-guess Goodeagle. A sharp ache invaded his chest. He fought it, filling his mind with hate. He thought he'd explode. Remembering.

He could see Goodeagle's face so clearly, see the almost Dreamy look in his eyes.

How could I have been so foolish?

"*You balance each other.*" Bramble's voice haunted him from the past. "*You are brutally practical. Goodeagle reminds you of the gentler aspect of life.*"

Ah, yes. So gentle. He winced at the memory of that hideous lance jutting out between Bramble's blood-smeared breasts.

Is that what you wanted, Goodeagle? She was your friend, too.

After a finger of time, he crawled to the bedding Dipper had laid down, stretched out on the hides, and stared at the shadowy ceiling as he examined his narrowing options.

Too often thoughts of Bramble intruded—he imagined touching her hair, her skin.

He'd trusted Goodeagle—trusted him like a brother.

It's my fault. I should have known.

Goodeagle had been dropping clues for moons: a missed meeting here, a lame excuse there, a change in his eyes.

Bramble had tried to warn him. . . .

Across a silken bridge of memory, he heard her say, "*Something's wrong with Goodeagle. He has a sickness in his heart.*"

He closed his eyes.

And now, I am going to bet all of our lives on him. On the things he'll tell Kakala.

Twenty-six

Sitting beside Kakala, Keresa studied the huge Council chamber, and slowly shook her head. The honeycomb of ice glittered in the light of the fire. The opulence of the place amazed her. The bluish dome of rock seemed to twinkle in the firelight.

Kakala moaned softly, and shifted painfully on the thick layer of buffalo, elk, and musk ox hides where they'd laid him.

The rest of her warriors had stared around uneasily at first, gawking at the painted parfleches, the wealth of hides, and paintings of the animal Spirits. These things were the plundered loot of the Sunpath People, carried here on the backs of captives, to create a display of Nightland might for Nashat, Ta'Hona, Satah, and Khepa to admire.

But at what cost to us and the Sunpath?

She shot a sidelong glance at the Guide, trying to ferret out his true motives. Thin and hollow-cheeked, Ti-Bish sat cross-legged on a plush giant beaver hide. His beautifully tanned caribou-fawn shirt had been decorated with images of Raven. He wore a cape made of the midnight black feathers over his shoulder. The man's hair was greasy, pulled back in a braid that snaked down his back.

The Guide periodically reached out when Kakala groaned, and at the mere touch, the war chief stilled, almost sighed with relief.

What sort of man is he? The question knotted in Keresa's soul. In the Guide's name, they had gone to war in a way that had been completely alien to her people. From hunters and occasional raiders, they had become dedicated killers. But at what cost?

She dared not count the dead, or remember their faces. All of those friends and companions, like Maga, whose souls now inhabited the camps of the Star People. How many women and children had been left fatherless? To what ultimate purpose?

She ground her teeth, watching the fire—a wealth of wood packed in on the backs of captives—burn into smoke that rose up through the ice.

A droplet of water spattered on the leather beside her.

"The hole in the ice is there, Deputy," the Guide said, as if reading her thoughts.

"Of course," she told him, masking her own doubts.

Ti-Bish gave her a knowing smile, his eyes warming. "If it helps, you won't be making that passage."

She started. "I won't?" A chill flowed through her, images of Maga's body filling her thoughts. *Please, tell me it won't be a gut wound!*

Ti-Bish fixed his understanding eyes on hers. "Power has another fate in store for you. You and the war chief are the lace that mends us."

"The lace . . . ? I don't understand."

"No, but you will. The lace must be wetted, then allowed to dry into a tight binding. Your soul isn't made for the paradise of the Long Dark. You must see the Raven Bundle to dry land."

"You speak in riddles, Guide." She took a deep breath, aware that most of her warriors, weary from days on the trail, had succumbed to the soft hides and dozed off.

In a soft voice, Ti-Bish said, "Follow your heart, Keresa. It will lead you in the right direction. This world is ending. Washed clean. Power is turning; something new is being born."

"And what would that be?"

"The future." He shrugged, reaching down again as Kakala gasped in his sleep.

"What did you give him?" she asked, indicating the little wooden cup beside Kakala.

"An herb tea made of moss, phlox, and a certain mushroom. He is Dreaming, allowing his soul to fly to the past."

"With his wife?" she asked curiously. Thoughts of her own youth, of being a misunderstood girl, filled her. Once again she could see her parents' disapproving stare as she returned from her first hunt. At nine, she'd run off, spent four days on the tundra, and returned with a brace of partridges, two hares, and a pika. The load had almost been more than she could carry.

She had expected praise, but her father had beaten her, insisting in no uncertain terms that such doings were for boys. Her older sisters had just rolled their eyes.

And where are they now? Both women were widows, with six children among them, living on the largess provided by Sunpath captives who bore food up from the forested lands to the south.

"Your children will be the binding," the Guide told her.

"I have no wish for a man." She almost snorted her derision. She had yet to meet one who could stand to put up with her ways. Well, all but Kakala, perhaps. And their souls, so close as warriors, would have rubbed raw as man and wife.

"And he has no wish for you," Ti-Bish added. Then he smiled. "Yet."

She chuckled. At least it wouldn't be Nashat!

At that moment, the Ash Clan chief, Khepa, entered the room, stopped short, and stared with startled eyes.

"Guide?" the old man asked, his right hand trembling uncontrollably.

"Greetings, Councilor," Ti-Bish said, suddenly uncomfortable.

"What are these warriors doing here?" The old man's glassy eyes took in the sleeping warriors. "And isn't Kakala supposed to be in a cage?"

"I . . . I freed him." Ti-Bish couldn't seem to meet Khepa's eyes.

"You . . . But, Nashat . . ."

"Nashat what?" came the sharp query as Nashat himself strode in, stopped short, and recognized Kakala. His eyebrows arched sharply, and his gaze fixed on Ti-Bish. "Guide? What is going on here?"

"Well, you see . . . Kakala . . . he was in a . . . cage."

"He *failed* you!"

"No . . . that is . . . ." Ti-Bish swallowed hard, his eyes fixed on his hands.

Dumbfounded, Keresa watched the Guide fumble with his fingers. She stood, kicked Kakala hard, and stepped between Nashat and Ti-Bish, who also stood, shifting awkwardly.

"There had better be a good explanation for this," Nashat growled.

Keresa braced her hands on her hips, stating, "The Guide ordered him freed."

Nashat stopped short, eyes half-lidded. "I thought you were hunting Windwolf, Deputy." Then he gave her a sly smile, his gaze lingering on her body. "But, for certain consideration, I might overlook your dereliction of duty. Perhaps we could discuss it later, in my chamber?"

"We will *not*," she snapped, caution vying with a sudden anger. She was aware of Kakala, awakened by her swift kick, sitting up on the hides, his eyes oddly unfocused as he peered around. Several of her warriors had awakened, and were nudging the others.

Keresa shot a hard look into Nashat's eyes. "The Guide asked us to help him remove Kakala from the cage." In a more serious tone, she added, "We *always* follow the Guide's orders without question. He said Kakala had to obtain the woman Skimmer."

"Yes, yes," Ti-Bish said, stepping up just behind Keresa's shoulder.

Giving Ti-Bish a withering glare, Nashat said, "Perhaps we should step outside, Guide. I would hear your reasons in a place where no idle stories could be mistakenly carried from this place."

Keresa's voice dropped. "The Guide has already given us *his* orders. They are clear, Councilor."

She met Nashat's hot stare, fully aware of Khepa's amazement. *Come on. Put your foot fully into the trap, Nashat!*

Instead, he gave her a crafty smile. "Of course, it shall be as the Guide wishes."

As he spoke, Satah and Ta'Hona stepped in.

"Good," Keresa said. "Then, as the Guide ordered, Kakala, as head war chief, will take all of his warriors south in the pursuit of Windwolf and the woman Skimmer." She turned, facing Ti-Bish. "We thank you, Guide. And wish you to know that we will pursue your goals with all of our soul and being. Upon my honor, we shall not return until Windwolf is dead and the woman Skimmer has been safely delivered to your care."

"Yes, of course. Thank you, Deputy." But Ti-Bish kept shooting frightened glances in Nashat's direction.

Keresa stepped close, voice a whisper. "Nashat serves *you*! If you need us, call."

Ti-Bish blinked, an odd relief in his expression. "Thank you, Deputy."

Keresa avoided the frothing anger stewing behind Nashat's hard face as she motioned to her warriors. "Come on, on your feet. Two of you, help Kakala. I need the rest of you to fan out. Find our people, collect packs, see to your weapons. I want us on the trail within two hands of time."

"And this time," Nashat added through gritted teeth, "you *will* teach the Lame Bull a lesson. And *bring back Windwolf's head!*"

Keresa gave him a slight bow. "And Skimmer, Councilor. Lest you forget."

Nashat's lips were twitching, a terrible promise burning within.

Keresa gave him a faint nod. *Don't even think it, Nashat. I'll rip your throat out before you lay a finger on me.*

She gave Ti-Bish a grateful smile. "Bless your wisdom, Guide."

Then she led her warriors from the room, wobbly Kakala supported between Bishka and Rana.

In the cold tunnel, Kakala asked, "What just happened back there?"

"I placed us between the lion and the bear, War Chief. But at least you'll face them standing up instead of doubled over."

In the middle of the night, Silvertip awakened suddenly. The rocky chamber was dimly lit, the coals little more than gleaming eyes in the hearth. He snuggled under his bear hide and felt Ashes' eyes upon him.

Cold seemed to creep from every part of the chamber, twining out of the rock to stroke his warm body. He shivered and pulled his hide up, leaving only his eyes showing. His breath came back warm.

The Wolf Bundle rested beside him. He kept glancing at it. He hadn't heard any voices since Grandfather put it in his hands, but his Dreams had been so vivid, a great black wolf telling him things that had splintered and slipped away as he awakened. Then he remembered: It was something terrible, about blood, and water, and crashing ice.

The wolf's voice came back with frightening certainty: *"You must die before you find the path!"*

He nervously crushed the hide with his fingers. The girl was still looking at him.

To his surprise, she shoved her hides off, put on her cape, and walked across the chamber.

Silvertip watched as she knelt beside him. Her beaverhide cape, with the hair turned in for warmth, had been painted blue with white stars. It was pretty. She was pretty, too. She had long black hair and an oval face with large black eyes. Her nose was small and narrow.

She leaned over him and whispered, "Did you really hear Wolf Dreamer's voice in that Spirit bundle?"

Silvertip nodded and stared up at her.

Ashes' eyes narrowed, as though she was thinking about it. "My mother says Wolf Dreamer is dead."

"Of course he's dead. He's a Spirit."

"Then how could you hear his voice? Are you a Dreamer?"

"I don't know." Silvertip propped himself up on his elbows and cocked his head. "The Wolf Bundle is like a trail. You can follow it to go visit Wolf Dreamer in his Spirit Lodge."

"In the skyworlds?"

He lifted a shoulder. "I guess so. But Grandfather told me that sometimes the trail also leads to the past or the future."

Ashes sat down cross-legged on his bedding hides, and scrutinized him as though he were a nasty bug. "Why would he want to talk to you? You're just a boy."

Silvertip lowered his gaze and brushed at a piece of gravel on the bear hide. "When the Bundle talks to me, Wolf Dreamer says that no one can hear him but me."

"I was watching you. You looked scared."

"I was scared."

Many times in the past Grandfather had playfully held the bundle to his ear, and he'd felt a prickle like sticky insect feet at the back of his neck. Tonight had been different. The deep voice had been soft and kind.

"Wolf Dreamer told you to pick up the bundle?" Ashes gave him a mean look.

"I don't know why . . . he just did."

"My father once told me a story about the Exile. He said that in the

Long Dark there were many Spirit bundles, and each one had a voice that helped to guide the people. But right after the emergence from the hole in the ice, the People of the Nightland stole all the bundles, so they were the only ones who could hear the voices." Her brows lifted. "If they stole them all, how did you get the Wolf Bundle?"

"It has always belonged to my clan. Foxfire, Wolf Dreamer's half brother, gave it to his son, and he gave it to his son, on down to my grandfather. When I become a man, it will belong to me."

"Wolf Dreamer is your ancestor?"

He nodded.

"Since he was the good twin, I guess that's all right."

"Yes, he was good, and Raven Hunter was bad. Wherever Wolf Dreamer goes, people are happy. Wherever Raven Hunter goes, there is war and suffering."

She exhaled and looked around the rockshelter at the sleeping people. "What did your mother mean when she said, 'Blessed Ancestors, not my son'?"

Silvertip wet his lips, and remembered what Wolf had told him in the Dream. *I have to die.* To Ashes, he said, "The prophecies say that when Raven Hunter sneaks into our world again, Wolf Dreamer will send a new Dreamer to save us. He will come from Foxfire's family line, my family. I think Mother is afraid it might be me."

"Would that be bad?"

He stammered, "It's just that being a Dreamer is very hard, and they're usually k-killed in awful ways."

She glared at the Wolf Bundle. "Why would Wolf Dreamer let his chosen Dreamer be killed?"

Silvertip sat up in his hides and reached for the Wolf Bundle. When his fingers touched it, a tingle ran up his arms and flared in his chest. "Here," he said, handing the bundle to Ashes. "Ask him."

She scrambled backward. "I don't want to talk to him!"

"Then stop asking me silly questions." He drew the bundle back and tucked it under the bear hide next to him.

As though frightened, she remained silent for a long time. Finally, she whispered, "If you're a Dreamer, have you had any Spirit Dreams?"

Was Wolf telling him he had to die in a Spirit Dream? "I'm not sure what a Spirit Dream is. I . . . I did have a strange Dream the night before Aunt Mossy was killed."

"What was it about?"

He patted the Wolf Bundle, and felt better, as though the bundle had given him courage. "It started out with horrible thunder . . . like the world was shaking apart. Then I saw Raven Hunter swooping down over Headswift Village. He was huge and flying very fast. His black wings filled all of Blue Sky Man. When he flew right over me, I looked up and his wings turned into a terrible wind. I've never felt anything like it before: black, howling, bringing a black darkness like death."

"Did it blow you away?"

"I don't know. I woke up. But I kept hearing a name in the wind's roar."

"What name?"

"Keresa. I don't know who that is."

Ashes got to her feet and gave him a scorching look. Like she didn't believe him. They stared at each other for ten heartbeats before she said, "Keresa is a terrible Nightland warrior. She's killed lots of boys like you."

Without another word she went back to her hides.

Silvertip lay down and petted the bundle. It felt suddenly warm. He lifted the bear hide to look at it. "Wolf Dreamer, are you in there?"

A mournful sound, like Wind Woman roaming the forests in winter, whispered from the bundle. As it did, he felt a sucking, as if it were trying to pull his soul out of his body.

Silvertip pressed his ear against the soft hide and yawned. "If I have to die to become a Dreamer, it's all right."

But down around his frantically beating heart, he was very much afraid.

Twenty-seven

A bitter wind roared out of the northwest. It ripped at clothing, clawed at the mossy tundra, and sent men staggering.

Keresa had picked a deep kettle, one of the depressions in the tundra that had formed after the retreat of the ice. Here, out of the wind, small fires consumed dry moss, wormwood, and willow stalks. Above them, the wind howled around the rocky outcrops and seemed to shake the very Star People so high above.

"How are you feeling?" Keresa asked.

Across from her, Kakala hunched under a caribou-fawn cape. He shot her a look of annoyance. "Everything aches."

She grinned, snugging her blanket—made of arctic fox hides—close about her shoulders. Around them, the rest of the warriors slept wrapped in hides, or huddled over the low fires, feeding just enough twigs, moss, and collected dung to keep the coals hot.

"I see. So, you'd prefer to be back in the cage?"

"I'd prefer to have you shut up." Then he relented, a strained smile curling his lips. "No, actually, I prefer your voice to the ones in the cage."

She lifted an enquiring eyebrow.

He gave a nervous shrug. "Just like last time . . . Well, I heard things. Voices."

"That told you what?"

"Nothing that would make either of us feel better." He changed the subject. "The Guide is an interesting sort."

"He is." She tucked the soft white hide around her chin. "But I'm more confused now than I was before. He doesn't give the orders; Nashat does."

"Maybe he's still just the same old Idiot that everyone thought he was."

"No, Kakala. He knows things. He said that you and I were the binding. Something about the two of us tying everything together. That somehow, we are supposed to heal things."

Kakala gave her a disdainful stare. "Of course. But first we'd better destroy Headswift Village, kill Windwolf, and find Skimmer. Who we both know was delivered to Nashat in the first place."

Keresa gave him a flat stare. "She's dead."

"Dead?"

"I asked around. Nashat sent a party of Karigi's warriors in one night and clubbed all the Nine Pipe women to death." She stared miserably into the flames. "The story was that the Council didn't want to feed them."

"Clubbed them to . . ." Kakala slowly shook his head. "Nashat kept Blue Wing. Remember her?"

"One of the women Goodeagle raped."

"Nashat sent her to the Guide instead of Skimmer." His expression hardened. "So, what happened to the bodies?"

"They were dragged out into the tundra for the wolves."

"Great. So we have to find a dead woman for the Guide."

"We'll have to tell Ti-Bish the truth when we get back. But first things first. Do you have a plan for attacking Headswift Village?"

He made a face. "Find Goodeagle."

Keresa set her cup down and rose to her feet.

Kakala watched her walk from one pile of sleeping hides to the next; finally she spoke to someone. When he didn't get up, she kicked him hard and a soft grunt sounded. Louder, she said, "Get up. The war chief wishes to speak with you."

A string of curses rose, but then Goodeagle crawled out of the hides. Very tall, with long black hair, he had a "pretty" face for man. It was just one of many things Kakala despised about him.

Goodeagle walked to Kakala's fire and impertinently asked, "What do you want?"

Keresa wanted to smack him in the back of the head.

Kakala ignored it. "Survivors from the Sunpath bands are flocking to Headswift Village. They—"

"I doubt it," Goodeagle interrupted. "Maybe the old and very young are flocking there for refuge, but any man, woman, or child who can wield an atlatl is running to join Windwolf's warriors. The man inspires loyalty the likes of which you will never know."

Kakala leveled a hard finger. "Don't interrupt me again, or I'll forget the part of our bargain that says you get to live."

Goodeagle stared at him. "Then don't lie to me. I know my people."

"I hope you know your former best friend as well. You must have some idea what he's up to."

"Where are his warriors?"

"Leaving the caves I heard that Karigi ambushed them on the trail west of Spineshank camp. Fighting was spirited. Silt managed to withdraw most of them. Karigi stopped to lick his wounds. When he sent his scouts out, they found several trails. All were headed west toward the Tills."

Goodeagle squeezed his eyes closed for several heartbeats.

Keresa watched the man. He had to be thinking about which friends had been killed. Perhaps he was telling himself it would never have happened if he hadn't betrayed his best friend at Walking Seal Village.

Goodeagle said, "Do you have any idea where Windwolf is?"

"No."

"All right, here's what I suspect is going on. Anyone who knows Windwolf understands the way his gut works. He's made an alliance with the Lame Bull."

"Yes, so?"

"You'd better hurry." Goodeagle slowly lifted his eyes to meet Kakala's.

"Explain that."

"When we attacked Headswift Village, we made our own future."

"And how did we do that?"

"By failing to take Windwolf." Goodeagle waved down Kakala's protest. "It doesn't matter. Windwolf *knows* we have to destroy it. He's expecting this attack, because you can't leave Headswift Village as a symbol of Nightland defeat."

Keresa scoffed, "Why would he stay there when his warriors are off to west?"

"Nonetheless, plan on it. He'll be there." Goodeagle's voice grew sarcastic. "He's a man of *honor.*"

Which you have never been. But she bit her lip.

Kakala exchanged a glance with Keresa. "And what would his strategy be? To delay us? The caves are an impregnable fortress. There are only two entries; both are heavily guarded. Will he wait for his warriors to arrive?"

Goodeagle ran a hand through his long hair and exhaled anxiously. "No, he'll do it alone. That way he's risking only himself. Unless . . ." He paused, clearly worried. "Unless he knows we have survivors flocking to Headswift Village. Then he'll want to make certain they are safe first."

"How?"

"I don't know."

"Will he try to talk the elders of Headswift Village into moving south?"

"He will, but I doubt they'd listen to him. The Lame Bull People consider their village to be as impregnable as you do the Nightland Caves. You will recall that once the villagers scurried into that rocky maze, you couldn't root them out."

Kakala glared at him. It was true, but he hated hearing it from Goodeagle. "I have forty-four warriors this time."

"And what would you have had when you began this mad venture?" Goodeagle asked. "Two hundred? More?"

Keresa ground her jaw. Yes, that would have been about right.

Kakala mused, "Spineshank Camp is eight days' *hard* run from Headswift Village. And Silt was west of that. We'll be there tomorrow. He can't—"

Goodeagle laughed. "Silt may have split his warriors long before Karigi hit them west of Spineshank territory. In fact, I suspect he did. Which means you have not inflicted nearly the losses you think. It also means Silt may have been on the trail for days, running straight for Headswift Village."

"Why would he go there?"

"I suspect it's the last place he saw Windwolf. And he's probably aware that many Sunpath People are scurrying there for protection." Goodeagle leaned forward with a smirk on his handsome face. "If Silt and Windwolf get together before you crush Headswift Village, you've lost, Kakala. Windwolf will box you in and destroy your forces just as you tried at Walking Seal Village."

Keresa studied Goodeagle's expression. Pride had stiffened the man's neck. Pride in his onetime good friend Windwolf's abilities, and for their warriors: people he'd loved and trusted with his life.

Can we use that against him?

It took mere moments for that look to vanish and be replaced by despair. Goodeagle's eyes went tight. He bowed his head and stared at the ground.

Keresa added, "Karigi's runner reported Silt was evacuating Spine-shank Camp. Which means he didn't split his forces before the attack. He has tens of villagers slowing him down. He can't travel fast or light. If he plans on protecting them, he must first feed them. That means sending out hunting parties every day."

"But that was days ago," Kakala mused.

A strange gleam entered Goodeagle's eyes, and a smile played at the corners of his mouth. "If Silt hasn't already split his warriors, he will. Once he knows where Windwolf is, he'll take half of his warriors and run hard to join him."

Keresa turned to Kakala. "Then we should send a runner to Karigi, tell him to expect that. He might be able to intercept Silt heading back east."

"Do it," Kakala ordered. "And tell our runner to instruct Karigi that once he's finished with that task, he is to bring his warriors straight to Headswift Village. The more warriors we have there, the better."

Keresa nodded, wary eyes on Goodeagle. The man looked frightened, but defiant. "Now help us think like Windwolf. Without his warriors, what will he do?"

"Hide the people in the rockshelters."

Kakala asked, "If I capture women and children and threaten to kill them unless he surrenders, what will he do?

"He'll be expecting that."

"Which means?"

Goodeagle shook his head. "I—I don't know, but for every move you plan to make, he's designed a countermove. If I were you, I'd stop thinking like a war chief and start thinking like a Prophet. The only way you're going to beat him is if you can see the future."

Again, that pride . . .

It certainly annoyed Kakala; Keresa could see it in the set of his lips. "If I capture ten tens of children and aim darts at their little chests, then he'll be cornered and he—"

Goodeagle laughed loud and long.

Kakala just watched him through flat eyes. "I gather you're trying to tell me something, Goodeagle."

"I'm surprised after fighting against him for so long, you could entertain something like that. If you put the Lame Bull children at risk like that, you've played right into Windwolf's hands. He'll order every man, woman, and child to take up weapons and rush you." He smirked. "And, they'll do it."

"That's suicidal."

"Of course, but he'll take a lot of you with him, and that will ease his conscience."

"Ridiculous! He wouldn't risk killing women and children."

"The Sunpath People aren't like you soft Nightland dogs, Kakala. After our women have used their hide scrapers on your warriors' faces for a time, you'll understand that." He tried to suppress the insane chuckle that shook him. Tears welled in his eyes—but not from amusement. "And if that doesn't stop your attack, Windwolf will just do something so totally unexpected that not even I can imagine it."

"Try?"

Goodeagle felt the smile fade from his face. "He'll be thinking of Walking Seal Village. It haunts his soul. He'll trap you, just as you tried to trap him."

"But you told me that he wanted to trap us at Walking Seal Village. That Bramble was the bait."

"Oh, yes, and what an irony this will be."

"But this time, he doesn't have any of my people for bait the way we had Bramble."

"He has himself."

Kakala snorted. "Impossible."

"I've told you. Go on, fall headlong into it." Goodeagle folded his arms tightly across his chest and squeezed, rocking back and forth, apparently trying to force the ache from his heart.

He's ready to fall apart. The realization took Keresa by surprise.

Kakala tossed the dregs of his tea into the fire and stood up. "Go back to your hides. You're of no use to me."

Goodeagle stood, his eyes moist, and walked away.

Keresa studied him across the distance. The man sat by the fire, staring at the flames while he rocked back and forth.

Windwolf rolled to his back and stared at the door curtain. Wind Woman breathed against it, making it sway. It would be dawn soon. A pale blue gleam lit the world outside.

He hadn't slept well. Goodeagle had filled his Dreams. All night long, vestiges of old and abiding friendship had vied with hatred. Even now, when he closed his eyes, he could see Goodeagle's smile, filled with warmth and friendship.

What did I do to you, Goodeagle? What did I do to hurt you so much that you'd—

Voices rose outside, and he heard people moving around Headswift Village, going about their morning duties. The smell of fish cooking drifted in with the wind.

He threw off his hides and got up.

It was time to face the village Elders.

They weren't going to like what he was about to tell them.

Twenty-eight

As Windwolf walked through one of the warrenlike passages, dawn light streamed between gaps in the boulders overhead. It dappled the silt-laden gravel at his feet. From the smooth surface of the rocks—they looked as though they'd been polished—he suspected these tunnels had once been filled with ice. When the ice melted, the boulders had collapsed on top of each other, forming the maze of passages.

Men's voices echoed down the tunnel. He walked toward them, rounded the bend, and saw War Chief Fish Hawk looking up at a big gap, perhaps a body length across. Two men stood on the boulders above, peering down.

Windwolf called up to them, "When you're finished, cover it with branches and dirt."

Fish Hawk said, "I pray this works."

"It will work. Just make sure you can trust every warrior you place at these critical spots."

Fish Hawk let out a breath. "I will. I'm still not convinced—"

"Windwolf?" Skimmer said.

He turned and saw her wending her way up the tunnel. Was this the same woman? Dipper must have given her clean clothing. The front of her foxhide cape was open, and he could see a green dress beneath, painted with soaring white seagulls.

When she got closer, she looked up at the gap and asked, "What are you doing?"

He gestured to the gap. "We don't want Nightland warriors to cast darts through these gaps."

"Or climb down," Fish Hawk added. "So we're covering them."

Skimmer frowned at the men on the boulders above, then said to Windwolf, "May I speak with you?"

"Of course."

On the other side of the gap, the tunnel narrowed, until it was just barely wide enough to walk through without turning sideways. He led her through it, and into another pool of dawn light, another gap they would have to fill.

A curious stinging sensation invaded his stomach. He glanced up at the gap again, and wondered if—

"I'm sorry to disturb you," she said. "I know you're trying to prepare the village."

"It's all right. What did you need?"

She appeared tired, as though she hadn't slept well. Long black hair clung to her face, framing her dark eyes and straight nose.

"Ashes told me something this morning, and I thought you should know about it."

"What is it?"

As though suddenly chilled, she pulled up her foxhide hood. "She and Silvertip spoke in the middle of the night. The boy told her that he'd had a Spirit Dream the night before his Aunt Mossy was killed."

Windwolf folded his arms, listening impatiently while he glanced at the gap and the narrow portion of the tunnel. "And?"

"In the dream, Silvertip saw Raven Hunter swooping down over this village, his black wings blotting out the sky."

He shifted his weight to his other foot. "Are you saying you think maybe the boy is a Spirit Dreamer? That he saw the future?"

"It just worries me. I think these people should leave here before it's too late."

"I've tried. They won't listen." He frowned up at the gap again. "Besides, I thought you didn't believe in Wolf Dreamer and Raven Hunter?"

"I—I don't."

She fumbled nervously with her cape ties, pulling them closed, but not bothering to lace them. Just watching her obvious discomfort made him uneasy.

"Was there something else?" he asked.

She stepped forward and whispered, "He mentioned Keresa."

He frowned at her for several moments. "Kakala's deputy war chief?"

She fixed him with a look that made his shoulder muscles contract.

"Is there something I should know?" Some undercurrent of emotion had stirred the depths of her voice. He couldn't quite figure out the source. "You were her captive."

"I never saw her up close."

He waved a hand. "Well, I don't know where to begin. First of all, thinking about her gives me a stomachache. Once upon a time, she and Bramble were friendly. They liked and respected each other. Secondly, I've often thought she might be the real talent behind Kakala's raiding strategies. Why do you care so much?"

Almost breathless, she said, "Silvertip heard her name repeated over and over in a great black wind that overwhelmed Headswift Village."

He grunted softly. "You're definitely a believer. You just don't want to admit it."

She ignored the accusation. "What could that possibly mean?"

He pointed to himself. "You expect me to answer that question? Go find a holy man. I'm just a warrior."

She took a couple of nervous paces, her hair flashing with a bluish fire when she passed through sunlight.

"Why does it matter, Skimmer?"

She brusquely waved a hand to silence him while she thought, and he lifted his brows. The only other woman who'd ever made him feel like a subordinate was Bramble.

Finally, she stopped and said, "May I ask you one last question?"

"Go ahead."

"Do you think happiness or suffering is more prevalent in the world? Does it depend on where you are? In some parts of the country is happiness on the increase?"

Almost mesmerized by her eyes, he responded softly. "I don't think so. Suffering seems to be increasing everywhere I've been."

"Oh . . ."

"Why did you ask?"

Tears glittered on her lashes. "You called me a 'believer.' I'm afraid I may be. Just not in Wolf Dreamer."

She turned and started to walk away.

Windwolf called, "Don't forget. In less than one hand of time, I want you, Dipper, Ashes, and Silvertip safely hidden in Dipper's chamber."

"I remember," she said without turning, and strode away down the tunnel. The last glimpse he had was a flutter of her foxhide cape as she disappeared into the darkness.

The Destruction

I huddle in the darkness, heart-stopped, breath-stopped, waiting to hear his whisper.

A Spirit of immense beauty, with a soothing voice and the power to convince frail humans of anything, he is also too beautiful to be real.

My heart aches from staring at the eerie shimmering blackness with mortal eyes.

"Soon, very soon, the first motions of the destruction will begin," he murmurs.

"What do you need me to do?"

"Disdain all those for whom your presence is a comfort and a blessing. Embrace those who see you as a fool."

"But . . . I don't like being treated as a fool. Why—"

"Because it will teach you to listen to the fool within: the man who loves too much, who believes too deeply, the man who shatters at a single harsh word. That man, Ti-Bish, is the only one who can lead his people through the hole in the ice. Without that fool, we are all lost."

"Including you?" I softly ask.

Raven Hunter's wings flash like black lightning, and thunder booms through the icy wilderness.

I shudder.

Almost inaudible, he breathes, "Especially me."

Twenty-nine

On his belly, Kakala sneaked up over the pile of boulders and scrutinized the village nestled in the rocks above him. Keresa slid up beside him. Dawn's lavender gleam sheathed Keresa's beautiful face and reflected in her hard eyes.

The morning was cold, mist hanging in pockets. A drizzly rain had fallen that night, turning into slushy snow before the clouds fled off to the east. Ice rimed the stone, making footing treacherous.

Not the best time to attack a hostile village.

"What do you see?" she asked.

"Nothing that looks like the kind of trap we laid for Windwolf at Walking Seal Village, that's for sure. Goodeagle is as crazy as a head-struck goose."

The entire hill was a mass of tumbled rocks, gravel, and scrawny spruce trees. Why would anyone wish to live here?

"Those must be the Sunpath People." Keresa pointed to the cluster of hastily thrown-up lodges at the foot of the slope. They looked like little more than broken branches leaned together and covered with ratty hides.

"Yes," Kakala answered. "If we send a handful of our warriors after them, they should run west, away from the village."

"And they'll probably keep running."

"If they're wise, they will." Kakala squinted against a fierce gust of wind. His bearhide cape flapped around him. "Remember: Tell our warriors they are not to kill *any* Sunpath People."

Her mouth quirked. "What if Sunpath warriors are casting darts at them?" She arched an eyebrow. "Can we wound them?"

"Yes, we can wound them." He chuckled. "We want them spreading the news that Headswift is destroyed, remember? So that Silt hears, and turns back."

Keresa heaved a sigh. "Assuming Karigi hasn't already stopped them." She paused. "Are you *sure* that changing your orders to have him come here was a good idea?"

"We came expecting a trap. Where is it?"

She shook her head, looking nervous.

Kakala gestured to the village. "Very few people are out in front of the rockshelters. Why?"

"It's still early. By midday, people will be everywhere."

"Then let's be about this. If three tens of our warriors hit the Lame Bull People fast, we can drive most away. That will make it easier to corner the rest."

She didn't say anything.

He scanned the valley, examining every possible place the fleeing survivors might take refuge.

Keresa's eyes narrowed, and Kakala's jaw muscles jumped at the look she gave him. They'd been arguing for moons now, debating the rights and wrongs of the curious orders they'd been getting. And just now, he could see that same rebellious gleam in her eyes.

"What are we doing, Kakala?"

"I'm trying to stay out of the cage for good. I'm not sure what you're doing."

"The Lame Bull People have never done anything to threaten us. Yet we're here to kill them."

"Some will survive. They always do." But his heart sided with her words.

She shook her head, and her long black braid sawed across her shoulder.

"I don't like this any better than you do, Keresa."

She hesitated for so long it set his teeth on edge. ". . . I know."

"The sooner this is over, the sooner we can go home."

She gave him a measuring look. "Home? To what?"

She slid down the rocks and trotted out to meet the warriors who waited at the base of the boulders.

Kakala scowled at her back. *What I would give to just turn around and leave this place.*

Thirty

In all the low places, mist had settled, cloaking the village in damp, intense cold. Icicles hung from the spruce boughs. The entire world looked iron gray in the lavender light of dawn.

Windwolf followed Lookingbill as he hobbled toward the back of the ceremonial chamber. The old man had pulled up the hood of his buckskin cape to shield his bald head from the frigid air. His fleshy nose had turned red.

"Dipper is ready. No one likes this, me most of all, but—"

"I don't like it, either," Windwolf said, "but it's the best I can do with the time I've had."

Lookingbill turned, and his wrinkled face pinched. "I had hoped you'd tell me it was infallible, that I needn't worry. Instead, you agree with me?"

"I try not to deceive chiefs."

Lookingbill smiled faintly and continued toward the rear of the chamber, where a number of weapons lay piled: Four tens of darts leaned against the wall, their sharp stone points glinting; atlatls were laid out on the floor, ready for warriors in need; and a mound of bone stilettos rested to the left of the atlatls.

Lookingbill pulled a dart, as long as he was tall, from the pile and checked its balance. As he bent to retrieve an atlatl, he said, "When do you—"

"*Chief!*" A young warrior dashed into the rockshelter and blinked while his eyes adjusted to the darkness.

"I'm here, Lone Eagle. What is it?"

"War Chief Fish Hawk said to tell you that our scouts have reported. The Nightland warriors are coming!"

"Very well. Get to your place."

"Yes, Elder."

The youth ran from the chamber, and Lookingbill expelled a breath. When he turned back to gaze at Windwolf, his eyes tightened. "War Chief, you look like you just stared into Raven Hunter's eyes and he stared back."

Windwolf did not smile. "Raven Hunter always stares back, Chief. That is my personal nightmare."

$\mathbf{S}$ilvertip huddled in the dark angle of two leaning rocks at the mouth of his mother's chamber. He stared down at his feet, clad in deerhide moccasins with mastodonhide soles. His feet looked small in the gloom.

In the rear, his mother sat across from Skimmer and Ashes, the women talking softly.

He reached out, running his fingers along the side of the Wolf Bundle. Every instinct urged him to stay here, to cower in the darkness and let the fighting pass by.

He wanted to shout: *I didn't mean it.*

But the Dream from which he had just awakened had been explicit. The black wolf had looked at him with glowing yellow eyes, and said, "*It is time for you to die.*"

He had stared in terror at the Spirit animal.

"*Do not be afraid,*" Wolf had told him. "*Death is the only passage from this world to the next.*"

He had just shaken his head.

"*But you must,*" Wolf had told him. "*You cannot find your future until you lose your past. You must give up this body for the One. Only then will you Dream.*"

He did want to Dream. For the moment, however, fear lay locked in his guts. His muscles were shaking, and all of his courage could barely keep him from throwing up.

Goodeagle used all of his skill to worm his way up the slope. He kept low, sometimes crawling between the rocks. There, to his surprise, he found a small shrine. Laid out on a piece of weathered hide, he discovered a collection of shiny pebbles, a long fluted point of sacred white chert, and several twists of mammoth hair. The leather on which they lay had once been painted in the image of a wolf.

A worthless offering, for an imaginary Spirit. He had a sudden urge to rip it up and throw it down the rocks behind him, but some impulse stayed his hand. Instead, he crawled wide around it, and wriggled up under the crest.

His gaze drifted over the jumble of rocks. The Thunder Sea came into view off to the northeast, glimmering, filled with icebergs. The white swell of the Ice Giants rode like a snowy range of mountains above the salt water.

Looking closer, he caught a glimpse of Kakala's warriors sneaking around the perimeter of the village.

No one seemed to notice them. Far down at the base of the slope, the Sunpath villagers went about their tasks, gathering wood, feeding the dogs, playing with their children.

It seemed odd, though, that there were so few Lame Bull People out. And, looking more closely at the Sunpath, he thought something was wrong. Their postures, the way they acted, was almost wooden.

Goodeagle untied his water bag from his belt and took a long swallow. Though food had been offered, he hadn't eaten in four days, and much of his pain had receded into a blessed haze. It was, perhaps, strange that going without food left a man's soul clear and calm. All the way here, he'd run at the rear of the war party with his two guards. While they'd eaten their daily rations, he'd watched and listened to the warriors boast about what honors they would win when they arrived at Headswift Village.

Honors? What honors were left to win when all the world was busy destroying itself?

At night, he had crawled into his hides, ill, but too numb to feel, or relive any of the nightmares that tormented him like evil Spirits with fiery darts. In too many, Bramble stared up at him, hatred marring the face he had once loved. He would see her choke on the blood welling from inside her. When she called out his name, it was in a crimson spray that coated his skin.

He didn't have to do the silent calculations of how many Sunpath lives had been lost, or would be lost in the moon ahead.

Windwolf, this is all your fault.

The ache in his gut started to rise again. He swallowed and forced it down.

Why were so few people out front? He shook his head. Could they be the bait? The thought affected him like a dart in his belly.

For several stunning moments, his thoughts riveted on strategy sessions held over campfires—just him, Windwolf, and Bramble. What fine times those had been. He could recall . . .

There are so few Lame Bull People out in front of the rockshelters.

He, Bramble, and Windwolf, they'd been stretched out on the dry grass near the Thunder Sea, watching the Nightland People pack up their camps, speculating on what it would take to get inside the Nightland Caves. Insane strategy—things to be tried only when they were already dead men, trapped, and no other path lay open to them. An ice-scented wind had blown off the Thunder Sea, rustling the grasses.

After the Nightland People had gone, he and Windwolf had explored every ice tunnel, trying to learn how the passageways connected.

Windwolf's deep voice rose in his thoughts: *"No, two tens would be too many. If you're going to take the caves, it'll have to be a small war party. Six men, with specific duties, and a crowd. That's all you will need. The war party will have no more than ten tens of heartbeats, but—"*

"Oh, no!" Goodeagle spun around and ran down the trail with his heart in his throat.

"You . . . fools! You stupid . . . stupid fools! Windwolf is going to . . . to kill all of you!"

Thirty-one

Cloud People filled the brightening sky. The queer leaden light lent an unearthly brilliance to the cold world, and turned the shawl of frost on the rockshelters into a glittering mantle.

Keresa trotted up and knelt beside Kakala, expecting a reprimand for being late. "It took longer than I expected, but our warriors are ready. As you instructed, I ordered the three tens of warriors going with us to capture any Elders they saw."

"Good. Did you dispatch a runner to inform the nearby villages that they will have refugees coming in?"

"I sent young Aniya. She's one of the best runners we have."

Kakala squinted up at the village. He looked as nervous as a big cat on a hunt. Sweat matted his black hair to his forehead. "Why aren't there more people outside?"

"I've been wondering that same thing. Something's wrong."

"Do you think they got word we were coming?"

She studied the few people who were outside, mostly women and children, one old man. They acted perfectly normal. The squealing children were playing a game of hoop-and-stick, running and trying to cast their sticks through the hoop to earn a point. The women who stood near the mouth of a small rockshelter were using jasper scrapers to clean the last bits of flesh from a buffalo hide. The old man dozed in the sunlight.

She said, "They look nervously calm."

Nervously calm? He shrugged it off. "They do. But then, given what the Sunpath People have been through, how could they look calmly calm?" A pause. "Maybe there's a ceremonial in one of the rockshelters—a burial rite, or a marriage."

Keresa whispered, "It's possible. We should at least hear drums and flutes." She stiffened. "I think they know we're here and have run into the rockshelters to hide."

Kakala nocked a dart in his atlatl. "Then . . . they would have taken the Sunpath People with them. Maybe it's a village Council meeting. That would explain why there's no music or Singing."

Keresa nodded reluctantly and took the opportunity to nock her own atlatl. "It would also explain why the Sunpath People are outside going about their day. They wouldn't have been invited."

Kakala said through a long exhalation, "That makes sense."

"Does it? I'm not so sure."

He started to rise, but suddenly ducked and stared up at the cloudy sky.

"What's wrong?"

He shook his head. "Nothing . . . I—I thought I saw a shadow. Something black . . . moving over me . . . the shadow of huge wings."

Keresa glanced up at the sky, then pinned him with cold eyes. "It's guilt."

Kakala turned to scowl at her. "Remind me to punish you for being insolent."

"I'll bring it up next time I find you in a cage."

Kakala hesitated for a few more heartbeats. "Do you see that woman in the pretty doehide dress?"

"Yes. What about her?"

"You're going to capture her. I'll get the old man. One of them is bound to be valuable to somebody."

He stood up, lifted his atlatl, and yelled a shrill war cry.

From everywhere warriors reared up from the rocks, leaped out of their hiding places, and flooded toward the village.

Two tens of warriors headed straight for the Sunpath People, screaming war cries. Keresa heard Goodeagle, coming from behind, screaming, "No! In the Guide's name, *no*!"

With amazing speed, the Sunpath People grabbed their children and vanished around the base of the boulders. The soft reverberations of screams and pounding feet carried on the wind.

"Victory!" Kakala cried as he charged up the slope on his thick legs.

She followed, but her gaze kept straying to the cloudy sky, expecting to see something monstrous and black swooping down upon them.

D eep in his rocky warren, Silvertip heard the shout of a warrior. Immediately, screams broke out on the still air. A chorus of war whoops and cries followed.

It is time. But he huddled, frightened and shaking. His tongue had gone thick, stuck to the roof of his mouth.

Clamping his eyes shut, he whispered, "I don't want to die."

"*It is time,*" Wolf's voice insisted softly from the air around him.

He didn't remember rising to his feet, or tottering out to the entrance. He blinked, half-blinded by the light, picked up a fist-sized rock, and hurried out onto the trail that led down to where warriors were running up through the boulders. His mother screamed somewhere behind him.

"I'm going to die," he kept repeating. Tears were leaking down his round cheeks, and the sobbing made it difficult to run.

K eresa charged straight for the woman in the doehide dress; the screaming children scattered, fleeing into the rockshelters.

The woman, running like a panicked deer, rounded a big boulder. Keresa frowned, staring at the rock formation. She could see no way out. It had to be a dead end. She was smiling as she slowed, expecting to find the woman cowering against a sheer stone wall.

Kakala shouted, "Degan, take ten men and pursue them into their hiding places! I want as many captives as you can catch. Kill anyone who's trouble!"

Goodeagle pounded toward them, shouting, "Go back! It's a trap! Pull back!"

Keresa hesitated. *What's he yammering on about?*

The warriors—grinning like wolves on a blood trail—had already ducked into the mouths of the rockshelters.

Only heartbeats later, new cries erupted, but they were not the cries of women and children, rather the cries of surprised warriors.

Keresa spun around.

Nightland warriors came flooding back out. Most had darts sticking in their bodies. Three warriors collapsed on the trail, screaming, while their wounded friends ran around them, trying to get away from the hail of darts that sailed after them. Five more men fell before they reached the safety of the rocks.

Goodeagle had stopped, his expression that of dismay.

Then, all along the rim above, whooping Sunpath warriors appeared and began casting darts down at the Nightland warriors milling below the rocks.

For one startled instant, Keresa froze. *It's a trap!*

"Pull back!" Kakala yelled. And Keresa saw a dart whistle past his ear to splinter on a boulder before him.

"They're behind us!" she cried, turning, seeing a line of advancing Lame Bull warriors. Even as she watched, the men nocked darts, bending their bodies into the deadly release.

"This way!" Keresa called, charging full tilt down a trail that led to the west. She could hear feet pounding behind her. A dart hissed past her shoulder, splintering on a rock to her right.

At least two of the warriors had taken captives, but they were hiding them in the rocks below.

In that instant, a boy of perhaps twelve stepped out of the rocks. Keresa had a momentary glimpse of his face, tear-streaked, his mouth racked with sobs. She watched as he drew back, and launched a rock straight at her. She ducked to the side, grabbed up her war club where it bobbed on her belt, and hammered the boy with a side-handed blow. She felt the smacking impact, saw his head jerk sideways under the impact, and charged past.

As she did, a woman emerged from a narrow trail, full into Kakala's path. He barely hesitated as he grabbed the screaming woman, spun her around, and propelled her forward.

As Keresa turned, caught sight of a pursuing warrior, and cast a dart in his direction, Kakala demanded, "Who are you?"

"I am Dipper! Daughter of Chief Lookingbill!"

Keresa caught a glimpse as Kakala's face slackened and a gleam entered his eyes. "It must have been your miserable sister I killed a few days ago. You don't wish to be next, do you?"

The tears in Dipper's eyes vanished. She gave Kakala a fierce look, but her voice shook when she said, "My son! You've killed my son!"

Kakala bellowed, "I want a woman named Skimmer, and I want Windwolf. I have heard they are both in your village. Is it true?"

"My boy, *you've killed*—"

Kakala slapped her hard across the mouth. *"Answer me!"*

Her split lips bled. She wiped her mouth on her blue-painted sleeve, and she looked up, eyes burning hate. "I'm *not* telling you anything."

Two darts hissed by to clatter on the rocks.

"Kakala!" Keresa shouted. "We've got to get out of here!"

He looked wildly around, shouting, "Quickly! Into those caves."

Keresa hesitated as the warriors charged past. On impulse, she reached down, grabbing the boy she'd clubbed. *Dipper's son? He could be of value to us. They won't know he's dead.*

Thirty-two

Keresa's shout—*"Kakala! Look out!"*—was his only warning. Wind-wolf dropped from a rock, feet impacting with a thud. Kakala spun, shoving the woman, Dipper, away. As she sprawled on the ground, Kakala tried to pull his dart back, only to lock eyes with Windwolf as the man recovered his balance, braced himself, and swung with a stone-headed ax. At the last instant Kakala threw himself backward, the deadly blow glancing across his temple.

Lightning flashed as his head snapped sideways.

"Dart him! Degan!" Keresa's shout seemed distant, as though heard from the bottom of a pond.

Kakala stumbled, careening forward, before he toppled face-first to the ground. In his wavering vision he glimpsed Dipper pulling her son off to the side. Windwolf was trading blows with Pega, their war clubs swinging.

The hills came alive. The Sunpath People ran from their hiding places carrying branches, throwing rocks, using sharpened sticks as stilettos. At the same time, the Lame Bull villagers flooded out of their rockshelters with weapons.

As though from a great distance, he heard Keresa shout, "Into those holes, hurry!" Then he felt her strong arm slide beneath his shoulders, and drag him to his feet. "Kakala? Kakala, hold onto me! We have to get out of here!"

His knees buckled beneath him.

Keresa dragged him; then other arms lifted his spinning body. He remembered rubbing against stone, then sagging heavily.

More and more warriors scrambled through the opening behind Keresa, bodies blocking the light. Each time it was as if someone drove a wedge through his numb head. And then he was falling in an endless spiral, the world turning gray.

He barely felt his gut heave, vomit spewing. His body was so distant, airy, floating . . .

And then the grayness faded to black.

Keresa had watched Windwolf strike Kakala down. Before he could strike again, Pega had charged forward, swinging a club. As Keresa tended to Kakala, she had glimpses of Windwolf and Pega trading blows, the clack of wood loud. Seeing Washani and Klah bear Kakala safely into the rock, she grabbed for her atlatl and one of the scattered darts where she'd dropped them. The boy's mother was tugging frantically at the boy's arm. No time for that now.

Keresa nocked a dart just as Windwolf struck Pega down. Her arm whipped back. From this distance, she couldn't miss. Their eyes met— an instant of mutual understanding.

I am going to kill you now.

His slight smile was as eloquent as if he'd shouted, *No, you're not!*

She threw her weight behind the cast. The dart flashed forward, the shaft flexing. Windwolf twisted to the side, her stone-tipped dart cutting through his war shirt, vanishing harmlessly behind him.

Corre and Degan rushed up, arms back, but even as they launched their darts Windwolf threw himself behind the rocks.

The hissing of a dart brought her back to the moment. Keresa heard its impact: a muffled slap as it drove itself into Corre's chest. He wavered on his feet, took a step back, and sank to the ground, staring in disbelief at the shaft quivering in his breastbone.

"Keresa!" Degan shouted. "Into the hole! Now!"

She looked for the dead boy, seeing drag marks.

No, he's no good to us now. She spun on her heel, a dart slicing through her cloak, and ducked into the rock as a volley of darts shattered on the stone behind her. Inside, back pressed to the wall, she panted, struggling for breath. Kakala lay on the gravel like a lump, blood running down the side of his head.

Goodeagle dove through on all fours, looked around, and lunged to pick up an abandoned war club. "Keresa! It's up to you! What are you going to do?"

Keresa, panting from exertion, hauled Kakala into a sitting position, looked into his vacant, half-lidded eyes, and propped him against the wall. Blood streaked his face and had soaked his war shirt until it clung to his muscular body in wet folds.

"Is it true?" Goodeagle demanded, and stared wild-eyed. "Did Windwolf escape?"

Keresa could only pant, staring out at the narrow opening. She could hear the screams and pleas of her wounded warriors. Despite clamping her eyes shut, she could see too clearly with the eye of her soul: They were writhing, bleeding, staring in horror at the wooden shafts sticking from their flesh.

One by one, the screams stopped. The Lame Bull were repaying blood with blood.

Goodeagle spun around, frantic eyes rising from Kakala to Keresa. "He's killed your *entire* war party. They're all dead. You fool! You let him kill your people! I tried to tell you—"

Keresa rose, drew back, and slammed a fist into Goodeagle's mouth.

Goodeagle staggered backward, sobbing as he hit the floor.

"Deputy?" Degan called. "There's a hole in the rear of this shelter."

She shook herself, gathering her scattered wits, and worked her way back along the narrow passage. In places she had to drop to her hands and knees. Then the tunnel opened, and she saw the high crevice. Bishka and Degan were staring up, their faces illuminated by diffused daylight.

Tell me it's a way out. "Degan, you and Klah carry the war chief. Follow me!"

It took all of her strength as she levered her body up the narrow crack, then poked her head up into the light. Some premonition warned her; a shadow moved on the rock. She loosened her hold as an adz whistled down to shatter on stone. She felt the wind of it, stone splinters pattering on her hair.

Keresa slid, her body bouncing off the rocks to land in a heap at the bottom. She winced, raising her hands to find raw and bleeding palms.

Feet shuffled behind her. She turned to see her frightened warriors emerge into the chamber. They manhandled the limp Kakala between them. Each was looking to her, desperation in their eyes.

She climbed painfully to her feet, turning her attention to where the tunnel forked. She glanced warily around the right bend. Up ahead, sunlight lit the tunnel.

Raven, let this be it!

Wiser now, she proceeded warily, her warriors creeping along behind her. The tunnel narrowed until barely wide enough to pass her shoulders. Looking up, she could see a wide, funnel-like opening, impossible to climb.

Pray no warrior is up there. He could drive a dart down through the top of my head and clear to my foot.

Once through, she turned, grabbed Kakala's arms, and hauled him forward to allow the warriors behind him to get through.

Kakala's eyes rolled. That much, at least, was an improvement. He reeled in her arms, disoriented. He kept saying, "What . . . what . . . what . . ."

Keresa called back, "There's sunlight up ahead. We're going to try to climb out!"

Warriors followed along after her, eyes wide as they stared at the forbidding stone around her.

She grabbed hold of the rocks, planted her feet, and started to climb. The hole at the top consisted of a gap between three boulders. This time, she peered around carefully, easing her way up, fearing an ambush.

She found it—saw the faces of tens of warriors above her, grinning. She jerked back as a stone-tipped dart snapped against the stone where her head had been. The shattered dart dropped past her.

The clattering sound of falling rock echoed through the tunnel. She slid back to the cavern floor, staring with the rest as Degan hurried back they way they had come.

"*Oh, gods, Keresa!*" Degan shouted, throwing himself back before a cloud of rock dust. The tunnel had been collapsed to seal them in.

The choking wall of dust continued to billow out as rocks and debris thundered down.

Above her, the Lame Bull warriors were rolling boulders into place, sealing the opening.

She breathed, "Blessed Raven Hunter, we're trapped."

Thirty-three

Goodeagle hunched in the rear of a chamber, surrounded by five other warriors. When the tunnel collapsed ahead of them, they'd been forced to turn around and go back. Somewhere in another tunnel, he heard shouts, but the voices were muted, as though coming from beneath a deep layer of earth and stone. He coughed and squinted at the veil of dust that filled the chamber.

The opening through which they'd entered mocked them. When Mong had eased up to the opening, a long dart had sailed in, opened a cut along his ribs, and clattered off the wall.

As long as warriors were out there, there would be no escape.

A loud thump gave them a start. Owl-eyed, they stared as yet another large rock hit the ground with a thud.

"What are they doing?" Mong asked.

"Sealing us in," Goodeagle said breathlessly.

Rana, who sat against the wall to his right, asked, "What happened to us?"

"Windwolf just destroyed your war party."

"We're still alive," Washani growled.

Goodeagle laughed; it was a low threatening sound, filled with self-loathing. "Not for long."

"Do you think the others survived? Keresa and the war chief?"

"Pray they're dead, Washani. If they lived, right now they're being sealed up in rock tombs."

The end would be long and difficult. They'd die from thirst first, but not before desperate men began killing their friends to drink their blood for the moisture it contained. Then they'd eat the meat . . . until only one man remained.

Windwolf found Dipper kneeling by Silvertip's side. She used a piece of damp hide to sponge the bulging lump on the side of the boy's head.

"You had a close call," he told her, kneeling opposite. "When I saw you running toward the fighting, my heart almost stopped."

"It was Silvertip," she said, sniffing. Her round face was tear-streaked, panic in her eyes. "I don't know what possessed him. He knew the orders. He was supposed to stay safe!"

Windwolf carefully turned the boy's head, pressing gently with his fingers. "There's a lot of swelling, but I don't think the skull is crushed."

"Will he live?"

He winced at the pain and worry in her voice.

"Dipper, I honestly don't know. Head wounds, well, they're hard to judge. For now, the best you can do is keep him quiet. Make sure that his body is warm, and use that cold compress on the wound."

She nodded, her hands shaking. "Thank you," she whispered. "But for you, they would have had us both."

"You and Silvertip were very brave."

Another tear slipped down her cheek. "I don't feel brave."

"That is generally the way of it."

A worried voice called, "Windwolf?"

He turned, seeing Ashes, some terrible distress behind her large brown eyes.

"What's wrong, Ashes?"

"It's Mother," she said, on the point of tears. "She's gone."

Skimmer bent under the weight of her pack, keeping to the low ground. She stopped when the sound of the fighting grew. Windwolf was springing his trap.

"May you win, War Chief." *And keep Ashes safe!*

She blinked back tears as she remembered her daughter's stunned expression.

Ashes' desperate pleading still rang in her ears. *"No! Mother, don't leave me!"*

"I had to, baby. This is the only way to ensure your future."

If she could do this thing, kill Ti-Bish, the heart would fade from the Nightland People. Their warriors would slip away, and her people could return to their lands once again.

It will all be over. And I will have saved us all.

She cast one last wistful glance over her shoulder. Then she turned her head back to the route. As she hurried along, her heart felt as if it were breaking. Ashes' face filled her thoughts. Every instinct told her to run back, to gather her daughter into her arms and never let her go.

But Ashes would be safe in Headswift Village. As safe as she would be anywhere. Windwolf would see to that. The man took his obligations seriously.

Now it's up to me. When she completed her task, if she lived, she would find her way back to Ashes.

She repeated the words she had told the girl. "I'll be back. I promise you. And then it will all be over. We can bury our dead, and grieve, and build ourselves a new life."

The way led along a drainage that wound through rocks. Stands of spruce and willows provided additional cover. From her calculations, if she continued, she should cross the trail that led back toward the Nightland villages.

You didn't trust me, Windwolf. Well, the decision is no longer yours to make. As she hurried along, memories of Hookmaker's body, of Blue Wing crying after the traitor Goodeagle had tired of her, and of the women in the pen fueled her anger.

She could imagine Ti-Bish's face as if it had been yesterday. She could see his large round eyes, the thin and pinched expression. He had looked up at her with a worship-filled gratitude, as if her kindness touched his very soul.

She would see him again, and look into his eyes as she drove some sharp pointed weapon between his ribs and through his foul heart.

What turned you into a monster?

She might even find that answer before she was finished.

A dead Guide is a false Prophet. Lookingbill's words drove her forward.

She wound through a stand of spruce, smelling the sweet scent of the trees, and turned onto the trail. Making better time, she continued at a fast walk.

The sounds of the fighting had vanished behind her, sealed by distance and the breeze in the trees.

"You there!" a sharp voice called.

She turned, fear leaping within, and saw four winded warriors trotting down the trail; two were already fanning out, ready to cut off her escape.

She focused her frightened eyes on the lead warrior. Yes, she knew him: one of Kakala's warriors. He had marched with them on that long walk up from the Nine Pipes camp.

"I am Skimmer," she called, trying to muster courage. "The Guide wishes to see me."

The warrior approached warily. He carried only one dart, and it was nocked, ready to be cast. Then, unexpectedly, he glanced worriedly over his shoulder.

He's as scared as I am!

"I take it the fight didn't go well?" she asked, trying to ignore the frightened beating of her heart.

He turned his attention back to her, making a hand signal to the other warriors. "No, it didn't go well at all."

The second warrior muttered, "I say we just kill her. After what we just survived, I'm ready to pay them back any way I can."

"No," the first replied. "I was in the Council chamber with Kakala and the Guide. He asked about Skimmer."

"So?" the second demanded.

Skimmer watched the remaining warriors close in from the sides; like the first man, each had only one dart left to him. They looked like they were more than eager to use them on her. She tensed every muscle in her body to keep from shivering.

"Are you a fool?" the first demanded. "If we go back to report Kakala's destruction, just who do you think is going into the cages? After what just happened at Headswift Village, Brookwood is nothing!"

"That's right," Skimmer said, fighting to think clearly. "But, well, say that you captured me before the fight. Say that Kakala sent you back with me. You'd have no part in what happened later, would you?"

The lead warrior tilted his head, running the idea through his soul. He rolled the long war dart in his fingers. "You would agree to that story?"

She nodded, hoping they didn't hear her dry swallow. "Let's just say that it has a certain appeal when the other option is being raped by four warriors, and then having my throat cut."

The warriors looked back and forth. Then the first nodded. "You're a smart woman."

She smiled, trying to keep her voice from breaking. "And you four would be even smarter by delivering me directly to the Guide. Last time, that fool Nashat almost killed me." The whistling sound of clubs shattering bone lived in her memory.

The warrior took a deep breath, shooting another worried look over his shoulder. "You may not be so glad you found us, woman. I have no idea how many warriors are following our trail. You're going to have to run like you never have before."

"I—I'll do my best." Then, in what she hoped was a firm voice, she added, "But the four of you had better remember that without me, you're headed for a miserable couple of moons in the cages."

"Oh, you can bet on that," the leader replied. "Now, let's see how fast you can run, woman."

Skimmer looked down. Her hands were trembling.

Come, Skimmer. You can do this.

Thirty-four

Keresa dusted off her cape and looked up at the rocks over her head. Between the gaps in the boulders, she saw the gray gleam of dusk. There were still men out there, moving around. She could hear them talking.

She shouted, "I want to talk to Windwolf!"

No one answered.

"Where's Windwolf? Tell him Deputy Keresa must speak with him!"

Whispers rose, as though they were discussing it; then she heard nothing but silence.

A short time later, a sliver of Windwolf's face appeared in one of the gaps. "What is it, Deputy?"

"Let's talk."

"I'm listening."

"I should think that telling you we surrender is a little ridiculous, but if you need to hear it—"

"I don't."

She exhaled hard. "What can I do to save the lives of the rest of my war party?"

Windwolf hesitated, and it occurred to her that he was about to tell her "nothing."

He asked, "How many warriors can the Nightland clan Elders gather to attack us?"

She stared up, confused at first, until it occurred to her that he was already thinking five steps ahead: *What will happen if I don't kill them? The Nightland Elders will catch wind of it. What will they do? They'll probably order Deputy Karigi to attack the village and free the hostages. What if they decide to make a full-scale assault? How many warriors can they muster?*

Keresa replied, "More than you can defend against, Windwolf. Even if Deputy Silt arrives with your warriors. Even if you manage to coerce every child into carrying a stick. You cannot win. Our warriors are coming, in overwhelming numbers."

Fish Hawk stood to Windwolf's left, watching.

Windwolf looked dead tired, drained of every shred of the strength that had kept them alive over the past few hands of time. His dark eyes were dull, lifeless. He propped a trembling fist on the rock, and said, "You've just helped me make a difficult decision, Deputy. I thank you. I was actually considering letting you live."

He got to his feet and walked away.

Keresa shouted, "Windwolf! Windwolf, wait! Talk to me! *Talk to me!*"

Confusion

I sit with my back against the ice wall and stare at the dark form five paces away. Against the faint gleam of the fiery lake, he looks tall and massive, almost blocking the tunnel when he spreads his wings.

In a very small voice, I say, "I don't understand."

"You don't have to. Just tell her."

Raven Hunter might stand right in front of me, but his voice sounds far away, like the distant rumble of thunder.

"Will she understand? About the feather?"

"Better than you know."

"You're sure she's alive?"

"Oh, yes."

I toy with the fringes on my cape for a few moments before rising to my feet. "I'll tell her as soon as she arrives."

"I know you will."

The blackness retreats down the tunnel, heading for the fiery lake, growing smaller and smaller, as though flying.

The scents of water and algae rise powerfully in the backwash of his wings.

I take a deep breath and watch until Raven Hunter is gone, and the pale gleam of the lake returns to waver over the ice walls like sunlight off water.

"Feathers and suffering," I whisper to myself. "I don't understand."

As I slowly head back up the tunnel, I wonder why Skimmer would understand when I do not. Is she smarter than I am? I feel a flush creep into my cheeks. Everyone is smarter than I am. Perhaps after I have told her the message, Skimmer will explain it to me.

"Yes, she'll explain it."

Thirty-five

Silvertip couldn't have explained it—not in words. He was sitting on top of the high boulders that rose over Headswift Village. How he had come to be there was beyond him. He didn't remember. The fact was: He sat on the stone, where he had been sitting, but with no idea of how long he had been there.

Nor could he explain his body. It lay before him, supine, with arms at the side, legs out straight. His hair had been washed, combed, and braided. A beautiful hunting shirt, stained blue with larkspur dye, had been dotted with white, signifying stars on a night sky.

A terrible wound marred the side of his head, and his eyes were opened to slits, dried and gray with death. The gray lips were parted, and he could see the tips of his teeth, starkly white. His belly was distended, swollen with death.

Silvertip studied his corpse, seeing the familiar scar in the web between thumb and forefinger on his right hand. He'd gotten it while learning to knap flint a year before. A long white chert flake had cut deeply, and when the scar slowly healed, left a bright white line on his skin.

How did this happen?

The memory seemed to seep into him, like water through moss.

I had to die.

He looked down at his Spirit hand, opening the fingers, remembering the feel of the stone. How, half crazy with fear, he'd run into the path of the woman warrior, and cast the stone with all his might. She had easily ducked it, and he remembered his terrible fear as she charged down on him, shifting her dart and atlatl, reaching for the club.

He had stood, frozen, watching the club lift, how it had flashed in the sunlight. Then, darkness.

And I am here.

He should have been afraid. Worried, or perhaps sad. Instead, he felt hollow, as if nothing were left.

"That is the way of it," a voice said gently.

Silvertip turned, startled, to find a great black wolf, its yellow eyes studying him intently.

"You were in my Dreams."

"The Spirit world lies beside yours. Separate, but touching. Power flows through them both, binding and pulsing. It beats with your heart, lives in the center of the stone, and flows with the sap in the trees. It waves with the grass in the wind. Then, sometimes, when the right kind of soul touches it, it fills a person."

"Like me?" Silvertip asked hopefully.

"Just like you." The wolf raised his eyes. "He comes."

Silvertip followed the wolf's gaze, seeing a dark dot high in the glowing sky. It circled slowly, hanging on the air, floating. As it drew nearer, the long black wings could be seen.

"Condor," Silvertip said at last.

"Condor," Wolf agreed. "The great bird of the dead." Then he added, "Do not be afraid. You must watch to understand."

Silvertip nodded. He'd never heard of a condor hurting anyone. They were shy things, awkward when taking flight from the ground. They much preferred roosting in high places where they could leap out and let the air fill their great wings.

The giant bird circled closer, cocking its ugly head, the brown eye glinting as it studied Silvertip's body.

In that instant, Silvertip understood. "It's coming to eat me."

"Oh, yes." Wolf's great yellow eyes were fixed on him. "And you must fulfill your role in the way of the world. Until you have experienced it, you will never understand."

Silvertip watched wide-eyed as the great bird backed air, and settled lightly to the rock. Cocking its head from side to side, it inspected the corpse. Then, with a tentative peck, it looked for any reaction.

Silvertip swallowed hard as his body remained inert.

He wanted to scream, "No!" but his voice was mute with horror.

The great curved beak shot down, neatly plucking one of the eyes from the socket, twisting and pulling to sever the resisting tissue before it gulped the prize.

Silvertip jerked, reaching up, aware that half of his vision had vanished.

"Do not fight it," Wolf cautioned. "You must only be."

Silvertip gasped as the great beak shot down, and then his world was black. All that remained was feeling. He tried to stand, to run, to escape from the sharp beak that now sliced into his skin.

But all he could do was sit there, feeling with exquisite sensation as his body was picked apart, piece by piece. Then the beak sliced into his belly, and he could feel his intestines being pulled, severed, and pulled some more.

Silvertip threw his head back, screaming. But no sound issued from his hollow throat.

Skimmer ran in the middle, with two warriors in front and two behind. They followed the beach trail that led around the western finger of the Thunder Sea. In Sister Moon's half-light, the dark surface of the salt water glimmered as though sprinkled with silver dust. Great bergs glistened with ethereal white where they had grounded off the littoral, stranded by low tide. The smell of the salty shore lingered, exotic in her nose.

She let the soft lapping of the waves soothe her.

Conversations had been brief, to the point. The previous night's camp had been a dreary affair, the warriors splitting up the rations in her pack. When the topic of her escape came up, she'd said, "Sleep. I'm not running away."

"And we are to believe that?" Kishkat had asked.

"My destiny lies with the Guide." Something in her voice had convinced them.

The two warriors in front, Homaldo and Tibo, kept up a steady distance-eating pace that was beginning to wear her down. Soon, she'd be stumbling.

Bless the Lame Bull for several days of rest and good food. She mouthed a silent hope that Lookingbill and the rest had survived.

She wondered about the battle. What had happened to Windwolf? Had he won? Was Ashes all right? Skimmer imagined her daughter eating supper with Dipper and Silvertip, pretending to be brave while worrying about her mother. Skimmer's heart ached. Ashes had just lost her father, her family, her clan, and village. Now her mother, too, was gone.

I am doing this for you, beloved daughter.

They hit a rocky section of the trail where waves had washed high. Skimmer's steps hammered the ground. She kept gazing out at the waters, looking so peaceful now, but few people lived along the strand. When great sections of ice were undercut by the warm tidal waters, they collapsed. Literal mountains of ice would slam down, sending giant waves to wash up, carrying everything before them.

As she looked out, she could see the cleanly scrubbed land, devoid of trees, with rocks piled here and there; deeply incised drainages had cut where the great waves drained away.

What would it be like? She imagined what a wall of water would look like, tall, its crest glistening in the sun as it swept forward. According to the tales from the few survivors, seeing such a thing was the most terrifying sight in the world.

They never survived anything like I did. The thought gave her a curious kind of courage.

As they reached a creek, Homaldo lifted a hand and called, "Time to drink."

They came to a halt, breathing hard, and Skimmer dropped to her knees. She dipped the cool stream water up in her hands and drank it greedily.

The warriors knelt, bending down to suck up the cold fresh water.

When Skimmer had drunk her fill, she sat down hard in the sand and heaved a sigh of relief. To the north, Sister Moon's gleam shadowed the trail. It resembled a gigantic black serpent winding along the shore.

"Why does the Guide want you so much? I heard that Nashat sent Blue Wing to him, and he turned her away." Kishkat shook his head. "She was a very beautiful woman."

The other warriors chuckled.

Skimmer shrugged. "I was kind to him once. In those days your people had cast him out . . . called him the Idiot."

Tapa cast a nervous glance over his shoulder. "We shouldn't linger."

Kishkat smiled. "I think Nashat still thinks he's an idiot." He took another drink from his cup and swallowed. "As to myself, I don't know. That night we found him trying to set Kakala free from the cage . . ." He shrugged. "Well, he just left me confused."

"Nashat is an evil man," Homaldo agreed. "It was his order that placed Kakala in the cage." He glanced at Skimmer. "And, but for this woman, he would have done the same to us."

"We had better hope the woman is enough," Tibo said.

Skimmer frowned. "Then the Guide doesn't issue all of these insane orders?"

"No." Kishkat bowed his head, looking weary to his bones. "The orders come from the Council. I think they come from Nashat. No one sees the Guide." He hesitated, looking at his companions, lowering his voice. "Sometimes I think the Guide is as much a captive as the rest of us."

To Skimmer's amazement, heads were nodding. "Captives? But you're the feared Nightland warriors!"

Tapa smiled wistfully. "I was a hunter. That's all I wanted to be. Then the Council made us 'hunters of men.'" He shook his head. "At first, it was exciting. I think we all got carried away with the glory. It makes a man feel great in the beginning. But then the fighting got harder." He looked at her with hopeless eyes. "My brothers are dead. My best friend, whom I grew up with and loved, is dead." He glanced back down the trail. "Now, even my war chief, whom I served and trusted with my life, is dead."

"We have all lost so much," Tibo agreed. "If I could have anything, I would ask to be the man I was before all of this began. I fear, however, that somehow, I am going to die a miserable death."

"Come." Kishkat climbed wearily to his feet. "What is, simply is. We can't change it. Our only hope is to follow the Guide to the paradise of the Long Dark."

Skimmer got to her feet and gazed out at the silver ribbons of waves rolling in. "Let's go."

The sooner I can find a way of killing him, the sooner all of this madness is over.

Thirty-six

The struggle had encompassed eternity. Silvertip could remember nothing beyond a desperate obsession with keeping himself whole. As the condor devoured his body, bits and pieces of his soul vanished. Nothing could convey the sensation of having his soul sliced up. One moment he would be frantically trying to retain some kind of hold on his very being, only to have a hole torn out of what remained . . . until the inevitable. But when had that been? When had the last tattered bits of his soul simply given up?

What remained of his body were bones. Little more than the scattered fragments of his soul, and then that, too, began to slip away as one by one, the ligaments rotted, and fingers, toes, legs, and arm bones rolled off the high stone, to drop . . . where?

Nothing remained to scream as Silvertip's loose jaw fell away to tumble down the rock. The skull finally slipped loose from the spine, clattering hollowly . . . falling. . . .

Moonglow filtered between the boulders, shooting a sliver of light across Goodeagle's face. He rolled uncomfortably to his back and struggled to sleep. Cramped between two warriors, he could barely stretch his legs to their full length. Worse, the constant low hum of distant voices chewed at the edges of his dreams like rodent teeth. Every time he drifted off, he heard Windwolf's soft baritone.

Would he never escape Dreaming the nightmare of Walking Seal Village? After an eternity of restless tossing and turning, he finally sat up, and slid back to lean against the wall. Weariness clung like a granite cape around his shoulders.

Stop torturing yourself. You did the right thing.

He braced his forehead on his drawn-up knees and closed his eyes. His breathing finally melted into soothing rhythms. The voices faded. . . .

He was back, standing in the great ceremonial lodge at Walking Seal Village. He could see the startled expression on Kakala's face, hear Keresa's bitter curses. Bramble lay naked, bitten, and raped, her eyes widening as she recognized him.

"Goodeagle!" Bramble sobbed. "Goodeagle . . . oh, no, get out!"

That was the moment his soul died, and with it, all that remained of the man once called Goodeagle.

In a tight voice, he said, "Kakala, you told me you wouldn't hurt her."

He couldn't tear his eyes away from hers as she looked up at him through stark horror, pain, and fear.

"Goodeagle?" Bramble called, as though he were suddenly the only thing she had to hold onto. The instant that she figured it out registered as a change in her eyes—a single frozen heartbeat of time. Her fear turned to hatred.

He backed up until he hit the wall. Why hadn't he realized Karigi would do something like this?

Through tear-blurred eyes, he saw Kakala's jaw harden.

"Deputy Karigi?" Kakala asked in a weirdly calm voice Goodeagle had never heard. "Why is she still here?"

Goodeagle remembered only Karigi's insolent smile. The words buried in the hatred that seemed to shoot from Bramble's eyes.

Kakala's barked order had penetrated Bramble's spell. "Tell your warriors to get out."

Karigi blinked. "What? Why?"

"Do it!"

Karigi took a step back, ordering, "Terengi, take your men and bring me Windwolf's head."

Glancing at each other, they filed out, striding past Goodeagle as if he didn't exist. He remembered Kakala, still and quiet. Karigi fidgeting, shooting nervous glances at Bramble.

"War Chief, I intended—"

The rest had been lost as Kakala drove a hard fist into Karigi's stomach. Goodeagle had watched in disbelief as Kakala kneed the man, lifting him clear of the floor. Karigi had dropped to his knees, his war dart flying.

As Kakala vented his wrath, Goodeagle had watched the dart, seen Bramble's desperate gaze fix on it.

As though his eyes were disembodied, he'd stared at the dart, vaguely aware of Kakala and Karigi ramming together, their screams of rage disjointed and unreal as they kicked, slugged, and abused each other.

Goodeagle's remote eyes followed Bramble as she edged a foot toward the dropped dart, toes questing for the shaft.

"She has a weapon!" Karigi's shout echoed in Goodeagle's soul. *Yes, use it Bramble! Kill him. Kill me!*

A shout came from outside; Keresa knocked him sideways as she hurried to stare out the doorway.

Bramble screamed.

Goodeagle's heart seemed to stop.

When he looked back, Karigi's dart was sticking out of Bramble's chest.

Goodeagle stumbled back against the wall, watching Kakala and Keresa race by, leaving him alone. For the last time, he looked at Bramble.

"I didn't know he'd do this, Bramble. I swear."

Faintly, almost inaudibly, he heard a voice plead, "Goodeagle?"

He took a fumbling step toward her—then blindly turned and ran. *Running. Running. I'm still running.*

He jerked bolt upright, panting.

"Just a . . . a dream," he whispered.

Shuddering as though from deadly cold, he folded his arms tightly over his aching stomach. Breath rushed in and out of his lungs in huge desperate gulps.

From the darkness, Washani said, "Yes, just a dream this time. But Windwolf is going to come for you."

Goodeagle tipped his head back against the cold stone wall, and breathed, ". . . I know."

Ashes looked up at the black ceiling, pretending to be asleep. Silvertip's cries had wakened her many times last night, but this time his soft whimpers twisted oddly in her belly.

She'd been in the middle of a Dream. The last image still lingered in her soul: She'd been crawling through a black tunnel on her hands and knees. She could hear the people in line behind her whimpering in fear. Silvertip had reached back and grasped her hand, holding it so tightly it ached.

"Ashes," he'd whispered, "I can't find the way, and I—I'm afraid. What should I do?"

"The Wolf Bundle," she'd whispered. "Ask Wolf Dreamer. He knows the way."

When Silvertip didn't respond, she'd reached forward and found his face. Tears dampened his cheeks.

"I'm gone," Silvertip whispered, barely audible, so no one else would hear. "Even the bones have been picked clean. I don't know what I've done. . . ."

And then Silvertip's cries had wakened her and she'd found herself staring at the ceiling. The sharp damp scent of the deep tunnel still clung in her nose.

Most of the night she'd Dreamed about her mother, wondering where Skimmer was, and if she would ever see her again. Loneliness made her feel like she had to throw up.

She slid a hand down to rub her belly, and stared at Silvertip. Even the Healer wasn't sure if he was alive or dead.

They had placed the Wolf Bundle atop his chest. His body now twitched, as though his soul were walking through a horrifying land.

She wondered if he was still crawling through the darkness, lost and frightened.

From right beside her ear, a deep voice whispered, *"Yes, he's always gone when you need him, but I'm right here, right here, Ashes."*

She tried to scream, but no sound came out of her mouth, so she dove under her hides, and lay there shaking, waiting for him to speak to her again.

Throughout the night, she jumped at every sound, but she never heard the voice again . . . just Silvertip's soft suffocating gasps for breath.

Thirty-seven

The pale lavender gleam of dawn filtered through the boulders, bleaching the faces of the warriors sitting around the chamber.

Keresa ran a hand through her long hair and paced back and forth. All attention was focused on Kakala.

The big war chief tossed and turned, writhing beneath his sweat-drenched cape, reaching pleadingly for people who weren't there. All night long he'd shrieked and wept.

"Hako?" Kakala cried. "Hako? Where . . . where are you? Tanta, where is she? Is she . . ."

Degan looked up at Keresa and said, "Hako sounds like a woman's name."

She nodded. "Yes, it is."

She'd never heard Kakala speak Hako's name with such desperation.

Degan said, "Have you known him to be with a woman named Hako?"

"She was his wife once, before—"

Kakala screamed, "You're dead . . . *dead!* Tanta get down! What . . . what are you . . . doing . . . ?"

The echoes of his voice rang through the chamber, almost covering the grating that came from above as one of the boulders was rolled aside.

Dawn light poured into the chamber. Keresa looked up. Against the brilliant background, she couldn't see any of the warriors' faces. Smart of them. Peering down could get the looker a dart through the face.

"Deputy Keresa," a voice called. "War Chief Windwolf has granted your request to speak with him."

"Thank the gods," she muttered. "Can I climb up?"

"After you remove all your weapons."

Keresa untied her weapons belt and let it fall to the floor; then she pulled out the stiletto she always kept in her right legging, and dropped it. "I've pulled my teeth."

"All right, climb."

Keresa climbed up, hesitated just below the scar in the rock where she had dodged death several days earlier. Nerving herself, she lifted her head, half expecting to duck another dart. The warriors just beyond the periphery of her vision were armed, alert, but none was set to skewer her. She pulled herself the rest of the way into the light. Eight warriors encircled her. A short burly man stepped forward.

"I am War Chief Fish Hawk. I need to search you."

"Of course you do." She spread her arms and legs, and waited while he ran his hands over her body. To her surprise, he was thorough, but took no inappropriate liberties.

Fish Hawk nodded sternly. "Be careful not to do anything foolish. We have more Sunpath refugees here today. They will not be happy to see you. One wrong move and we might just let them have you."

"Fish Hawk, you've never met a more careful warrior than me."

They'd overheard the warriors who'd guarded them talking about Windwolf. The tone of voice would have been more appropriate to Old Man Above than a human war chief.

She looked around at them, at the glow in their eyes. *By Raven Hunter's balls, they've made a mystical Spirit out of the man.*

According to the story Windwolf had personally gone to speak with the refugee chiefs and clan Elders, asking questions, assuring them they were safe here. It was said among the guards that many had fastened themselves to his legs, pleading for his leadership.

Is there anything we can do to use that against him?

Keresa started forward, but Fish Hawk's hard hand on her forearm stopped her.

"I think it's better if you follow me. Windwolf is concerned about your safety."

Fish Hawk had said Windwolf's name with such reverence, she ground her teeth. And why not? Her own warriors were starting to speak of him the same way.

Fish Hawk stepped out in front of her while the other two warriors fell in behind. Her spine prickled, knowing they had their darts centered on her back.

They followed the trail over the top of the rockshelters that composed Headswift Village. Below, she heard children talking, and the voices of elders. A dog barked happily.

Fish Hawk led her around the base of the boulders and straight through the Sunpath village—if it could be called a village. When the people saw her, they ran forward to stare and call insults. Her knees trembled, but she kept her head high.

As she rounded a corner, groans and sobs filled the air. Many people wore bandages. Black bloody tatters of hides wrapped heads and legs. One old man—with a face like a weather-beaten mountain—gazed at her through hate-filled eyes, watching her every movement.

As she passed, an old woman with a missing eye spat at her, crying, "Nightland *filth*! You killed my family. You killed my *whole* family!"

Keresa's heart skipped. Had she been on that raid? There had been so many.

Memories rose of a Hunting Horse camp they'd attacked in the early days. After they'd burned it to the ground, they'd gone down to inspect what remained, and she remembered too clearly the multitudes of orphaned children wandering among the ruins, crying, searching for family they'd never find again. Kakala's eyes had possessed a haunted gleam for days.

She said, "You have *many* more refugees."

Fish Hawk replied stiffly, "Karigi and Blackta are still attacking Sunpath camps. The people who can make it here, do."

With this many mouths to feed, they'll be running short of food soon.

Fish Hawk led her around the boulders and onto the path in front of the rockshelters.

They had placed the dead Nightland warriors in a pile at the bottom of the hill. Looking down she could see they were naked. Had they stolen even the clothing? Many of the bodies had been brutalized—objects of the hatred these people lived. Two guards now stood to protect the dead. Blood trails marked the paths where they'd dragged the bodies. The Lame Bull dead must be in the ceremonial cave, being ritually prepared for the journey to the afterlife.

Fish Hawk stopped. "Wait here." He ducked through a low oblong opening.

She leaned against the stone wall, pressing her hot cheek against the cool rock while she fought the overwhelming urge to vomit. The two warriors stared at her with cold eyes.

Pull yourself together. You can't let Windwolf see you like this.

Arranging this meeting had been nearly impossible. Through two long days, she'd begged every person who'd stood guard to let her speak with Windwolf.

Think, rot you! You don't have time to feel sorry for yourself. Look, learn, plan.

As she forced herself to study the village, something struck her as odd. The two guards at the corpse pile were barely more than boys. Eight men guarded her people. Where were the rest of the warriors? Surely some of the Sunpath refugees had been warriors? When mixed with the Headswift Village warriors, there should be many men and women with atlatls and darts walking around. She tallied a total of ten. Then she noted an eleventh, down working with a group of older boys and girls, training them how to use a war club. *Children?*

Fish Hawk ducked out and held the door curtain aside. "Go in. He's waiting for you."

She rubbed her sweaty palms on her cape, called on all of her courage, and ducked beneath the leather curtain.

Inside she stood face-to-face with the one man she'd feared for most of her adult life. Their eyes met: that same challenge crackling between them as it had when they'd tried to kill each other just a few days past.

He wore a clean blue war shirt painted with red buffalo on either breast. Then she looked closer. His eyes might have struck fire, but his face was haggard, lined with fatigue. His muscular legs were locked the way a man did to fight exhaustion. Black hair clung to his forehead in clean wisps, as though he'd just bathed.

"Deputy, please sit down." He gestured to the hides around the fire hearth where a small blaze burned.

She walked to the hides, but remained standing. The firelight cast a pale amber glow over bare rock walls. The chamber spread about four paces across. He apparently had few belongings. His atlatl and a stack of darts—many of them belonging to her warriors—leaned against the wall. Beside the fire a tripod with a hide bag stood. Wooden cups rested near the hearthstones. A rolled buffalo hide had been shoved against the wall to her right.

Windwolf went to stand in the middle of the chamber, and the heavy weapons belt he wore clattered. He gestured to the bag hanging on the tripod. "You must be thirsty. Please fill yourself a cup of tea."

She crouched, picked up a cup, and dipped it into the tea bag. The tea, made of rosehips and dried berries, smelled sweet and warm.

She straightened and studied the knives, stilettos, and two war clubs he carried. "I assure you, War Chief, I'm in no position to be dangerous. They forced me to leave my weapons in the chamber."

"I don't meet any Nightland warrior unarmed. You in particular. You're dangerous no matter what."

Her stomach cramped threateningly. She tipped her cup up, drained it dry, and dipped it into the bag again. She might not get anything else to drink for days—or forever.

Through the laces of his shirt, she could see his chest was streaked with deep cuts. Hurt and tired. Could she find a way to use that? Wring information from him he wouldn't ordinarily reveal?

She knelt on the hides.

A brief expression of relief crossed his face. He lowered himself across the fire from her, and stifled a weary sigh.

"War Chief," she began, "thank you for agreeing to meet with me."

He nodded. "How is Kakala?"

"Delirious. As I'm sure your spies have told you. He keeps reliving old battles. All night long he called for Hako and Tanta, and screamed things about Brookwood Village."

Windwolf reached over and dipped himself a cup of tea. As he swirled the liquid, he said, "He was placed in a cage as punishment, wasn't he?"

"Yes. Our Council of Elders ordered that every warrior involved in the battle be locked in a wooden cage. Since War Chief Gowinn was killed in the battle, Kakala, his deputy, was singled out for punishment. They tortured him for two moons. When he was finally freed, he crawled out of his cage a changed man, they said. He spent several moons living alone in the mountains."

Windwolf sipped his tea and casually said, "Why did the Nightland Elders do that?"

She lifted a shoulder. "If you punish people for losing battles, they won't lose as many."

"If you escape, will they do that to you?"

A cold sensation filtered through her, as though ice water had just been poured into her veins. "Let's . . . let's talk about something else."

He slowly shook his head. "Once, before the coming of Nashat and the Prophet, the Nightland People were envied. Your people harvested the waterfowl, fished the Thunder Sea, hunted the seasonal migrations of the caribou, and stored their wealth of food in the ice caves for winter. You crafted the finest artwork, conducted the most elaborate rituals. Your Dreamers charted the paths of Father Sun, Sister Moon, and the Star People. You made the finest boats out of wood we Traded north in return for your dressed hides, paintings, and shell jewelry."

She sat silently, remembering.

Windwolf clapped a weary hand to his knee. "And now your Council orders its finest warriors placed in cages." His gaze bored into hers. "I have just learned that they had Kakala locked in a cage again because he failed to take Headswift Village with ten and eight warriors. How he was returned to leadership is a little hazy, but tell me, are your chiefs mad?"

She caught herself on the verge of speaking, and bit her lip.

"I thought so," he added, reading her expression too well. "Tell me, how did Kakala get out this time?"

"On the Guide's orders."

"He didn't order him placed there?"

She gave him a narrow-eyed glare.

"Nashat," Windwolf guessed.

At her silence, he asked, "What do you think of this Guide of yours?"

"He will lead us to the paradise of the Long Dark." It was a safe answer.

Windwolf stared at her for a long time before saying, "Kakala is interesting, isn't he? After the Sprucebell massacre, did he really send runners to the surrounding Sunpath villages telling the chiefs to be ready for the survivors?"

"He did."

"Thoughtful of him, considering that the Nightland Elders might have had him killed for it."

"He knew that."

"Then why did he take the chance?"

"To save a few worthless Sunpath lives."

Windwolf ran a hand through his damp hair. "That's difficult to believe, considering the tens of tens he's taken in the past few summers. But I'm sure he has his reasons. I've promised myself that after I've had a thick buffalo steak and slept for three days, I'll think about it."

She lifted a brow. "Why don't you just ask him? When he gets better."

"If he gets better. I really was trying to kill him."

Just like I tried to kill you. She clamped her jaw and watched the way the dim light shadowed his forearm above his wrist. His hand shook slightly from exhaustion. "You're not very subtle."

"But I'm a good host. Your cup is empty. Please fill it again. Some of the refugees killed an elk on the way. They would think poorly of me were they to learn, but you are welcome to the piece offered to me." He raised his voice. "Fish Hawk?"

"Yes, War Chief?"

"Could you bring that roasted elk to me?"

"Of course."

She dipped her tea, thinking, *Keep him talking on friendly terms; think of something.*

"That was a crazy stunt you pulled at Jayhawk Village."

He looked at her curiously, aware of the change of subject. "You were holding my people hostage. What did you expect me to do?"

"Something saner. You rushed a heavily armed camp with six warriors to rescue *two* people?"

"I liked them."

"You must have. Your escape at Star Tree Camp, however, was brilliant." She gave him a small smile.

He smiled back, as though he saw right into her soul. "I didn't know you were so devoted to me, Deputy."

She lifted a shoulder. At Star Tree they'd had his warriors boxed tight in a narrow valley, outnumbered five to one. Rather than surrendering like any sane war chief who knows he's lost, Windwolf stationed eight warriors in strategic locations, then stampeded a herd of buffalo right through the middle of Kakala's camp. When their warriors scattered in every direction, Windwolf's people had picked them off like wingless ducks.

"You killed ten of our warriors that day," Keresa said.

"I'm disappointed. I thought it was more."

"Hopefully Wolf Dreamer heard that and will make sure your soul becomes a homeless ghost, wandering the forests forever."

He tilted his head and smiled. "Wolf Dreamer, Deputy? I've heard that you follow a different Spirit."

She ground her teeth. She'd always had what Kakala called "a noxious interest" in Sunpath beliefs. "I'm not a disbeliever."

Windwolf laughed softly. "You're a surprise, Deputy. Though I don't see what that has to do—"

"Your vision is very limited, isn't it? Yours and Goodeagle's. Is that a Sunpath trait?"

He set his cup on a hearthstone and looked her over in detail.

At that moment, a boy, perhaps eight summers old, entered with a bark plate on which a thick section of elk backstrap rested. The aroma drifting off the hot meat sent the juices flowing in Keresa's mouth.

"Bless you, War Chief," the boy said in awe. "We saved the best for you." Then he shot a worried glance at Keresa, and fled.

She took another long drink, letting the warm tea wash away her sudden craving for the meat. It didn't work.

Windwolf extended the bark plate, setting it before her. "Oh, go ahead. If you're going to escape, destroy me with the handful of warriors you have left, you're going to need your strength."

She lifted the piece of meat, tearing into it, trying not to look like a starved wolf, but failing, as the twinkle of amusement in Windwolf's eyes communicated too well.

As she ate, he said, "Deputy, let's discuss what you and I are doing here. I'm trying to protect both Sunpath and Lame Bull People from the brutal orders your Prophet, Council, or whoever, has been giving. I'd lie, cheat, steal, do anything, say anything, to kill him and every one of your clan Elders. I—"

"Leave the Guide out of it!" She cursed herself as that look of understanding glinted in his eyes.

He continued. "I've watched tens of tens of my people die under your darts, Deputy. Do you know what it's like to witness old men, women, and helpless children running in terror before they're slaughtered by warriors from the far north? Do you have any idea—"

Desperate rage smothered her. Unthinkingly, she rose to her knees and slammed a fist into the tripod, sending the tea bag splashing across the floor. "You just murdered two tens of my warriors, Windwolf! They're lying in a pile, naked, hacked, and stabbed. Don't be so righteous!"

He leaned forward tiredly, and his blue-painted shirt rustled in the sudden quiet. "And you've destroyed seven of our bands since last summer, Deputy. We kill warriors, not babies. Didn't you ever feel a twinge of conscience murdering children?"

She sank to the hides again, hearing her own words in his mouth. "No warrior enjoys killing children."

"Well, maybe the Nightland warriors are human after all. Some of my people have begun to whisper that you're evil Spirits straight from the Long Dark that your Prophet preaches about."

She gripped her cup hard and took another long drink. "Windwolf, what are you going to do with all the refugees here?"

"Find some way to feed them."

"And then?"

"Explain."

"I'm no fool. I suspect your warriors, what's left of them, are on their way here right now." *Are they?* "When they arrive, are you going to use me and my warriors as sacrificial offerings in the stead of our clan Elders?"

"Sunpath warriors have souls, Deputy, despite what you've heard."

"Does that mean your men won't rape me and torture my people?"

When she'd said the word *rape*, he'd flinched. Thinking about Bramble, no doubt.

Through a long exhalation, he said, "As to torture, that depends on whether or not you tell us what we need to know."

She shook her head, picking up the meat again. Her stomach had started to ache again; perhaps filling it would help. "We're not going to tell you anything."

"Then what are you doing here? You asked for this meeting."

"I . . ." She squared her shoulders and took a deep breath. "I need your help."

His dark eyes glittered as though he was wondering how she had the guts to ask.

Keresa swallowed the last of the succulent elk. When she looked up, she found him watching her like a cat at a mouse hole. "We need water. We drank all that remained in our water bags yesterday."

He thumped his finger against his cup. "And what will I get in return?"

Keresa swallowed hard. "I'll order my warriors to lay down their weapons; then I'll turn the weapons over to you."

"All of them? No tricks?"

"No tricks."

A suave brutality tinged his voice when he asked, "And will your warriors obey you?"

Keresa glared. "Yes."

He smiled as though intrigued by the entire conversation. "Let me make certain I understand. I'll give you water, and you'll willingly become my prisoners. Is that it?"

"Willingly? I said we'd give you our weapons, not our hearts. We'll fight to the last to kill you and escape. We'll just have to use our hands to do it."

"These are the kind of warriors the Nightland Council would put in a cage?" A small smile touched his lips. "I agree to give you water."

She bowed her head in relief. "One other thing."

"Yes?"

"Kakala . . . I fear he may be dying. While I know this may not disappoint you, it does me. If there is a Healer in this village, I would appreciate—"

"If I send a Healer to care for him, what will I get in return?"

"What do you want?"

He drummed his fingers on his cup, as though trying to decide. "A map of the Nightland Caves."

The boldness of the request made her laugh. "Is that all?"

"No. It's just the beginning." His face showed no more emotion than a dead panther's.

"I can't do that," she said. "And my map wouldn't be much good to you anyway. I—"

"If it wouldn't be any good, what's the harm in giving it to me?"

"I've been in the caves a few times, but I know only the main passageways. There are tens of tens that I've never seen. You don't want a map from me."

He looked regretful. "Then I can't send a Healer."

Fear soured her belly. She wasn't sure Kakala would survive without a Healer. Nor was she sure he'd survive with one. Windwolf's blow may have crushed his skull, and he was already dead; his body just didn't know it.

She said, "I'll draw you a map of the main passageways. After the Healer treats Kakala."

"A true map. No tricks?"

"I give you my word." She frowned before saying, "I won't have to worry about the Healer murdering Kakala in his sleep, will I?"

"I'll make certain the Healer understands that will be my privilege, and mine alone."

Bizarrely, that made her feel better. "I thank you for the food and drink."

She rose to her feet, and he quickly got up to face her. *He takes no chances. . . .*

He reeled slightly before he caught himself. Even in exhaustion, his physical presence was daunting. He moved with a leashed power that made her wish she had her war club in her fist.

As she walked for the mouth of the rockshelter, he said, "I have one question for you."

She stopped and turned. "What is it?"

He stared at her, and it went straight to her soul.

"Is Goodeagle in the cave with you?"

She blinked, surprised. *That means there are other caves where my warriors are trapped? How many?* She remembered Goodeagle screaming at her, asking her what they were going to do. "No. I don't know where he is."

She couldn't read his expression when he said, "That must mean he's dead." Then he called, "Fish Hawk, the deputy is leaving."

Fish Hawk drew the curtain aside and said, "Come with me."

Before she exited, she looked at him. Their gazes held.

Just beneath that calm confident surface . . . he was as terrified as she was.

Thirty-eight

In an endless gray, Silvertip thought: *I am.*

The sensation was of floating, rising and falling, buoyed by something.

"You are," a voice told him from the gray. "You can only be after you have ceased being everything else."

The odd lack of sensation surprised him. He couldn't feel cold or heat, just being.

"Where am I?"

"Nowhere, lost in the Dream of the One."

"I died."

"You did."

Silvertip let the questions flow away. He could feel a slight pulsing now, a faint sensation of movement.

"You are coming into the Dream," the voice told him. "It will happen slowly. Do not think, just be One."

"One," Silvertip agreed, feeling resistance as his arms spread. The first sensation was of being suspended, as though his arms bore what little weight he had. Then he recognized the rushing sensation, as though he slipped through a delicate resistance.

Wind, he felt wind!

"Just accept," the voice told him. "You are One."

"I am One."

He tried to stop the sudden rising of his arms.

"Do not resist," the voice told him. "Accept. Allow the feelings to flow through you. Become One."

Silvertip steadied himself, aware of his arms rising and falling, but something was odd about his hands and fingers: When he tried to splay them, the air pulled, causing a slight roaring.

"Accept, Silvertip. Simply be."

The soothing words allowed him to relax, feeling the resistance fade. Again he slipped effortlessly through the air.

His arms lifted, stroking down, and experienced the lift, could feel the pressure beneath, the subtle vibrations that quivered in his skin.

"That's right. Learn, allow the knowledge to flow through you."

"I am flying."

"Very good. Accept that."

And he did. Flying. Not arms, but wings.

Awed, he raised the wings, stroking, feeling the lift, the sudden surge forward.

At a sudden gust, his tail shifted, the experience unsettling.

"Accept. Learn."

Silvertip allowed his new tail to adjust and felt the rightness as he came back level.

Time had no meaning as he tried different movements, flapping, twisting his tail, marveling in the movement of his body through air.

"Where am I going?" he asked.

"Up there."

A faint glow suffused the gray. He focused on the glow, stroking with his wings, feeling air rushing past his body.

"Slowly, Silvertip. There is no need to rush. You are outside of time. Accept."

He stiffened his wings, allowing his beating heart to settle, simply soaring toward the glow. As he did, it grew brighter, the foggy image of clouds appearing. The way it did through mist, the round ball of the sun could be seen emerging above and to the right.

"You are One," the voice insisted.

"I am One. I accept."

He turned his head, glancing down through the silvered mist, aware of patches of trees barely visible so far below. In fascination, he felt himself slip, his body beginning to fall.

"Extend, Silvertip. Do not think. Simply be."

He reached out with his wings, feeling them catch the air, and recovered his balance with a twist of his tail.

"Now, rise."

He took a cautious stroke, then another, feeling the lift. Yes, this was easy.

"Of course it is. But only if you simply accept."

The world below was clearer now, forest and lakes, grassy meadows, the meandering lines of streams like veins upon the land. To his right, he could see the ragged, cracked expanse of the Ice Giants. They looked so odd from up here: dirty, broken, extending to the north in a jumble of peaks, blocks, and dark crevasses. He could see the long inlet of the Thunder Sea, its dark, silty water filled with dots of white ice.

The tundra stretched as a gray-green belt, undulating over hillocks and pocked with holes. Clusters of boulders jutted up, and to the south, the spruce lands of his youth were carpeted with dark green patches of trees. The great freshwater lakes to the west gleamed a greenish blue. Strips of beach were catching the white froth of waves. Sparkles of smaller lakes and ponds caught the sunlight, glimmering as he soared overhead.

"That is not our goal."

He slipped into complete clarity, the wind rushing past as he sailed out high over the land.

Something caught his eye, just off to the left.

"Do not be startled," the voice told him.

The sense of vision was odd, taking in the entire world as he coasted through the crystal air. A great eagle slipped sideways, dropping down toward him.

"You're an eagle?"

"In the One, yes."

He tried to crane his head, only to lose his balance. But he knew now, and corrected. "What am I?"

"Condor."

Memory came to him. "A condor ate my body."

"That is the lesson, Silvertip. Life is the One. You have become what you feared the most. Through death, you live again, in a different form. That is the way of the Dream. We are all the One."

Silvertip took a breath, allowing his worry to dissolve, and cocked his head, focusing with extraordinary clarity on the eagle that soared off to his left. The sky hunter stared at him with a familiar piercing yellow eye.

"You are the Spirit Wolf."

"Sometimes, yes." A pause. "But you will never see me as a Raven."

"Wolf Dreamer!"

"Come, try your wings. I have something to show you."

The eagle flapped great wings, the white tail correcting its flight into a turn.

Goodeagle leaned against the wall, desperately thirsty, trying to catch some sleep. A hornet's nest of emotions hummed inside him. He dropped his face in his hands and watched the memories that ran across his soul.

His thoughts kept returning to the firelit rockshelter near Walking Seal Village.

He and Windwolf had been sitting in the mouth of the overhang, gazing up at the magnificent pines that seemed to pierce Sister Moon's heart. Light penetrated the soughing trees, carelessly throwing moonglow like silver nuggets over the valley. He remembered so clearly, so very clearly, the forest-scented winds that had ruffled their sleeves, the strong handclasps they'd shared.

When had it all gone wrong?

He couldn't quite place the exact moment, but sometime, somewhere, they had stopped defending Sunpath villages, and started attacking Nightland warriors. Blind. Desperate. Hitting hard and running fast.

He'd pleaded with Windwolf to stop and take a good look at what they'd become. But he never did—couldn't, he said. Even now, he could hear Windwolf's deep voice: "The whirlwind has caught us up and twisted us around so much, Goodeagle, the only way out I can see is to fly into the storm."

"But Windwolf . . ."

The hands pressing against Goodeagle's face trembled. He dug his fingers into his flesh to still the nervous attack. How many innocent people had died while they'd been out attacking Kakala's camps? They'd kept Kakala busy, but that had freed Karigi to wipe out one band after another. If they'd divided their warriors and sent them to guard vulnerable bands, perhaps those people would have been spared.

For a while Windwolf had been satisfied with a life for a life; then it had escalated to two Nightland warriors for every Sunpath killed. Making up for the past murders, he'd said. Then three to one, because they'd lost so many pregnant women and little girls. . . .

"All we have to do is find out what they want!" he'd pleaded. "If we go on this way, there will be no one left!"

"They *want* our destruction!" Windwolf had insisted.

"But how can we even *ask* if all we do is kill each other over revenge?"

Goodeagle couldn't bear it any longer. When they'd been planning the defense of Walking Seal Village, he'd shriveled in upon himself, so staggered by the anticipated bloodbath he could no longer turn his head.

"You will go to Karigi?" Windwolf had asked. "Tell him we wish to meet in Walking Seal Village?"

"Yes," he'd whispered hoarsely, knowing he'd planted the seeds of the ambush in Windwolf's mind.

"Good. Bring him here in six days. It will take me four to get our warriors assembled and in position. I will arrive on the fifth, ensuring we have plenty of time to prepare for Karigi's arrival. If we do this right, only a few will ever see their families again."

He'd gotten up from the Council meeting and been sick, sick to death with the horror, the screams that filled his dreams, the terrified faces of little children running, running along trails filled with corpses.

"Windwolf," he'd begged, "let's go talk somewhere alone. I need to talk to you. Let me talk to you!"

Windwolf had frowned, his eyes distant—already lost in springing the great trap, mind weaving the strategy he devised so well. He'd warmly grabbed Goodeagle's shoulder and murmured, "I promised to have dinner with Bramble. We have so little time together anymore. Later? Maybe tomorrow after we've . . ."

But there'd been no tomorrow.

He whispered, "Why wouldn't you listen, Windwolf? I begged you."

Tendrils of the friendship he'd tried so desperately to kill wrapped around his heart. He hurt as though he'd been bludgeoned.

He brought up his knees and rested his forehead on them.

Why didn't you talk to me?

Thirty-nine

As night fell, Skimmer followed Kishkat around the last curve in the trail. To her left, the jagged peaks of the Ice Giants rose so high they disappeared into the bellies of the Cloud People. Their mournful groans and squeals echoed, sounding like lost ghosts.

"We're almost home," tall Homaldo called, and gestured toward the orange campfires that bordered the ice. The fires seemed to blink, and Skimmer realized that tens of people must be walking back and forth in front of them.

"Thank Raven Hunter," Tapa said. "I miss my wife and boy."

"At least we'll see them again."

The warriors glanced back and forth, fear behind their grim expressions.

"Remember," Kishkat reminded, "we were sent with Skimmer before the attack."

They trotted straight toward the Ice Giants, and Skimmer saw the black maw that led into the Nightland Caves. Last time, she had been held farther south and never brought this close to the famed cavern. It was a huge opening, perhaps four body lengths across. Passing Traders had told her that once a person went through that maw, the ice tunnels branched many times, flowing out in every direction. One of them was reputedly "the hole in the ice" that led back to the Long Dark where Raven Hunter still lived and breathed.

Her legs had been shaking for the past four or five hands of time. Skimmer longed to sit. . . .

"Stop!" Kishkat called, peering into the half-light. "Who's there?"

The warriors surrounded her, the move almost protective. For days now, they had traveled together, sharing meals, water, and stories.

When did I begin to see them as friends? The notion stunned her.

Rocks and gravel scalloped the edge of Thunder Sea. Some of the boulders were three times the height of a man.

Skimmer struggled to see what had alarmed Kishkat. Near the rocks ahead, a human form slipped through the shadows.

"We said stop!" Tapa insisted, and lifted his single dart.

The man kept coming, and finally a soft voice called, "Kishkat? Is that you?"

Kishkat's eyes went wide. He stepped forward and whispered, "Blessed Spirits! Guide? Is that you?"

The warriors fell to their knees, and long-legged Homaldo called, "Guide! We've brought the woman you wanted. Kakala dispatched her when we encountered her on the trail."

The Guide walked gracefully, hands clasped behind his back, apparently deep in thought.

The warriors hissed back and forth, wondering how Ti-Bish had known Kishkat. It was too dark to see their faces.

Homaldo shot a frightened glance at the other warriors and said, "Guide? How did you know it was us? No runner could have beaten us here. No one knew."

"I've known from the moment Skimmer slipped away from the Lame Bull caves," the Guide said.

Hatred and fear burned through Skimmer's veins like a Spirit plant, paralyzing her trembling legs. She could only stare as he walked nearer.

When no more than two body lengths away, he stopped and looked at her. She couldn't be sure in the darkness, but she thought a faint smile curled his lips. He spoke gently, "Raven Hunter said you'd be here tonight, Skimmer. I've been waiting for you for a long time."

"Ti-Bish, I must talk with you. Don't . . . don't hurt me."

He stepped closer, took her arm, and led her up the trail, as though they were friends of many summers.

The warriors followed a few paces behind them.

"Don't worry. You're safe now." Then he bent down to whisper, "Raven Hunter told me to wait for you here. He didn't want Nashat to see you first."

As the words sank in, a wave of nausea tormented her. "Why?"

"He said Nashat would frighten you."

She looked at his gentle hand on her arm and the kindness in his eyes. "Why would you care?"

In the silver gleam of light that reflected from the Ice Giants, she saw his jaw tremble. "You need me, Skimmer. Raven Hunter helped me see that truth. He wants you close before the first motions of the destruction begin."

"The . . . destruction? Of what?"

"Oh." He smiled boyishly. "Everything."

Skimmer's stomach threatened to empty itself. She'd walked into the lair of a madman.

Windwolf had been right. She couldn't see this thing through.

Run! Now!

The desire made her shiver. He noticed, turned, and wrapped his arms around her. His bearskin cape felt warm, but smelled of darkness, of things that grew deep underground where sunlight never reached.

"Don't run. Please? You don't know the whole truth yet." He murmured softly, "Come. Let me take you inside where it's out of the wind and we'll talk." To the warriors he said, "Thank you for being so kind to Skimmer on the way here. You may go home to your families. You will be rewarded for your service."

"Thank you, Guide," Kishkat bowed deeply, and backed away.

As the warriors trotted out toward the campfires scattered across the tundra, Ti-Bish led Skimmer through looming shadows toward a small cave. "Raven Hunter wants you to know that your daughter is safe. Ashes is staying with Dipper and Lookingbill."

"How do you know?" Her suspicion burned brightly.

"Because Windwolf won the fight." He waved it away. "It doesn't matter. I think Keresa was Traded for you."

"Keresa?" She frowned, remembering young Silvertip's Dream.

"I don't understand all of the details, but they are fighting over the end of the world."

Of course, the end of the world. Skimmer pointed to the huge maw. "Aren't we going through there?"

"No. I have a chamber prepared for you in a different part of the caves. No one will know where you are until I tell them. It may take some time before I can teach you some of the things Raven Hunter has taught me. I want you to be happy during that time."

She stared at him. He wanted to keep her all to himself, locked in the bowels of the Ice Giants?

"Ti-Bish, the warriors will tell Nashat I'm here. He'll search the caves until he finds me."

He timidly lifted a hand to stroke her long hair, and she forced herself not to shudder. "He won't find you, Skimmer. No one will."

Forty

The Council chamber smelled of sweat and damp hides. Lookingbill smoothed a hand over his bald head and gazed at the warrior who stood guard outside the entrance.

Tens of people walked along the tunnels. The rockshelters were already packed. Where in Wolf Dreamer's name would they put any more? He thanked the gods that Dipper was making those decisions. After the past few days, he felt hollow, as though his insides had been eaten out.

"I don't know which hole to aim for," Ashes said.

He looked back and frowned at the holes in the floor and the positions of the round stone balls. The goal of the game was to roll the balls into the holes with a flick of the wrist. The stones couldn't be bowled. It wasn't easy.

"You're just tired, Ashes. Would you rather take a nap, like Silvertip?"

His wounded grandson lay on a hide on the far side of the chamber, next to his elderly cousin Loon Spot. The old woman had been snoring for a hand of time.

He tried not to look at Silvertip. The Healer had drawn sacred designs on his face and forehead, each but a desperate attempt to keep his soul contained in the body. The swelling on the side of the boy's head had finally receded, but the high fever remained.

Old Loon Spot had taken to continually dribbling water between the boy's lips. Any more than a couple of drops at a time, and he'd choke, unable to swallow.

More than once, Lookingbill had feared the boy was dead, but placing his ear to the thin chest, he could hear the heartbeat, frighteningly slow, but there nonetheless.

"No," Ashes said, maintaining the fiction of Silvertip's "nap." "I—I have bad Dreams when I close my eyes."

"What kind of bad Dreams?"

She shrugged. He'd tried to get her to discuss her Dreams since dawn, hoping he could ease some of the girl's terror, but she'd refused.

Lookingbill saw her mouth quiver before she clamped her jaw. "Your mother is all right, Ashes. She's a strong woman, and she knows what she's doing." He hoped.

"I was thinking about my father." She swallowed hard to keep tears at bay. "Wishing he were here."

"When was the last time you saw him?"

"The day the Nightland warriors burst into the ceremonial lodge and started killing people."

No wonder she had no desire to sleep.

Ashes flicked one of the stone balls. It rolled across the hard-packed floor and settled in a hole.

"Good aim, Ashes. Well done."

She didn't look happy, just relieved. "I don't want to play any longer."

"We don't have to play. Would you like to do something else?"

"No, I just—"

Loon Spot woke suddenly—stared at them as though she'd never seen them before—and threw a basket with all her might.

Lookingbill dodged just in time; it went sailing across the chamber toward the warrior who stood guard. The poor man must have thought it sounded like a dart cutting the air, because he dove for cover.

"Loon Spot, what are you *doing*?" Lookingbill demanded.

The willowy old woman had a shriveled triangular face tucked beneath a gray mop of hair. A broad smile creased her lips.

"I Dreamed you were a dog," she said.

Lookingbill scowled and thrust a hand toward the guard, who peered nervously through entrance. "Look what you made the guard do."

She grinned. "He moves fast. That makes me feel safer."

"I wish you'd go find another chamber to sleep in. I'm tired of you *and* your snoring."

With all the dignity he could manage, the guard pulled himself to his feet and straightened his war shirt. Beneath his breath, he murmured, "Crazy old—"

Loon Spot said, "He's not crazy. He's senile. There's a big difference."

"He meant *you*, Cousin."

She gave him a disgruntled look. "Just wait until you've seen six tens of summers. Your aim won't be so good either."

Ashes smiled, and it warmed Lookingbill's heart. She had a soft, luminous look in her dark eyes, betraying the desperately tired little girl beneath.

"It's good to see somebody around here has a sense of humor." Loon Spot leaned across the floor to pat Ashes' arm affectionately.

"How come you aren't sleeping?" Loon Spot pointed a crooked finger reprovingly. "When I went to sleep, you said you were going to take a nap."

Ashes' smile faded, and she stared down at her restlessly twisting hands. "I can't sleep, Loon Spot. My Dreams are bad."

"Well, whose aren't? You should have seen what Lookingbill looked like as a dog."

Ashes laughed, and it made Lookingbill smile. From the instant they'd met yesterday afternoon, Ashes and Loon Spot had been fast friends.

Loon Spot waved to her. "Come here. Tell me about these Dreams."

Ashes walked over and sat down. Loon Spot put a skinny arm around her shoulders and whispered in her ear. Ashes sniffled in response.

Gradually, their two low voices intertwined, barely audible, and he could tell the little girl's fears had ebbed. Her tone grew calmer, brighter. Lookingbill shook his head. Who knew that gruff, sharp-tongued Loon Spot could speak so kindly to anyone?

Loon Spot whispered, "So he came and floated over your bed?"

Ashes nodded, twining her fingers in her cape. "Mother said he was dead. Just like Wolf Dreamer."

"Did he look dead?"

"Only a little. He had eyes like black stones." Ashes' mouth puckered, and tears glistened on her lashes. "Why is he coming to see me? I don't *want* to see him."

"Tell him that; maybe he'll go away."

Ashes toyed with the fringes on her leggings. "I'll try to sleep . . . if you stay here and watch."

"Oh, you bet I will. Someone bring me another basket. I'll toss it at any nasty raven that flutters close."

A raven? Lookingbill wondered.

Ashes curled up on the hide and closed her eyes. Loon Spot gently kissed her forehead. It seemed only moments before the girl was sleeping soundly.

Lookingbill whispered, "You two get along too well to have been strangers only yesterday. Are you sure you haven't been giving her gifts in secret?"

"I don't have to buy friendship. You're just jealous because you've never had a way with women."

"For once in your life, you're right."

They sat in silence for a time; then Ashes moaned.

Loon Spot waited until the girl's face slackened, then she whispered, "Did you know Raven Hunter was speaking to her in Dreams?"

Lookingbill's breathing stopped. "That's what she told you?"

"That's why she doesn't want to sleep."

"Blessed gods." Lookingbill massaged his brow. "I'm so tired. It never occurred to me to ask why—"

"Of course you're tired," she interrupted. "A few days ago you were sitting around enjoying the sun on your face. Now you're in a fight to the death with the Nightland Elders."

He lowered his hand to his lap. "I had to help the Sunpath People, Loon Spot. Someone had to."

"Dipper says the food stores down in the ice caves will be gone by the next quarter moon."

"She's right." He gave her a dull appraisal. "Windwolf has been meeting with the chiefs. He's preparing the refugees to head west. They're to leave in small groups, escorted by warriors. He thinks that in small bands, traveling by different trails, many can make it to safety in the Tills."

"How soon do you think the Nightland Elders will find out Windwolf defeated Kakala and took him captive?"

Lookingbill picked up one of the stone balls and tossed it toward a hole. He missed. It kept rolling until it hit the wall.

"Two or three days, if we're lucky. Then they have to gather warriors, depending on where Karigi and Blackta have gotten to. Windwolf calculates that it may take as long as a moon to assemble the number necessary."

"And then?"

He gave her a sad look. "By then, we'll be a quarter moon's travel west of here, making the best time we can toward the Tills."

THEY DID NOT HAVE BOWS AND ARROWS THEN

Forty-one

Kakala weakly pushed the hide off his chest and rolled onto his side, blinking at the hazy ceiling. His flesh burned with fever. Thirst plagued him. Dim silver light came from somewhere.

How long had his soul been out wandering? Days? A moon?

He took a deep breath, and the room swirled around him. "What a . . . headache."

His skull throbbed agonizingly. Gently, he tried to push up on one elbow to reach for his blurry pack, but the effort sent his soul tumbling, thought after thought, memory after memory. From the corner of his eye, he saw someone move. He blinked and fell back to his sweat-soaked hide. Closing his eyes, he struggled to control the cascading images.

"Are you finally awake?" Keresa asked.

"You don't . . . sound happy about it."

He pried an eye open; even that hurt. A blue spot wavered in the direction of her voice.

"I am happy. Now I can stop wasting my strength cursing you."

"Glad to . . . to finally be of some use. How long . . . how long has it been?"

"Since the battle? This is our fifth night here."

Keresa cautiously stepped over sleeping warriors to reach him. He closed his eyes and listened to her quiet movements.

"Where . . . are we?"

"In a rotted hole beneath Headswift Village."

He opened his eyes and saw the blue spot hovering above him. He squinted and thought he could make out the shape of her face. Her eyes looked more red than brown.

"You look terrible," he commented.

"Probably because I've been slaving to keep our warriors from killing each other while worrying myself sick about you."

He smiled. "Is there . . . water?"

She made noise, and he heard water splashing into a cup. Keresa sat beside him, slid an arm beneath his shoulders, and gently lifted him. Then he felt the cup touch his lips. He drank greedily. Liquid spilled from the corners of his mouth and ran coolly over his chest. He finished it and let his head fall back against her arm.

"Better?" she asked.

He nodded, but as she pulled her arm from beneath his shoulders, his mind tumbled again, confused memories flying close, then soaring away.

"Wh-where am I?"

Suddenly, he couldn't remember. He shook his head, struggling to recall. In the background he heard the shrill whine of the Ice Giants . . . didn't he?

"Kakala, are you all right?"

"Hako?" Hope burst his heart. He reached out for her.

"No, War Chief. It's Keresa."

Images of lightning-filled skies pulsed behind his closed eyes. He could smell the vile odors of blood and torn intestines. Hako looked at him in utter terror.

"Hako, I told you to run! *Run!*"

Darts cracked on the rocks all around them. Someone screamed. . . .

"War Chief. Do you remember that Windwolf captured us at Headswift Village?"

"Windwolf?" His mind struggled to sort images of many battles. "He . . . he what?"

"There was a battle. We lost. He took us hostage."

Not Hako. *Hako's dead. Dead for too many summers.*

He shuddered, twining fingers in his damp hide. The battle at Headswift Village . . . Windwolf bashing him with his war club . . . Trap, ambush . . . Keresa's hard voice demanding, "Kakala? Kakala, hold onto me! We have to get out of here!"

"I remember . . . Keresa."

"Good. Lie still. A Healer will be coming to check on you. He's been here twice."

"Healer? What Healer?"

"A man from Headswift Village. I don't know his name."

He threw her a questioning look. "Search him . . . before he touches me, all right?"

"Forget it. Windwolf assured me he wanted to finish you off himself."

He felt like laughing, but figured it would kill him. "How are our warriors?"

She exhaled hard. "Not well. In order to get a Healer to come and see you, I had to order them to turn over their weapons. No one is happy about it."

"But they . . . did it?"

"Of course. I threatened to kill each man who hesitated."

"Keresa? What do the warriors . . . think . . . I . . . ?"

Even in his haze and pain, he'd been worried to death about that. Surely the ones who'd lost friends would be blaming him, praying he'd die. When he was able to take control again, would they obey his commands?

"Some have misgivings. But most of them are with you. I'm with you."

"I . . . I know that."

With hushed violence Keresa said, "The world out there has gone mad, Kakala. There are tens of refugees crawling all over Headswift Village, and more appear every hand of time. Windwolf's forces are growing rapidly."

He sucked in a deep breath. "Have we . . . heard . . ."

"We've heard nothing. Windwolf must have ordered the warriors who guard us to keep their mouths closed. At first I heard many interesting things, but since then, nothing."

"What about Goodeagle. Did he . . . did he survive?"

She stopped pacing to stare down at him. "Did you want him to?"

"Not really. I just . . . thought he might suddenly . . . be of use."

Keresa laughed, but it was a strange, near-desperate sound. Since he felt the same way, he chuckled with her—and instantly regretted it. His head shattered like a block of ice dropped from a mountaintop.

She said, "Windwolf did say something that made me think he might be alive."

"What?"

"He asked me if Goodeagle was in this chamber with us, which made me think he meant there were other chambers where our warriors were being held."

"Keresa . . . when possible . . . try to find Goodeagle. . . . Get organized."

He thought he saw Keresa run a hand through her hair, but it was a splotch-on-splotch movement so he couldn't be sure. Her voice came out soft, strained. "I've missed you, Kakala."

He smiled. "You . . . scared?"

"Terrified."

"Don't be. Windwolf . . . may have taken . . . us hostage, but he can't . . . can't hold us. We'll escape."

"I think you're right. If he keeps taking in more and more refugees, it won't be long. When the people here are going hungry, tensions will rise. He'll have his hands full just managing his own refugees' quarrels. And it won't be long until the Nightland Elders realize we haven't returned from this raid. We might be dead before they get here, but surely—"

"No . . . we won't."

She took a deep breath and spread her feet, looking like she'd just braced herself for hand-to-hand combat.

"You have more faith in our Elders than I do." A treasonous tone invaded her voice.

Why did she do that to him? It set him on edge, and she knew it.

He lay still, thinking until he felt the silence so desperately he knew he had to get up—get the warriors organized. He pushed up on his elbows, and a sharp pain nearly fragmented his skull. He fell back weakly, thoughts rolling, jumbling, pieces of images swirling, slips of different voices shouting. . . .

Keresa watched him writhe; her fists clenched in futility. She should have let him sleep. But she'd needed to talk to him, to bolster her own flagging spirits.

Many of her warriors were awake now. Their eyes gleamed in the faint slivers of light that fell through the boulders.

"Hako?" Kakala called. "Don't . . . don't leave me." He feebly lifted a hand, reaching out.

Keresa felt like she intruded on some private memory, but she knelt and—

Footsteps grated on the rocks above, probably warriors changing watches, but in Kakala's soul they were enemy warriors.

"No!" he screamed. "No! Don't! Oh, gods, not . . . our fault!" He raised his hands to his head, squeezing hard as he tossed from side to side.

"Kakala," she called. "It's Keresa. You're here with me. You're safe!" What a lie that was.

"Safe?"

"Yes."

He shook his head, as though clearing the feverish fog. "No. Even if we . . . Hako?"

He turned toward her, and the soft pained look in his usually hard eyes made her feel like he'd ripped her guts out.

"Kakala," she assured him, "Calm down. Try to sleep."

"No, I . . . I'm frightened, Hako. I—I don't . . . Hold me?"

He weakly lifted his arms to her. She sat down and let him wrap his arms around her.

Warriors whispered, and she didn't like the sound of their voices.

"You're safe, Kakala. Get some sleep."

He tightened his arms around her back and feebly pulled her against his chest, tenderly rubbing his chin in her hair. "Never safe . . . no . . . never."

Drained from his outburst, he blinked wearily and drifted off. His arms slowly slid back to his sides.

Keresa got up and looked around the chamber, her eyes squinted. "Any warrior here who thinks what I just did makes me weak had better never turn his back on me."

Laughter rose. Some of the tension eased.

Footsteps grated above her again, and this time there were voices.

She looked up as one of the boulders was rolled aside.

Windwolf loomed tall and hard-eyed in the moonlight. A shorter man stood behind him, a bag beneath his arm. "Deputy," Windwolf greeted. "How's the war chief?"

"Bad."

"I've brought the Healer, Flathead, again. Just like last time, before he comes down I want all of your warriors to gather on the far side of the chamber."

She turned. "Do it."

Her men rose and moved to the rear, muttering unpleasantly to each other. They should be used to it by now.

A pine pole ladder was lowered into the chamber; then an old man descended one step at a time. He had a small pack on his back. The Healer immediately went to Kakala's side and put a hand to his fevered brow.

"Now, Deputy," Windwolf said, "I want you to climb out."

"Me?" Keresa asked.

"If you're no longer deputy war chief, I'll take your successor. Someone has to keep a promise you made."

The map of the caves . . .

Keresa glanced nervously at her warriors. "All right. I'm coming up."

She climbed and stepped out onto the boulders. Eight warriors surrounded the entry to the chamber. Four clutched war clubs; four held nocked atlatls. Just in case any of her people escaped.

She heard Kakala whimper; then the Healer said something soft.

Windwolf crouched over the opening and looked down.

"Hako?" Kakala called feebly. "No . . . no. Reach . . . farther. I can almost touch . . . Don't! I—I need you. I—"

"It's all right," the Healer soothed. "You're going to be all right."

"No! Please . . . please no more. I can't . . ."

Keresa shifted uncomfortably. Windwolf had no right—*no right!*— to see Kakala like this. She tried to impale him with her fiery glare, but he kept looking thoughtfully at Kakala.

He rose suddenly, said, "Come with me," and walked away.

She followed him. Two guards fell in line behind her.

What had he felt? His expression had betrayed deep, grudging emotion.

By instinct, she studied the high points, noting every place a war-rior stood silhouetted. Frowning, she looked again. No good warrior would allow himself to be seen so easily. And these warriors looked very slender, and short.

When Windwolf turned around and caught her scrutinizing the high points, he said, "Deputy, I would prefer that you walk beside me. We can talk on the way to my chamber."

Forty-two

Windwolf almost breathed an audible sigh of relief when Keresa finally followed him into his chamber. Once he had wondered how the Lame Bull People could live in these holes. Now he felt distinctly uncomfortable out in the open—especially with so many refugees filling the valley.

Most were just reverent, but too many insisted on crowding around him, reaching out to touch him, demanding his attention. The look in their eyes left him shaken; each and every one believed that he could save them.

By Wolf Dreamer's sacred breath, it will be a relief when the first groups leave tomorrow.

Too many things disturbed him these days. As he had watched Kakala, his heart had saddened. Why would his old enemy's suffering bother him so? Was it just the things he'd learned? That Kakala had tried to kill Karigi for what he'd done to Bramble? Or that somehow, he'd gone from a heartless butcher to a vulnerable captive?

I can't afford sympathy for a man who'd love nothing more than parading me into the Nightland Council.

But what about Keresa?

He studied her as someone down in the camps started playing a wooden flute. The mournful lilting notes made him stop and listen. It was too beautiful for this time and place.

She stood by the fire, arms folded tightly across her chest. Her red doehide war shirt conformed to her body, accenting every curve. He couldn't keep from staring at her, wishing so desperately that this able woman was anyone but his foe. Something about her manner, the way she handled herself, spoke to his loneliness. How long had it been since he'd spoken to anyone as frankly as he did to her? If only . . .

"Those acorn nut cakes smell wonderful," she said, breaking the spell and pointing to the basket that rested beside the hearth.

"I'm sure they do, since you haven't had anything but water for two days. Please, eat some."

She didn't waste any time, but knelt, unfolded the hide wrapping, and pulled out one of the cakes. She gobbled it down as fast as she could and reached for another.

Windwolf walked across the chamber and picked up the hide he'd chosen earlier. As he walked back, he asked, "Do you like them?"

Crumbs had fallen onto her dress. She didn't take any time to brush them away. Around a mouthful of food, she replied, "Wonderful."

"They were made for me by a woman who once lived in Walking Seal Village."

She stopped chewing.

Well, that tells me something about your conscience. He sat down on the opposite side of the fire, and watched her.

She swallowed, and said, "I'm grateful for the food."

"You're welcome."

She finished the cake, sank to the floor, and exhaled slowly. "May I dip myself a cup of tea?"

"Please."

As she did, he unrolled the deer hide and found the piece of charcoal he'd been saving from the fire.

She shifted positions, brought one knee up, and propped her cup on it. From this side view she seemed all the more slender. It touched something inside him, some illogical masculine need to protect—as if this warrior needed anybody's protection. Nonetheless, it softened his guarded responses to her.

"Windwolf, tell me something?"

He lifted his brows, expecting something unpleasant. "Go on?"

"Why is it that Sunpath People keep plotting to kill our Guide? We've wiped out one nest of conspirators after another, but more spring up immediately."

He listened to the lilting note of the flute. If he let himself, he could almost feel as though he'd stepped backward in time, and Bramble was still alive. He could hear their son laughing. . . .

"Your Guide preaches the extermination of anyone who believes in Wolf Dreamer. What do you expect my people to do?"

"Some have converted. Like the Seadog band."

"Yes," he said. "I remember. It was the first day I took my son into the forest and started teaching him how to throw a dart and swing a war club."

In a graceful motion, she made a sweeping gesture to Headswift Village. "So, he owes all this to you? Is he grateful in his praise?"

He lightly stroked the fine hairs on the deer hide. "My son is dead."

Her stony expression melted. "Forgive me. I didn't know." After a few heartbeats, she added, "The earlier a boy learns to fight, the better. You were clearly a good father."

She looked like she wanted to ask him what had happened, but restrained herself.

He was thankful for that. It might have been one of her darts that had killed Lion Boy four summers ago. The fight had been swift and hot. Nightland warriors had struck the Hunting Horse camp fast and hard before they dashed away into the forest like cowardly dogs.

In the fireglow, her hair had shaded golden, as though a glistening web of real summer sunlight netted her head. He fumbled with the piece of hide, suppressing an ache for the family he'd lost, for the scents of wet dirt and wildflowers, the rustling of wind through pines around the Hunting Horse camp.

"What have we done to ourselves?" she asked softly.

He said, "That almost sounded friendly."

"Did it? I must be exhausted beyond good sense. But I'm not blind, Windwolf. My angle of vision is just different from yours. I've seen the Sunpath People kill many of our children, too."

"*I've* never killed your children."

She smoothed her fingers down the side of her cup. "No, you haven't."

Thoughtfully, he rolled up the hide, then unrolled it again. "Deputy,

I know some of the stories of the Nightland People. Do you any Sun-path stories?"

"I know about the Exile and the climb through the hole in the ice to this world of light. I know about Wolf Dreamer, and his battle with Raven Hunter." She smiled wistfully. "They used to be our stories, too."

"There are others. Every time my people got settled into a nice comfortable place, something went wrong, and we ended up running for our lives. It was as though Wolf Dreamer had abandoned us. So we dedicated ourselves to seeking the One. We . . ."

She put a hand to her mouth to cover a yawn, and Windwolf said, "Am I boring you?"

"No, it's not you. It's just . . . I've never been this exhausted in my entire life."

He unrolled the hide again. "Draw this map for me and you can go."

He started to rise; to hand her the hide and charcoal, but she reached around the fire to touch his sleeve. He could feel the chill of her delicate fingers through his shirt.

"I'm sorry; it's not you." She laughed, as if amused at herself, eyes softening. "Odd, isn't it? Here I am, facing my enemy, and I feel at ease." She hesitated. "Can we talk while I draw?"

He lowered himself back to the hide. "Of course."

"For just this one moment, can we forget who we really are?"

He lifted a shoulder noncommittally. "What would you like to discuss?"

"Only things that don't matter. Tell me . . ." She drew a line on the hide and shrugged. "If you could have one wish, what would it be?"

"To be left alone." He looked down at his hands. "The problem with life is that you never know what to miss until it's gone."

She nodded sympathetically. "And your favorite food?"

"Nothing you'd like. It's a plant so spicy almost no one but me can eat it. It's called beeweed and comes from the far west."

"How do you get it?"

"From the river Traders. One summer they brought a sack of bee-weed to our camp in the Hunting Horse territory. That's the only time I've had beeweed, but I remember the flavor."

She smiled, a true gesture, not one of those carefully contrived to ease tension. It made him feel better. She drew a black curving line on the hide. "The Waterthrush People make an acorn bread that they serve with bumblebee honey. That's my favorite."

He leaned forward. "I'll have to try it the next time I'm there."

She smiled, white teeth flashing behind her lips. "Do. You'll like it."

They fell silent, gazing across the fire at each other.

Who is this woman? As he looked into her eyes, it was as if to touch her soul. He could sense her fear and the worry that chewed away at her. For that moment, she wasn't deadly, didn't mask her insecurity in the face of the future. In the firelight, he watched her pupils expand, her lips part. Then, self-consciously, she took a breath and went back to drawing.

A long silence stretched.

"Windwolf . . ." She pressed her lips tightly together. "I'm sorry that all this . . ." She bit it off, averting her eyes, irritated with herself.

"You did what you had to, Deputy." He smiled wearily. "We all do."

He watched the fire dance over her smooth cheeks, wondering why no man had devoted himself to her.

As if in defeat, she murmured, "As Kakala says, we have to be Nightland warriors."

"You sound like you'd rather not."

"Like you, I'm tired of it." She met his eyes, that curious vulnerability calling to him. "Do you believe in what you're doing?"

He made a helpless gesture. "If I don't save my people, who will?"

"Can't they save themselves?"

He shook his head. "I don't know. Think about what we were: loosely knit bands of hunters and gatherers, moving our villages from place to place. All anyone wanted was enough to eat, to watch our children grow, to appease the Spirits of the animals we hunted and the plants we ate. Most of our time was spent squabbling with each other over trivialities." He paused, staring into her eyes with a desperation of his own. "Now it all seems so silly."

She broke the connection, frowning as she bent down to trace another line, scowled, and spit on her palm to rub it out. "Tell me . . . do you ever long to just run away? Maybe travel south to the nut forests, or out to the grassy plains?"

"More than you could know," he said sadly. "Were it not for my responsibility to save my people, I would be gone." He rubbed the back of his neck, feeling curiously uneasy. "There's nothing left here now.

Only painful memories of my wife and child, dead friends, and a happy life that is lost."

She nodded, lips pursed. He decided he liked the pouting frown in her forehead.

"Do you and Kakala wish to run away, too?"

"I do. Kakala . . ." She looked up, slightly startled. "No, Kakala and I aren't like that. It's hard to explain. We're . . ." The frown was back, a mirror for her own confusion. "Closest friends." She gave a dismissive gesture. "There's no man in my life."

"Are they all fools?"

She laughed, genuinely amused. "No, and I guess that's the problem. You'd have to be a fool to want a woman like me. Few men can stand a woman who runs faster, throws harder, or hunts better."

"Some do." He glanced down at his hands again. "Once, I had a woman like that."

"I know." She shook her head, voice dropping. "Bramble was my friend."

"Then you know what they did to her?"

She nodded. "Karigi." She swallowed hard. "When Kakala saw . . ."

"Go on." He felt his chest tightening.

"If you hadn't attacked, Kakala would have killed Karigi. I've never seen him in such a rage. He was in the process of beating him to death. It wasn't just that Karigi had disobeyed orders."

"Why?"

She looked up at him, eyes liquid. "Because Kakala liked and respected Bramble. It takes a great deal to earn Kakala's respect. But Bramble did. Seeing . . . It wounded him." She rolled the charcoal in her fingers, staring into his eyes, the corners of her lips twitching.

"What was Kakala's plan at Walking Seal Village?"

"He thought if he could take Bramble, hand you a crushing defeat, it would be an incentive for your people to leave without more killing. If the Sunpath just went away, left, the Nightland would have only the Lame Bull to convince. With no enemies, the Council would have no reason to send out war parties. No one who believed in Wolf Dreamer could follow us when the Guide took us into the paradise of the Long Dark."

"A quick way to end the killing?"

"Kakala sometimes has grand notions." She returned to her drawing.

Windwolf frowned, thinking back. Bramble had broached the subject of leaving. He had even been considering it before Walking Seal Village. Now, all these years later, what was he doing, but sending parties of refugees west to the Tills?

Kakala tried to kill Karigi? Would have, had Silt and I not arrived when we did?

"Have you ever thought about changing sides?"

She lifted a brow and laughed softly. "Don't be ridiculous. You're doomed."

"We could use you."

"I'm intrigued by your faith in the future." She laughed again and shook her head, as though she doubted his sincerity, while she drew several more curving lines. "But I'll keep it in mind."

"I'm serious."

Something about the softness of her expression touched him. He wanted her to stay, to talk, to just let him look at her.

He pointed at the map. "How are you doing?"

"I'm finished." She handed it to him.

When he reached for the map, he accidentally grasped her hand where it held the hide. Time seemed to stop. Conflicting emotions danced across her beautiful face: a magnetic attraction to him, fear, confusion. They might have been frozen, the physical contact lasting for five heartbeats, then ten. Her cool skin under his sent blood rushing in his ears.

Finally, Keresa gently pulled her hand back and said, "That's the best I can do."

Windwolf looked at it, pulse pounding, short of breath. "Is this the eastern entrance to the caves?"

"Yes." She tapped the map. "And this is the western entrance."

She'd drawn many more passageways than he'd thought she would, and based upon his own explorations, they looked accurate. It told him something very valuable about her sense of honor.

Her dark eyes fixed on his. He could see the question there that she dared not ask.

"Yes?" he prompted.

"About Kakala, back at the cavern. You shouldn't have stared like that."

He sighed. "All these moons I have wanted him dead. And now . . ."

"Go on."

He shook his head. "Keresa, I—"

"May I go now?" She refused to meet his eyes, but he could see the pulse racing in her neck.

"Of course." He went to the entry to hold the curtain aside for her. She ducked outside and was gone.

Forty-three

Silvertip fought his way through a thick haze of gray, images of the Dream living within him.

Each of Wolf Dreamer's words remained fresh and clear, as though they had become a living part of Silvertip's soul.

He blinked his eyes open and winced at the grating feel, as if sand had been poured behind his lids. He reached up with a feathered wing, oddly surprised to find a very human hand at his control. It took a moment to remember how to work his fingers as he rubbed his dry eyes. His tongue stuck to the roof of his mouth, and a terrible pain filled his head.

Unlike his Spirit body, this one hurt; his bones ached. His bones, the same ones he'd seen slowly bleach, and fall away. Making a fist, he savored the miracle of muscle, tendon, and bone. He felt stiff, but he was whole.

When he turned onto his side, it wasn't with a simple twist of his tail, but the more ponderous movements of a dull and clumsy body.

It took a moment for his eyes to focus. Then he knew were he was: the Spirit Chamber.

Glancing at the door he determined it was night. The fire in the center had burned down to coals. Grandfather Lookingbill lay wrapped in his buffalohide blanket. Loon Spot sat just to his side. Her head drooped at an odd angle, mouth open to expose a few peglike teeth, a rasping snore rising from her wattled throat.

I'm back. He looked down at his small body, so poorly human. But in his soul, the magic of flight still ran through him like a beam of morning light.

Tears brimmed in his eyes, silvering his vision. He blinked at them, and sniffed, a profound grief welling within. The sense of loss grew, encompassing a sorrow he didn't know his breast could contain.

"Give me back my wings. Please, Wolf Dreamer!"

In the middle of the night, Keresa heard a familiar voice. She sat up and rubbed the sleep from her eyes. All around her warriors lay stretched out across the floor with their capes tucked closely about their bodies for warmth. Kakala whispered and whimpered, lost in some dream.

The familiar voice came again, and she realized it wasn't coming from this chamber.

A thrill went through her.

She got to her feet and picked her way between the sleeping men to the blocked tunnel. The debris, composed of several large boulders and tens of small rocks, felt icy cold.

Two voices: both soft, but familiar.

Why hadn't she heard them before? Voices carried farther at night, especially when it was as quiet as it was tonight. There was no wind. The warriors above her were silent.

She used her hand to dig out some of the gravel and dirt that filled the space between two of the large boulders. It crackled as it hit the floor, but none of the sleeping men seemed to hear it.

When she'd created a hole as deep as her arm was long, she pressed her mouth into a gap and called, "Washani?"

The voices stopped.

"Washani?" she called again, as loud as she dared.

Silence.

Then Washani called, "Deputy Keresa? Is that you?"

She leaned her forehead against the wall and smiled.

Skimmer lay on the thick pile of buffalo hides and stared at the utter blackness. She had no idea where she was, but she had to be very close to the beating hearts of the Ice Giants. Their cries and groans seemed louder here, more grief-stricken.

She rolled to her side and tried to sleep.

Ti-Bish had led her through the dark tunnels for hands of time, feeling the way. At each fork, he would sniff the air, as though the tunnels had a distinctive scent. She had funneled all of her concentration into the task, but had no more chance of retracing her path than she did of flying.

When they'd finally arrived here, he'd taken her hand and placed it on the items in the cave: the sleeping hides; a water bag; a basket of pemmican, consisting of a length of intestine stuffed with meat, berries, and fat; and wild rice cakes.

Then he'd left her alone.

The darkness pressed on her eyes and ears as though it had heavy hands.

"Did Windwolf really win?" she whispered, and her voice seemed to ring in the silence, bouncing back from the ice walls. Ti-Bish had assured her he had, and that Ashes was safe. But how could he know for sure?

If Windwolf had lost the battle, what had happened to Ashes? Had Lookingbill gotten her out before the end?

Horrifying images flashed: Ashes being raped by Nightland warriors . . . Ashes being herded northward with the other orphans to become slaves in Nightland villages . . . Ashes lying dead in the Spirit Chamber with her head bashed in. . . .

"He won," she said sternly. "Windwolf won. He killed Kakala and destroyed his war party to the last warrior."

She had to believe it.

But whatever had happened, she still had a terrible task ahead of her.

She had to kill Ti-Bish. Perhaps in the chaos afterward, Windwolf would be able to storm the Nightland Caves and force their Elders to halt the attacks on the remaining Sunpath bands. Or, with the Guide dead, maybe the Nightland would simply lose heart, their warriors withdrawing meekly to leave her people alone.

A strange tapping began. It echoed from some distant tunnel. She listened, hoping it was Ti-Bish returning with a lamp. The tapping turned into a forceful thudding, and she realized it was water.

Had a new crack opened in the bellies of the Ice Giants and allowed a pool of meltwater to escape?

Would it flood her cave?

Is this how I'll die? Drowned in ice water, here, deep in the darkness?

She bent her head, tears of despair streaking down her cheeks. She sobbed, wishing for sunlight, air, and the feel of wind on her face.

The Ice Giants let out an ear-splitting groan, then trembled, shaking the floor beneath her . . . and the thudding stopped.

Skimmer clamped her jaw to keep her teeth from chattering.

Pain

She doesn't know I'm here, sitting just outside her chamber.

Raven Hunter told me long ago that I needn't fear the darkness; that I walked with Death every instant of my life, and if I could just keep staring at it, I would never be afraid again.

But I worry about Skimmer.

She is a creature of light and warmth.

Raven Hunter tells me that I must force her to live in perpetual darkness for at least one moon. That she has to get used to it, because it is the nature of Raven Hunter's world and the sooner she learns what that means, the better.

I haven't the heart.

She's tearing herself apart in there. Her breathing is rapid and shallow. She keeps whimpering as though she can feel the hands of monsters stroking her body.

Doubt consumes me.

I asked Raven Hunter today why it was taking so long, why he couldn't just show me the hole in the ice and let me lead our people back to that paradise.

For the first time, he grew angry. The earthquake that followed his outburst lasted for nearly three tens of heartbeats. I was terrified that the Ice Giants were going to collapse around me, burying me in the darkness forever.

He told me he was struggling to assure that everything happened at the right moment and ordered me never to question him again.

I won't.

Skimmer has started crying.

I am afraid for her.

And for me, if I don't obey Raven Hunter.

Forty-four

Windwolf leaned against the mouth of the rockshelter and stared out at the boulders that created Headswift Village. In the sunlight, they gleamed wetly with the morning dew. Down the hill—at the base of the outcrop—Sunpath People went about their morning duties, cooked breakfast, and played with their children. A pack of dogs raced through the village, barking.

He sighed heavily. Two camps had already headed out on the trail west, but another three had arrived. It was an awkward way to move people. Those who came north to Headswift Village might have a couple of days of recuperation, only to be sent off west, knowing they had to ford the great river at the western edge of Loon Lake. They could have saved a moon's travel or more by simply traveling straight west along the southern margins of the lakes.

But Karigi and Blackta were out there, somewhere.

"I do not understand," Fish Hawk said. "I just told you that we heard boulders being moved in the chambers where we've trapped the Nightland warriors. Doesn't that disturb you?"

Windwolf kept his gaze on the Sunpath villagers. "I know my orders sound . . . unusual, but I have my reasons."

"Please help me to understand them."

A boy ran down the trail in front of them. His dog, a puppy, trotted happily at his heels. Windwolf waited until they'd passed.

"Deputy Keresa needs to speak with her people. Let her."

Fish Hawk studied him curiously. "They'll be plotting against us."

"I'm counting on it. I'm also counting on their growing desperation."

Fish Hawk propped his hand on his belted war club. "If they work hard enough, they may open a tunnel connecting the chambers."

"If they do, pretend you don't know about it."

Fish Hawk's brows knitted. "They'll think we're fools."

Windwolf nodded. "Perhaps. But desperation grows with numbers. I want them all sharing each other's doubts."

"Then . . . you want Kakala's warriors all in the same chamber?"

"Now you're getting the idea."

Fish Hawk shook his head as though he hadn't heard right. Long black hair fell over his shoulders. "If I were making the decisions, I would be trying very hard to keep them separated. The warriors in the new chamber must still have weapons. We don't know how many there are, but if they get together, they are much more powerful. They'll be plotting to escape, and if they escape, they will surely kill some of us."

Windwolf pushed away from the wall and stepped out into the sunlight. Cold wind gusted up the trail and flapped the collar of his buffalo coat. "That's a chance I'm forced to take."

Fish Hawk held his gaze. "Why don't we kill them?"

"Because the longer we hold them, the more time they have to think, to lose hope. They know the cages are waiting for them. As soon as I know how the Nightland Elders will respond to our hostages, I'll explain my bizarre orders." He clapped a hand on Fish Hawk's shoulder. "In the meantime, I must ask you to trust me."

"Well," Fish Hawk said through a long exhalation. "I hope you're being brilliant, not stupid. If they escape, Kakala won't rest until he kills you."

Windwolf tightened his arms over his chest and gave Fish Hawk a tired smile. "Then, we had best not let them escape."

I'll bet you want to kill Keresa," Ashes said as she knotted fibers cut from spruce roots. Her nimble fingers were occupied making a net bag.

"No," Silvertip told her as he clutched the Wolf Bundle to his chest. He mostly kept his right eye closed, since it was hard to focus. And the headache didn't make talking easier.

"Why not? She tried to kill you."

Silvertip pursed his lips, giving her a squint-eyed appraisal. "She only did what Power wished."

Ashes gave him the sort of look she'd give the demented. "Power wanted you to have your head bashed in?"

He glanced around, seeing none of the adults close. "I had to die."

"Well, you came pretty close."

He gave the slightest shake of his head. "No. I died. I saw my dead body . . . watched as a condor came down and . . ." He pressed the Wolf Bundle against his stomach, remembering the sensation of the condor's beak pulling out his guts. "I had to watch until my bones fell away."

"Why?" Her eyes were wide, the partially finished net bag forgotten in her hands.

"To learn to fly," he said wistfully. "It was the only way I could become Condor."

"Condor?" She hesitated. "Did you eat dead things?"

"It's not so bad." He gave her a somber look. "What was wonderful was Dreaming the One. And don't ask. I can't explain. It's a . . . harmony. A sharing of life and light." He clamped his eyes shut. "If I could only go back."

"Go throw another rock at Keresa."

He smiled, but it hurt. "It's tempting. But I have things to do."

"Like what?"

He stared into her eyes. "The voice you hear in your Dreams is Raven Hunter's."

Her interest was replaced by suspicion, and not a little fear. "Loon Spot told you?"

"No. I saw us. In the future."

Her expression had turned wary. "In the future?"

"After our world is destroyed."

"You're starting to sound like the Prophet."

"He is Raven Hunter's tool. Wolf Dreamer was lost in the One,

Dreaming the harmony. He didn't understand. Opposites crossed. There's great Power in that. Harmony and order must be crossed with chaos and creativity. Life must be balanced by death. Only when male and female are joined can new life be created. Wolf Dreamer didn't understand. The battle between him and his brother was just beginning."

"He's not the only one who's confused. You're sounding peculiar yourself."

"The Ice Giants are melting."

"Tell me something that I don't know."

"You've heard of the great lakes beyond the Southwind People's lands?"

"Of course. The Traders tell how the whole southern rim of the Ice Giants is one endless lake after another."

"Water runs downhill."

She laughed. "That was a good bump on the head. If you didn't know that before, you needed it."

"And all that holds it back is a narrow dam of ice."

She stared at him, thinking. "But the Ice Giants are melting."

"As Condor, I flew over the last dam, looked down at the cracks and tunnels. Wolf Dreamer and I saw it. In the One, I watched it give way." He looked down at the Wolf Bundle, hearing its soft whispers and feeling its growing warmth.

"You have to warn people."

He nodded. "Many will listen. Others won't believe a boy who was hit on the head. They will say I'm too young to be a Dreamer."

"Then what will you do?" She was giving him a serious look that he would come to love.

"I'll take you with me."

"But . . . what about my mother? She'll come looking for me here."

"That's just it, Ashes. There will be no 'here' left." He looked around. "All of this, it will all be washed away."

She gave him a skeptical look. "And what if I don't go?"

"Then you will never become my wife, and our children will never struggle to find the balance between Wolf Dreamer and Raven Hunter."

Forty-five

*S*kimmer . . . *Skimmer* . . . *Skimmer* . . ."

She jerked awake at the sound of her name being repeated over and
over, and stared up into Ti-Bish's worried eyes. He carried an oil lamp
with a moss wick. Two long braids framed his boyish face and hung
down over the front of his bearskin cape. In the fluttering light, the
tiny black ravens painted on the cape seemed to move, to be flying.

"Is it morning?" she asked, and sat up.

"There is no morning here. Are you hungry?" He lifted the basket
in his left hand, and she smelled the distinctive aroma of roasted fish.

"Starving."

Ti-Bish started for the mouth of the cave. "Come, I want you to
see something. We'll eat there."

Skimmer rose, swung her cape around her shoulders, and followed
him out into the tunnel. The endless moaning of air flowing through
the crevasses and tunnels mixed with the low groaning of the ice.

Her mouth dropped open at the size of the winding irregular passage. She'd had no idea when she followed him here in the darkness.
This stunned her. The tunnel arched three body lengths over her head

and spread five wide. Sand and gravel dotted the floors and walls. Occasionally a massive boulder jutted out through the ice.

"I thought the Nightland Caves were pure ice," she said.

"The ones near the surface are," he replied softly, but his voice reverberated from the walls, almost as though he'd shouted. "Here, in the lowest tunnels, the Stone People live with the Ice Giants."

The tunnel forked. Ti-Bish took the passageway to the left, the one that slanted sharply down. Skimmer was happy for the gravel in the floor; it kept her moccasins from slipping.

"It's not much farther," he said.

"Where are we going?"

"To my secret place."

She kept her eyes on Ti-Bish. He had a gawky walk, like a blue heron hunting shallow water.

In another six tens of heartbeats, the tunnel seemed to fade, but as Ti-Bish carried his lamp closer, she saw the truth.

Ti-Bish stepped out onto a gravel shore and looked up. A pained howl rose from the bellies of the Ice Giants and shook the world.

"Blessed gods." Skimmer had to brace her hand against the tunnel wall to stay on her feet. When the tremor stopped, she walked out behind him . . . and her breath caught.

The coal-black water rippled in the aftereffects of the quake; it spread before them like an endless ocean. An ocean of living light. Tens of fish swam near the surface, driving billows of light with their heads and, in their wakes, leaving milky veils behind. As far as her eye could see, the water had a faint glow; and the ice ceiling above, scalloped and sculpted by eons of water, gleamed.

"It's . . . unbelievable," she whispered. Her heart began to pound. "No one could ever Dream such a place."

Ti-Bish knelt on the gravel and set his basket down. "Grandmother Earth is alive, Skimmer. The mountains have souls. The trees Sing late at night. Grains of sand can speak. It's just that no one listens."

Her gaze followed a sinuous trail of light created by a very large fish. She had heard elderly Traders speak of the far oceans as living seas of light, but she'd never imagined this. "Where are we, Ti-Bish?"

"Beneath the Ice Giants."

"You mean . . ." Terror killed her voice. In a bare whisper she said, "You mean that massive bulk of ice sits on top of us?"

"Yes. This lake is their tears. Every time they cry, the water level rises." He pointed to the ledges that had been carved into the ice from the rising and falling water.

"Do they know we're here?" she whispered.

"Oh, yes, they called me here—to this very spot—ten summers ago." That mad gleam had entered his eyes again.

"Called you?"

"Please, sit beside me. Let's eat and talk." Ti-Bish laid out shell bowls. With care he unwrapped four roasted fish and divided them into the bowls. Finally, he drew out two wooden cups and handed her one.

Skimmer took it and sat down cross-legged.

Ti-Bish pulled out a water bag and filled his cup as he said, "The water here is salty, so you can't drink it."

"How can it be salty when it's melted ice?"

"Because it's part of the Thunder Sea. At high tide, salt water rushes in, and fresh water drains out at low tide. Those are ocean fish. And sometimes I see seals and walrus in here."

Skimmer let him fill her cup from the bag and drank. It tasted good. "This must dazzle everyone you bring here."

He gave her a hopeful look and softly said, "I have never brought anyone here before."

For the moment the awesome vista overwhelmed her hunger. He picked one of the bowls up and handed it to her.

Skimmer set her water cup down, took the bowl, and rested it in her lap. When she took a bite, she found the fish still warm, the meat flaky and delicious.

Ti-Bish said, "I come here when I'm afraid or worried. When I'm here none of the terrible burdens of being the Guide weigh my soul down. I feel like I've already gone through the hole in the ice and returned to the sanctuary of the Long Dark."

Her thoughts shifted briefly to Headswift Village, and worry began to nibble at her heart. She ate more of her fish, trying to force the thoughts away, but when she looked up, she found him studying her anxiously.

"I'm glad you're here, Skimmer."

The air around her shifted, as though moving in response to the wind outside, and the faintest of ripples brushed the shore. "Why, Ti-Bish?"

"I need to be with you. To pray with you."

She gave him a hard look. "I thought you wanted me for other reasons."

"What other reasons?"

"As a man wants a woman. The way Nightland warriors usually do with women captives." She watched his eyes widen as she added, "If that's the price I must pay for my people, I will lie with you."

"You would . . ." He looked completely stunned. "I . . . I . . ." He swallowed hard, turning his eyes away in embarrassment. In an oddly squeaking voice he barely managed to say, "I only want to pray with you."

"Pray?" she asked, confused.

His eyes widened. "Yes, you . . . you're important. To me, and especially . . ." His excited voice stopped suddenly as though he'd been hushed by invisible Spirits.

"Yes, Ti-Bish?"

"You would . . ." He blinked his eyes, as though suddenly tortured. "I *can't* lie with you."

She sighed relief, ate another bite of fish, and swallowed. "We live in a terrible world, Ti-Bish. I'm sorry I—"

"Terrible?"

She blinked. "Filled with rape, sadness, and death. Suffering is the heart of everything."

Ti-Bish pulled a long strip of crispy skin from his fish and ate it before he replied. "Fortunately there is darkness to kill that terrible light."

She frowned. "What did you say?"

"Sadness and death . . . they are sharp daggers of light that blind the soul. Darkness eases the pain." He spread his arms to the dark womb that held them. "Raven Hunter's black wings make it go away."

He inhaled the scents of the darkness as though they soothed him.

Skimmer finished her first fish and tossed the bones into the lake. An eerie glow expanded in its wake.

She watched it fade before she started on her second fish. "Do you actually see Raven Hunter?"

He smiled and bowed his head. "No one believes me. But, yes, of course I do."

Fascinated, and frightened, she asked, "What does he tell you?"

"Oh, things I'm too stupid to understand. A few days ago, he told me that Wolf Dreamer has touched the Spiral and it's twisting down into nothingness. Like a child's top, winding down."

Hesitantly, he reached over and caressed her hand. The warmth of his skin, the tenderness of his touch, made her turn her palm up so they could twine fingers. He gripped her hand tightly and heaved what sounded like a sigh of relief. Then he closed his eyes as though drowning in the feel of her flesh against his.

"What's wrong?" she asked.

"I . . ." He lifted his gaze and shyly said, "I need to talk with you."

"Then talk."

He gazed at her through dark eyes that glowed with a haunted light. "Do you remember when I brought you the feather?"

"I remember."

"You laughed, but you had tears in your eyes." He hesitantly reached out and touched her hand where it rested in the sand, caressing her fingers. "I asked you why beauty made you cry."

She didn't remember any of this. "What did I say?"

For an instant, his heavily lidded eyes reminded her of deep dark holes. He dropped his gaze to examine the twig of driftwood. "You said that beauty died."

"Why did my words about the feather bother you, Ti-Bish?"

"Because"—his voice sounded pained, unsure—"it has a bearing on our lives, doesn't it? I mean, if you believe that all beauty dies, then you're never happy."

The hollowness in Skimmer's breast seemed to boom. She said nothing.

He pressed. "Why do you think there's so much suffering?"

"You're the holy man. You tell me."

Ripples undulated across the surface like swirls of luminous frost.

"I asked Raven Hunter." He gazed up at her with childlike innocence, but his eyes seemed haunted. "He told me it's the fault of the Sunpath People."

"Our fault? Why?"

He tenderly stroked the long black hair that fell down her back. After the consternation her offer to bed him had caused, she allowed it. "Because you believe in Wolf Dreamer."

"Well, the next time you see Raven Hunter, tell him there is one fewer believer."

"You . . . you've stopped believing in Wolf Dreamer?"

"He's just a story our Ancestors created to entertain children."

Sounds from the lake drifted to them: a fish jumping, water dripping, the deep aching groans of the Ice Giants.

Ti-Bish looked at her through eyes filled with so much sorrow that she felt wounded. "Oh, no, he exists, Skimmer. He's just wicked."

A curiously empty sensation invaded her. "If he exists, I agree with you." *And there's no sense in telling you what I think about Raven Hunter. Not after what I survived in the pen that night.*

Ti-Bish reached around and pulled the basket onto his lap. As he unfolded the hide that had kept the fish warm, he said, "This is for you."

He handed her a beautifully painted bundle.

Skimmer took it and examined the designs. The paintings looked ancient. In many places the colors had flaked off, leaving gaps in the picture, but she could still make out the two men hurling lightning bolts at each other. "Where did you get this? It's very old."

Ti-Bish wet his lips and stammered, "I—I found it. I've never opened it, though, and I don't think you should either. Just . . . keep it. As a gift."

A strange phosphorescent fog formed on the far side of the lake and moved toward them, as though being pushed by Wind Woman's breath.

Ti-Bish said, "Father Sun has risen. He's warming the sea outside."

Skimmer stared at the fog. "Do people come in here in boats?"

"No. You can't see the opening from outside because the Ice Giants have fallen into the water, blocking the way for boats. But I think once, a long time ago, people rowed their canoes in here. I've found skeletons on the shore."

"Skeletons? Of people?"

"People and animals. Some of the monsters are frightening. They're huge, and their bones are rock."

A fluttering like bats overhead sounded, and Skimmer looked up. The ice vault shimmered, but nothing alive flew around up there.

Ti-Bish abruptly got to his feet, picked up his oil lamp, and said, "I have to take you back to your chamber now."

"Why?"

"It's necessary."

Skimmer clutched the bundle as she rose. "I hate the darkness, Ti-Bish. Could you bring me a lamp?"

As he led the way back up the tunnel, he said, "Not yet. Soon, I hope. Raven Hunter says you need the darkness right now."

"Why?"

"To smother the spark of Wolf Dreamer that lives in your soul."

There is no spark of Wolf Dreamer left, Ti-Bish. He is as dead in my heart as Hookmaker is.

As they walked back toward her chamber, the darkness grew heavy, leaden, weighing down her shoulders like a granite cape. The worst part was the fear. . . .

Forty-six

Silvertip sat with his legs dangling over the sharp edge of a boulder that perched high on the slope overlooking Headswift Village. Below him, yet another of the Sunpath camps was packing up their few pitiful possessions. The two warriors who would lead them west were talking to the Elders, pointing at this and that.

They are the lucky ones. But how can I tell them that by having lost everything but their lives, they have gained a future?

Craning his head, he could look out over Thunder Sea. In the distance, across the gray water, the Ice Giants shot their cracked, piled, and tumbled heights into the sky. No human could cross that.

But I flew. He longed for the sensation of wings.

"What a gift, just to have known it."

He could hear the soft whisperings of assent from the Wolf Bundle where he clutched it tightly in his lap.

Wind tugged at his hair, sending cold fingers past his hunting shirt and along his skin. *To feel is to live.*

He heard Ashes as she climbed up and immodestly seated herself beside him. She looked out at the camps, then turned her eyes west, where the faintest rim of Loon Lake could be seen.

"Why do you think I even want to be your wife?"

He smiled, knowing full well that she'd been puzzling over that.

"Because you and I are matched by Power. After what happened to you in the Nightland pen, you have no illusions about this world. After I died and Dreamed the One, I have no illusions about the Spirit World. Both of us were changed, Ashes. We have both lost everything, and gained everything."

She gave him that probing look. "Your family is alive. You have people who still love you."

"You've never Dreamed the One, only to lose it." He closed his eyes, savoring the memory. "I had wings, Ashes. *Wings!*" A tear crept past his cheek.

She was silent, considering that. Finally, she said, "Well, what about Mother? You said you'd seen the future?"

He nodded. "She will come back to you." He paused. "But you won't know her."

"That's silly. Of course I'll know her. She's my mother!"

"She's Raven Hunter's. As I am Wolf Dreamer's."

"But you said that I'm Raven Hunter's, too."

"You are. But he will never own your soul like he does Skimmer's."

"I don't understand."

"She has no balance. You have me, and I have you. I will bring order and peace to your life, while you bring chaos and creativity to mine. Together, we will balance our Power, and lay the seeds for a new world."

"Don't bet on it." Wind teased strands of her black hair across her face. Her eyes were fixed on the distance to the south, where spruce gave way to pine, maple, and oak. "Somewhere out there are warriors who wish nothing more than to kill us."

"But we can Dream a new way."

"Only if you have the darts to back it up." She shrugged. "My father was like you. He thought that if we left the Nightland alone, they'd do the same to us."

"But your mother wanted to kill the Guide."

"Mother dragged Father into that kicking and screaming. Up until the end, he thought he could keep his world the same." She glanced at him. "It doesn't work that way, Silvertip."

"No," he whispered, "it doesn't. And you're right. As much as I dislike the thought, we will have to have warriors who protect what we create. But unlike the Nightland and Sunpath, we can't forget that Power fills the world."

She shifted on the rock. "It must have been a wonderful thing . . . to fly."

"The world looks different from up there." He raised his eyes to the sky, seeing a hawk gliding on the thermals.

"Well, what if I really do love you? Among my people, Dreamers avoid women. In the myths, it was love that killed First Woman. If I slip into your blankets some night while you're Dreaming, are you going to lose your soul in the One like she did?"

He reached out, taking her cool hand in his. "Nothing comes without a price, Ashes. I agreed to that when I came back. To do what I must, I can't Dream the One again. Not like I did."

"Good," she answered simply. "Because I remember how it was between Mother and Father. They thought I was asleep, but they liked coupling." She grinned. "They used to have this look, something special in their eyes before they sneaked off to lie together. I think I'm going to like coupling when I'm finally a woman."

He laughed. "I'll do my best to keep you happy."

"I suppose you've seen it?"

He nodded. "But that's all right, because I already know you've imagined it."

She punched him playfully in the shoulder. "I've imagined a lot." Then she sobered. "But for a while, during that terrible night in the Nightland pen, I thought they were going to kill me."

He searched her eyes, seeing the wounded soul behind them. "Then you know, as few others do, that every moment is a blessing."

Goodeagle sat in the near darkness with his jaw clenched. Scents of wet dirt, human feces, and sweat tainted the air. Kakala and Keresa had been taking turns questioning him for over a hand of time. Keresa's questions confused him the most. She kept asking things about Bramble: How did she wear her hair? Did she tilt her head in a certain way when she smiled? What sort of hand gestures did she use? He felt crazed, on the verge of violence.

As soon as Kakala had crawled through the recently opened tunnel, he'd ordered his warriors, and Goodeagle, to remove and pile all of their weapons in the far corner—out of sight, but within reach. Then he'd told his people to leave. They'd crawled into the adjacent chamber and Goodeagle had heard them guzzling water from water bags, laughing and joking with their friends.

He would have given anything for one sip of their water.

"Why is he leaving us alive down here?" Kakala asked. The side of his head looked terrible: cut, swollen, and scabbed with dried pus.

"I—I don't know, Kakala."

The war chief sat on the floor, looking ill. Blood-matted hair hung in greasy strands around his scarred face.

"You are truly worthless. Windwolf is asking questions about the Nightland Caves, and you haven't any notion of what he might be up to? What's he doing?"

"I *don't* know. Leave me *alone*!" Discussing Windwolf made his stomach cramp. He kept seeing the man's eyes, and he couldn't shake the remnant of old and abiding friendship.

Goodeagle glared up at Kakala and Keresa. Every word he spoke to them made him feel like he was reliving that terrible day at Walking Seal Village when he'd first made the deal with Karigi to betray Windwolf. His stomach cramped again. He bent forward in agony.

Kakala looked at Keresa, then tilted his head toward Goodeagle. She walked lithely forward.

"Goodeagle," she said, "let's lay out what we know. Windwolf has totally reorganized this village. He's ordered the Elders to stay inside and posted guards around them. He's set up a warriors' training school for young boys and girls. Nearly all of the true warriors here, both Lame Bull and Sunpath warriors, seem to be missing. He's kept a few critical people—like War Chief Fish Hawk—but his own green child warriors are currently standing guard on the high points. What's he doing? Is this a ruse to distract us from something else? Is it possible he's already sent warriors to attack the Nightland Caves?"

Goodeagle examined her from head to toe. She'd said "Windwolf" with a hint of softness in her voice.

He ran a hand through his moist black hair and forced himself to respond. "Windwolf would never dispatch a war party to the Nightland Caves unless he was leading it."

"What about the missing warriors?"

"I suspect they're involved in finding food for the refugees." He looked up and smiled gloatingly at Kakala. "You already told me they've looted the dead."

Kakala's nostrils flared. "I would do the same thing. Let me ask you this: Is it possible Windwolf is planning on exchanging us for some of the hostages Karigi is holding? Or perhaps the Sunpath slaves at the Nightland Caves?"

Goodeagle chuckled. "If somebody corners him, he'll try arranging an exchange—your people's freedom for his. If that doesn't work . . . well, you won't have to worry about anything ever again." But then, even if they were exchanged, they only had the cages to look forward to.

He paused. Was Windwolf counting on that?

Kakala's gaze drifted to Keresa. She wandered slowly around the edges of the chamber, grimacing at the walls and floor. Goodeagle's eyes narrowed. He'd watched her go about her duties for moons; he knew her style: brusque and honest. What was this new feminine allure? He shook his head, fighting against the clear similarities between her graceful movements and Bramble's. Did they affect Windwolf in the same way? He felt suddenly numb—the thought like a stiletto driven into his soul.

Perhaps her newfound allure reflected exactly what she knew Windwolf liked? Or was it his direct, if subtle, coaching? *Whose side are you on, beauty?* He had to know, and fast.

"I'm worried," Keresa said. "I think the missing warriors are on their way to the Nightland Caves, and if we don't get out of here to warn our people—"

"Really?" Goodeagle gave a low laugh that made his own blood run cold. "Did Windwolf tell you that? In personal discussions? He's a rare man, isn't he? Gentle, willing to bend over backward to compromise so he doesn't have to hurt you. Yes, I can hear it now, 'Keresa, just help me and I'll guarantee the safety of everyone you love. Help me, Keresa.'"

She seemed to stop breathing. He leaned forward. "And he has a reputation for being an expert beneath the hides. Oh, I'll bet you like that, don't you? Did he promise you riches as well?"

Kakala glanced at his deputy, and Goodeagle could see the lurking doubts surface. Kakala suspected it, too.

In a warning voice, Kakala said, "Goodeagle, if I were you, I wouldn't—"

"You're not me! And this is too amusing. Don't you disapprove of treason, Kakala?" He thrust a hand out at Keresa. "Blessed Ancestors, I've seen this so many times!" he lied, pushing, trying to force her cool confidence to break. He ignored the slight shift of her body, the cold glare she gave him. "Seducing women warriors is a game with Windwolf, he—"

In a graceful dancer's whirl, she kicked out. Her right foot slammed into Goodeagle's shoulder and sent him sprawling. He struggled to his knees, but she kicked him down on his stomach, landed on top of him, and her arm tightened around his windpipe. He gasped for breath.

From the corner of his eye, he could see her smile. "You're dead, Goodeagle."

"Keresa," Kakala said sternly. He tried to pull her off, but her arm just constricted tighter.

"Keresa! Let him go! We're all crazy from the tension. Don't let this—"

"You'll back me, won't you, Kakala? Goodeagle was obviously suffering from a bout of Sunpath conscience. He was trying to escape . . . to go warn Windwolf about our plans."

Kakala hesitated, then nodded. "Make it quick and clean; I don't want any noise."

The cool way Kakala had spoken left Goodeagle reeling. "Wait!" he rasped. "The Nightland Elders promised me sanctuary! Kakala, you can't—"

"No, but I can." Keresa smiled again, speaking to Goodeagle in a caressing voice as she lessened the pressure. "Let's have a final talk, shall we? If I get the right answers, you might even live. Hmm? What do you say?"

He twisted to gaze up into Keresa's icy eyes. "What—what do you want to know?"

"Details. Just minor details of the Walking Seal Village battle." She toyed with him, smoothing her deadly fingers down his neck like a lover's hand. Every muscle in his body went rigid. Kakala looked on as though bored.

May the Spirits curse him! He's a Nightland war chief, and the Council promised me sanctuary!

He blinked at the pressure at his throat. *But that's not why I did it. No. No!*

"For example," Keresa said in a silken voice. "We had Walking Seal Village surrounded. When Windwolf's warriors ambushed us, it was a terrible battle. But in the midst of all the killing, he ran straight for the ceremonial lodge—abandoning his warriors. Why?"

Goodeagle's breathing came in shallow gasps now; sweat stung his eyes. If he could get to his knees, he might be able to take her. He considered it. No, no, even if he managed to take Keresa, Kakala would probably kill him out of some bizarre sense of loyalty to his deputy. "To rescue Bramble."

"I don't believe that. He's too good a war chief to endanger his warriors simply out of—"

"You're a fool, Keresa." Goodeagle shook his head, chuckling hysterically. Maybe he could talk his way out. "I'd have thought you'd know this by now! Windwolf has some fundamental flaws. He's a cool calculating war chief only up to a point. He can recover from any surprise, but if he takes a blow to the heart, he stumbles. He *loved* her!"

"Let's discuss Bramble. Try to imagine, Goodeagle; try to see what her last discussion with Windwolf must have been like. He let her go into a situation where he knew she might die."

He shook his head. "I—I never really liked her. I don't—"

Her arm pressed coolly into his windpipe. He swallowed convulsively, belly threatening to empty itself. "He . . . He probably said something about how dangerous it was. And . . . And she told him he was too valuable to risk . . . that she was the right choice."

Keresa asked, "Would she have discussed you? Women tend to be more perceptive about people than men. She had suspicions you weren't the loyal friend Windwolf thought, didn't she?"

"Bramble and I never got along. She was always so fanatically dedicated to Windwolf that it sickened me. I couldn't even have a decent argument with him without her tongue—"

"But he *let* her take the risk?"

"You didn't know Bramble like I did."

"And how was that?"

"She was strong-willed like a man. How he could love a woman like that . . ."

Keresa released him and stood. She glared down, disgust and hatred marring her normally striking face. Her full lips pursed as though she wanted to spit on him. "I've heard enough."

Kakala nodded. "Go. I need to question him for a time longer."

She briskly strode away.

Goodeagle collapsed to the floor, gasping for breath and rubbing his throat. "Kakala, if you push Windwolf, he'll head straight for the Nightland Elders. None of them will be alive when he leaves."

"And how will he accomplish that feat of magic? Did the two of you ever plan such an attack?"

"Yes. Many times, and in great detail." Goodeagle rolled to his stomach and wiped sweat from his eyes, trying to catch his breath. "But before I tell you, I need water. Bring me some water!"

A few heartbeats later, a water bag sailed through the tunnel and thudded on the floor.

Forty-seven

Nashat rolled his hips, enjoying the pressure of Blue Wing's pubis against his. The woman had her long legs wrapped around his buttocks as he had instructed the first night he'd taken her. Some deep-seated comfort filled his chest, augmented by the sensations of his shaft moving inside her. He liked full-breasted women, and pressed his chest into hers.

When the tingle began in his loins, he stiffened, eyes closed. As waves of pleasure spasmed, he gasped, "Gods, yes, Keresa, yes!"

He lay spent, then lifted himself on an arm, looking down at the woman.

"I am Keresa again?" she asked emotionlessly.

"It's an expression among my people." He rolled off her, then watched as she stood, wiped herself, and listlessly pulled a dress over her head. He watched her breath fogging in the cold, wondering if it reflected the disgust in her soul, and added, "I would take it as most inappropriate if I heard that you made mention of such things among the slave women." He smiled. "And I will know."

She nodded, the defeated expression on her lovely face sharpening.

"Oh, come, Blue Wing. At least you're fed . . . and alive."

"Is that what I am?"

"Would you rather have remained in the pen with the others? I hear the wolves have even taken the bones."

She gave him a dull look, as if she didn't really know.

And to think the Guide just told her to go home?

He dressed as she ducked out through the hanging. He shivered, stepping over to the woodpile and tossing three pieces onto the coals. Would he never be warm again? Glancing at the pile, he noticed how low it was. What were the slaves doing on their half-moon-long trips down to the forests and back to keep him supplied?

He heard someone clear his throat beyond the hanging. "Yes?"

"The warriors you requested are here, Councilor."

Nashat straightened his long war shirt, hung a string of shell beads with an intricately carved ivory pendant about his neck, and slicked his hair back. "Enter."

He watched as a nervous Kishkat and Tapa stepped in, wary eyes taking in his opulent surroundings. Neither one seemed to have any idea what to do with his hands.

"Ah, Kishkat, Tapa, how nice of you to accept my summons."

"Thank you, Councilor," Kishkat said, trying to mask the deep-seated fear behind his too-quick movements.

Nashat stood, fingering his chin, letting them stew as he gave them a half-lidded glare.

The pressure got to them. Kishkat stammered, "C-Can we help you, Councilor?"

"Imagine my surprise when I learned just recently that you were at home with your wives and families instead of on the war trail with Kakala."

Tapa looked like a trapped hare. "Is . . . is that a problem, Councilor?"

"Why don't you tell me?" he asked pleasantly.

Kishkat spread his arms. "We brought the woman, Skimmer! Under . . . under War Chief Kakala's orders." He swallowed too hard.

"Skimmer is dead."

"Oh, no, Councilor," Tapa protested. "We . . . we found her just outside Headswift Village. On . . . on the trail." He looked pleadingly at Kishkat. "Isn't that right?"

Kishkat took a breath. "Yes, Councilor. Kakala, in accordance with the Guide's orders, sent us here with the woman."

"With a dead woman."

"But she's not *dead*!" Kishkat insisted. "We delivered her to the Guide! Go ask him."

Nashat narrowed an eye. "Just where did you do this?"

"Beyond the caves!" Kishkat swallowed hard. "He was waiting for us in the dark. Skimmer told us he wished to see her. And we brought her. He took the woman and told us that we should go home, and that we'd be rewarded."

"We just did what the Guide said, Councilor." Tapa's voice sounded like something squeezed out from under a rock.

Skimmer is alive? He frowned, taking a couple of paces before the fire. Shooting a glance at the warriors, he could tell that that much was true.

"Why didn't you come to tell me this?"

Kishkat spread helpless arms. "We . . . we serve the Guide."

"We *all* serve the Guide," Nashat snapped. "At least in our own way." He took a deep breath, the tension he'd shed lying with Blue Wing rebuilt in his chest. "Where is the woman now?"

The two warriors glanced at each other and shrugged. Kishkat said, "Wherever the Guide took her, Councilor."

Skimmer has been with Ti-Bish for several days? And I've heard no word of it? By Raven Hunter's breath, is the Idiot still alive?

"And what of Kakala? I have heard no word."

Kishkat took a deep breath. "I can honestly say that I have no idea what has happened to the war chief."

Nashat gave him a nasty smile. "Then tell me dishonestly."

Kishkat blinked. "What?"

"What was he doing when you saw him last?"

Tapa had sweat beading on his brow. "P-Preparing to attack Headswift Village."

"Did you know that Skimmer was plotting to murder the Guide?"

Both warriors looked stunned.

Kishkat shook his head. "They talked like friends. Nor did Skimmer say anything unkind about the Guide during the days we were on the trail with her."

Nashat could feel a headache coming on. "Go. Get out of here. And if the Guide is harmed in any way, you will bear the blame."

They bolted headlong from the chamber.

He reached for his cloak, calling, "Guard! Prepare me a lamp."

Of all things, he hated climbing down into the dark ice tunnels like some sort of misbegotten rat.

Ti-Bish, you idiot, if you are dead through this foolishness, it is going to really complicate my life.

War Chief Fish Hawk called, "Windwolf? Are you awake?"

Windwolf blinked, yawned, and tried to shed fragments of his Dream. In it, Bramble and Keresa kept merging together: sometimes one, sometimes the other. An odd mixing of grief and hope left him muddled as he stared around his stone-lined chamber.

He wearily threw off his hides and rose to his feet. As he reached for his buffalo coat and slipped it on, he called, "I'm awake, Fish Hawk. What is it?"

"Deputy Keresa wishes to speak with you."

He frowned. Why would she request a meeting at this time of night? He blinked at the firelight that flickered over the stone walls. How long had he been asleep? If the fire was still burning, not long. "Is she with you?'

"Yes. She told me it was urgent."

"Let her enter, Fish Hawk."

The curtain was drawn back, and she ducked under it. Her red doehide war shirt looked faintly orange in the dim glow of the fire. She wore her long hair loose about her shoulders. The style made her seem more frail—an illusion he dared not fall prey to.

He gestured to one of the hides on the other side of the fire. "Sit. May I get you a cup of tea?"

"Yes, thank you."

"What may I do for you?"

"You may set me and my warriors free."

"Try as I might, I can't quite talk myself into believing that's a good idea." He paused. "Assuming, that is, that they wish to continue attacks on my people."

She walked over and stood beside him as he dipped the cup. He gave her a sidelong look. In the fire's gleam, her tightly clenched fists shone starkly white. He examined her more closely. She was fighting to keep her breathing even, but it wasn't working. His brows lowered.

Either the stakes were uncommonly high—or she wasn't particularly practiced at this. Maybe both. Was she covering for someone? Kakala? A moment of panic set his heart to racing.

He stood and handed her the cup, noting with interest how long she allowed their fingers to touch before taking it. The touch sent a small tingle through him; just as she'd intended. Interesting.

"Did you decide not to sit down?" he asked.

"I think I'll stand."

He eyed her speculatively as he sipped his tea. "What can I help you with?"

"The tension among my people is growing. Fights are breaking out over nothing. Just moments ago one warrior was very tempted to choke another to death."

He lifted an eyebrow. "And *I* should think that's a bad idea?"

"Nevertheless—"

"I suppose I could climb down and give them a lecture on the intricacy of good manners while awaiting the inevitable."

"I think . . ." She paused. "That might make things worse."

He nodded amiably. "What do you suggest we do about it?"

She gave him an uncertain glance. Were his suspicions that plain? Or was she just uncomfortable with the role of trickster? Lifting her cup, she finished it to the last drop, and handed it to him for a refill.

He dipped another for her. "Is this discussion difficult for you?"

"Not yet."

"Do you expect it to be?"

"I don't know."

"Really? I'm disappointed."

"Disappointed?" She gave him an irritated look that he thought completely charming.

"You're a warrior. You should have had your strategy worked out before you came in."

She fixed him with a penetrating but uneasy stare. "What do you mean?"

He shook his head and tossed more branches onto the fire, stalling; giving her time to stew.

Silence stretched; she started to fidget.

He relented. "Tell me something? How distracted am I supposed to be? Enough to forget myself completely?" He brazenly looked her up and down. "I hope you're not counting on my sense of honor."

"I've already heard about your honor when it comes to women." Her cheeks turned a rosy hue. She exhaled haltingly and ran a nervous hand through her hair.

My honor when it comes to women? He smiled. *Goodeagle, working his poison!*

"I think you are one of the most attractive and capable women I have ever known, Keresa, but don't count on me losing my senses just because I find you fascinating."

"Counting on you in any manner seems risky."

He scrutinized her unmercifully. She stood quietly, staring into her tea cup, as though vaguely embarrassed.

"Do you wish to tell me what we're really discussing?"

"Not particularly."

"Then why don't you let me start?" He took three steps to stand directly in front of her. "Let's discuss how Kakala is plotting to escape."

"We've tried. It's impossible. We can't—"

"No good war chief ever gives up. And my old adversary is a very good war chief."

She opened her mouth to say something, then thought better of it. He took the opportunity to refill his cup. As he straightened again, he ordered, "Sit down, Deputy. It's not working."

She stood defiantly for a moment, then knelt across the fire, eyes sharp as if to see into his soul. "If it's not working, why don't you throw me out?"

He grinned. "I like you."

"Is that supposed to ease my tension?"

"Not particularly." Toying with his tea, he asked, "So Kakala's finally decided he needs Goodeagle's knowledge?"

"Goodeagle's dead. You said it yourself."

"Goodeagle knows the rules too well to be dead. Surely he'll fill you in on all of my plans. It's in his interest to get out and as far away from me as he can get."

She let out a frustrated breath. "I don't understand you, Windwolf. Why are you just sitting here? Goodeagle—assuming he's alive—can *hurt* you."

A small thread of warm emotion tinged that last. He noted her flushed cheeks, the anxious movements of her hands around her cup. She was good.

"Maybe I'm foolish enough to believe in old friendships."

"You're going to let him work his poison? Just like he did at Walking Seal Village?"

His control crumbled. She'd done that deliberately, taking charge of the conversation.

"Careful," he advised. "Be very careful. What are you getting at?"

He saw the change in her eyes, as though she'd come to a difficult decision. When she lifted her head, her tanned skin gleamed in the firelight. "At Walking Seal Village, you knew he was off plotting behind your back, didn't you? Surely someone tried to tell you that your best friend—"

"Bramble tried to tell me. Didn't matter. I trusted him."

"Like now? If you lose this gamble, they'll *kill* you!"

His gaze drifted slowly from his cup to her piercing eyes.

Blessed gods, does she know what I'm doing?

She was a shrewd warrior. Had he misread her motives? The possibility struck him like a blow to the belly. "What are you trying to say?"

She rubbed both hands over her delicate face as though in disbelief. "Nothing, I—I've lost my wits."

"Are . . . are you trying to help me, Deputy?"

She stared down at her hands, slowly shaking her head. "I don't know what I'm doing. I don't know what you're doing. If you think that because you and Goodeagle were friends once . . . well, don't! There is no redemption. Not in his worthless soul."

She looked suddenly weary, weary beyond exhaustion. After peering interminably at the floor, she lifted her right hand—her throwing hand—and opened the palm to the soft light. A somber expression came over her face. She stared at it, then slowly closed it to a tight fist and shook it at some inner foe. He understood that gesture better than any of her spoken words. Tens of times in battles, he'd cursed fate with that same soundless ferocity.

She said, "I hated you for summers. You killed so many of my friends."

A familiar ache swelled in his chest. He stared at the fire, letting her finish.

"But as I watched what you did, I came to grudgingly admire you. You were so perfect. Every move was clean, precise, no emotion."

"That's how it looked from the outside?"

"Yes, and I suggest you continue the practice. You're in an impossible situation. What are you going to do? Nashat may already know what's happened here. He will combine Karigi's and Blackta's war parties, and together they will overrun these caves." She thrust her arm out. "All of those faithful camps out there are going to be destroyed, the people murdered. And you're just sitting here like . . ."

She closed her eyes, a look of defeat on her face.

"Then, what would you suggest?"

"If you wish to stop these attacks, you have to do it at the source: our Elders. But you'll have tens of warriors waiting for you at the Nightland Caves. You can't—"

"Maybe I can."

"Windwolf, think! No matter how well these children fight, they'll never be good enough to match Nightland warriors. And you sent all of the other warriors away, didn't you? All of the adults? So they're waiting, expecting orders to attack the Nightland Caves. But what if Karigi locates them in the meantime?"

He blinked at the question. "Shall I tell you all the details of my plan?"

She met his gaze with a severity that stopped him short. "I'll know soon enough. Your best friend, Goodeagle—if he's alive—will undoubtedly tell Kakala exactly what he expects you to do. And here you are—"

"Being *far* too honest with a woman I like far too much."

Their gazes held, and he noticed how hers softened. He shook his head sternly. "You should go. Otherwise we'll both make fools of ourselves."

"Don't hate me for asking about your strategy. I figured you needed help."

He chuckled softly, unsure now if she really cared, or if they were still sparring for advantage. "As a matter of fact, I do. Tell me how Kakala plans to escape."

His heart pounded at the look on her face. She paused almost as if she wanted to. A ploy? It was a good one. He would do anything to help her step across that silken bridge of loyalty to his side.

Her voice was little more than a whisper. "Were I to stay with you, help you, would there be a way that Kakala and my warriors could leave in peace?"

"Could they promise me that none of them would ever lift a weapon against my people again?" His heart began to pound. Was this the way?

"I don't . . ." She shook her head. "They fear the Council too much. Doing that would mean a worse punishment than the cages."

"Keresa, just tell me . . ."

She shook her head miserably. "You're right. I have to leave."

She rose and walked toward the door, a defeated slump in her shoulders.

"Keresa?" He saw her turn, eyes moist. "There has to be a way out of this. Help stop the killing. Some way, any way, that turns good people like you, me, and Kakala back from being the monsters we've become."

He stepped toward her, taking her hand in his. He rubbed his fingers over the smooth skin, his desperate gaze boring into hers. "If we follow the same old path, there will be nothing left for any of us."

She pulled hard against his grip. He refused to let go. They stood eye to eye for ten heartbeats, and he could feel her pulse increasing until it raced as rapidly as his own.

He reached up with his other hand, gently running it down her long hair. What had she done to him? How had she worked her way into his heart?

Her lips parted, eyes widening. The telltale pulse in her neck was throbbing. Abruptly she seemed to melt against him, her body conforming to the hollows of his. She tightened her hold, as though he were the last thing she had left to cling to. A surge of warmth flooded Windwolf's veins.

In the back of his mind a voice whispered: *A game. This is all a game. We'll both use whatever leverage we can . . . but what harm is there in soothing each other for a few moments? What harm . . . ?*

He slowly disengaged himself and backed away. She was watching him, tears rimming her large dark eyes. Her breasts rose and fell with each rapid breath.

"Keresa," he said in a strained voice, "tell Kakala that Goodeagle's right about one thing: If I can't find a way out of this, I won't leave anything alive in the Nightland Caves."

She hesitated for an excruciating amount of time.

"Windwolf, if I . . ."

He balled his fists. "I need you, Keresa."

Without a word she ducked beneath the door curtain and disappeared. He caught a glimpse of Fish Hawk's curious face before the curtain fell closed again.

Keresa walked down the trail with Fish Hawk at her heels. The warrior followed a good pace behind her.

The sensation of Windwolf's strong arms around her had stirred feelings that terrified her.

Too deep, she'd gotten in too deep. How had that happened? How had she let it happen?

The game was going awry. . . .

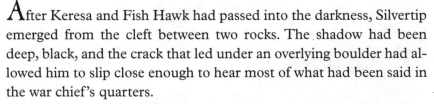

After Keresa and Fish Hawk had passed into the darkness, Silvertip emerged from the cleft between two rocks. The shadow had been deep, black, and the crack that led under an overlying boulder had allowed him to slip close enough to hear most of what had been said in the war chief's quarters.

Now he cradled the Wolf Bundle, and stared after the dark forms. "We all have our parts to play. I hope that you have bargained well, Wolf Dreamer. If we all Dreamed the future, would any of us find the will to live?"

He ducked back into the shadows as Windwolf emerged to stalk down the trail like a man with a purpose.

As the man's footsteps faded Silvertip looked up into the night sky. He could hear Raven wings gliding through the dark air overhead.

Forty-eight

Kakala slept soundly, dreaming of the pleasant lazy days of his youth. . . .

The sweet pungent scent of tundra blossoms drifted on the warm wind. Hako was stretched out at his side beneath a huge boulder. From their vantage overlooking the Thunder Sea, they could hear the soft singing of the Ice Giants. Gulls flew overhead screaming. Pilot whales, six of them, were coursing among the bergs just off shore. A warm southern breeze was blowing across the land, driving the black flies to cover. The rock's soft shadow smoothed Hako's triangular face, and jet black hair hung like a cape around her shoulders. She gave him a reproachful look.

"Kakala, you're the best warrior in the village. You can throw a dart farther than anyone else . . . swing a war club harder. But when it comes to finding your way back from Little Lake, you get lost."

He chuckled in amusement. "I'm only good at useless accomplishments. Killing people and—"

"Someday, when you're the high war chief, you're going to regret that your deputy has to lead every war party."

"Then I'd better pick you as my deputy. You can always find your way. I don't understand it."

Her laughter reminded him of warm winds through autumn-brittle leaves. He cherished it, engraving it in his memory to hear again and again. When he thought he could bear no more of the horrors of war, or the futility of command, recalling her laughter soothed him.

Somewhere, down deep in his soul, scenes of her death struggled to rise, flitting like butterfly wings through the Dream. Desperate to avoid them, he looked into her mischievous eyes.

"Hako," he said. "I love you. I wish we could—"

Faintly, he heard the boulder above him being rolled away. Hako's face began to fade. He fought against it, not wanting to wake up. The ladder thudded as it struck the floor, and all around him warriors leaped to their feet cursing.

Kakala rolled to his back and grimaced at everything in the chamber: the warriors backed against the walls; silver streaks of moonlight painted the floor; the hated ladder was like a lance through the heart of his domain.

He noted Keresa's strained expression as she dropped to the floor. He knew that stiff posture, and the thunder reflected on her lined brow. Something had her terribly upset.

His spine went stiff when a deep voice called from above, "Kakala? It's Windwolf."

Kakala pulled himself to his feet. "What do you want?"

Windwolf stepped into the gap and looked down. Behind him, Sister Moon's face gleamed, giving the air a silver sheen.

From the corner of Kakala's eye, he saw Keresa hug herself.

Windwolf coldly said, "I need to speak with you, War Chief."

"I have nothing to say."

They held each other's gaze like two bull mammoths during the rut. Windwolf yielded first, shifting his attention to one of the warriors who stood guard. Windwolf said something that Kakala couldn't hear, but he understood when two armed warriors climbed down the ladder. Six others stood over the opening with their darts aimed down.

The tall warrior said, "Climb up. Now."

Kakala looked at his own warriors. None of them seemed to be breathing.

Keresa said, "Just go, Kakala. Find out what he wants."

Kakala muttered a curse and climbed. When he stepped onto the boulders, two men took particular pleasure in searching him.

Windwolf said, "Tie his hands."

One of the warriors pulled out a twisted hide rope and tied Kakala's hands in front of him.

"Do you see that flat boulder up the slope?" Windwolf pointed.

Kakala turned to look. It was perhaps three body lengths long and two wide. "I can see it just fine, thank you."

"Walk toward it."

Is it my time to die?

He smiled grimly. For days, he'd been trying to figure out why he was still alive—now he wished he'd enjoyed them more.

When he reached the flat rock, Windwolf ordered, "Sit down."

Four warriors surrounded him, taking up positions eight body lengths away—which he found interesting. Windwolf must have told them he wanted privacy. Another warrior placed a basket on the rock, then trotted back toward the village.

Kakala took a moment to appreciate the stunning view. To the north, the peaks of the Ice Giants glowed in the moonlight as though lit from within. Thunder Sea looked liquid silver. A fringe of dark spruce trees rimmed his high perch, resembling a buffalo's beard curving beneath a pristine stone face.

"If I have to tell you to sit down again, you'll be standing up for the rest of the night," Windwolf said.

Kakala eased down onto the rock. In the moonlight, Windwolf looked haggard, his eyes red-rimmed from lack of sleep, but he wore a clean blue war shirt, painted with red buffalo, and he'd bathed recently. His short black hair shone.

For that alone, Kakala detested him.

He'd actually been dreaming of taking baths in rivers, pools, waterfalls, even the icy Thunder Sea. Anywhere to wash away the blood, grime, and stink that clung to his body.

Windwolf spread his legs; the weapons clattered on his belt. "That basket contains food and water. The Healer, Flathead, said you needed to eat."

Kakala studied the basket, and his mouth started to water. For two days, he'd felt like his navel had melted into his spine.

He held up his bound hands. "How am I supposed to eat with my hands tied?"

"A clever man like you? I'm sure you'll discover a way."

Kakala slid over, grabbed the basket, and brought it back to his lap. As he unfolded the hide inside, the smell of roasted arctic hare rose. He pulled it out, delighted with an entire rabbit roasted on a skewer.

He lifted it to take a big bite, but stopped, letting the hare hover right in front of his teeth. By Raven Hunter's breath, that would be a cruel twist, wouldn't it?

"Oh, I see," Windwolf said irritably. He walked up, pulled off a strip of meat, and ate it. "Feel better?"

"I will in another six tens of heartbeats. I'm sure you'd only use the best poison."

"Of course I would. Why would I want you to suffer for days? After everything you've done for my people, I'd want your death to be quick and painless, wouldn't I?"

The irony in his voice made Kakala's skin creep. "Your cunning in war is legendary. Your sense of humor needs work."

Kakala took a big bite of the juicy white meat and swallowed it whole, barely chewing. Then he attacked the carcass.

Windwolf squared his shoulders, standing rigid as a wooden statue.

With a greasy hand, Kakala gestured to the far side of the flat rock. "Why don't you sit down? You look like you need to."

Windwolf just stared at him.

While Kakala ate, Windwolf meandered around the boulders, glancing frequently back to make sure Kakala still sat eating his hare. The night breeze was sharp with the scent of spruce needles.

Kakala asked, "Have you already sent warriors to the Nightland Caves?"

"No."

Kakala laughed condescendingly. "You should run there right now and throw yourself at the feet of the Guide to beg for mercy. If you surrender, he might spare your life."

"And after two botched attacks on Headswift Village, maybe Nashat would show the same leniency to you. Why don't we go together?" He paused. "Or we could ask Karigi what punishment he would prefer."

At the thought of Karigi—and the disaster at Walking Seal Village—Kakala's belly soured. He took another bite, but it didn't taste nearly as good.

Windwolf wandered to the far side of the flat rock, and his gaze settled on Kakala's cape, the red war shirt visible through the open front. A strange expression tensed his face. He pointed to the painted sash that belted Kakala's waist. "That's from the Star Tree band, isn't it? It looks like their painting style."

Kakala took another big bite of his hare and, as he chewed, looked down at his sash. "The Star Tree painters were some of the best anywhere. I always appreciated their work."

Windwolf studied the sash. "Just when did you develop this appreciation? Before or after you killed every living thing in Star Tree Village?"

A chilling tingle filled Kakala's breast, like icy ants crawling around inside him. "Insults between us are useless at this point, Windwolf. Why did you wish to speak with me?"

Windwolf inhaled a deep breath, as though preparing himself for a lengthy conversation. "Your warriors are holding up better than I'd have thought. You trained them well."

Kakala wiped his mouth on his sleeve and eyed Windwolf speculatively. The compliment sounded honest—a gesture from one war chief to another. It made him even more uneasy. "Keresa kept them together while I was ill. She deserves the credit."

"We could all wish for so talented a deputy."

Kakala gently rested the hare bones on the rock beside him. A curious light gleamed in Windwolf's eyes at the mention of Keresa's name. Kakala noted it, then pulled out the gut water bag that rested in the basket and took a long drink.

"Come and sit down, Windwolf. You make me nervous pacing around."

He continued standing. "How are you feeling?"

"Concerned about your skill with a war club?"

"A bit. You should be dead."

"I've had a great deal of practice fighting with you. It's made me fast on my feet."

Windwolf actually chuckled. "Me, too."

"Flathead is a good Healer. I'm doing better. How are your refugees?"

For several painfully quiet moments, Windwolf bowed his head. "Several are dying. Some with agonizing slowness. Others too swiftly for their families to mourn. Why do you care? Worried about your skill with an atlatl?"

From some crack in Kakala's soul, hysterical voices rose, pleading with him not to kill them. "I've never liked attacking defenseless people."

"No? You've certainly done it often enough. When did you decide you didn't like it? Somewhere between ten children and ten tens? Perhaps it was the women who bothered you? Not enough of them to rape and mutilate?"

"Let me know when it's my turn. I have a few things I'd like to tell you, too."

"Yes, I'm sure you do."

Windwolf walked back and forth in front of the rock with his brow furrowed. "You've never enjoyed murdering my people, or trying to take our lands? I'm glad to hear it. Perhaps you wouldn't mind, then, telling me what other orders you've received lately regarding Sunpath bands?"

Kakala laughed incredulously. "You're bold."

With unsettling silence, Windwolf walked over and seated himself. He stared hard into Kakala's eyes. "Let's discuss your last couple of days in the cage."

Kakala barely moved. "Why?"

"I assume it's bothering you."

His gut tried to tie itself in knots. "And?"

"I'd rather it didn't."

Kakala stared his disbelief. "Why would *you* care?"

"How can I keep that from happening to you and your warriors?"

Kakala shook his head as though he hadn't heard right. This had to be some ploy to gain leverage. "What's this? Don't tell me you've started to believe the rumors circulating among broken Sunpath refugees that you're the promised Dreamer sent to save the world from the coming cataclysm?"

"If I let you go, Elder Nashat will certainly order you captured and hauled off to cages—"

"Not . . . ! Not . . . certainly." Blood had started to surge deafeningly in his ears. "Why are we discussing this?"

Windwolf's face fell into stiff lines. "Because I thought if we could solve that problem you would be able to make decisions more clearly."

"Which decisions did you have in mind?"

Windwolf looked up without moving a muscle. "Decisions regarding the Sunpath People and the Lame Bull People."

"You think *I* have any influence on that?"

They stared unforgivingly at each other for a time, each silently trying to guess the other's strategy.

In cynical amusement, Kakala asked, "Why don't you just tell me what you're offering? If I betray my people, you will . . . what?"

Windwolf bowed his head and stared at the smooth surface of the rock. In a curious voice, he asked, "After the attack on the Sprucebell band, why did you send runners to the neighboring Sunpath villages telling them to expect survivors? I've heard you did the same thing at other places."

Kakala frowned. The man changed subjects as quickly as a cougar could its charge. Was it designed to fluster him? He studied Windwolf's bland expression.

In a mockingly conspiratorial voice, he said, "Perhaps *I'm* the promised Dreamer who's going to save the world."

Windwolf stiffened. "Let me know when you decide to talk to me as one leader to another." Then the man rose, turned his back on Kakala, and walked away. Over his shoulder, he said, "Get some sleep, War Chief."

The guards trotted forward. Kakala took another long drink from the water bag before he rose unsteadily to his feet.

"Walk," the tall warrior ordered.

Distress

*M*y slave girl, Pipe, is dead. That beautiful little girl torn to shreds by some mad Spirit. I found pieces of her scattered through the lower tunnels. I buried her head at the fiery lake. My heart aches so much that I can barely force myself to keep going. Raven Hunter says it's Wolf Dreamer's work.

I don't believe it.

I told him yesterday that she loved Wolf Dreamer and didn't wish to return to the Long Dark—that she had vowed to serve me well until the time came for us to go, then she begged me to let her return to her own Sunpath band.

Ancestors, forgive me. I didn't know how insanely desperate he has become.

Now I fear he'll do anything to keep me believing.

Forty-nine

Sunrise remained hidden behind the high ridge to the east, but a luminous halo arced over the horizon and turned the bellies of the drifting Cloud People a glittering gold.

"Very well, let's begin," War Chief Fish Hawk said, and started swinging his war club. He'd twisted his black hair into a bun at the nape of his neck and wore a tattered deerhide shirt that reached to his knees. From his cord belt a variety of weapons hung: a stiletto, atlatl, and shining black chert knife. "First, a warrior must loosen his shoulder muscles."

Silvertip followed Fish Hawk's moves, swinging his club back and forth with his right hand, then switching it to his left hand. Two tens of boys and girls, including Ashes, circled Fish Hawk, all swinging their clubs.

As he swung it upward in an arc, Silvertip studied his club. It had belonged to his dead father. Beautifully crafted from hickory, the shaft, as long as his arm, had been carefully thinned and polished. The warhead was fashioned from a splinter of mammoth's tusk, the ivory ground to a sharp point, then grooved and attached to the hickory shaft with green sinew. As the sinew dried, it had shrunk, binding the tusk and wood together. Immediately below the warhead, his father had embedded a large finely flaked quartzite spike. It glinted as he swung the club up and around, now making circular motions.

From the corner of his eye, Silvertip glimpsed Windwolf. The war chief sat near a fire at the edge of the Sunpath lodges, talking with two men. New lodges filled the forest. More Sunpath people had trickled into the village last night. Many were wounded. Their cries rode the cold morning breeze.

Ashes leaned sideways and whispered, "Who is Windwolf talking with?"

"Just before I ran down here to practice, Grandfather told me his name. He's Chief Sacred Feathers."

"What band is he from?"

"Moon Rock. I don't know where their territory is."

Ashes said, "It's far to the west, on the border between Sunpath and Southwind lands. Was it attacked?"

Silvertip nodded. "Karigi."

In the middle of the circle, Fish Hawk perched on the balls of his feet and began weaving and feinting, leaping from foot to foot, shifting his club from hand to hand, twirling it faster and faster. Silvertip tried to do it, as did the other children, but no one was having much luck. In one final leap, Fish Hawk launched himself into the air and landed in a crouch. His club flashed down to within a hair's breadth of the ground.

As he rose, Fish Hawk said, "I don't expect you to be able to do that today, but keep practicing. You must train your muscles before you'll be able to control the club."

Silvertip balanced on the balls of his feet, as Fish Hawk had done, and listened to his club whir as he spun it from one hand to the other, then pirouetted and slashed down.

The other children made surprised sounds, and pointed at him. Fish Hawk grinned. "Very good, Silvertip. If you keep that up, you will master the club before you become a man."

Silvertip smiled and ducked his head at the praise. Next summer he would have been initiated in the Men's Lodge. A summer that would never come.

Fish Hawk called, "I'll return shortly. In the meantime, continue practicing."

Ashes walked closer to Silvertip and asked, "Can you teach me to do that?"

He nodded. "It's easy. I'll do it slowly. See if you can follow."

She concentrated on his movements, trying to duplicate them.

"That was good, Ashes. Now, you just have to do it faster."

Silvertip spun his club again, pirouetted, and landed in a crouch while he slashed down with his club.

Ashes did it, but lost her balance at the last instant and fell over. She laughed and said, "I need a lot more practice than you do."

"You will do it. Better than I. You will make it like graceful Dance, swift like a striking falcon, but balanced, like a cougar that leaps and lands with total control."

She gave him that sober look. "Sometimes, when you talk like that, it sends shivers down my spine." She glanced warily around. "Why haven't you told anyone about your Vision?"

He straightened, and his gaze drifted again to where Windwolf sat talking with the two men. "When they are ready."

Ashes gave him an askance look, rose to her feet, and watched Windwolf for a time before she whispered, "You cried a lot last night."

He bit his lip, and to hide it, began twirling his club. "It's the only time I can weep for the people."

She watched his club for a time, then said, "This is really going to happen, isn't it?"

Silvertip let his club swing to a stop and propped it over his shoulder. Throughout the night, the Ancestors had slipped through the walls and walked around his bed as though he didn't exist. As the ghosts murmured to each other, he'd heard other things: mammoths trumpeting; giant buffalo roaring like lions, the way they did in the rut; and a young man talking. He thought it was Wolf Dreamer's voice, but wasn't sure.

He said, "It will happen. Just as I said. Before I came to bed, I watched part of the future unfold. Just like Wolf Dreamer showed me. Windwolf met Keresa, and then he went to speak to Kakala."

She cocked her head. "Why?"

Silvertip exhaled hard, and his breath condensed into a frosty cloud. "They are struggling over the future."

As Father Sun rose higher into the morning sky, more and more people came out of their lodges. The aroma of breakfast cooking carried on the cold breeze.

The other children drifted farther away, meandering down the slope as they practiced with their clubs, until Silvertip and Ashes stood alone.

Ashes reached up to touch her earlobe, and Silvertip's eyes went wide. As she rubbed it, she flinched, and he could see that she'd cut off the bottom of her lobe. A person did that as an offering to the Spirit World. Usually it was done for success in Trading, or in hopes of curing a sick relative, but often people made the offering in mourning.

He gestured to her ear. "Did you do that for your father?"

"No." Ashes pulled her hand down, frowned, and looked away. "For Mother. You said she would never be the woman I knew. If I admit that now, it won't hurt as much later."

Though she tried to blink them away before he could see, tears filled her eyes.

Silvertip gently said, "I have already come to love that practical way of yours."

She wiped her eyes on her sleeve and gazed down the hill at Windwolf. As he listened to the Elders, the muscles in his massive shoulders corded and rippled beneath his cape. "They must be saying terrible things. Do you think the raiding is going to get worse?"

Silvertip lifted a shoulder. "Karigi and Blackta are soulless."

To the north a dire wolf barked, then howled. The deep-throated sound echoed through the forests. Moments later another answered. Silvertip listened to them.

"It's almost time now."

He had no sooner spoken, than a scream rent the air. He turned, having seen it, just this way. Bear Boy lay sprawled, his war club off to one side. Little Crow stared in horror, first at Bear Boy, and then at his club. He dropped the weapon, crying, "I didn't mean it!"

Windwolf was on his feet, sprinting. The children that had gathered made way for him, watching as he lifted the boy, staring grimly at the side of his head.

"Help me," Silvertip said as he started forward. "Keep them from interfering." He stopped only long enough to retrieve the Wolf Bundle from where it lay on his coat. Then, Ashes, behind him, he walked up to the crowd, calling, "War Chief? I can help."

Windwolf looked up at him, Bear Boy's head still cradled on his lap. "I don't think so, Silvertip. I've seen head wounds before. He's not breathing, and the heart isn't beating."

Silvertip crouched, staring into Windwolf's eyes. "You have asked many people for their trust in the last couple of moons, War Chief. Now I will ask for yours."

"Silvertip, this isn't a game. Let me call the Healer."

"I am here," he said simply. "Please, lower him gently. Someone, bring a wolf hide to lay his head on. His spirit is still close. There is time to call it back."

One of the girls hesitantly pulled her wolfhide coat over her head, extending it, then wrapped her arms over her bare chest against the cold.

Silvertip met Windwolf's piercing gaze with his own, then watched the war chief lower Bear Boy, carefully resting his head on the folds of the wolf coat.

Silvertip bent, looking into Bear Boy's vacant, half-lidded eyes. Bear Boy's tongue lolled behind parted lips.

I have seen this look. When I lay dead on the high rocks, before Condor came.

Silvertip closed his eyes, lifting the Wolf Bundle. The Song rose in his throat. He willed his soul into it, digging down into himself, believing, willing the Power to flow down from the Wolf Bundle. He felt it, growing, prickling. Like a warm rush of water it coursed through him, Singing with him, its Song mixing with his.

In that instant, Silvertip felt wings, and he stretched out, the familiar feel of them bringing a brimming ecstasy to his body.

Bear Boy's soul hovered above the body, dark, frightened, and poised to flee.

Gently, so as not to panic him, Silvertip closed his wings around the Spirit, wrapping his warmth and goodwill around the fear.

"Go back," Silvertip coaxed. "This is not your time. We are here, loving you, calling for you. Go back, Bear Boy. Your body needs you. Do not fear; you will live. We all need you."

He could feel the confusion, and curled his wings tighter, willing his love and warmth into the soul.

Slowly, carefully, he eased it down with his mighty wings. Felt it slide back into the body, and pressed down, keeping it there while it seeped into its familiar shell.

"Live, Bear Boy. Breathe. Feel the beat of your heart, and let the blood flow through your veins."

The gasp came from somewhere distant, as though heard through a thick fog. The sense of rightness swirled around him, and he looked up, seeing the sky filled with color.

"Silvertip!" Windwolf's barked command broke the trance.

He blinked, almost crying out as he felt the wings slip away. He tried to make sense of the blurry face above him. Windwolf!

"Stay back!" Ashes was saying. "He's Dreaming! Are you fools? Don't disturb a Dreamer when he's sending his soul to the Spirit World."

"Silvertip?" Windwolf asked again.

"Tired." He groaned and sat up, the Wolf Bundle warm in his hands. "Bear Boy?"

"He's alive," Windwolf told him. "But, I think he'll have a headache for a while."

"Yes. Me, too."

Silvertip was vaguely aware of Ashes, still haranguing people to stay back.

"You Dreamed the One," Windwolf said reverently. "How long have you been doing this?"

"Since I died, and Wolf Dreamer showed me the way."

"And you told no one?"

"Who would have believed me?"

"Come, let's get you back to your bed."

Silvertip stood on wobbly legs, his vision still swimming. He could make out Bear Boy, tears running down his face as his mother dabbed at his head with the hem of her dress. Ashes looked like a warrior, brandishing her war club, keeping people back. Then he noticed the expressions, people in the crowd staring, struggling to believe what they had just seen.

Silvertip almost made a full step before he bent double and threw up.

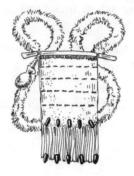

Fifty

Windwolf glanced across at Dipper, where she hovered beside Silvertip's bed, a stricken look on her face. Then he glanced at Lookingbill. The old man's lined expression and distant eyes reflected sober thoughts. Ashes looked oddly cowed as she sat with her war club across her lap.

Outside, Fish Hawk said yet again, "The chief is in Council with Windwolf. You may not go in. We will send news when they have finished."

More questions were called, to which Fish Hawk replied, "Silvertip used the Wolf Bundle to Dream the boy's soul back into his body. Beyond that, I don't know."

Windwolf ignored it, turned his attention to the roast haunch of beaver, and took a bite. With this new development, who knew when he'd get to eat again. He chewed the sweet dark meat, swallowed, and looked at Ashes.

"Tell us the whole story. How long have you known?"

She glanced nervously at him and then Lookingbill. "Since the night he woke up. He was different."

"We thought that was due to the wound," Lookingbill said. "People are often introspective after such a blow to the head."

"Tell us everything," Windwolf coaxed.

"He says he died." Ashes fingered the handle of her war club. "That he watched his body laid out on the high rocks, and then Condor came and ate him." She made a face. "He told me it was horrifying as it pulled out his insides and swallowed them. Then, when the bones were picked clean, he watched them fall apart, and then everything went gray. That's when Wolf Dreamer came to him and told him he was dead."

Lookingbill nodded. "Great Dreamers often have to die to be reborn. What did Silvertip come back as?"

"Condor. Wolf Dreamer taught him how to fly, and then they flew west, along the Ice Giants. He saw big lakes, and then, the biggest of all, somewhere beyond the Southwind People."

"I know the lake," Windwolf said. "A huge thing—to skirt it takes moons of travel."

Ashes nodded. "Silvertip saw a great ice dam, a place where the water is backed up." She looked up at him with a piercing stare. "He says the ice is melting. Sometime soon, this entire country is going to be washed away."

Lookingbill frowned. "That's impossible!"

"Our world is ending," Ashes snapped. "I believe Silvertip."

"But Raven Hunter whispers in your Dreams," Lookingbill snapped back.

"We are opposites." She narrowed an eye. "Silvertip and me. That is what is going to make our marriage so Powerful."

Windwolf raised a hand, stilling Lookingbill's response. "Your ear is bleeding. Did that happen this morning?"

She shook her head. "It's for my mother."

"But you don't know she's . . . Did Silvertip tell you she's dead?"

Ashes pursed her lips, then shook her head. "He said that she would come back, but the mother I knew wouldn't be there." She raised her eyes. "By offering for her soul now, it won't be as hard when she comes back."

"So you're saying she survives this flood?" Lookingbill asked skeptically.

"Silvertip does."

"What about the rest of us?" Windwolf asked. "Did he tell you anything about the people?"

"Only that they have to go west. Some will follow him to safety; others won't."

Windwolf nodded. "What about me? What does he say I'm supposed to do?"

Ashes shook her head. "I don't know. He just said that you, Kakala, and Keresa were struggling over the future. Something about bargaining between Wolf Dreamer and Raven Hunter."

"I see."

"Well, I don't," Lookingbill muttered. "He's just a boy!"

"One who carries the Wolf Bundle," Windwolf corrected. "And apparently speaks with it." He took another bite of his breakfast. Swallowing, he added, "I was there this morning. Bear Boy was dead. What I felt . . ."

"Yes?" Lookingbill prodded.

Windwolf shrugged. "I've never been what you would call a strong believer in Power, Chief. But I felt it. Silvertip called it to him, and then, I'd swear, I saw great wings."

"Raven Hunter?"

He met Lookingbill's eyes. "Condor. I think the boy called his Spirit Helper, and used Power to save Bear Boy's life."

Lookingbill shot a worried glance at his grandson, now sleeping soundly on the hides. "But he's still a boy. What do I do?"

"Begin preparing your people to travel west, Chief. Until Silvertip wakes, we're not going to know how much time we have left. Meanwhile, I need to hear what the new refugees have to say."

Keresa sat with her back to the stone, as far as she could get from the others. She had pulled her cape tightly around her shoulders, attempting to keep some sort of warmth around her body, because her soul was most definitely shivering.

She glanced up at the thin spear of light shining down from the mouth of their prison.

She gave Kakala a warning glance as he stepped over and lowered himself beside her. He had a puzzled look as he draped his hands on his knees.

In a kind voice, he asked, "How are you doing?"

"Confused," she admitted.

He made a halfhearted gesture toward the high opening. "Kind of them to lower food down this morning. But it was almost a fight to ensure it was portioned out fairly."

"Half of a yearling caribou." She rubbed her face. "It was generous, considering the mouths he has to feed."

"How many camps?"

"The hollow below the hill is filled with them. Too many, Kakala. He could have found plenty of reasons to ignore our wants."

Kakala grunted assent. "I'm beginning to understand how he wins the hearts of so many." He glanced at her. "What happened last night? When you came back, you looked terrible."

She shot a look at the warriors, thankful they knew enough to give their war chief and deputy privacy. "I don't know. That's why I'm so confused. But I can tell you now, the ruse of playing Bramble isn't a good idea."

"Oh?"

"Kakala? Do you trust me?"

"With my life." He smiled. "I'm sorry you thought you had to ask."

She lowered her voice. "I offered to stay with him last night if he would let you and the rest go. He said he would, provided you swore never to raise your hands against the Sunpath or Lame Bull again."

He studied his hands, flexing his fingers and watching the tendons work under his scarred skin. "He offered me that same option. He asked if there was a way we could go back without ending up in the cages. I thought it was some sort of trick."

She shook her head. "I don't think it's a trick."

"Why?"

"Because he respects us. Isn't that odd . . . after the things we've done to him and his people?"

"We did as our Council ordered. Nothing more, and as it turns out, often less." He gave her a knowing appraisal. "I've watched you since you've been meeting with him. I was curiously affected when you tried to kill Goodeagle yesterday. This offer to stay, was it more than just acting for the rest of us?"

She felt her soul tumble. "I would love to lie and tell you it was a cal-culating move to enable you to escape." She stared at her hands. "But I am drawn to him as I have been to no other man I've ever met."

"I see."

"Do you?" She searched his face. "I feel torn in two, Kakala. I don't know what's right anymore."

His lips curled in a faint smile. "I know you, Keresa. Perhaps bet-ter than I have ever known anyone . . . even Hako. You need a man who is your equal."

She gave him a sidelong stare. "No jealousy?"

"A little. But not like that. We share our souls, our trust, and hopes. I depend on you. But our lives are separate." He met her gaze. "If you can find more with Windwolf, take it." He glanced away, "Though, Raven Hunter knows, it might be short and miserable. The Council has no doubt learned what has happened to us by now. Ka-rigi will be coming, and this time, not even Windwolf can stop him."

"And when Karigi frees us?"

"You and I both know the penalty for failure." He swallowed hard, a shiver tracing down his spine. "I won't . . . can't . . ." She saw his great muscles knotting, swelling the war shirt under his cloak.

"There is a sickness in our people," she said bluntly. "It began with the return of Nashat, and has grown worse with the rise of the Guide."

"Who do you serve, Keresa?"

"You, and these warriors here." She gestured toward the huddled men who now used stones to smash the marrow bones of the cari-bou. They lifted the fragments, sucking out the pink delicacy. "Who do you serve, Kakala?"

His voice was wistful. "I don't know anymore."

She stared at her hand, remembering Windwolf's touch. She had gone to his arms willingly, and for that one blessed moment, her soul had been at peace.

"I'd almost think I was witched. Could that be it?"

"It was that way with Hako and me." He smiled, remembering.

"I don't even know him."

"Oh, yes you do. You just can't find it in your soul to trust him. He's fed us one bitter meal after another each time we've tried to kill him." He lowered his head. "And then there's Walking Seal Village."

"It haunts him." *As it haunts us.* She couldn't help but shoot a glance toward the back, where Goodeagle sat, his eyes focused on the distance.

Kakala placed a hand gently on her shoulder. "It's a terrible problem, isn't it? No matter what we choose, we will condemn ourselves in the end."

She nodded, glancing back at Goodeagle. That was the price of betraying one's people. *But if I help Kakala kill Windwolf, I will never forgive myself.*

Fifty-one

Windwolf leaned forward to warm his hands over the flames. In the slanting afternoon light, the crude lodges thrown up by the Sunpath refugees resembled dark round dots scattered through the forest. Tens of new lodges had appeared overnight. As soon as he'd stepped out of his chamber at dawn, he'd sent a runner to arrange a meeting with the village chief, a man named Sacred Feathers. They had barely begun their discussion when Bear Boy was struck down.

Sacred Feathers sat across the fire from Windwolf next to his grandfather. Sacred Feathers had seen perhaps three tens of summers. His grandfather, Drummer, had seen at least two tens more.

"So you think the boy is a Dreamer?" Drummer asked.

"You saw what he did." Windwolf studied the old man. "I was beside him; I *felt* the Power."

"We couldn't get close," Sacred Feathers muttered. "That little girl would have broken our knees with that war club she was swinging around."

"I have heard the boy's story." Windwolf shifted. "I saw his body after the fighting. I thought he was dead. His recovery is as much a miracle as his saving Bear Boy this morning."

"It is the talk of the camp."

"The Wolf Bundle speaks to him," Windwolf added. "Chief Look-ingbill gave it to him for safekeeping during the attack. Silvertip be-longs to it now."

"Then perhaps the prophecy is true?" Drummer mused.

"Perhaps. We will see. But for the moment, I need to know what happened at your village. Tell me everything."

Drummer nodded, thinking for a moment. "I told my grandson people were missing from the surrounding camps. He wouldn't be-lieve me."

His face had a skeletal appearance. Every bone stuck out through the thin layer of skin, which made his deeply set brown eyes look cav-ernous. Two long gray braids fell over the front of his worn tigerhide cape. He shook a fist at Windwolf. "Old Woman Rust never missed the meetings we held every full moon to worship Wolf Dreamer. First she disappeared, then Coal Lion vanished. I knew something was happening."

"They were old and from nearby camps," Sacred Feathers pointed out. "I thought maybe they'd gotten sick or hurt, or just couldn't make the walk any longer."

Windwolf said, "What happened to them?"

Sacred Feathers waved a hand in a helpless gesture. "We found out that just before Deputy Karigi attacked their villages, he sent war-riors in to kidnap a few of the Elders."

Sacred Feathers had a birdlike face with closely set eyes and shoulder-length black hair. "He used them as hostages. He told peo-ple to put down their weapons or the Elders would be killed. Many people did." Sacred Feathers' head fell forward. He stared blindly at the fire. "Then he killed everyone."

A cold breeze blew through the spruce trees, fluttering the lodge door curtains, and carrying the aroma of roasting grouse.

Drummer glared at his grandson. "They did the same thing to us."

Sacred Feathers crossed his arms over his yellow-painted cape. "I thought if we just did as Karigi said, we'd be all right. For many sum-mers, I've been telling my people that the Nightland clan Elders are not monsters. They're human beings, just like us. I hoped that if we treated them with dignity, they would leave us alone."

"Fool!" Drummer's wrinkled face tensed. "The Nightland People are monsters straight out of Raven Hunter's Long Dark."

346   W. Michael Gear and Kathleen O'Neal Gear

Sacred Feathers pointed to an old woman sitting in front of a lodge scraping a fresh deer hide. She used her hafted chert scraper to carefully remove the last bits of flesh, preparing the hide for tanning. "The morning before our band was attacked, a Nightland warrior ran through, gave her a freshly killed snowshoe hare, and ran away. I thought it was kindness. A gesture of—"

"He was a *spy*! It got him into our camp so he could look around. I told you we should have killed him before he could run away."

Sacred Feathers threw up his arms in exasperation. "Grandfather, Nightland warriors have been traveling through our territory for many summers. They stopped, they Traded, they told stories. Most Nightland warriors are peaceful!"

Drummer leaned forward and squinted an eye malevolently. "It's a lot easier to kill people when they still think you want peace."

Windwolf watched the conversation with an ache in his chest. He'd heard these same words so many times. There was always a peacemaker and a warrior. And depending upon the circumstances, each might be right.

"When did Karigi strike?" Windwolf asked.

Sacred Feathers threw another branch on the fire and watched the flames. "Two moons ago. We didn't know what to do. We just crept northward, hunting, fishing, hiding by day, hoping to find sanctuary in other Sunpath territories." He hung his head. "Most of them had already been abandoned."

"What brought you here?" Windwolf said.

"We met other fleeing people on the trails. They said Chief Lookingbill had promised sanctuary. And we heard you were here."

Windwolf let out a breath. "You are safe here. For the moment. But you can only have a couple of days to regain your strength. I will appoint a couple of warriors to escort you west. We are building a new home in the Tills."

Sacred Feathers ran a hand through his hair and shook his head. "I don't know. This is the land of our Ancestors. I've always believed that we could negotiate with the Nightland People, establish agreements for Trade, or the use of certain hunting or gathering grounds, but now . . . now, I don't know."

Drummer banged his foot on the hearthstones, as though to get everyone's attention. "The only time talk has ever helped the Sunpath

People was when Windwolf rammed it down their throats with a war party at his back."

Windwolf nodded in gratitude, but deep inside him, a voice asked, *"There are fewer Sunpath bands now than when I started protecting our people. Have I helped them?"*

Drummer continued, "The only reason Karigi didn't capture me is because I was afraid to return to my lodge. After the snowshoe hare was delivered, I walked all day to get to Walnut Creek Camp, spent one day there, and moved on. I just kept moving."

"How did you hear about the attack?" Windwolf asked.

Drummer extended a hand to his grandson. "The great chief, Sacred Feathers—his tail stuck between his legs—and a handful of survivors came running into the village where I was staying."

"Oh, Grandfather." Sacred Feathers exhaled the words.

Windwolf interrupted. "I need you to help me understand what Karigi is doing." He pulled his stiletto from his belt and started drawing in the dirt around the firepit. "These are the bands I know he has recently attacked." He poked holes into the soil. "Do you know of any others?"

"Yes," Sacred Feathers said. He used his fingers to poke two more holes. "Both of these. We met survivors on the trails."

"The survivors were not headed here?"

Sacred Feathers shook his head. "No. Many people do not believe that the Lame Bull Elders will keep their word when Karigi finally arrives here. But they haven't heard you are here, either. Or that you've trapped Kakala."

Why do they have such faith in me? I've failed them all. "Given what you've heard, where is Karigi now?"

Sacred Feathers seemed to be thinking about it. Finally he said, "He could be on his way back to the Nightland country. He's moving very fast."

"How many warriors does he have?" Windwolf's stomach muscles clenched in preparation.

"Six tens, maybe seven tens. We didn't have time to count."

Six tens? With Hawhak and Blackta's warriors, plus any others the Council can scrap up, they could hit us with more than ten tens. Were it he, he'd attack with two tens of warriors coming from five different directions. There could be no defense. *But Karigi's moving fast. His men will be worn out.*

Down the slope in the village, a little girl let out a shriek, then broke into tears. Sacred Feathers whirled to look.

Windwolf followed his gaze. A girl, perhaps eight summers, ran up the trail, whimpering. Tears streamed down her face.

Sacred Feathers opened his arms, and the girl ran straight to him and climbed into his lap, sobbing, "Father, he *hit* me!"

Sacred Feathers examined the scrape on his daughter's cheek. "Oh, Elk Leaf, what happened? Did you get into a fight?"

She nodded against his shoulder, trying to suppress her tears.

"You didn't hit first, did you?"

"No, Father, no."

"All right. Hush, now." He stroked her back tenderly, and kissed her forehead. "Did you say something you didn't mean and somebody—"

"No, I don't know why Little Calf hit me! But Tusk Boy hit him back."

"Good for Tusk Boy," Drummer muttered furiously. His ancient face had taken on the alert, dangerous look of a wolf on the hunt.

Sacred Feathers glared at him. "Elk Leaf, next time Little Calf hits you, you just cover your head with your hands and tell him you're sorry—even if you didn't do anything. He'll stop hitting you."

"I will, Father," she moaned and sniffed, burying her face in his shirt.

From the corner of his eye, Windwolf caught Drummer's enraged expression.

"I love you, Elk Leaf," Sacred Feathers said. "Are you better now?"

She sucked in a deep halting breath and looked up, giving him a frail little-girl smile. "A little."

"Good. Why don't you run down to Aunt Wren's lodge. She made cattail root bread this morning."

"Does she have any left?"

He winked at her excited expression and set her on the ground. "Go see for yourself."

She smiled broadly and ran away down the trail.

Once Elk Leaf had vanished, Drummer violently shoved Sacred Feathers' shoulder, swinging him around to face him. The old man's cheeks blazed. "You want to get her killed?"

"No, I want to keep her safe!"

"You're teaching her to be a mouse. You think she should get used to being a victim? That she should come to like it, maybe?"

Sacred Feathers met Drummer's hot stare with one of his own. "Maybe being a victim isn't as bad as being dead."

The anger drained from Drummer's face. He stood up and straightened to his full sapling-thin height. They stared at each other in silence.

Then Drummer's hard eyes turned to Windwolf. "Tell him, will you? Tell my grandson that all the *I'm sorry's* in the world won't make murderers put down their clubs."

Drummer turned and stamped away down the trail, following behind Elk Leaf.

Sacred Feathers had his eyes closed and his teeth gritted. "He's old," Sacred Feathers said. "He doesn't think as well as he used to."

"I'm afraid he's right, Chief. When your enemy is bent on killing you and taking your lands, you must fight."

"But that is Raven Hunter's way!"

Ashes' words from that morning echoed in his head. "I fear that we have lost our balance."

Windwolf looked out at the village. Sunpath children played in the trees, chasing each other and laughing. Old men knapped out new stone tools in front of the lodges. One of the women sat weaving a basket from strips of tree root: a fine basket, the weave tight enough to hold water.

Windwolf said, "The search for the One does us no good if we Dream it as dead men."

Sacred Feathers frowned at the Headswift Village rockshelters. "Well, you won't have to worry about my people. We will start for the Tills today. And you don't need to provide warriors."

Fifty-two

When you bore each of your children, Mother, it was a painful experience, wasn't it?" Silvertip lay back on his thick mat of hides and stared at the firelight playing on the soot-coated rocks above. He could hear the din outside where warriors guarded the entrance to the great chamber. But for them, the room would have been chaos as people tried to get to him.

"Of course," Dipper replied, stroking his hand with loving fingers. She glanced uneasily at Ashes, who squatted to his left, her war club perched on her lap.

"All that pain, and blood, and fluid." He smiled. "In the end, was it worth it?"

"Of course, Silvertip! How can you even ask that?"

"So that you will know that creating a new life, be it a person, or calf, or chick . . . or even a people, is difficult and painful. For everything, Mother, there is a price."

Ashes nodded soberly, watching him with her now-possessive eyes.

"But why should you—"

He waved Dipper's protest away. "There is no second-guessing Power, or the Dance of the One."

The growing sounds of the crowd indicated some sort of disturbance. He tucked the Wolf Bundle tightly against his left side, feeling the warmth, the rhythm that beat to the time of his heart.

"Make way!" Fish Hawk ordered. "The next person who tries to spit on her will get a taste of my club!"

Dipper's head turned as silhouetted forms blocked the entrance.

"I've brought her, Silvertip. Just as you ordered. But I'll say again, I think it's a bad idea."

"Thank you, War Chief." Silvertip sat up, feeling weak, but somehow rejuvenated. "Come closer, Keresa."

The woman walked hesitantly, squinting in the darkness. Fish Hawk stood close behind her, his war club half-raised to strike at any false move the warrior woman might make.

"You!" Dipper gasped, starting to rise.

Silvertip tightened his grip on her hand. "Mother! No!" He forced Power into his voice. "You will sit, *and listen*!"

Dipper blinked, nodded, and sank back to the floor.

Keresa stopped just beyond the bedding, her surprised eyes recognizing him. "How are you feeling?"

He smiled at her courage. "Very tired."

"Why did you send for me?" She stood tall, head back, her matted long hair falling around her shoulders. He could see the resolve coursing through her like a glowing light.

"I wished to thank you."

A slight frown marred her forehead. "Do not expect an apology."

"You need not apologize for serving the needs of Power, Deputy. You could not have played your part better."

"You *wanted* to be killed?"

"There is no greater gift than the one you gave me. Come, sit." He released Dipper's hand. "Mother, if you would make room for my guest?"

Reluctantly, Dipper scuttled off to the side, her eyes burning with threat as she watched the Nightland woman seat herself.

"You're saying . . . what? That Power planned this all?"

Silvertip looked into Keresa's controlled features. "You served my purpose well."

"Your purpose?" Keresa asked cautiously.

"I had to die to be reborn. The proof of the lesson lies all around us. The cycle of life and death and life is the heartbeat of Power.

Yet, distracted by our physical needs, we see, but do not understand."

"I don't—"

"I first heard your name in a Dream, Keresa. One that I did not understand. You are the Wind, Mother of Legends. Kakala is the Fire, and Windwolf is the Water. Together, you act upon the earth."

He watched her eyes narrow the way they would if she were listening to mindless babble. "I see."

Silvertip smiled. "Why is it that you, Mother of Legends, who have so much trouble believing in anything, cannot even believe in yourself?"

He could see the confusion in her eyes. "Mother of Legends?"

"Believe in yourself, Keresa. Step out, and place that first step on the trail to your destiny. Stretch your arms wide, and gather the winds."

She peered closely, trying to see his eyes, wondering, no doubt if the pupils were the same size.

"I am quite well, thank you." He reached out, taking her hand. At the touch, she stiffened, expression shocked.

When he released her, she might have been frozen, stunned. Her eyes had lost focus, as though her vision was swimming.

When she finally blinked and steadied herself, he said, "I asked you here to thank you for helping me to find the One. As a warrior, it will be counter to everything you believe, but to surrender yourself is to achieve victory."

"You're right. I . . . I don't understand."

"You will wish to see Windwolf when I am finished with him." He looked up. "Fish Hawk, would you escort Keresa to the war chief's chamber? And when you pass through the crowd tell them they are making way for the Wind."

"Of course, Silvertip."

Keresa had trouble standing, as though her legs wobbled beneath her.

Windwolf peered up in the gathering gloom. The trail was a mass of humanity. If Karigi attacked now, they would kill themselves trying to get down the steep hill.

"Make way for the war chief!" Fish Hawk shouted. "Make way for Windwolf!"

"Windwolf!" The awe, the sudden silence, unnerved him. He climbed carefully through the press, people squeezing aside to make room. Some reached out, touching him, as though he were something precious.

When he could take no more, he turned on them. "What are you doing? By Wolf Dreamer's breath, *get back to your camps*! Go! Now. Or so help me, I'll have warriors clear this whole trail!"

"But the Dreamer?" one old man cried. "He's here!"

"And when he's ready to address you, he will!"

They wavered, watching him expectantly.

He pulled his war club, waving it. "I said, *go!*"

As if herding ground sloths, he bullied them off the steep trail, balking only at the few who cowered before him, willing to take a blow rather than leave their precious Dreamer.

"Wolf Dreamer bless you," one of the guards at the top said. "We've been hard-pressed to keep them back."

Windwolf rubbed his face. "How can you blame them? They've lost everything, and now, suddenly, they have hope."

He ducked inside to find a fire, the pungent odor of spruce smoke thick in the air. He walked back, nodding to Lookingbill. The chief still looked confused.

Gods, aren't we all?

Ashes sat, her war club on her lap, one hand holding Silvertip's. She nodded severely as he walked up. When he looked into her eyes, it wasn't to find a girl. Her captivity, the terrible events in the pen, and the subsequent flight had burned childhood away.

"Windwolf, thank you for coming." Silvertip was seated, his back to a roll of hides.

When Windwolf looked into the boy's eyes, it was to receive a second shock. Something glowed behind that young face, as if the Power were flowing freely through his body.

"I have been talking with some of the refugees. Karigi has a larger force than I thought. We may not have as much time as I had hoped."

"No, we do not," Silvertip replied. "Our people must leave by the quarter moon."

Windwolf settled himself wearily, sighing with relief at the soft hides. "You saved that boy's life this morning."

Silvertip frowned. "I didn't know it would be so draining."

"Ashes told me most of the story. Your Vision about the ice, is it true?"

Silvertip nodded, then glanced at Windwolf. "That you accept Power so easily is unusual." He smiled. "No questions?"

"Hundreds of them. If we survive this, I'll have time to ask each and every one." He paused. "When will you order the people to head west?"

Silvertip's eyes seemed to lose focus. "Soon."

"Then this really is the end of our world?"

"As we know it. Raven Hunter waited, let us fall into the Dream. Now it is his time."

"So he has won?"

Silvertip reached out, touching the back of Windwolf's hand. His skin seemed to crackle like rubbed fox fur. "You don't understand Power, War Chief. Is day more Powerful than night? Will winter destroy summer? They are equal but opposite, order and chaos, harmony and creativity; they ebb and flow, ultimately opposed, and forever invincible."

"Then, how do we choose?"

"Balance," he said, reaching out with his other hand to take Ashes'. He looked at Windwolf. "You know the answer, War Chief. You—of all people—have finally found the balance. You are a creature of compromise. Most of all, you dislike extremes. Karigi, you would kill. Kakala, you would save."

He looked up. "Save, how?"

"That is for the Wind to blow."

"I don't understand."

"You are Water, War Chief."

"Water?"

"Without you, there can be no life; all would be drought and death. And, as you will see, unleashed, there is only flood. Balance is so elusive, and so important."

"And Kakala?"

"He is the Fire."

Windwolf took a deep breath. "Of course." He frowned.

"Yes?" Silvertip prompted.

"It's easier when I don't have to look at you. I am unsettled to hear wisdom granted to so few Elders from a mouth so young."

"Opposites crossed, War Chief. As you know so deeply in your soul. Male and female, enemies to lovers . . . Raven Hunter and Wolf Dreamer."

"Fire and Water."

"You have plans to pursue, War Chief. You may go."

As Windwolf stood, Silvertip added, "I must warn you, nothing comes without a price. What will you pay?"

He swallowed hard. "Haven't I already given enough?"

Fifty-three

Keresa drew her buckskin cape more tightly around her shoulders and paced Windwolf's chamber. Three guards stood outside the entry. She could hear them talking quietly. In the distance, the happy squeals of playing children rose.

Her soul might have been in turmoil after her visit to the boy Dreamer, but her wits hadn't deserted her. She heard plenty, about parties headed west, the Tills, and preparations to leave Headswift Village. Rumors were already passing that the Dreamer would order it.

What does that mean for Kakala and our warriors?

She rubbed her face, remembering the pulse of energy that had run from Silvertip's touch through her body: a sensation of peace and harmony.

Mother of Legends? The Wind? To surrender is to achieve victory?

She shook it off, trying to think. Windwolf's atlatl and quiver were not leaning against the wall where she'd seen them before. His bedding hides lay tangled, as though he'd risen quickly.

Where are you? What's happened?

She walked over and extended her hands to the small fire. The scent of boiled mastodon meat rose from the bag hanging on the tripod. She considered helping herself but decided against it. Instead, she took the opportunity to thoroughly search the chamber. Not that there was much to search. Overhead, a crack between the boulders created a smokehole. Wisps of blue smoke clung to the high ceiling before being sucked out.

She picked up one of his moccasins and sniffed it, finding his scent. "You're being a fool." She cast the moccasin down. "Sniffing old shoes, by Raven Hunter's balls! How could you have let this happen?"

But she hadn't *let* it happen; it just had. She was supposed to be a hard-eyed, ruthless warrior. She had no ability to pretend to be vulnerable. No, she had to *be* vulnerable.

She'd been shocked that Windwolf had responded to her the way he had.

And I responded to him.

She sank down to the hide in front of the fire and drew up one knee. The sooty shadows clinging in the corners wavered in the fire's glow.

Silently, she cursed herself. She could imagine the amusement in his eyes, as though he were watching her. And behind that lay a warm caring.

"You need a man who is your equal." Kakala's words echoed within her.

"Reach out and gather the Wind." She snorted. "I've drawn a storm."

Karigi was coming. Refugees were fleeing westward toward some stronghold in the Tills. If Karigi arrived, Windwolf would attempt to barter his captives. Karigi would accept, but only to parade them through the Nightland villages in disgrace before locking them all in the cages. She didn't have much time for pleasant feelings of self-pity.

She slipped a hand beneath her braid and massaged the back of her neck, easing the tension in the muscles. How could this happen now when everything she'd ever cared about in her life was in danger? They had to escape. And they had to capture or kill Windwolf.

Voices rose outside. Windwolf's deep voice said, "Fish Hawk, I need you to speak with young Silvertip. He will want to address the people. We have to prepare to leave Headswift Village."

"Yes, War Chief."

Footsteps pounded away.

When Windwolf ducked beneath the door curtain, she stared at him through tortured eyes.

Windwolf stood uncomfortably before the door.

As his eyes adjusted to the darkness, he clenched his hands into fists. She sat by the fire in the center of the chamber, dressed in her buckskin cape with long fringes. Her braid hung over her right shoulder. Through the lacing on her cape he could see her war shirt beneath.

"Forgive me for not being here when you arrived. Karigi has been very busy. More refugees poured in just a short time ago."

"Which band this time?"

"Moon Rock."

He watched her expression. Her soul must be following the same trails his was, tracing Karigi's path. The deputy was attacking the southern Sunpath bands, pushing people north toward Headswift Village.

Windwolf quietly walked to the opposite side of the fire. "What's Karigi doing?"

"Clearing the southern territories so that the Sunpath cannot follow the Nightland People to the paradise of the Long Dark." She shrugged unhappily. "Or so we were told."

"Doubts, Deputy?"

"Too many to count. Your Dreamer told me to trust myself, to be the Wind. I'm that, all right. Blown every which way."

He fought the urge to step forward and hold her again, to soothe her doubts.

No, she is still Keresa. Get too close, and she'll split your head open with a rock.

The chamber smelled of fat-rich meat. He hadn't eaten yet this morning. His stomach growled to remind him.

"Fish Hawk told me you no longer wished to be my go-between with Kakala. I'd like to know why."

She crushed the fringes of her cape in nervous fingers. He watched with amusement as she said, "Kakala is feeling better. You should be meeting with him. He's the war chief."

"We met last night. Somehow we get on each other's nerves."

"It's because you are both so alike."

"Really?"

She smiled. "You've seen buffalo bulls? The big dominant ones? They swell up, step lightly around each other, and then one makes a sound like *Phiisst!* and they both go at each other."

He folded his arms and stood silently, thinking. She expertly evaded his gaze, pretending to have found something fascinating on the floor.

Windwolf absently studied the way the shell beads on his moccasins reflected the firelight. "Keresa, let's be honest. We both know the reason you want me to deal with Kakala. You haven't been able to kill me."

"Is that what you think?" she asked sharply.

He reached to his belt, plucking a long stiletto shaped from a sliver of bone. This he tossed at her feet.

She looked away quickly, but not before he caught the buried desperation. Shaking her head, as if angry with herself, she stood in a whirl of fringed cape and strode toward him.

He was on his feet in a heartbeat. "More doubts, Keresa?"

"If not Kakala, then pick another warrior. Degan would be good." In the dusty radiance of the firelight, her eyes glinted.

"No."

"Why not?" she demanded.

"I want you." Gods, could he say it more clearly?

"You don't . . . You confuse me." She stalked away. The fireglow cast her shadow like a huge beast on the far wall.

"Keresa, talk to me. We don't have time for useless games. Tell me why—"

"You are such a fool."

He started to say something, but decided against it. Instead, he propped his hands on his hips, hoping she'd finish that thought and enlighten him. But she clamped her jaws.

A malevolent gleam filled her eyes. "You know, in that position, I could kill you with one swift punch to the throat. You wouldn't know you were dead until you hit the floor."

Uneasily, he glanced down, seeing the bare floor where the stiletto had lain. "I appreciate the warning."

"You should. Two days ago, I wouldn't have given you one."

"Two days ago you wouldn't have needed to."

She exhaled hard, flipping the stiletto into her fingers from where she'd palmed it. "I wish . . . I wish desperately that you were the monster I used to believe in."

"The Dreamer says I'm a compromise."

"Well, he says I'm the Wind, whatever that means. And you're Water."

"I heard he asked to see you."

"He wanted to thank me."

"For trying to kill him?"

"For getting the job done, according to him." She shook her head. "He touched me. It was . . . dazzling."

"What else did he tell you?"

"That surrender was the way to victory."

"I think," he said softly, "that to be a good Dreamer, you have to speak in riddles?"

A warm, worried expression strained her beautiful face. He walked over to her. The fire cast a yellow glow around them. Keresa observed him quietly. Flickers of gold glimmered in her eyes.

"I heard talk of a great flood. That Headswift Village is to be abandoned."

"Silvertip says this place is going to be washed away."

She suppressed a shiver, and he instinctively lifted an arm to drape it around her shoulders. When he realized what he was doing, he glanced down at the stiletto in her hand. After two or three agonizing instants, she took a small step forward and eased into his arms.

He pulled her close and let himself drown in the fragrance of her hair and the feel of her breasts against his chest. A hot tide flooded his veins. "Keresa, neither of us can afford—"

"No." She looked up at him, and he saw desire and something more in her eyes, soft, fearful. "Between floods and Karigi, we may not have much time. Kakala, himself, said that it might be short . . . and miserable in the end."

"Kakala said that?"

"He's my friend, Windwolf." She smiled wearily. "My only friend in the world."

"And I am . . ."

"I don't know yet." She shook her head lightly, as though denying some inner admonition. "But I think I want to find out. Who knows?

Maybe after we get past this attraction, we'll decide it was a bad decision."

He closed in upon himself, hiding. Her words echoed around the chasm in his soul, swirling, images of Bramble flashing.

"Don't. Don't need me. Don't care about me. Just . . . don't."

"I think it's too late." She took a deep breath, stepping back to remove her cloak. "I suppose it's time to put my foot squarely on the path to destiny."

"The path to what?"

"I don't know. Something the Dreamer said." She pulled her war shirt over her head, flipping her braid back to stand naked but for her moccasins. "Kakala says I need a man who is my equal."

Windwolf's breath came in short gasps as he fixed on her body. "He does?"

"So," she asked brazenly, "do we do this with you on your back . . . or me on mine?"

As the fire burned low, they lay twined in each other's arms beneath his hides. Her forehead pressed against his chin, while her long hair flowed over his chest and arm. He stroked her naked back slowly, letting the silken texture of her skin soothe him.

"You asked about freedom," he murmured. "I think it means being free to fight with all your heart without ever expecting—"

"You mean being free to die for your people, don't you?"

She lifted her head, and he gazed into her eyes. They shone now with a strange warm light.

"There is no greater freedom than that."

She lay her head back down and nuzzled her cheek against his shoulder. "Hallowed Ancestors, I think I'm beginning to understand the Sunpath nation."

She'd said it with such a tone of reluctance, his breathing went shallow. "Sorry you stayed?"

"Not at all. I've never been so comfortable with a man. You weren't even timid when it came time to touch me."

"Where's the stiletto?"

"Within easy reach."

"Maybe that's why I dared not disappoint you."

"You didn't." She snuggled closer, resting her long thigh over his belly. "Assuming you can get the people out before Karigi comes, what are you going to do with my warriors?"

"Honestly, I don't know. Your Council doesn't give me many options. Kakala can't go back without a victory to clear his name. I can't let him have one because it means having my people killed. We can't take them with us. Too many people hate them. They'd be rushed with sticks, stones, anything at hand to repay them for dead relatives and the pain they've caused."

"Why do you care?" She ran her fingers down his chest. "We did terrible things."

He smiled thinly. "Because I was headed down that same trail. That was the lesson Goodeagle tried to teach me. His betrayal brought me back . . . but it took longer than it should have."

He felt her tense. "If we are serious about trusting each other, you have to know. Kakala and I were there. We saw what Karigi did to Bramble."

"I know."

She shifted, raising up to look at him in the dim light. Her eyes were shadowed in the spill of her hair. "I will not have what happened to Bramble lie between us like a thorn that slowly festers. In the end, Windwolf, it was our fault, Kakala's and mine. We trusted Karigi, and we should have known better."

He reached up, cupping her shoulder with his palm. "You said Kakala would have killed him?"

"Oh, yes." She hesitated. "I should have done it myself. But sometimes things happen so fast we can't understand the implications."

"No. We can't."

"And what are the implications of you and me, together?"

"Difficult." He slid his hand down to envelop her breast. "But if this night is all that we have, I'm going to fill it with you."

Dislocation

*H*e *won't come in the day anymore. But at night, he touches me, his ghostly fingers gliding like fox fur over my flesh to wake me. I think . . . but I shouldn't . . . if he could hear my thoughts . . . no, he doesn't care as long as I keep making plans to take our people back to the Long Dark. I . . . I'm safe. I'm sure of it. And my thoughts are my only refuge.*

I'm not sure he's Raven Hunter. He may be an evil Spirit hiding behind the name. Though, Ancestors help me, he's so persuasive. The horror stories he tells about Wolf Dreamer seem true. When I look around me, all I see is suffering.

If I only knew for certain that he was Raven Hunter, I'd go out and challenge Wolf Dreamer myself. I'd ask him why, if he truly could save his people, he hasn't already done it.

Raven Hunter tells me that the only way I can speak to Wolf Dreamer is if I have the Wolf Bundle. It's the door to Wolf Dreamer's Spirit lodge. He says a little Lame Bull boy has the bundle, and tells me that I should send warriors to get it and destroy it.

I don't know. I just don't know what to do. . . .

Fifty-four

*T*hey know you're here."

The voice seemed to seep from the ice walls and echo around her chamber.

Skimmer sat up in her hides and stared at the utter darkness. It had started to press in upon her like black smothering smoke. If she hadn't experienced it, she would never have believed that mere darkness could become the enemy: a living ominous creature that stalked her. It moved and breathed. It spoke to her in a soft muted voice that rang in her ears.

She called, "Ti-Bish? Is that you?"

Moccasins on ice.

"They know you're here," he repeated from no more than two or three paces away.

"Who?"

"The Four Old Men, the Elders." Ti-Bish shifted uneasily. "The warriors who brought you here have been talking."

Skimmer drew the worn softness of the hides up around her throat. She'd started to shiver. But it wasn't the cold; it was the memory of Nashat's voice coming from just outside the enclosure.

"H-How long have I been here, Ti-Bish?" she asked. The anguish in her voice surprised her. "I can't tell how many days have passed."

"The Elders want to see you."

Why wasn't he answering her questions?

"Ti-Bish . . . where have you been? It seems like I've been alone forever."

His steps padded closer, and he knelt down. "It's not easy to get to. But Raven Hunter showed me the way."

His scent filled the air, something deep and dark, like moss that had been growing in a cave for tens of tens of summers.

"The way?"

He didn't answer.

Tiny flashes of light, like a distant torch reflecting from midnight-colored feathers, surrounded Ti-Bish. She could clearly see the outline of his body as he stood up.

Reflections from the Thunder Sea? This far away?

"We have to go," he whispered. "The clan Elders are waiting."

Skimmer fought to suppress the shudder that climbed her spine. If they killed her before she had a chance to kill Ti-Bish, what would happen to the Sunpath People? To Ashes?

"Ti-Bish," she said as she braced a hand against the wall and rose. "The darkness . . . has taught me many things."

"Raven Hunter said it would," he breathed, and spread his arms, as though opening them to the black world. "It has become the one ally I can rely upon."

Fear tingled through her. His soul seemed to be loose, flying somewhere far away where it couldn't hear her.

She moved toward him. "You were right. I have seen the truth of Raven Hunter's vision. I *believe* we must go back through the hole in the ice to the Long Dark."

The words terrified her. If the Long Dark was anything like living in this black cave, it would drive her mad. It would drive every normal human being mad.

Ti-Bish took a quick step backward, as though stunned. "Has . . . has he picked you?"

Nothing he said was making sense.

"Who?"

"C-Come," he whispered. "Let's . . . let's get this over with. We must prepare for the way."

She shook her head in confusion, but said, "All right. I will try to follow you, but it's difficult. I wish you'd brought a lamp. The darkness . . ."

Ti-Bish took her hand in a tight grip, and said, "I'll lead you."

As they climbed the sloping tunnels, the Ice Giants groaned and squealed.

Skimmer stopped suddenly when Wind Woman moved around her, blowing her long hair. "Are we nearing the surface?"

"Yes."

The darkness began to recede, and a faint glow lit the tunnels. Ti-Bish still held her hand, leading her up through the maze and around enormous pools of meltwater.

"It won't be long now," he said, and walked around a curve.

As they headed up a steep tunnel, her feet repeatedly slipped on the ice. Ti-Bish kept a tight hold on her hand to keep her from falling. They rounded a bend to find the ice parted, the rough walls split vertically. She stared into the chasm created by the giant crack.

"Is that . . . ?" She sucked in a breath.

"Yes," he said. "There are crevasses everywhere. And more open every summer."

Skimmer tipped her head far back to look up. Sunlight filtered through the fissures overhead. A feeling of ecstasy and freedom swelled her heart. It was as if Father Sun himself had reached down and touched her. For the first time since she'd arrived, she could get a full breath into her lungs.

"That is my *secret* crevasse," he whispered to her, as though sharing a bit of precious knowledge. "Remember it, Skimmer. Someday, you may need to know how to get back here."

They veered left at the next split in the tunnels, and as they continued on up the steep incline, Father Sun faded, but the flickering light of a fire began to waver over the pale blue walls like invisible wings.

The narrow ice tunnels opened to magnificent arched passageways and huge rounded chambers.

When she heard voices, her stomach muscles tensed.

"We're almost to the Council Chamber," Ti-Bish said, and turned to look at her. "Don't worry. I won't let them hurt you."

"I—I believe you."

But she wondered if he had any real authority to stop them.

From within the chamber, she heard laughter, the rustle of hides, and the clacking of wooden tea cups.

She looked down at her soiled doehide cape. The white moons painted around the bottom had grown dim from soot and dirt. She was meeting the Nightland Clan Elders, and she looked like a slave. Using her fingers, she combed her long hair and tucked it behind her ears. It was the best she could do.

Ti-Bish led her into the chamber, and the voices stopped.

The Four Old Men sat around a stone bowl of warming coals with tea cups in their hands. The tea bag hung from a tripod at the edge of the bowl. Two were bald; two had white hair that hung down their backs in long braids. Each was dressed regally. Their capes had been smoked a beautiful golden hue, then covered with elk ivories, circlets of mammoth tusk, and painted with their clan symbols. She recognized each Elder by those symbols: *Elder Nashat from the Night Clan, Elder Satah from the Wolverine Clan, Elder Ta'Hona of the Loon Clan, and Elder Khepa of the Ash Clan.*

The hem of Nashat's cape was decorated with white fox tails that almost dragged the floor. He seemed to be the youngest of the Elders. Though he had a long white braid, his face bore few deep lines. The other Elders resembled shriveled winter-killed carcasses.

Just the sight of Nashat's face brought back that terrible night in the pen. She swallowed hard, willing her hands not to tremble. And from somewhere, perhaps the very blackness she had feared, courage came.

Skimmer's gaze was drawn upward to the high ceiling, which arched five body lengths over her head. Firelight fluttered over the dome. Truly, the Nightland Caves were staggeringly beautiful.

"Forgive us for being late," Ti-Bish said, and bowed to the elders. "A servant caught me just before I started down and—"

Nashat asked, "Was it that ugly little girl, Pipe? I haven't seen her for a while. I thought maybe you'd murdered her and I was finally rid of her."

Ti-Bish stood as if frozen. He didn't even blink.

Nashat turned to Skimmer and scowled as though he'd scraped her off his moccasins just that morning. "Please, step forward so that the Elders may see this 'Skimmer from the Nine Pipes band.'"

"It's all right," Ti-Bish whispered nervously, and gestured for Skimmer to walk forward. "They wish to speak with you."

Skimmer managed to keep from quaking as she stepped closer to the seated Elders. They whispered darkly to each other as she stopped before them.

Clenching her fists, she asked, "What do you want?"

Nashat strolled toward her, the fox tails on his exquisite cape swaying, the fur glinting wildly in the filtered daylight. His white hair had been freshly washed and braided. It shone.

"Did you organize your people to kill our Blessed Guide?" Nashat circled her like an eagle ready to dive for an unsuspecting rabbit.

She glanced at Ti-Bish, who stood near the entry with his shoulders hunched and his head down. He reminded her of a puppy beaten so often it always expected to be struck at any moment.

"I did," she answered.

The Elders hissed to each other and looked at her through narrowed hateful eyes.

Elder Ta'Hona turned his scarred face to look up at her, and the spotted loon painted on the front of his cape folded in the middle. He cradled a withered right arm in his left. "You wanted to kill our Guide. Why?"

"Because you're trying to steal our lands and have ordered the destruction of my people. Your warriors are murdering women, children, and elders. People who never wished the Nightland or their Guide ill until you butchered their relatives." She glared at them, feeling her hatred. "Can you think of a better reason for murder?"

Nashat grinned, and she fought the urge to spit on him.

Ti-Bish spread his feet, and his shoulders hunched more, as though he were trying to hide in plain sight.

Elder Khepa waved a trembling hand. "If you don't want to die, move. Then we won't have to kill you."

"Yes." Elder Satah turned white eyes on her. "We have far more people to feed than you do. We need your nut forests and hunting grounds. You can go somewhere else. Move farther south."

"I thought you were following the Guide to the Long Dark. Or are you just using him for an excuse?"

"Oh," Nashat responded, "we take the Guide very seriously."

A potent brew of anger and desperation seared her veins. "Why can't you go around us? You should move farther south, not us. The Sunpath People have lived in the nut forests since Wolf Dreamer first led us up through the hole in the ice. Our Ancestors lived and died on that land."

Nashat chuckled from her left. She turned to look at him. He tilted his head in an oddly seductive way and pinned her with cold black eyes. "It doesn't matter now anyway. In the past moon, War Chief Kakala and Deputy Karigi have destroyed most of your insignificant little bands. The few pitiful survivors have dispersed across the land. The Sunpath People are no more."

Skimmer's heart raced. Could it be true? Or a clever lie?

Ta'Hona ran a hand over his bald head and said, "Soon, we will head south and move into your old lands, perhaps even into your old lodges, those that are left standing. There's nothing you can do to stop—"

"No," Ti-Bish softly said, and his eyes went wide. "We won't."

Nashat scowled at him. "How dare you contradict an Elder? What do you mean?"

Ti-Bish stepped forward. His voice was like buffalo wool, soft and warm. "I've found it."

All of the Elders turned to face him. "Found what?" Khepa asked.

"The way."

Nashat turned to the other Elders and exchanged glances. No one seemed to know what the Guide meant.

Nashat said, "The way . . . to do what?"

"The way." Ti-Bish swallowed hard and lifted his chin. "The hole in the ice. I can lead our people to the paradise of the Long Dark!"

Fifty-five

Skimmer stared at Ti-Bish in disbelief. *The Paradise of the Long Dark? It was real?*

The Council chamber was silent for a moment, the expressions of the Elders that of shock. Even Nashat was speechless.

Khepa and Ta'Hona were on their feet in a heartbeat.

Satah walked up to Ti-Bish, and in a reverent voice said, "You've found the way to the Long Dark?"

"Raven Hunter showed it to me. He said I'd been good."

Gasps were followed by cheers; then laughter rose. Tears streaked their elderly faces. Nashat, however, sat to the side, fingering his chin, eyes narrowed to slits.

Ta'Hona asked, "When can we leave?"

"Soon. Raven Hunter told me that our people must start packing. But they can only take their most precious things. The trip is long and difficult."

Satah spun around, and the other Elders smiled toothlessly at him. "We must tell our people immediately. We're going back. Back through the hole in the ice to the Land of the Long Dark, where we will never be hungry again."

Laughter again, joyous. The Elders rose to their feet, and as they filed out, each gently touched Ti-Bish's shoulder.

Skimmer watched, amazed. *They are old fools! Men who no longer think, no longer walk in the world like the rest of us!* The image of puppets, the sort that adults used to entertain children, flickered in her soul. *And the one who guides them . . . ?*

Only Nashat remained. He waited until the voices of the other Elders had vanished before he said, "Now that the foolishness is over, let's discuss Headswift Village."

Skimmer blinked. His entire demeanor had changed. His cold eyes fixed on Ti-Bish, and he said, "Guide, come and sit down. It makes me nervous when you stand by the door as though you're going to bolt at any instant." He pointed to the buffalo hides.

Ti-Bish came forward with a frightened look on his face and sat down as he'd been ordered.

Skimmer frowned, the memory of stone hammers whistling in the night, sounding in her head. Where once it would have brought horror, it now stirred a terrible anger.

Nashat . . . someday, I will repay you for all of this.

Nashat said, "First, what's this idiocy about the hole in the ice?"

Ti-Bish bowed his head. "I found it."

"You're going to have all of our people racing around stuffing their packs full preparing for a journey they will never take."

Trembling, Ti-Bish had the courage to lift his gaze and look at Nashat. "We need to go soon. Very soon. Raven Hunter says—"

"Oh, Blessed Spirits, you're talking to *me* now, not the fools who believe you're going to lead them to the promised Long Dark. We have more important issues to discuss." He thrust an arm out at Skimmer. "It's a good deal more critical that we push the Sunpath People out of the nut forests, than it is—"

"We're going," Ti-Bish whispered. "I'm going to lead our people through the hole in the ice and back to the Long Dark, where tens of tens of mammoths, giant buffalo, and bears live. We don't need the nut forests. We'll never be hungry again. Raven Hunter will be there to watch over—"

"Ti-Bish." Nashat propped his hands on his hips and shook his head as though terribly disappointed. "Try to listen for a time."

Ti-Bish kept quiet.

Nashat turned to Skimmer and malevolently said, "What's the last thing you saw at Headswift Village?"

Skimmer wet her lips. She could sense his hidden joy, as though he was about to reveal some terrible bit of knowledge that he knew would hurt her. "Windwolf was preparing to fight Kakala."

Nashat walked to the tea bag and dipped himself a cupful. He took his time swirling it before he said, "After that, Kakala overran the place. He tortured Windwolf to death, then hunted down and killed every man, woman, and child who had sheltered Windwolf. Including your daughter," he said pointedly.

Skimmer had to lock her knees to keep standing. *No, he's lying. He's lying!*

Ti-Bish shakily got to his feet, and stared at Nashat with his mouth open. "You . . . you ordered Kakala to kill the Lame Bull People?"

"Of course I did. They deserved it. But I also did as you instructed and told Kakala not to harm any Sunpath People. Though that was certainly a mistake."

"A mistake?" Ti-Bish asked in a tortured voice.

Nashat heaved a breath. "Ti-Bish, did Skimmer tell you that her friends, the Lame Bull People, sent her here to kill you? Did she mention that Windwolf was planning on attacking these caves, and hoped to kill us all?"

"What?" Ti-Bish whirled to stare at her. Every line in his face tensed with hurt.

She gave Ti-Bish a narrow-eyed appraisal, saying, "Don't worry, Guide. You're still alive. I think we both know the source of the problem." Her voice hardened. "And so does Raven Hunter."

Nashat ignored her, continuing to say, "Oh, yes, they sent her here specifically to keep you distracted while they organized their forces; then, at the last instant before they attacked, she was supposed to assassinate you."

Ti-Bish gaped at her. "Is that true?"

"I came to kill you in revenge for the murder of Nine Pipes women in the pen just south of the Nightland Caves. You ordered Kakala to destroy the Nine Pipes and have me brought here. Nashat took a woman called Blue Wing from the pen. The rest were clubbed in the head by Karigi's warriors. Murdered. When Nashat ordered it, he said it was *your* wish."

Nashat was giving her a slit-eyed stare. "Then how did you survive?"

"By hiding under the corpses of the dead, you piece of filth. If so many hadn't died of thirst, hunger, and cold, you would have got us all."

At the still, ravaged expression on Ti-Bish's face, she walked toward him and knelt at his feet. "I am telling you the truth, Ti-Bish. I came to kill the person responsible. And you are not he."

Nashat squeezed the bridge of his nose. "Don't be a fool, Ti-Bish. She's using your emotions against you. Can't you see that?"

Ti-Bish stuttered, "If S-Skimmer says she's telling the truth, I trust her." He looked up, stunned, tears beginning to leak down his cheeks. "But these other things? All of these horrible things? You have *murdered* in my name?"

"Of course," Nashat laughed, throwing up his hands. "It was necessary. We needed the supplies. What do you think you've been eating for the last two winters? It's food taken from the Sunpath camps! And as to your friend, Kakala, a rumor has come that the fool managed to get himself trapped at Headswift Village. I have sent runners for Karigi and Blackta. We'll deal with the Lame Bull threat once and for all."

"No." Ti-Bish stiffened. "Send runners to bring our warriors home so that they can prepare for the journey to the Long Dark."

Nashat rolled his eyes and grinned, inspecting Skimmer. "With a bath and a clean dress—"

"No!" Ti-Bish cried. "You send those runners! If you don't I—I'll tell the other Elders that you're trying to leave members of their clans behind!"

Nashat stopped and gave Ti-Bish an evil look. "Do you wish to challenge me?"

Skimmer stepped between Ti-Bish and Nashat. "He does. Come on, Nashat, you and me. Right here. Let us see who serves the Guide. I call on Raven Hunter's Power to aid me. What do you call on, you foul wretch?"

She saw his eyes widen, the first tremble of fear glittering behind his eyes.

"I need only call the guard," he said softly. "And you will be servicing the warriors one after another until you come to wish you'd died in that pen."

"I *did* die in that pen. I came here for justice, you pus-licking scum. And now I'm going to *have* it." She stepped forward, all of the anger washing up through her soul.

Nashat scrambled back, hands up, eyes wide with disbelief.

Ti-Bish grabbed Skimmer's collar, pulling her back. "No, no, let him go, Skimmer. This isn't the time." She heard him swallow, desperation in his voice. "*Please, Skimmer!*"

She hesitated, trembling with the desire to choke the very life out of Nashat.

"Skimmer?" Ti-Bish asked weakly. "Please? It's not the time."

"But it will be," she promised. "And soon."

Nashat fled to the doorway, calling, "Time, Guide, is a very fluid thing." Then he was gone, running for all he was worth.

Tears welled in Ti-Bish's eyes. Softly, he said, "Skimmer, come. We've got to go."

He pulled her after him, taking a side passage out of the chamber.

When they'd followed the tunnel around the first curve, he broke into a run.

"Why are you running?"

"Because as soon as he finds the right warriors, they'll be coming to kill you."

Fifty-six

Nashat hurried down the tunnel and out the front entrance, heading straight for the Night Clan's camp. He hadn't been so frightened in years. He'd looked into Skimmer's eyes and seen death there.

She would have killed me! The knowledge sent a shiver down his spine and turned his guts runny.

The round lodges made of bent saplings tied together at the top and covered with hides looked tawdry in the bright sunlight. The paintings had faded to dull, indistinguishable images. And the soot of many campfires had furred the lodge tops, turning them black.

Get a hold of yourself! He forced himself to slow, to breathe normally. Gods, he was Councilor Nashat! Not some simpering slave. For a moment, he stood, letting his heart resume its normal beat. Here, out of the caves, his old self returned.

The tall man standing with his friends before the fire stopped suddenly when he saw Nashat.

"Elder," he said, and bowed deeply. "You honor us with your—"

"What's the last thing you saw at Headswift Village, Homaldo?"

The muscular warrior straightened, fear behind his eyes. "War Chief Kakala was preparing to attack Headswift Village." He waved his hand uncertainly. "After that, Kakala ordered us to leave immediately, to bring Skimmer to the Guide."

A stiff wind gusted off the lake, flapping Nashat's cape around his long legs. "Would it surprise you to hear that Kakala walked into a trap? Perhaps it would shock you even more to learn he's holed up in some rocks, surrounded?"

Homaldo looked at the other warriors in the circle. They shrugged or shook their heads. Homaldo said, "Alive? He's alive?"

"That seems to surprise you?"

"Well, I mean . . . if what you say is true."

"I'll know soon enough. I've sent a runner to have Karigi's deputy, Ewin, take a war party to Headswift Village on his way back here." He enjoyed the expression of terror on Homaldo's face. "But I have another task for you and your friends."

Homaldo swallowed hard. "Y-Yes?"

"You can go to the cages—you Kishkat, Tapa, and the other one. Or you can do me a slight service. Which would you choose?" When Homaldo just stood there looking at him, Nashat barked, *"Which!"*

"Yes, Elder, of course. We are honored to do you any service. Let me get my weapons and my pack. Kishkat, Tapa, and Tibo will be most anxious to help."

While Homaldo ducked into his lodge, Nashat gazed around the camp. Curse the other Elders. The news must have already reached the people. Everywhere he looked, men and women ran from lodge to lodge, and happy voices rang out. Several people Danced and Sang. Before he knew it, they would be taking down their lodges and packing up for the journey through the hole in the ice to the Long Dark.

The fools.

Homaldo ducked out of his lodge carrying his weapons. His small warrior's pack rode his back beneath his cape, making him resemble a hunchback. His wife ducked out behind him, and gave Nashat a scathing look. A little boy came out behind her with tears in his eyes. He gazed up at Homaldo and started to sob.

Homaldo knelt and hugged the boy one last time, then said, "Elder, what do you wish us to do?"

Nashat flipped up his hood against the ferocious wind. "You will take your friends and search the tunnels under the ice until you find the woman Skimmer. I think you remember what she looks like? Then, you will bring me her head."

W here are we going, Ti-Bish?" Skimmer called up to him. The trail that twisted through his "secret" crevasse was steep and slick. Rivulets of meltwater ran down the trail. Her moccasins kept slipping on the wet ice.

"We're almost there." Ti-Bish gripped her hand and pulled her out into the bright gleam of Father Sun.

Skimmer climbed to the crest of the dirty, gravel-encrusted ice, and gazed westward. A rocky ridge thrust up in the distance, rising perhaps ten tens of hands above the tundra. Sunlight sheathed the boulders, turning them into a glimmering wall. To the south, lodges covered the tundra. Already, runners were sprinting from lodge to lodge, probably relaying the news about the sacred hole in the ice.

Ti-Bish sank down onto a boulder and lowered his face to his hands.

Skimmer said, "Are you all right?"

"No." He looked up at her, soul sick.

"I'm sorry you had to hear those things," she said, laying a gentle hand on his head. "But you needed to know. Nashat has done terrible things in your name. Half the world hates you. I hated you."

In a tight voice, he replied, "I just need to pray for a time."

"I don't think praying is the answer, Ti-Bish. Nashat obviously disdains you and your Dream."

He paused as though judging his words before he murmured, "Prayer is always the answer. The problem is that humans no longer know how to pray."

She studied his tormented face. "Probably because so few people try these days."

"I know." His voice was small. He lifted his face and gazed out across the tundra at a herd of caribou grazing its way along the distant shore of Thunder Sea. Their shiny coats glinted in the sun. "Humans don't pray. But the world prays all the time."

"It does?"

He gestured to the lake. "Prayers are Sung every moment on the lips of breaking waves, and windblown branches, the whispering of leaves in the moonlight."

A strange tingling sensation began in her hip. She looked down at the old Spirit bundle tied to her belt. A mixture of fear and curiosity tormented her. Very faintly she heard a voice. A man's voice, deep and rich.

"Ti-Bish, I—I . . ." Her gaze was glued to the bundle as though attached with boiled pine pitch. "I hear . . ."

"Yes, I hear him, too." Ti-Bish swallowed hard. "No wonder he wished you to have it. He wants to speak with you."

"Who does?"

As though trying to decide if he should tell her or not, he twisted his hands in his lap. "Skimmer, I didn't tell you the whole truth when I gave you that bundle. I'm sorry. I was afraid of what you might do."

The tingling sensation had grown fiery. "Tell me now."

"Raven Hunter gave me that bundle, and told me to give it to you. He wanted you to have it."

Blood began to pound in her ears. "Why?"

"He didn't tell me that. I think he worried that I was too stupid to understand."

"You're not stupid, Ti-Bish. Just innocent."

"No, but there are times when I—I lose the"—he waved a hand uncertainly—"the boundary between myself and the world; it melts away, and I'm no longer sure if I'm seeing with my own eyes, or hearing with my own ears. I get confused."

Skimmer looked down at the bundle. The tingling had stopped. The voice was gone. Had she merely imagined it?

"Ti-Bish, whose eyes would you be seeing with if not your own?"

He grimaced down at his hands. "That's the problem. I don't know. There are times when I feel as though every rock and river, bird and buffalo, everything that has ever lived, has always been there in my soul. I could be seeing through any of their eyes. And they through mine."

"That doesn't mean you're stupid."

Ti-Bish said, "*Stupid* may have been the wrong word. What I meant is that Raven Hunter can't rely on the fact that 'I' am actually there when he explains things to me. So"—he sighed—"often he doesn't."

Skimmer flinched at the pain in his voice. "Why do you think he wishes to speak with me?"

"He speaks to a person when they need to hear him. Perhaps today you needed him."

In the villages below, voices had risen and there was a flurry of activity. People raced around shouting and weeping in what sounded like joy.

"The word is traveling," she said.

Ti-Bish nodded, then tenderly asked, "Skimmer, why didn't you kill me?"

As though all of her strength had vanished in a heartbeat, she hunched forward and braced her elbows on her knees. "I . . ." The words came hard. "I came to get justice. To pay you back for the horror in the pen. For the dead babies and husbands, and ruined lives." She paused. "Instead I found an innocent, a holy man. One doesn't kill the innocent and holy, Ti-Bish. No matter how many lives your death would save."

"My death would save lives?"

She made a sweeping gesture to the villages. "The warriors would no longer have a reason to kill. You were the symbol, the heart, the Spiritual reason that drove them to do terrible things." She sighed. "And all along, it was Nashat."

"He is the leader of the Council of Elders. I am just the Guide. I have no right to give orders, though sometimes I make requests, and hope that Nashat will approve them. As he did when I asked for War Chief Kakala to bring you here."

"I have hated you for summers for things that were never your fault," she said. "Forgive me. If I had known the truth moons ago, my people would have assassinated Nashat, or the other Elders, but not you, Ti-Bish. I've never wished for the innocent to suffer evil—"

"Suffering is not evil, Skimmer." He turned to her and his mouth smiled, but his eyes remained sad abysses. "All suffering forces us, in utter humility, to return to our own hearts. And that is where truth resides."

"You think suffering leads to truth?" She stared into his wide, appealing eyes. He seemed to beam at her with an inner peace that touched her soul.

"Oh, yes. Truth can never be found out there." He waved a hand to the world. "It's here, and here alone." He tapped his chest.

Her heart began to swell. "I don't know why your own people haven't killed you. What you say sounds like a rejection of Nightland beliefs. They should consider you a false Prophet, not a sacred Guide."

He tilted his head and nodded. "Some do. But not as many these days. It's taken so long to find the hole in the ice. And so many warriors have died. People lose faith when fathers, sons, and brothers are taken from them."

"As did I." She sighed. "Perhaps, since I'm not going to kill you, I should go home. My daughter needs me." She looked back at the soaring spires of the Ice Giants. "And something tells me Nashat isn't going to let me get my hands around his throat, or sneak close enough to run a dart through his pus-dripping heart."

Ti-Bish stood up. "You will go home. Soon. Raven Hunter told me you can't go with us to the Long Dark. But there's something magical I wish to show you before you go."

He extended a hand. She took it and got to her feet. At his touch, a sensation of peace and longing filled her. When had Ti-Bish wound himself so deeply into her heart?

"Where is this thing?"

"Deep in the belly of the Ice Giants." He fixed his warm eyes on hers. "It is the last, and greatest, wonder. I have longed for it, and now, I will be able to share it with you. For that, my soul is filled with joy."

Fifty-seven

Windwolf sat on the hides before his fire, occasionally throwing branches onto the dwindling flames to fight the early-morning chill. The gray stone walls and high ceiling seemed to suck all his warmth away, leaving him bone-cold and weary.

He couldn't explain it, but he sensed something growing in the dark silence—some malignancy without form.

He cursed under his breath. One night with Keresa, and suddenly, for the first time since Bramble's death, he realized he had something to lose.

He stared at the fire, and then back to his bedding, imagining her there, seeing her smile up at him.

Windwolf lowered his head to his hands and massaged his forehead. He longed to send for Keresa, to start west for the Tills and a new life; but he couldn't just walk away from the people here. Without him, there was no telling what the Nightland warriors might be able to do. One tiny error and Kakala would be out of his cage and killing Lame Bull and Sunpath children in a frantic bid to save himself from the cages.

Voices came from the trail outside, and he heard someone running. He was on his feet headed for the door before he'd even realized it. Fish Hawk called, "Windwolf?"

He threw the door curtain back. It was still mostly dark. The last of the Star People twinkled overhead. "What's wrong?"

Fish Hawk caught his breath—he'd obviously run flat-out to get here. "Our scouts just reported in. There's a runner coming." While he sucked in a breath, a momentary flash of relief went through Windwolf. Silt, sending word that he'd reached the Tills. Then Fish Hawk finished, "He's definitely a *Nightland* warrior."

Windwolf's jaw clenched. He said, "Relax. Follow the plan. Notify the refugees. They know what they must do. Tell your men to get dressed. I'll take care of the rest."

"Yes, War Chief." Fish Hawk took off at a fast run, careening down the hill toward the Sunpath camps.

Windwolf let the curtain fall closed . . . and leaned heavily against the stone wall.

Kakala, tell me you value your hide as much as I suddenly do.

Goodeagle lounged on the floor, head propped on his hand, watching Kakala and Keresa. They knelt on the opposite side of the chamber. The thin veil of dawn penetrated the rocks over their heads and cast a pale blue tracery across the floor. They were drawing in the dirt at their feet, whispering to each other. Plotting their escape.

A chuckle shook him.

The fools thought they could escape.

All around him warriors talked about their families, wondering if their wives and children were safe. The plans they made remained blissfully free of references to the cages when they finally returned home.

Goodeagle wiped his mouth with the back of his filthy hand. Since the deaths of his parents when he'd seen ten and four summers, he'd never had any family . . . except Windwolf. Windwolf and the friends who'd fought and hunted beside him those many summers. An ache built in his belly and climbed into his chest.

He glanced back at the tunnel they'd opened between the chambers. He ought to crawl back through to his own chamber, but two rocks covered the entrance. It was Kakala's order. They *always* rolled rocks over the entrance, coming or going. Kakala didn't want the guards above to know how many warriors he had in here. Since it was too much effort to roll them aside by himself, he stayed put.

Kakala said to Keresa, "If you're right that he only has a handful of real warriors and a gaggle of children playing at being warriors, we might have a chance if we . . ."

His voice went too low for Goodeagle to hear, but Keresa nodded and said, "We'll have to wait until he lowers the ladder again and hope he only has a few guards posted."

Goodeagle laughed; it was such a desperate sound that everyone turned in his direction. He said, "That moment will never come, Deputy. He will always have more warriors than necessary posted around this chamber. The greatest threat to his plans lies in here."

"But the last time I was out I saw only—"

"Of course you didn't see them," he said. Then, as though speaking to a child, he leaned toward her and continued in a condescending voice, "He will never let you count his warriors. That would give you an advantage he doesn't wish you to have. If he's let you see ten warriors, he has three tens, maybe four. The instant you think you know what he's doing, Deputy, you are dead."

Keresa started to comment, but the rocks overhead grated shrilly. She hissed, "Goodeagle, get back to your own—"

He and two other warriors leaped to shove away the boulder that covered the entry to the next chamber. They moved it just enough for one warrior to slide through . . . then dawn light poured into the chamber as the rocks above them were rolled aside. Goodeagle and Mong froze, using their bodies to block the entrance.

Keresa shot Goodeagle a knowing glance, but kept her face blank.

Windwolf stood silhouetted against the dark blue sky—and looked Goodeagle right in the eye.

Goodeagle's heart stopped dead in his breast; he dared not even to breathe. He saw the instant recognition. Windwolf's expression hardened—painful remnants of old friendship mixed with hatred and silent questions of "why?"

Then Windwolf's gaze turned emotionless and passed to Kakala.

Goodeagle sank back against the wall, forcing himself to take deep breaths while he pretended to stare at the floor.

If Windwolf knew, why hadn't he . . .

Blessed gods, he—he's counting on me. He needs me.

"Kakala, Keresa," Windwolf ordered, "we have a problem."

Fifty-eight

Kakala dragged himself to his feet and held up a hand, shielding his eyes against the gleam that poured in. He counted four warriors with war clubs in their fists.

Standing above, looking down, Windwolf carried a dart.

"What do you want, Windwolf?"

"Both of you."

The tall man's jaw was clamped so hard, his entire face seemed skewed. Whatever this was, wasn't good. Kakala straightened. "What for?"

"My scouts just reported that there's a runner coming."

"And you need my help to talk to a runner?"

Windwolf used the point of his dart to motion to every warrior in the chamber. "It's a Nightland runner. I need all of you on your feet. Hurry. We haven't much time."

Kakala nodded to his warriors and said, "We're hurrying. Don't get nervous."

His warriors glanced at each other, obviously thinking the same thing he was—that this might be their chance. Keresa subtly held out five fingers, meaning "There are five of them." He nodded. Granted,

Windwolf's people had weapons, but if the right opportunity arose . . .

Kakala gestured for his warriors to climb the ladder first. All the while, Windwolf stood rigidly, eyes glued to Kakala's every movement. Only when Keresa passed by him did his gaze shift. He glanced at her with a softness in his eyes.

Kakala climbed out last . . . and walked straight into three tens of warriors with clubs and nocked atlatls. Keresa bowed her head and smiled wearily.

Kakala grimaced. "What are we doing?" He took another look at the warriors, seeing no more than ten adults among them. Some looked as if they were hiding wounds. The rest were women and children, but each seemed to know how to hold a weapon.

Windwolf gave him a piercing look, almost pleading. "First, order your warriors to follow my directions."

"Why?" *If I ordered a sudden rush, we could probably break that pitiful bunch of warriors, seize enough weapons to make a real fight of it.*

More to Kakala's warriors than him, Windwolf said, "Working with me does two things. First, it saves your lives, and perhaps the runner's as well. Second, it gives us a chance to keep you out of the cages." In a louder voice, he said, "Do you understand?"

Kakala looked back at his warriors, who shot questioning gazes in his direction. He turned to Windwolf. "You could just kill the runner."

A faint smile crossed the man's lips. "Nashat will *know* the rumors are true." He gave Kakala a challenging look. "You help me; I help you."

"Outside of keeping out of the cages, is there a reason I should?" He shot another measuring look at the pitiful band of warriors, women, and children.

"No games, Kakala. We don't have time for it. You choose: back in the hole, and I kill the runner, or we work together to find a solution that leaves everyone breathing, and with a future."

"We await your orders, War Chief Kakala," Keresa said formally. She managed to keep her expression wooden, but he could see the anguish behind her eyes.

She's leaving the choice to me. In that instant, his soul swelled with heartfelt appreciation. If she would do this for him, he could do no less for her.

"We do as War Chief Windwolf instructs! No tricks, no foolishness.

That is my order," Kakala shouted loudly enough for the rest. To Windwolf he said, "Tell me what you want me to do."

"You'll meet the messenger in the ceremonial cave, where everything will look perfectly normal."

"All right." Kakala started walking. His warriors followed. The Lame Bull warriors surrounded them with their darts knocked.

Windwolf matched his pace to Kakala's. "Let's discuss your conduct."

"I think I know how to act with another Nightland warrior."

"One wrong word, one suspicious move—if you blink too quickly, Kakala, I'll do what I have to do. But I'll keep you alive to the last. Do we understand each other?"

Rage flared, but he controlled it. "We do." Then he asked softly, "Keresa, too?"

His shot went home. He saw the scream behind Windwolf's eyes.

"I die with my warriors," Keresa said stiffly. "No favors."

Kakala and Windwolf locked gazes, each taking the other's measure. A silent tug-of-war ensued.

Keresa noticed, averted her head, and made a *phiisst!* sound with her lips.

Then Windwolf broke the gaze, almost laughing. Softly, he said, "I want you to ask the runner one question for me."

Kakala squinted suspiciously. "What is it?"

"Ask him if anyone has reported the location of my warriors."

The question seemed to have a special importance to Windwolf. *By Raven Hunter, he doesn't know.* Kakala laughed. "And to think I've been worried—"

Windwolf's muscular arm slammed Kakala painfully against a boulder. His warriors started forward.

Keresa shouted, "Keep your places!" Then in a lower voice, "Windwolf, that isn't necessary."

To Kakala's surprise, Windwolf backed off, saying, "Just ask him."

"Of course," Kakala responded mildly. A seed of hope lodged in his breast, quickening his breathing. If Windwolf didn't know, they could be days away. Or dead.

He shot a quizzical look at Keresa, who lifted her eyebrows in a shrug.

Windwolf took a deep breath, remarking, "Keresa's right. You bring out the worst in me."

In a voice too low for Keresa to hear, Kakala said, "We don't have to like each other, but if this goes bad, you will make sure Keresa is safe?"

"Kakala," he said with a sigh, "I am a flawed man. For reasons I do not fully understand, I even want you safe."

They walked around the base of the rockshelters, and passed through totally empty Sunpath camps. Every person was gone. Their belongings lay strewn in front of the lodges as though dropped by fleeing people. A few dogs skulked unhappily through the garbage, sniffing and growling at anything that moved.

"Where are all the—?"

"Keep walking," Windwolf said.

Kakala looked at him with new appreciation. "You've known someone would be coming."

Windwolf shot him a sidelong look. "And you didn't? Holding an entire Nightland war party is big news."

Kakala sighed. *I've been so busy keeping my people together and worrying about the cages, I haven't thought about those parties of Sunpath People headed west. Not all of them would have made it past Karigi.*

"You irritate me," Kakala muttered. Then he laughed, more at himself than anything else.

"Good," Windwolf replied. Then he gave Kakala a serious look. "When I capture Karigi, you can have what's left of him when I'm through."

Kakala narrowed an eye. "When I take you back to the Council, I might let your bindings slip when we see him."

"Keresa told you about the Dreamer's vision?"

"The flood coming? Yes. She seems to believe it."

"So do I." Windwolf rocked his jaw. "But for the death, suffering, and misery, it makes our war appear even more insane."

"Assuming your Dreamer is correct." Kakala shrugged. "The Guide has been promising to lead us back to the Long Dark for a long time, now. It doesn't seem to ever happen."

"Maybe he serves the wrong Spirit."

"Or yours does." Kakala arched an eyebrow.

From behind, Keresa said, "Have either of you thought that perhaps they are both right? Raven Hunter wants to take his people into the ice, just as Wolf Dreamer wishes his people to flee to the Tills in the west?"

"Perhaps," Windwolf agreed.

They strode up the trail toward the ceremonial cave near the crest of the hill.

Kakala's eyes widened when he saw that every high point around the village had a red-shirted warrior standing on it. He grimaced. "So that's what you did with the shirts you took from my dead warriors. It might work. If the runner doesn't look too closely."

"After you speak with him, I want you to order him to run straight back home."

"What reason shall I give?"

"You have a message for the Nightland Elders."

Kakala exhaled unhappily. "What is it?"

"You're still hunting down some of the survivors, but upon your return you will personally be bringing me back alive as a present to the Elders."

Kakala studied his hard expression. "I will?"

"Just tell him."

"Windwolf?" Keresa asked in surprise. "By Raven Hunter, do you know what they'll do to you?"

Kakala stared in open shock. "Nashat will order you tortured to death."

"No," Keresa hissed. "Windwolf, you do not have to do this thing for me! Have you lost your mind?"

"Probably," Windwolf said gruffly.

When they reached the ceremonial chamber, Windwolf gripped him by the arm. "Order your warriors to sit down in a circle around the fire and start having a delightful conversation."

Kakala roughly shook Windwolf's arm loose, walking out into the room. "You heard him. I want you to look tired. Think of this as the first rest we've had in a long time." He met their eyes, letting his stare bore into Goodeagle's. "Are you with me?"

"Yes, War Chief," they shouted in unison.

Kakala nodded. *He ignores Goodeagle, acts as if he doesn't exist. Is there something I can use here?*

His warriors sat, delighted to find a skewered elk haunch slowly roasting. They dipped themselves cups of warm tea from the bag on the tripod and started whispering to each other.

Windwolf jerked his chin at his own warriors, and they slipped into the shadows of the cavern's walls.

Windwolf eased back to Kakala's right, hiding behind the lip of the cave, but his dart point stabbed uncomfortably into Kakala's kidney. He said, "Don't forget: Your warriors' lives are at stake."

Kakala shot a glare over his shoulder. "Do you think I'm an idiot?"

"That is a fascinating discussion we'll save for another time."

Kakala pulled himself straight. Forgetting where he was, his head struck the stone. At the impact he almost passed out. Trembling, he fought the urge to cry out. His warriors noticed. They looked at him breathlessly, some obviously worried that he was too ill to handle things. It made his gut ache as badly as his head.

Keresa's hard eyes assessed the Lame Bull warriors, then shifted to Kakala. "Are you all right?"

Kakala nodded, and in the calmest tone he could muster, said, "We'll proceed just as though this were a casual conversation with a runner from the Elders. No heroics, or our friend Windwolf will order his warriors to kill us all."

Windwolf said to Keresa, "Deputy, when the runner arrives, I would appreciate it if you would walk out and greet him."

She gave him a wary look. "I'll make him feel right at home."

I would appreciate? Kakala looked back and forth between them, seeing the worry and concern in their eyes. *Oh, Keresa, what have you gotten yourself into?*

On the hilltop across from the ceremonial chamber, the guard waved a hand.

"He's coming, Kakala. Are you ready?" Windwolf asked in a strained voice.

"As ready as I ever am when I have to answer ridiculous questions from the Elders."

A small round of nervous laughter went through his warriors, just as he'd intended. They all knew how much he hated clan politics.

"All right, Keresa," Windwolf said with a sigh. "He's running up the trail."

She stepped over to stand beside Kakala, looking down at the runner.

"Homaldo?" she called, and lifted a hand. "What are you doing here? Where are the others? What happened to you?"

"We thought the fight was lost, got cut off from the rest of you," he called back, and pounded up the trail grinning.

When he got close, Keresa stepped out and smiled. "You should be home playing hoop-and-stick with your son."

Homaldo stopped in front of Keresa and took her hand in a strong grip. "We thought you were all dead! It's good to see you alive."

"Of course we're alive," Kakala said indignantly. "Do our Elders judge me so poorly?"

Homaldo's smile faded. "No, War Chief, not at all. I'm not supposed to be here. And if Nashat learns that I have come, the cages will be a merciful alternative to what he will do to me. Kishkat, Tapa, and Tibo are searching the caves for the woman Skimmer. We found her on the trail, and . . ." He glanced away. "We thought you were all dead, War Chief. But we took her to the Guide."

Kakala narrowed an eye. "With an eye to saving your necks, no doubt."

He gestured to the bandage on Kakala's head. "It must have been a tough fight."

"Windwolf jumped me at the last instant, but we got him. Even without your help." He pointed to his head. "I have been unable to travel."

Keresa added, "We're still hunting down a few survivors. We should be headed home tomorrow or the next day."

"With Windwolf," Kakala said, and lifted his chin proudly. "I will personally be bringing him back alive as a gift to our Elders."

Homaldo smiled broadly. "They will be glad to hear it. It's another piece of good news."

"Another?" Keresa asked.

Excitedly, Homaldo said, "Just before I left, the Elders came out and told us that the Guide has found the hole in the ice! We're all packing to return to the Long Dark."

The warriors sitting around the fire behind Kakala gasped and turned to listen.

Windwolf's dart pressed into Kakala's kidney. He winced and said, "Have you heard from Karigi? Where are Windwolf's warriors? We've been expecting them to show up at any time."

Homaldo spread his arms. "The news is mixed. They destroyed Hawhak's war party. He, his deputy, and the rest are in the cages. Nashat says that because of their disgrace, they cannot accompany the Guide to the Long Dark."

"And Windwolf's warriors?"

"Karigi sent word that they all fled west. Karigi attacked three more camps and is herding tens of captives to the Nightland Caves, where he's been ordered to set up a pen for them. And Deputy Ewin's war party is on its way here. He should arrive tomorrow."

From the corner of his eye, Kakala saw Windwolf's expression slacken, as though he'd just heard his own Death Song being sung.

"Why is Ewin coming here?" Kakala demanded. "Do the Elders think I am so incompetent that I require *his* assistance?"

Behind him, his warriors responded to his outrage by shifting disgustedly. Moans and curses laced the air. He wanted to kiss them.

Homaldo wet his lips nervously. "War Chief, I don't know. But there is a rumor that you had been captured. I, well, I'd die for you. We cast gaming pieces to see which one of us would come to see if it was true. I won the honor."

Anxiety tingled in Kakala's chest. If Ewin was headed here, Nashat knew of his failure.

Hawhak and his warriors are in the cages! They cannot accompany our people?

Kakala sagged against the cave wall, which forced Windwolf to pull his dart back. Unfortunately, he resettled it on Kakala's spine. "Homaldo, I want you to run home immediately and tell the Elders we will be right behind you with our 'gift.' "

Keresa pointed a finger like a bone stiletto at Homaldo. "And tell my clan not to return to the Long Dark without me."

Homaldo frowned. "I'll have to figure something out. I'm supposed to be searching the caves for Skimmer."

"Why?" Kakala asked. "This part, I do not understand."

Homaldo lowered his voice. "The guard at the Council is my cousin. As we were entering the caves, he told me that Skimmer was accused of plotting to kill the Guide. But in the Council, she accused Nashat of misdeeds. And then, after the Elders left, Nashat threatened the Guide. Skimmer protected Ti-Bish! Dared Nashat to try and harm him!" He blinked. "Can you believe that?"

Kakala and Keresa traded glances, and Kakala felt the dart point fall away, as if Windwolf had lost interest in holding it against him.

Kakala took the opportunity to step forward, out of visible range of the dart. "When it comes to Nashat, I can believe anything. Kishkat was there the night the Guide freed me. Ask him."

Keresa said, "War Chief? Perhaps it would be a good idea if Homaldo met Ewin? He could save him the trip here, urge him to hurry home and prepare to follow the Guide?"

Kakala gave her the expected look of irritation and said, "Homaldo, can you find Ewin?"

"I think so, War Chief." He frowned. "But who will carry your message to the Elders?"

"One of these lazy warriors back here." Kakala barked, "Washani! Bring Homaldo some of that meat to stuff in his pack. We have plenty."

"Yes, War Chief."

Kakala took a gamble, and walked over to clap his hand on Homaldo's shoulder. "Thank you, my friend. We all appreciate the risks you have taken on our behalf. I would ask you as a favor, find Ewin. Tell him the rumor of our capture is a lie formulated by the Sunpath. We are fine, and he shouldn't waste precious time coming here. By the time he arrives, we'll almost be home. Can you do that?"

"Yes, War Chief!" Homaldo cried with a grin. "Especially if it keeps me out of Nashat's way!"

A chorus of shouts rose behind him.

Washani emerged with a pack stuffed full of meat. He cast an inquisitive glance at Kakala, as if expecting some instruction, like, *Run off with Homaldo and tell him the whole story.*

"Thank you, Washani," Kakala said. "That will be all. Go back and fill your lazy belly."

"Yes, War Chief."

Kakala watched Homaldo turn and trot back down the trail. He called, "Find Ewin!"

"I will!" Homaldo waved over his back.

The Lame Bull warriors eased from the shadows with their nocked atlatls up.

Windwolf stepped forward and peered over Kakala's shoulder, watching Homaldo until he vanished down the trail. His voice came out unsettlingly soft. "That was good thinking."

Kakala blurted, "Well, someone had to save all of our skins. You'd just better hope Homaldo finds Ewin."

"The Guide has found the hole!" warriors called back and forth, excitement in their eyes.

"Yes!" Kakala snapped. "And Hawhak and his warriors aren't going!

The Council has heard that we've been captured. If they believe it, we're not going either!"

They stared at him soberly.

Kakala turned. "All right, Windwolf. The other night, you said that when we could talk like men, we should talk. Perhaps that time is now."

"What are you thinking?" Windwolf asked.

"I'm thinking it's not a coincidence that the Guide finds the hole in the ice just after your Dreamer warns of a great flood." He looked down at his fingers. "My people live on the Thunder Sea. Have you ever seen what happens when a mountain of ice falls into the water? A huge wave washes everything before it. My family died in one of those." He smiled wryly. "Perhaps, as you said, our war is insignificant."

At that moment, a low rumble rolled over the land; the ground shook. Kakala could see the warriors glancing nervously at the rock over their heads. Bits of gravel pelted them.

And then it was gone.

Fifty-nine

Windwolf watched Fish Hawk climb up the trail. "Did it all go well?"

"They did exactly as Kakala ordered, War Chief. They walked right up to the hole and climbed down. I have already sent warriors to bring them robes and firewood." Fish Hawk fixed him with curious eyes. "War Chief, are you sure this is a smart thing to do?"

Windwolf turned and fixed him with knowing eyes. "I just met with Lookingbill. He understands that Homaldo may not be able to find Ewin. At Silvertip's urging, he reluctantly agreed that it was time to leave. I want every person packed and ready to move by first light."

"You mean, before Ewin's war party arrives?"

Windwolf nodded. "We can't fight them, Fish Hawk. We have only a few adult warriors; it's not enough. And our young warriors will fall like dry grass before a powerful hailstorm. You know it as well as I."

Fish Hawk swallowed hard, gaze inexorably drawn to the children playing at the base of the rock shelters. He could hear their laughter rising on the gusts of wind. "This has been my home for all of my life. The idea of leaving . . . it just doesn't seem possible."

Windwolf asked, "Can you do it, War Chief?"

Fish Hawk nodded. "I can, but . . . where will we go? The Tills? I know nothing about them. My clan has been here forever."

A powerful gust of wind swept up the slope, and Windwolf's short black hair blew around his face. "I need to talk with Kakala and Keresa."

Fish Hawk jerked a nod. "My people will be packed by first light."

"And, in case I forget, you make sure you have a screen of scouts out. It wouldn't do to stumble into Ewin's war party on the way."

"Of course, War Chief." He hesitated. "Do you need guards for your talk with the Nightland?"

"No." He smiled at the irony. "Not anymore."

As Fish Hawk trotted away, Windwolf eased down on a flat rock and closed his eyes. So much had to happen so quickly.

Skimmer followed Ti-Bish along the sandy shore of the fiery lake, her way lit only by the luminous streamers that snaked through the water. The Ice Giants who stretched high overhead groaned, and the very air trembled with their pain. New cracks, like black lightning bolts, had split the ceiling since the last time she'd been down here. Some were over two tens of body lengths wide.

"Ti-Bish," she called, frightened. "Where are we going?"

"It's not much farther. Are you tired?"

They'd been walking for a long time, though she could not say just how long. The lack of sunlight and darkness left her completely bewildered. "No, I'm not tired; I'm just concerned. Won't your Elders wonder where you are?"

He shook his head. "They're busy packing for the journey. They know I'll return."

In the damp air, his two black braids had turned frizzy, but his dark eyes glowed as though a blaze had flared to life in his soul.

He pointed. "Do you see the bones ahead?"

Skimmer looked to where he pointed.

"That's the Monster Bone Trail," he explained in a whisper, as though the long-dead beasts might hear him. "I want you to see the path."

Skimmer's mouth dropped open when they walked through the rib cage of a huge animal; the bones arched over her head. From snout to tail, the beast must have stretched at least five or six body lengths. "What is this creature?"

He shrugged and stepped around a human skull. "One of the monsters that lived just after the creation, I think."

As Skimmer passed another human skull, she stared into the dark eye sockets, wondering who the man might have been. Another Dreamer? Someone else seeking the hole in the ice?

Then she saw the ax. It had been laid on an ice shelf. She stepped over, and picked it up, looking back at the skull. *Was this yours? A tool no longer needed?*

She hefted it, staring at the handle. The wood had been carved with long grooves and drilled with dots. The binding, made of sinew, was crusted with frost. The stone head had been set in a Y in the wood and daubed with pitch. It had been chipped from a translucent brown chert she'd never seen before. She pressed her thumb to the sharp edge.

How long had it been since this had rested in human hands? Tightening her grip on the handle, she followed after Ti-Bish.

They walked in silence until Ti-Bish said, "There. Do you see it?"

"What?"

He gestured to the dark cavern ahead. A river spilled out through it and ran into the fiery lake.

She said, "It's a river."

Ti-Bish frowned at her. "Yes, but . . . that's the hole."

"The hole?" she said in confusion.

"The hole in the ice. We must go through it to get to the Land of the Long Dark."

Terror crept up around her heart. She stared at him. "That's it?"

He smiled tenderly. "Yes. That's it. It's a difficult journey. It will take many, many days, but—"

"How do you know how long it will take? Have you made the trip before?"

"Oh, yes," he murmured. "In a Spirit Dream. Raven Hunter took me."

"It's cold water, Ti-Bish. Walk in that for more than a couple of hands' time, and people's legs will go numb. If someone trips and falls, they'll be wet clear through. You can't stop and make a fire to dry out. The children will die first."

"Raven Hunter will find a way. Perhaps, at the last moment, he'll divert the water." He searched the ice roof over their heads, as though expecting to see Raven Hunter swooping down to speak with him.

Skimmer pulled her cape more tightly around her shoulders and shivered. "Have you seen him lately?"

"Yes, often."

"Ti-Bish, doesn't it frighten your people when you tell them that?"

"Does it frighten you?"

"I . . . I don't know."

He bowed his head and smiled. "Skimmer, every man walks away from the herd sometime. When he chooses to stand alone in the meadow, he knows the predators will see him. He also knows they will be waiting. There was a time"—he hesitated—"a time when I moved too far from the herd. I'll never do that again. I only tell my people what they need to know. It keeps them at bay."

How strange that he thought of his own people as predators. But why wouldn't he? It had been only ten summers ago that he'd been a homeless outcast, loathed by almost everyone, chased from village to village.

They walked closer to the black cavern, and Skimmer said, "You once told me that you'd brought me here to pray with you. But we haven't prayed together. Not yet."

He stopped and looked at her with luminous eyes. "Prayer is . . . not what you think. Not what most people think. It isn't begging the gods for something. It isn't undertaken to enlighten, or bring tranquility. It is an act of service done for the sake of the world. If people truly work to maintain harmony, the world will stay in balance. If they don't, the Spiral of life will tilt, and everything will wither and die."

Sorrow tinged the last few words, and tears welled in his eyes.

"Is that why there's been so much war and sadness? The Spiral has tilted?"

"Yes, Raven Hunter has been trying to bring it back into balance, but his evil brother won't allow it, and that's why we must go back."

"Back to the Long Dark?"

"Yes, back to a time before the brothers fought. Back to a time before they were even born."

As though in response, a deep agonizing groan shook the Ice Giants, and massive slabs of ice cracked loose from the ceiling and crashed down. When they splashed into the lake, brilliant sprays of light burst into the air. Waves washed high onto the shore, wetting her to the knees. She felt the sand slide under her.

Skimmer lurched back against the wall, panting like a hunted animal.

Ti-Bish just smiled. "It's all right," he said softly. "The pain is almost over."

Sixty

Nashat caught his balance as the quake hit. Impulsively, he cast a quick glance up at the ice overhead. Only a couple of gravel pellets clattered down around him. He could hear the ice moan, screech, and crack.

"Blessed Raven Hunter, I can't *wait* to get out of this death trap!" Then he glanced around to make sure no one was close.

A sensation of doom was closing in around him, making breathing difficult. He hurried along, passed the opening to the Council Chamber, and stopped short. A huge block of ice had smashed down on his robes. White, and crusted with bands of gravel, it had shattered to send angular chunks of ice around half the room.

If I had been sitting there . . . No, don't even think it.

In half panic, he trotted down the tunnel, feet crunching the gravel underfoot.

At the great opening, he stopped, staring. People had been coming from all over. Literal mountains of packs stood beside small camps. But for the moment, the people were congregated down at the shore. It took a moment for the meaning of the darkened sand to sink in. A large wave had washed up and then receded.

He glanced out at the Thunder Sea. He could see debris bobbing in the choppy water. Among the packs, boats, and floating hides, people splashed around. Some clung to wreckage, calling desperately.

Those on shore were dragging bull boats down to the water, intent on rescuing the survivors before the cold water claimed them.

He took a deep breath. When strong quakes shook the ice, it often broke off, splashing down into the Thunder Sea. His people knew better than to camp too close to the beach.

"Fools! Serves them right."

Then he returned his attention to the piled packs. The people were ready to move. He shifted his glance to the south, as if seeing beyond the tundra and spruce barrens to the oak and maple forest beyond. A land abandoned, ready for a new people to move in and enjoy the bounty, far from this miserable ice and cold.

"I am sorry, Ti-Bish. But I think it's time that Skimmer finally served her purpose." He actually felt a sense of delightful relief. His long ordeal was over. At last, he need no longer endure the wide-eyed innocence of the Idiot.

Keresa tossed a stick into Windwolf's fire. As the flames licked around it, she studied Kakala. He walked around, staring at the stone, fingering the bedding, and idly ran a finger down one of the long war darts leaned against the wall.

Kakala glanced at her as he studied the darts. "Do you think he remembered these were in here?"

"He's getting tired. Making mistakes." She flipped the bone stiletto from the top of her tall moccasin. "He never asked for this back, either."

Kakala picked up one of the darts, glancing down its polished length with a practiced eye. "You two must have spent an interesting night."

Keresa glanced at the fire. "I just hope it wasn't the *only* night we ever have together." Coolly she asked, "Why didn't you order us to rush Windwolf's pitiful little band of warriors when we climbed out of the hole?"

"Maybe it was curiosity. Maybe I wanted to see what Windwolf would do." Kakala was balancing the dart experimentally. "What does *pssst* mean?"

"*Phiisst!* It's the sound that one buffalo bull makes when another dominant bull walks up. You've heard it."

Kakala nodded. "And watched them tear up half the scenery. Is that what you think Windwolf and I are? Buffalo bulls?"

"You act like it when you get together."

"Well, at least he didn't kill me when I stepped out to clap Homaldo on the shoulder." He paused, bouncing the dart up and down in his hand. "Do you think the Guide has really found the way to the paradise of the Long Dark?"

Keresa shrugged. "I don't know."

Kakala searched her eyes. "Are you going?"

She shook her head slowly. "As much as it will break my heart not to be close to you, no. I've been different all of my life, Kakala. The only place I felt at home was with warriors. If the Guide is right, and the Long Dark is paradise, where will the warriors be?"

"Hunting." He grinned. "And I will never have to look at another dead child and say, 'I did that.'"

"I wish you all the happiness in paradise, Kakala. You, of all people, deserve a little." She shot him a sidelong look. "Give my regards to Karigi."

His expression fell. "Somehow, I forgot. I hope paradise is large enough that I can live on one side, and he on the other."

Keresa frowned. "What is this nonsense about Windwolf going with us as our captive?"

"I have no idea, but I will enjoy the reversal of roles."

Keresa gestured impotence. "It's madness. He doesn't have to do this! Our warriors can just leave. We can promise never to raid another Sunpath band. They're going west; our people are going into the ice."

She looked up as Windwolf—looking weary and concerned—stepped in. He stopped short, seeing the dart in Kakala's hand. "I hope you're not having creative thoughts about that."

Kakala balanced the shaft, feet braced. "Actually, I was. I was thinking how happy I am that it isn't sticking in one of my warriors' guts."

"Or your own," Windwolf said warily, ready to duck.

Kakala neatly bounced the shaft off his hard palm, caught it, and laid it back against the wall. "After all we've been through, War Chief, it appears that I am as flawed as you are. For some reason that defeats me, I don't wish you dead either." He smiled. "I'm tired, Windwolf. Sick of it. And after the last couple of summers wondering what it was all for."

"Don't we all?" Windwolf asked, and finally seated himself beside Keresa. He reached out and took her hand. "How are you?"

She smiled, tightening her grip in his. "Still confused." The smile fell. "Why do you think you have to go with Kakala to the Nightland villages? I don't understand. My warriors can take their chances, and by returning, no one will believe that they were captives. Homaldo can tell them otherwise."

Windwolf's probing look sent a shiver through her. "They have my people. Tell me, Keresa: Why would Karigi be herding still more captives north? Why do they need more women and children?"

Kakala exhaled bitterly. "The captives are to carry the Nightland possessions into the Long Dark."

Windwolf narrowed his eyes. "But I thought the reason you killed so many of us, destroyed our happiness, was to ensure that no Sunpath People followed you through the ice. Every one of those captives believes, Kakala."

Keresa saw Kakala nod slowly. Then he walked over and seated himself across the fire from them. "It is Nashat's order. Probably without the Guide's knowledge."

Windwolf's look was grim. "The same Nashat who ordered the Nine Pipes women clubbed to death in the pen they were being held in?"

Kakala rubbed his face. "How did you hear about that?"

"Skimmer and her daughter, Ashes, escaped. They hid under the dead. Nashat ordered the attack in the middle of the night. Just before dawn, Skimmer and her daughter slipped away."

Keresa felt her heart sink. She glanced at Kakala. "And you wonder why I am not going with our people? They have lied to us from the beginning. We are sick, Kakala. Sick in our souls."

"They are our people, Keresa."

"The same ones who put you into the cage! And for what? Following Nashat's orders to attack Headswift Village with a force we both knew was too small for the task?"

"We have *had* this discussion before."

"And we're going to have it again," she insisted. "We have obeyed, followed their orders, and they put you in the cage for it. But for the Guide and me, you'd still be there!"

Kakala's expression had grayed. "Don't *remind* me!"

Keresa glanced apologetically at Windwolf. "Forgive us."

"You sound like a married couple."

Kakala shot him a warning look. "You're the one who wants to marry her. I'd never have let myself in for that kind of irritation."

Keresa shot him a smile. "Marry? Windwolf might be as disgusted with me in next moon as you've been for summers."

Windwolf's amused smile died. "I still have to save as many of my people as I can." He looked at Kakala. "Unless you have some objection to that?"

"If my warriors can go free, and you can find a way of doing this without killing my people, I have no objection." Kakala frowned. "If the Long Dark is such a paradise, why do we need to take so many things with us?"

"The journey is supposed to be long," Keresa answered. "The captives carry the extra food."

"And what do they eat?" Windwolf asked. "Each other?"

Keresa met Kakala's suddenly dull eyes. "Nashat wouldn't care about feeding slaves. That's why he had the Nine Pipes women murdered."

Kakala propped his chin on his knee. He glanced curiously at Windwolf. "You sent your warriors to the Tills?"

"It kept them alive. And, with party after party of refugees, they're so busy hunting and getting people settled that they don't have time to come back and get themselves killed over misguided heroics."

"So, it's just us?" Keresa asked.

"Just me," he amended.

"I'm with you," she insisted. "I helped put a lot of those women in there."

Kakala gave a harsh laugh. "Windwolf, you've been so lucky you've come to believe you can't die. Well, you can. I could have killed you when you walked through that opening. You're tired, making mistakes. And one man isn't going to free tens of tens of captives. Not from under Karigi's very nose."

Windwolf's eyes hardened. "Karigi? It's even more tempting. I have an old score to settle with him."

"We both do," Kakala insisted. Then he threw his arms up. "*What* am I doing?" He gave Keresa a pleading look. "He's a madman!" Then, "Windwolf, you can't help them by dying!"

She watched Windwolf and Kakala lock gazes. Then Windwolf said in a soft voice, "They're my people, Kakala. If they were yours, what would you do?"

Kakala's mouth opened, then slowly closed. He shrugged in weary defeat.

Keresa said, "Kakala, after all the planning we've done, and the raids we've pulled off, this shouldn't be that difficult."

He climbed stiffly to his feet. "I don't know. My head has been aching since I banged it on that rock." He looked at Windwolf. "I'm going back to my warriors. Do I need a guard?"

"It would be a good idea. First, it would stop you from entertaining any foolish ideas. Second, it would keep some angry Sunpath or Lame Bull widow from taking out her wrath on you."

Keresa sighed, pulled her hand from Windwolf's, and stopped when Kakala smiled. "Stay, Keresa. Maybe you can talk some sense into him."

Windwolf smiled at her. "I'll escort him myself."

"No guard at the door?" Kakala asked.

"Why would I need one?" Windwolf replied. "I assume Keresa still has that stiletto tucked in her moccasin."

Sixty-one

The pain is almost over. Skimmer ran the words through her soul as she stared at the forbidding blackness of Ti-Bish's chamber. She could feel his warm body pressed against hers where they lay together under the hides.

Upon their return from the long trek to the hole in the ice, the fire had been burned out. Ti-Bish had been concerned that no wood had been carried in, and he refused to discuss what had happened to his slave girl, Pipe.

Skimmer, still wet from the wave that had washed up her legs after the quake, had been shivering, exhausted, and heedless of anything but getting warm. Ti-Bish, too, had been nearly blue from cold. She had removed her moccasins and damp dress to climb under the hides.

Unable to bear his shivering, she had looked across the room where he'd sat back against the wall. In the flickering light of the little lamp, he'd looked pathetic as he huddled and shivered.

On impulse, she'd invited him to share the hides.

The pain is almost over.

But what had it been for? She stared out at the darkness, sensing a presence in the very air. The little lamp had long ago burned out. Did something hover in the room?

She almost turned over to wake Ti-Bish, then felt a movement in the air, as if a great wing had spread over her. The sensation was oddly reassuring, as if a covering against her thoughts.

I am alive when so many are dead.

She closed her eyes, remembering with clarity the attack on Nine Pipes Village, the shock of her captivity and the long journey north. She relived each instant of the horror of the pen, right down to the snapping of skulls as Karigi's warriors waded into the captives. Again, she smelled the cloying odor of death.

So I came here to kill, and found a humble and honest man who Dreams of peace.

The Song of the Ice Giants changed harmonics, little creaks and groans of the ice adding to the effect. Why did she feel so at peace?

"Ti-Bish loves you with all of his lonely heart."

Did she hear, or just imagine the soft voice in the darkness?

"Loves me?" she asked under her breath.

She thought back to Hookmaker, and what they'd shared.

"You live," the faint whisper from the darkness assured. *"Take the moment."*

She closed her eyes, trading one darkness for another. She was aware of the beating of her heart, the blood in her veins. She reveled in the air filling her lungs. She could sense Ti-Bish, feel his warmth and life, where it pressed against her.

Alive.

At that moment, Ti-Bish rolled over to mold his body against hers. A delighted sigh escaped his throat as he slid his arm over the curve of her waist.

She should have stiffened, repulsed by his body against hers. Instead, the disarming memory of his worshiping eyes lingered within her. She could recall each of his gentle movements, the joy that filled his face when he looked out at the marvels of his world.

She had never known a soul as pure as his. That left her oddly disturbed, but with a curious warmth down in her core.

How odd that she'd instinctively placed herself between Ti-Bish and Nashat, understanding the role that Power had cast for her.

Her eyes opened as she felt his penis harden against her buttocks, and from the purling of his warm breath on her neck, knew that he still slept.

How long did she lie there, aware of his hard shaft? Considering its implications?

She had come expecting this, believing it was part of the ruse to gain his trust.

And now?

Without thought she rolled onto her back and wrapped her hand around his stiff manhood.

He started, coming awake.

"What . . . ?" The words froze in his throat.

"Don't speak," she told him softly, and tightened her hold.

She heard him swallow. With her other hand, she took his, laying it on the swell of her breast. He moved awkwardly as he explored her, the touch reverent and gentle. Then, hesitantly, he settled onto her body. As he slid into her ready sheath he took a deep breath, whispering, "I love you."

"I know."

Keresa blinked awake, aware of the dull gray light that filtered in around the door hanging. She lay for the moment, deeply content with the warmth from Windwolf's body. She could hear his deep breathing, feel his back pressed against hers.

If only we could stay like this forever. What a joyous miracle that would be.

She replayed their coupling during the night, relishing the memory of their bodies moving in unison. She had tried to pull him inside, as if to press his body right through bone and muscle. If only she could keep him there, inside her, somewhere close to her heart.

Turning over, she pressed herself against his back, scooting her knees behind his and hugging him tightly.

"Morning?" he asked gently.

"It is."

He groaned. "Got to get up."

"Can't we take time?"

"The Lame Bull are packing."

"They don't need you to put blankets in packs. I'm sure they can do that on their own." She hesitated. "This might be our last chance."

Her inquisitive fingers snaked down past his navel to find him. She had greater powers of persuasion than logic.

When they finally lay spent, the glow fading from their loins, he propped himself up to stare down at her. "If anything should happen, if we are separated, I'll wait for you at the Tills." He arched an eyebrow, "But I wouldn't travel there dressed in a Nightland war shirt."

She laughed. "Come, let's get on with the day."

"War Chief?" a voice called from outside.

"Silvertip?" Windwolf asked. "A moment please, and then I will be out."

"I need to see you both," the boy said. "Call me when you are ready."

"How long has he been out there?" Keresa whispered. "He would have heard everything."

"I don't think he heard anything he didn't already know," Windwolf muttered, reaching for his war shirt.

Keresa pulled on her dress, running fingers through her hair. What she'd give for a proper washing. The miracle was that Windwolf didn't hold his nose when he was coupling with her.

"Enter, Dreamer," Windwolf called.

Ashes ducked beneath the hanging, her careful eyes taking in the room's contents. The war club filled her hands.

Silvertip followed, his face expressionless, but when Keresa looked into his eyes, it was like staring into deep pools, knowing that the bottom might be an illusion.

"Dreamer," Windwolf greeted. "Can I help you?"

Silvertip walked over and settled by the cold fire. "I am leading my people west, War Chief. Some insist on staying, though I have told them the price they will pay."

"People must make their own choices, Dreamer."

He smiled. "That they must." His young face lined. "Wind, Water, and Fire. It is a Powerful combination. Opposites crossed." He stared right at Keresa, and her soul shivered. "When you are in the north, you will find the Earth."

"The Earth?" Windwolf and Keresa asked in unison.

Silvertip smiled. "Power comes in fours: the directions, the great forces, the seasons, it is all part of the unity."

"Some say six, Dreamer," Keresa replied. "The four directions, and up and down."

"Or light and dark," Silvertip agreed. "Darkness and light. I am one; the Guide is the other. Do you begin to understand?"

Keresa frowned. "He is Raven Hunter's. You serve Wolf Dreamer."

"I walk in the light," Silvertip told her, a question in the set of his lips.

". . . And he walks in darkness."

"Opposites crossed. We all serve Power."

Windwolf nodded, as if some great revelation had been born in his soul. "What is my role, Dreamer?"

"To serve Power, War Chief." Silvertip leaned his head back. "In the end, our peoples will have paid the cost of disharmony, as Wolf Dreamer and Raven Hunter are paying."

"I don't understand." Keresa frowned. "How do Spirits pay?"

"By finally understanding that neither can win." He smiled. "Opposites cannot exist without the other. Can men exist without women? The very existence of light can never be pure by itself. Look beneath the rock, Deputy, and you will find shadow. Revel in the blackness of midnight, but it will yield to morning."

"And Wolf Dreamer and Raven Hunter are bound by this?" She gave him an uneasy look.

"Oh, yes. Though it has taken time for them to realize that while they must, by their very nature, oppose one another, they are brothers, born of the same womb. Is it possible, Deputy, to receive without something being given?"

Windwolf took her hand, giving it a press. "We understand, Dreamer."

"Good. The lesson is surprisingly simple, but infinitely difficult at the same time." Silvertip pressed his palms together.

"Isn't that always the way of it?"

"The final pieces are in place," Silvertip told him. "Opposites crossed. When you find the Earth, you must head south. The west will be impassable. I would urge you to make all haste. You will not have time to tarry. Once across the river, you will have to follow the southern margins of the lakes to the Tills."

"I see," Windwolf replied.

"What of my people, Dreamer?" Keresa asked. "We have heard that the Guide has found the way to the Long Dark."

He smiled at her, eyes seeing somewhere in the distance of his Dream. "The Sunpath People ignored Raven Hunter, and cast his teachings from their souls. They have paid dearly for that."

"But my people have turned their backs on Wolf Dreamer!"

"And now, the balance must be restored," Silvertip said sadly. "Deputy, remember, there is no life without death. Sometimes, terrible steps must be taken to restore the harmony."

Keresa's fumbling thoughts tried to make sense of it. The Sunpath and Lame Bull were beaten, leaving. Who could possibly challenge the Nightland now? She was about to ask, but Silvertip had stood, nodding politely at them.

"Dreamer?" Windwolf asked, rising. "Will we see you again?"

He looked back, one hand on the door hanging. "That depends on Wind and Water, Fire and Earth." And then he was gone, Ashes silently following behind.

Sixty-two

What have I become? Who have I become?

Skimmer sat in the darkness, her back to the contoured wall of Ti-Bish's chamber. She had placed a folded hide to both cushion and insulate her back from the ice.

She felt Ti-Bish shift, his head cradled on her lap. Her fingers carefully smoothed his hair, running strands of it between them the way she had once done with Ashes.

"Are you still alive, Daughter?" she asked the darkness.

"She is."

Skimmer heard the voice from the Raven Bundle, could feel its pulsing warmth.

"Where is she?"

"Headed west, toward the Tills."

"Why should I believe you?"

"Because I have no reason to lie."

"Oh? You have Ti-Bish believing he can lead the Nightland People up an icy river to find paradise."

"And Wolf Dreamer led your people to believe that through peace, and the search for the One, they, too, could find paradise."

"We were fools."

"That is the lesson you needed to learn."

She heard the shift in his voice, and looking through the darkness, thought a darker shadow moved in the room. She could feel the change in the air on her cheek. "So, what are you going to do? Let all those people climb into that hole, splash around, and wash out as corpses?"

"No. The Dream, my Dream, is about to die. The bargain is struck. Opposites crossed. I have taken from Wolf Dreamer; he has taken from me. I have given him his Dreamer; he has given me mine."

"And what comes next?"

"The struggle begins again. It is the nature of creation."

"Why struggle?"

"Why not just live in the One?"

"Because it becomes stagnation. It leads to weakness and death."

"You begin to understand."

"So all that is left is war and struggle?"

"Until you met Ti-Bish, what did you have?"

"Hatred and rage." She smiled at the darkness. "And I still have it."

"Good." A pause. *"But you now have something to go with it."*

She frowned, and then nodded, aware of the spark deep in her breast. "Hope."

"My mistake . . . I failed to anticipate the Power of it."

"You should have listened to your Prophet. Ti-Bish is full of it."

"Ti-Bish is not my Prophet."

"Spirits take me, if it's Nashat, I'm going to burn your bundle."

"Oh, no." The soft voice sounded amused. *"Nashat cares nothing for Spirit Power. He lives only to serve Nashat."* A pause. *"I sought a Dreamer who believes but has a strength of soul and dedication. Someone who would offer his life and happiness to a cause he believed in. My Dreamer had to understand down to the soul's core why the One, tranquility, and order were flawed, like tool stone riddled with cracks."*

"Have you looked closely at Karigi?"

"Karigi is too much like Nashat."

She saw the darkness shift, felt movement in the still air.

"Come. Let me show you something."

"I'll wake Ti-Bish if I get up."

"He sleeps more soundly than he has since he was a child. He loves you with all of his heart."

She carefully lifted his head, slipped to the side, and eased it to the hides. Standing, she followed, oddly aware of his black presence. To her surprise, she could sense the corridor, as though her soul reached out and touched the ice walls, could feel the twists and turns in the passages.

"It's as if I can see in the dark."

"It is my gift."

"Do you give such gifts often?"

"As often as you do." A pause. *"You have given the greatest gift to Ti-Bish. He has loved you for a long time."*

"He once said that lying with me would have dire consequences."

"It was your final decision."

"And that means . . . what?"

"Pleasure, creation, fertility, love, and sharing. The balance of harmony, peace, and order. To seek the One is to deny the needs of the flesh."

She wound around a sharp twist, the tunnel leading upward. It took all of her concentration to scramble over a fallen boulder.

"I should have felt guilty. My husband isn't that long dead."

"You have survived a lifetime's worth since Hookmaker's death. You have learned a valuable lesson."

"All I have learned is that moments can be precious."

"Come. Climb up here."

She frowned. "That looks steep. What if I fall?"

"You won't. The water has washed just so, leaving stones exposed that will hold your weight."

She watched the dark shadow rise, felt puffs of air, heard the flapping of wings. Then, following her instinct, grasped a protruding stone and levered herself up. How long she climbed was hard to assess, but finally she struggled out, amazed to find herself in a narrow valley between masses of jumbled ice. A trail of gravel, stone, and silt showed where meltwater had run before a crack drained the runoff away.

"That takes you to tundra. Trust me, you need only follow it."

"My way out?" She turned back, seeing a human form, a great black-feathered cape falling down from his shoulders. His face, achingly handsome, seemed to glow with the same radiance as the waters in Ti-Bish's hidden lake. He watched her with knowing dark eyes.

"Raven Hunter?" She placed one hand to her heart, the other dropping to the bundle tied to her belt. She could hear it Singing, as if with tens of tens of voices.

He extended a dark wing, pointing off to the east. "The crack is opening there. When it goes, it will wash most of the Thunder Sea south. Imagine slapping your hand into a puddle, but on a much grander scale."

She stared off to the east, aware only of jagged spires of the ice rising toward the night sky.

Raven Hunter's other long wing unfolded and extended to the west. "There, a moon's travel to the west, the ice dam has given way. That was the quake you felt in Ti-Bish's chamber. The huge lake it held back is already washing everything before it. When you find the others, you will need to hurry south. Once past Lake River, find high ground. You will be safe."

"But what about the people?" She stared out to the south, seeing the distant high point that marked Headswift Village.

"Ask Wolf Dreamer. He's the one who is supposed to be merciful."

She heard the change in his voice, but when she looked back, it was to see a dark form flapping up into the night sky.

They heard the unearthly Singing of the Ice Giants—like tens of voices Singing slightly different notes—long before the trail ran down the rugged tundra to the Thunder Sea. But there was a new sound today, like bones cracking deep inside the Giants. Occasionally, the earth trembled.

Kakala glanced behind him, watching his warriors follow in a winding line. *At least they're alive.*

He noticed Goodeagle at the rear, and glanced speculatively at Windwolf. The man pointedly ignored his old friend, acted as if he didn't exist. And that, Kakala realized, tortured Goodeagle even more than outright looks of disgust would have.

Keresa led them through the maze of boulders that littered the shoreline. To his left, the massive peaks of the Ice Giants rose like gleaming white shark's teeth. Icebergs floated in the deep blue water. He lifted a hand to shield his eyes and, in the far distance, thought he saw bull boats out on the sea, people fishing, or hunting seals.

Keresa had been keeping up a steady pace, just fast enough, but not too fast to drain Kakala's strength—though his head had been pounding nauseatingly all day.

Kakala tried not to stare at Windwolf. The red shirt the man wore irked. He kept wondering which of his dead friends it had belonged to. Somehow, the war club, stiletto, and darts the man carried didn't seem as menacing anymore. Even the warriors accepted the presence of an armed enemy, and one by one, they had been sidling up to Windwolf, making introductions, almost anxious to talk to the legend they had hunted, fought, and hated for so long.

The grudging respect they showed each other came as a revelation. *But for the Elders, and their insistence on war, we would have been friends.*

"It's not much farther," Kakala said. "One hand of time, maybe."

"I know."

The closer they got to the Nightland Caves, the harder Windwolf's expression became. This afternoon, his square-jawed face might have been carved from wood, and the statue set with glittering stone eyes.

The path curved around to the bizarre side of the Thunder Sea, where drifting icebergs had grounded offshore and melted into strange shapes. They resembled a forest of dirty half-human monsters. As Father Sun descended in the west, sunlight reflected from the ice sculptures with a fringe of opalescent fire.

"Let me stop, just for a moment," Kakala said. "I need to drink."

Keresa nodded, panting. "How's your head?"

"Feels like a Sunpath warrior split it in two."

The faintest of smiles flickered and died on Windwolf's lips.

The rest of the warriors dropped into squats, conserving their energy, taking the time to sort through their packs. The pickings in Headswift Village had been lean after the grand exodus.

Kakala dropped to his knees by a large pool of fresh water

spawned by the melting icebergs that had come ashore. He dipped up water with his hand. As he drank, he watched Windwolf and Keresa trade desperate glances. Their longing brought a pang to his heart. He remembered sharing the same with Hako, two cages down.

And the way that ended ruined my life.

Kakala wiped his wet hand on his pants leg. "Gather around. We have planning to do." The old familiarity of his warriors gathering, the looks of anticipation in their eyes, brought a surge to his heart. "All right, my warriors, here's the situation: We must assume that Homaldo found Ewin, since we didn't see his ugly, fat warriors drifting into Headswift Village. That being the case, he is probably off to the west somewhere, running straight home with Homaldo. He may even beat us there, which means the Council will hear directly from him that all went well at Headswift Village."

They grunted assent.

Kakala narrowed an eye at Windwolf. "We owe a debt to Windwolf. He could have killed us. The Lame Bull and the refugees were most anxious to pay us back for our attacks."

Another grunting of assent.

"My warriors do not leave debts unpaid." He walked around, looking them in the eyes, one by one. "Many of you know that I have often disliked the orders we have received. You know that I often warned Sunpath villages to expect people seeking refuge after our attacks."

The grunting was muted this time.

"This is the situation: Nashat is going to try and use Sunpath slaves to carry our possessions through the ice to the Long Dark. He is doing so in violation of the Guide's direction that no Sunpath should follow us, bringing their beliefs about Wolf Dreamer to soil the Long Dark."

He got worried looks in return, and nodded. "Yes, you see the problem. We all know that Nashat, for reasons I can only guess at, changes the Guide's orders to suit himself."

Sour chuckles erupted.

"I would cast one stone to knock several birds from the sky at once." He ground his fist into his palm. "So, my warriors, here is what we are going to do. Just at dusk, we will approach the slave compound.

As high war chief, I will order the guards to leave, to return to their villages for the purpose of packing their belongings, or, if they've done so, to ensure that their belongings are carried to the Nightland Caves in preparation for leaving."

He looked from face to face, emphasizing his words. "When they are safely out of sight, you will simply go home."

They gave him a puzzled look.

"That's right," Kakala said. "Go home." He made a gesture. "It's over. We're finished. Go to your families, pack your things, and join the rest of the people. Say nothing about what we have been through. Say nothing about me, or the deputy. You have done all . . . no, *more* than your duty to your people. You have earned the right to live the Guide's promise."

"And what of you, War Chief?" Corre asked.

"When I have ensured that Windwolf has his people headed south, I will be along." He smiled. "I, too, will have fulfilled my obligations." He glanced at Windwolf. "All of them."

They nodded. Only Goodeagle looked perplexed. But since traveling with Windwolf, the man had remained unusually quiet. Contemplating his faults, no doubt.

"Any questions?"

Keresa asked, "What if one or more guards refuse to leave?"

Kakala shrugged. "He might be surprised to wake up after taking a short but very unexpected nap. You know, caught by surprise from behind when the Sunpath made their break."

"If that happens, War Chief," Bishka pointed out, "the Elders might put you in a cage with Hawhak."

Kakala shrugged. "I'll take my chances. I owe a debt to Windwolf. I have given him my word that he can take his people home." He searched their eyes. "We all know the fate of those women and girls if they enter the Long Dark. The war is over. We have won. Having fought this from the beginning to the end, I say it is not too much to let them go."

He could see the agreement.

"Very well, warriors, you have your last orders from me. I ask only that Raven Hunter bless you all, and especially those who are not with us today. They will live in our memories forever."

More grunts followed. Kakala gave Windwolf a slight nod, then gestured to Keresa. "Lead the way, Deputy."

Windwolf trotted along behind Kakala, asking, "That's it? Just walk in, tell the guards to leave, and open the gates?"

Kakala said, "What do you expect? I lay awake that last night at Headswift Village, asking, 'What would Windwolf do?'"

Sixty-three

Skimmer glanced up at the rounded ceiling of ice over her head. The fact that she could see so well in pitch blackness still amazed her.

Raven Hunter's gift!

She prowled up the winding tunnel, awed by the way it rose and fell, only to twist to the left or right. The place reminded her of the wormholes she had observed in a clod of freshly turned earth.

"And now I am a human worm." Was this how the little beasts felt? Oddly safe and protected? She had never thought of the earth as a thing to live *in*, but something to walk on.

She closed her eyes, letting her soul drift, feeling the cold eternity of the ice, but this, too, was passing. Year by year, it melted, the waters draining away. One needed only walk north from the distant oak and pine forests to see the moraines, kettles, and boulders left behind.

"Where will it end?" she mused. "With all of the world's ice melted?"

She remembered the ever-present winds blowing up from the distant south, warm and balmy, even in winter. The world was changing, warming. The old ways were about to die, and how were people to adapt? Could they become one with the new land, the new plants? And what of the animals, creatures like the mammoth, sloth, and short-faced bear who clung to the spruce barrens?

"We live with death," she murmured. "Everything in its time." But now time was running out.

So she stood, savoring the darkness, feeling the ice. It moaned and creaked, the wind keening through the tunnels, forever drawing warm air into the depths, only to have it cool, and suck more warm air down into the slowly melting ice.

For that moment, she felt eternal.

A voice broke the peace.

She turned, hearing someone say, "This way, Kishkat . . . I think."

The faint flicker of a light shone around the tunnel's curve.

Skimmer reached down and slipped the ax from where it rode on her belt beside the Raven Bundle.

"Kishkat?" she called. "Is that you?"

Silence. Then a tentative voice called, "Skimmer?"

"I'm just around the corner."

She squinted at the faint light the warrior held before him. His eyes widened in surprise as he stared at her.

"You have no lamp!" he stated.

She looked past him. "Greetings, Tapa. But what are the two of you doing here?"

Kishka lowered his eyes. "Looking for you."

She smiled grimly. "Missed my company?"

Kishkat sighed, and to her surprise, slumped to the floor. "We're supposed to kill you."

"I see."

"Where's your lamp, Skimmer?" Tapa asked.

"I don't need one."

"You don't?" Kishkat wondered; then he stared down at his flickering flame. "This is the last of our fat. When it burns out . . ." He closed his eyes. "What seems like an eternity ago, when the big quake struck, it blocked the tunnel we were in." A pause. "Tibo was on the other side."

"I just want out," Tapa said fervently. "Nashat can lock me in a cage. Break my back, but I'll be able to see the stars."

"Nashat," Skimmer said softly. "He ordered you to murder me?"

Kishkat nodded. "We found out why. It's because you protected the Guide." He looked up. "But I guess you're as lost as we are."

"Nashat ordered you to kill me . . ." She stiffened. "Ti-Bish!"

"What?" Kishkat asked.

"Come. We have to hurry."

"Is it on the way out?" Tapa asked anxiously.

"It is. Follow me. As soon as we know the Guide is safe, I'll show you the way out."

She left at a run, chafing at the slow progress they made trying to follow her. They didn't dare let their precious flame blow out in the draft rushing through the tunnel.

W ith his light flickering before him, Nashat stalked down the tunnel, gleamings of yellow reflected on the ice around him.

He took the familiar turn, watching his footing as he descended a steep slope, then rounded a bend. He paused, listening.

No voices could be heard.

He swallowed hard, hating the fact that he couldn't bring a warrior with him. He'd thought about Karigi, but wasn't sure he could trust the man in the long run. Karigi had an utterly practical streak, one that might be held against Nashat in the future.

Nashat crept closer, holding his lamp behind him to shield the light, and peeked past the hanging. Ti-Bish sat, back straight, eyes closed. He had a slight smile on his lips, and wore a ragged-looking hide shirt.

Nashat could see no one else as he slipped his head back and forth. Relieved, he let the flap fall, calling, "Guide? Are you there?"

"Y-Yes?"

Nashat pulled the hanging back and stepped into the room, satisfied that his first impression was correct. No woman waited to ambush him.

"I'm surprised to find you still alive. I would have thought Skimmer would have murdered you by now."

Ti-Bish stood, then gave a small shrug. "She's off with Raven Hunter."

"Oh, is she?" He fought the urge to smile.

"Are the people ready?"

Nashat paced idly around the room, staring in disdain at the shabby hides, the piles of clothing. "They have most of their things packed. In fact, that's what I've come to discuss with you."

"We can leave in the morning. Raven Hunter told me the water is coming."

"Water?" Nashat frowned. He had no interest in water.

"We don't have much time to get everyone into the tunnels."

"Yes, well, Ti-Bish, that's the problem."

"H-How?" He swallowed hard. "The Councilors told them, didn't they?"

"Oh, yes. Everyone is excited. Ready to go. Even the Lame Bull People are gone. The Sunpath have fled west to the Tills. All of the south is open. Ewin sent a runner with that information, and Karigi arrived last night with a large contingent of slaves."

Ti-Bish frowned. "Then what is the problem?"

Nashat reached down to his belt, fingering the handle of a stiletto crafted from an elk's brow tine. "The caves, Guide. We don't want to go starve ourselves to death in some hole in the ice that leads to who knows what kind of disaster."

Ti-Bish gave him a look of absolute incomprehension. "But that was Raven Hunter's Vision."

"I'm sure it was." Nashat smiled. "But it is certainly not mine."

Ti-Bish's confusion grew. "But, you heard—"

"Of course, and it worked splendidly! We have opened the entire south, driven the Sunpath People out. All of those nice forests are ours for the taking. The people are packed, just ready for their Guide to walk out and give them a new vision."

"I don't . . . What new vision?"

"The one where you raise your arms and tell them that Raven Hunter has changed his mind. That instead of into the ice, we're headed south, to spread the word of Raven Hunter throughout the great forests of the south."

"That wasn't the Dream."

"Ti-Bish, it doesn't matter. They will believe anything you tell them."

Ti-Bish closed his eyes, shoulders slumping. In a voice little more than a whimper he said, "You have never believed."

"Oh, I believed. I believed in you. Now, come, like a good Guide, and tell the people we are headed south."

Ti-Bish shook his head. "It's too late, Nashat. The water is coming. A fast warrior might make it, but women and children carrying loads, and the elderly and frail, they'll be washed away."

"We can take the high trails," Nashat mused. "It might even make the tale easier to accept."

Ti-Bish opened his mouth, but words seemed trapped behind his tongue.

"It's not so bad," Nashat told him, his finger tapping on the stiletto top. "You will have everything you need. Just do as I say and you can even keep Skimmer. What do I care who you fill your bed with? As long as she keeps a decent tongue in her mouth and stays out of my way, I won't even insist on taking a turn or two with her myself. You'll have more—"

"No!"

"What did you say?"

"I said no, Nashat. I am going up and telling the people to pick up their packs and start into the tunnels." Ti-Bish crossed his skinny arms.

"That is your final word?"

"It is. You've worked your poison long enough. You've broken the Dream, muddied the Vision, and I have let you."

"I'd reconsider," Nashat said as Ti-Bish walked past him.

"No. Raven Hunter protects me." Ti-Bish reached for the door hanging as Nashat spun on his heel and drove the sharpened tip into Ti-Bish's back.

Nashat watched Ti-Bish stiffen as he twisted the antler cruelly, pulled it out, and drove it in again. Then he grasped Ti-Bish's collar, thrust the stiletto in a third time, and jerked the man back into the room.

Ti-Bish sprawled on the hides, staring up in pain and disbelief. His mouth hung open in a surprised circle. With one hand, he reached around and felt the crimson rush that poured from the punctures in his back.

"Raven Hunter protects you?" Nashat laughed. "It seems he doesn't do a very good job."

Ti-Bish made a gurgling sound, eyes blinking.

"That punctured your liver, and most likely the bottom of your lung. It won't take long."

"Why?" Ti-Bish croaked.

"Because, with you dead, we have no choice but to head south. No Guide . . . no way to find the way to the Long Dark." He made a face. "Long Dark? Who'd want to live there?"

"Those who believe," a sober voice said from behind.

Nashat whirled to find Skimmer, breathing hard, standing behind him. He backed up, raising the stiletto. "This time I'm armed. And, well, your timing is perfect. A Sunpath assassin has taken our Guide from us. All the more reason for the people to joyously head south. It makes reaping the benefit of your old lands even more precious to them."

Skimmer smiled coldly, stepping forward.

Nashat caught the cold glow of her large dark eyes, as if they no longer had pupils, but watched him like some great raven's. "Better that you ran, Skimmer. You'd at least have a chance before we hunt you down."

"There's no running, Nashat."

Even as she spoke, Kishkat and Tapa stumbled in behind her, staring first at him, then at the bloody stiletto he held, and finally at the Guide, flat on his back, blood pooling blackly on the hides.

"Take her," Nashat said. "Drag her out to the people. Let them tear her apart. She's killed the Guide."

Skimmer's smile grew. "It's too late, Nashat. You've uttered your last lie." She cocked her head as a low wailing rose from the ice tunnels. The sound was eerie, keening, one he'd never heard before.

Skimmer fixed him with her liquid-dark eyes. "Hear them? Those are the voices of the Sunpath dead. The Nine Pipes women are screaming for your soul." The smile widened. "And I'm going to give you to them."

He watched her pull an old ax from her belt, raising it. Then, she jerked her head toward the door. "Go on, run. But leave the lamp behind. They're waiting for you. Just out there in the darkness."

Nashat swallowed hard, hearing the eerie wail rise like a thousand screaming voices.

"Kishkat, Tapa, seize her. I'll give you anything you want. Women? I have them. Would you like to be war chiefs? Elders? I can make it happen."

"Go," Skimmer ordered, her voice little more than a whisper. "Run! They're reaching out, their fingers as cold as the very ice."

"Skimmer?" Kishkat asked, staring in horror at the Guide.

"Let him go." She continued to glare at Nashat. "Death at the hands of the ghosts will be more horrible than anything we could imagine."

Nashat turned, threw down the stiletto, and bolted for the doorway. He shoved past the two warriors, scrambling down the tunnel, slipping, falling, grunting as he ran headlong into the walls.

Then something cold plucked at him from the solid blackness. . . .

William he make it back to the main caves?" Kishkat asked. He glanced at Tapa, finding his friend wide-eyed, speechless.

"No," she said softly, crouching down beside Ti-Bish. "He only thinks he knows the way." She turned, looking up at Kishkat, her large eyes as black as the caverns themselves. He stepped back. It was as if he'd looked into some night creature's face, something not quite human.

He felt Tapa's reassuring grip on his arm. Then, mustering his courage, he bent down, lifting the Guide, seeing the blood draining from the back of his shirt.

Ti-Bish coughed, frothy red bubbling on his lips. "Too late," the Guide whispered.

"I know," Skimmer told him. "The world is dying. You understand, don't you?"

Ti-Bish jerked a slight nod, crimson leaking past his lips. "Skimmer? Do . . . do you love me?"

"Yes, Ti-Bish."

He smiled slightly; then his voice changed. "Raven Hunter, is that you?" His eyes had widened, sightless. "Thank you, the light was getting to be too much." He coughed, spewing red. Then he whispered, ". . . Let's fly now . . ."

Skimmer reached out, running her fingers along his blood-smeared cheek. Then she closed her eyes.

Kishkat watched for a long moment, and then saw her nod. She said, "He's reached the Long Dark. Raven Hunter kept his promise."

Somewhere from down the tunnel, they heard Nashat's terrified scream.

Skimmer turned her strange black eyes on Kishkat, and his blood ran cold. "Nashat has found the dead," she said simply.

Scream after hideous scream echoed from the darkness.

Sixty-four

Ashes sat with her war club across her lap. Throughout the long day's walk, she had kept it in hand, swinging it, practicing a leap, skip, strike, and then whirling, preparing to block a blow.

Silvertip had watched her, as if he'd seen it all before. Once she'd raised an eyebrow, asking, "Problem?"

"Nothing that will not fix itself over time."

She had swung the club up onto her shoulder, shooting him a side-long look. "It's been four days now. Why did you turn us to the south?"

"You will know soon enough."

"I suppose." She matched her pace with his. "I thought I heard Mother's voice last night."

"I'm sure you did," he had said simply.

She had pondered that, wondering what it would be like to know everything, including another person's Dreams. The idea of it was unsettling.

Now, as they sat by the evening fire, Lookingbill snored softly, his mouth open. Dipper placed the last of the wooden bowls in her pack and shot a curious smile at her father, saying, "He's not as young as he used to be. A full day's walk used to be nothing for him."

Silvertip watched the fire crackle and spit, and then looked out toward the north again. He had insisted that they camp on the highest point. Across the moonlit night, the distant waters of Loon Lake could be seen, its surface silver against the black land.

"He will make it, Mother. Most of the danger is past now." Silvertip rubbed his nose, as if it itched.

Dipper glanced at Ashes. "Are you ever going to lay that club down?"

"No," she replied. "They put me in a pen once. They will never do it again."

Silvertip turned his large eyes on hers. "The pens will be gone soon. No others will be built in our lifetimes."

"Idiocy," Dipper murmured, "putting people in pens. We don't even do that to animals."

Ashes felt the sudden tension in Silvertip, watched him rise to his feet, staring out at the darkness. Then he started to walk out past the fire.

"Where are you going?" Dipper called.

"I have to speak with someone."

"You don't go past the line of guards," she insisted.

Ashes walked a step behind, casting suspicious glances around. The Lame Bull camps had been laid out in a large circle, and Silvertip walked past one after another until he reached the outer edge.

People watched them pass, pointing, some whispering, others smiling and waving. Ashes carefully nodded, her gaze roving, searching for danger.

Passing the last camp, she said, "Going beyond the fires could be dangerous."

"No," he answered. "Not tonight." He glanced at her. "If you weren't Raven Hunter's perhaps you could hear him as clearly as I can."

"Hear who?" She shifted her war club, trying to widen her eyes to the dark forest beyond the camp. The way led downhill now, winding around spruce and patches of sumac. Moonlight limned the prickly spruce needles and silvered the sumac, budded now with the first hints of spring.

Ashes gasped, tightening her grip on the club.

A large black wolf stood in a clearing where a great spruce had toppled and now lay rotting into the duff. Even in the moonlight, the animal's eyes seemed to glow an odd yellow, as if lit from within.

"Greetings, Grandfather," Silvertip said respectfully. For a long time, he and the wolf stared at each other, Silvertip whispering under his breath, then pausing, as if receiving an answer.

Finally, Silvertip nodded, saying, "I understand."

Ashes felt rather than heard the rasping of feathers on the cool night air. She looked up, seeing her breath cloud in the moon's white light.

The raven sailed around the clearing, gliding on midnight wings to perch on an old branch that stuck up from the long-fallen tree. The raven—a bird comfortable in the daylight—now peered intently at the wolf, as if distrustful.

Silvertip nodded respectfully to the bird, turned to Ashes, and said, "The Guide is dead."

For a moment, Ashes wanted to leap and scream out a whoop of victory, but something held her back. "Did Mother kill him?"

Silvertip shook his head. "She would have saved him."

"Why? She hates him. *I* hate him."

He reached down, fingers tracing the old worn sides of the Wolf Bundle. "She has accepted her destiny. Another part of the balance is restored."

"How?"

"Keresa came to Wolf Dreamer; your mother has gone to Raven Hunter. A trade—opposites crossed. Keresa has turned to peace and light, your mother to chaos and darkness."

"What does that mean?"

"It means that she now carries the Raven Bundle."

Ashes pointed at the raven. "Is that why he is here?"

He nodded. "You are Raven Hunter's. He has sent a Spirit Helper to ensure the balance is kept."

She walked out toward the bird, fully aware of the wolf watching her intently. She lifted the club. "I can take care of myself. But thank you."

Silvertip grinned in the moonlight. "In many ways, yes. But we have a long way to go. Listen to him, Ashes. He was sent for you."

To the north, a low rumble could be heard.

"It comes," Silvertip said. "I would see this."

"What?" she asked.

"The end of the world."

He led the way down a little farther. From a rocky knoll, they could see Loon Lake, glowing silver in the light. It came from the west. The surface seemed to roil, changing slightly in color.

"Can you see the beach down there?"

She followed his finger to the pale strip of sand in the distance.

"Watch it," Silvertip said, seating himself. He seemed oblivious to the wolf and raven, as they perched beside them, and watched as the sandy strand slowly disappeared.

Evening gloom lay on the land as Windwolf followed Keresa toward the compound that held the Sunpath captives. He could just make out dark forms through the gaps in the fence. The enclosure had been constructed of rocks, sections of mammoth rib, and long bones all laced together with roots and strips of old hide. It was the sort of thing the Nightland people cobbled up for caribou drives.

And, like caribou drives, he suspected that the warriors gleefully darted anything that tried to wiggle through the flimsy barrier.

As Kakala trotted toward the fence, he glanced up at the scattered puffs of cloud that blew steadily northward to blot the early-evening stars.

Windwolf could just see Kakala's ironic smile. "Thinking of something, War Chief?"

"Only that you must have your guts tied in knots, Windwolf. One wrong word from me, and you'll be in there with the rest. I'll be a hero. You'll be the captive."

Windwolf's thin smile reeked of danger. "Perhaps you shouldn't have allowed me to keep my weapons."

"A couple of darts won't do you much good."

"Good enough," Windwolf said softly. "You'll be dying at the same time I am."

Kakala chuckled under his breath. "Well then, perhaps we should just do it my way. Unlike Karigi, I keep my word."

When they got to within atlatl range, shouts went up from the compound, and two warriors trotted out toward them.

Kakala said, "It's time to Dance. I hope you brought your sacred mask."

"I'm wearing it," Windwolf muttered.

A skinny bald warrior called, "War Chief Kakala! What are you doing here?" Then he smiled. "It is good to see you here. You wouldn't believe the rumors that have been flying about you."

"Rumors are like songbirds; they sound filling but make a poor feast." Kakala stepped out to meet the men and said, "What is your name, warrior?"

"Jaron." The man bowed, nodded to Keresa, and looked at Windwolf.

Kakala quickly said, "This is . . . Water."

Jaron bowed slightly. "The Elders said they would send someone to inspect the slaves, but we didn't know it would be you."

He thinks the Elders sent us. . . .

"Thank you, Jaron," Kakala said. "But I come with orders of my own. Have your warriors seen to the packing of their things?"

"Yes, War Chief."

"Then you are to take your warriors, have them return to their camps, and carry all of their belongings to the caves."

Jaron hesitated. "But Karigi said—"

Coldly, Kakala said, "I was unaware that Karigi had been appointed high war chief by the Council."

"He has not, H-High War Chief." Jaron swallowed. "As you order, High War Chief." He glanced past Kakala. "I assume you will take responsibility for the captives?"

Kakala looked back. "Fan out; take the others' places so they can get about their business."

Windwolf watched Kakala's warriors trot out to either side, gesturing the others to head home. He could hear calls of greeting in the night. But then, Kakala's men had always been well trained.

Only after Jaron trotted off after the others did Keresa say, "Well, that went easily."

Windwolf muttered, "I'm not used to things being easy." He glanced around worriedly. "Let's see what we've got."

They walked up to the narrow gate, little more than a couple of worn poles that marked the entrance. Inside he could see people squatting, huddling together for warmth. In the gloom, he couldn't make out faces.

"Are Jaron's warriors far enough away?" Kakala asked.

"I think so." Keresa stared off into the distance. "Bishka, keep a watch for us."

"Yes, Deputy." He trotted off around the curve of the enclosure.

Windwolf laid his darts to the side and began sliding the poles off the rocks on which they'd been braced. To those closest to the opening, he said, "These are your orders. You will walk out with your belongings. You are to head straight south. No one is to speak; no one is to laugh or shout. You must be across Lake River by no later than four days."

"Who are you?" a man asked.

"I am called Water. The Council has decided that they have no need for captives." Then he added, "But that could change at any moment. If you're going, go. Anyone who lingers might be called back."

People rose, filing past him. He watched as they hurried along, slipping out into the night, heading back south.

Windwolf stepped back and turned to Kakala. "Thank you for this, War Chief."

Kakala nodded, an anxious set to his shoulders. "You're not finished yet, Win . . . Water. They only have a night's head start. Karigi will be after them as soon as he discovers the escape."

"Hopefully, he'll be too anxious to follow the Guide."

"We can hope."

A woman paused. "There are some who cannot walk." She gestured. "Back there."

"I'll see to them." Windwolf nodded, and watched the trickle of people passing by.

"I'll come, too." Kakala turned. "Keep watch, Keresa."

"Of course. I think our people are fidgeting to get home."

"Dismiss them. Tell them I will speak with them later."

"Yes, War Chief." She turned, trotting away.

Sixty-five

As he entered the compound Windwolf caught the stench of feces, urine, and human fear. "How did we come to this?"

"Arrogance," Kakala muttered, "and Nashat's poison."

They walked into the enclosure, peering around. A hide-covered hut sat in the back, a low fire burning before it.

Kakala prodded a human form on the ground. "Come on, get up." Then he bent down, fingering the body. "Dead," he said. "A young woman. Club wound to the head."

"Nightland honor?" Windwolf asked.

"Karigi's sort," Kakala replied, failing to take the bait.

Several more dead lay here and there; two of them, Windwolf noted, were children. Kakala said nothing as they passed.

The hide-covered hut was a low-domed thing made of willow stems bent over and tied together.

Windwolf stepped up to the fire. In the feeble light it cast, he could see three naked women and a little girl. They sat, backs to the wall, hunched over for warmth.

A warrior lay sleeping opposite them, his body covered with a bearhide robe.

The little girl stared up with horrified eyes, and said, "Not again. Please?"

Kakala asked, "Again?"

Not realizing it was a question, the little girl crawled out onto a filthy hide, settled on her back, and spread her thin legs. Windwolf's heart sank as he watched the child, no more than eight summers of age, opening herself to the next man who demanded her.

"By Raven Hunter's balls," Kakala growled. "Put some clothes on, child."

The warrior blinked, sat up, and yawned. As he stretched lazily, the women lowered their heads, doing anything to avoid the man's attention.

"Come for your turn?" the warrior asked muzzily. "I recommend the woman on the right to start with. She's—"

"My turn?" Kakala asked, stepping forward. "How does this work?"

Windwolf cast a sidelong glance at Kakala, surprised by the deadly calm in his voice.

"We each get a couple of hands' time." The warrior rolled his shoulders as he stood up. "Compensation for having to do this stinking duty. Most of us have taken a turn or two already. Sorry for the leftovers."

"And the child?" Windwolf asked in a mild voice.

"She's tight. You'll have to spit on your shaft first." The man was ducking through the low doorway.

Windwolf sensed Kakala's bunching muscles, heard the whistle and crack as Kakala's war club crushed the back of the man's head.

The warrior dropped with a hollow thud, his limbs twitching. Kakala stood over him, raising the club and bringing it down again and again on the back of the man's head. The body jerked with each sodden impact.

"Worried he might still get up, War Chief?" Windwolf asked dryly as Kakala raised himself for another blow.

"I just can't . . ." The war club hammed the pulped head again. ". . . abide . . ."

Windwolf watched the women flinch at the snapping impact of the club as it continued to hammer at the man's crushed skull. He reached out and laid a restraining hand on Kakala's bulging arm, feeling the rage.

"The captives have been freed," Windwolf told the women. "Find your clothing, or take what you need from here. The robes will be a comfort during the cold. But go now. Stay silent until you are far away. Head south. Follow the others."

The little girl still lay on her back, legs spread, her naked body pathetically vulnerable in the flickering light.

"See to her!" Windwolf ordered. "I am making you responsible! And, by the Spirits, if you fail me . . ."

"Yes, warrior," one of the women said, and they bundled the little girl up as they stripped the lodge and hurried out into the night.

Kakala sank down beside the fire, his face working. He looked up. "Are you made of wood?"

"It splinters too easily. What do you mean: Am I made of wood?"

"How can you be so calm after seeing this?"

Windwolf sighed. "It is nothing new, Kakala."

"It is among my warriors. A child. *A little child!*"

"Are you telling me you didn't hear the stories?"

Kakala spread his hands, looking at the palms. "Somehow, it was different this time."

"Then perhaps you have finally found your soul. You will have plenty of time to become acquainted with it in the Long Dark."

Kakala smiled bitterly. "The Long Dark? What right do I have to enter paradise?" Then he slapped his knees and rose. "Come. Let's see if there are any others, and then you and Keresa can be on your way."

Passing occasional corpses, Windwolf almost dismissed the huddled forms at the distant end of the enclosure. He walked over, kicking at a foot.

"What?" a man asked, sitting up in the darkness.

"You're leaving, quietly."

"Windwolf?" the man asked incredulously.

"Quiet. Just get up and walk. Leave and head south. Make no noise. You have to get as far as you can by morning."

"Yes. *Yes!*" The man turned the next figure, trying to rouse the sleeping man. "Wake up! Grandfather, let's go!"

Windwolf pressed on, kicking each corpse, investigating each pile of clothing.

He met Kakala and Keresa at the gate. "I think that's the last of them. Did the women take the girl with them?"

"They did." Kakala was still looking downcast, staring at his hands.

"All of our warriors have gone," Keresa added. "I don't want to remind you about Silvertip's flood. We don't have much time to get south."

"No," Windwolf agreed. He glanced around, noticing that more clouds had moved in, the darkness increasing. "Kakala, I thank you for this."

"My debt is repaid, Windwolf."

"What debt is that?" a voice asked from the darkness.

Kakala spun. "Blackta?"

Dark shapes formed in the night. Windwolf eased his war club from his belt. How many? Four? Five?

"So, you've captured Windwolf after all?" Blackta walked up, peering in the darkness. "Brought him to the slave compound? Not the Council chambers? Are you insane? He'll give the slaves hope after we've taken so much time to beat it out of them."

Windwolf gripped the handle of his war club, feeling the familiar smooth grain of the wood. He started forward, only to feel Keresa's restraining hand grip his forearm.

Kakala stepped breast to breast with Blackta. "You are dismissed, War Chief. Get away from me before I break your neck!"

Blackta seemed to consider it, then cocked his head. "Quiet in there." He bent, craning, trying to see into the compound.

"Like you said, you beat half the life out of them." Kakala seemed to swell in the night. "You make me sick."

"Oh, do I?" Blackta chuckled. "You've been in the cages how many times? Twice?" He turned, "Tanga, see to the slaves. Make sure they're not up to mischief."

Kakala barked, "Tanga! You, and the war chief will return immediately to your camps. As high war chief, *I* order it."

"No," Blackta said crisply. "Check, Tanga. Now."

"You would disobey me?" Kakala demanded.

Tanga stepped to the side, lifting himself above the wall to say, "I think it's empty!"

Blackta's movement was a blur in the night. Kakala snapped back from the impact as Blackta drove a fist into his jaw. Then the man was on him, kicking, beating.

Windwolf whipped his war club up, pivoted, and caught the surprised Tanga on the side of the head, knocking the man back. From the feel of the blow, he could tell it hadn't connected well, but might be enough to stun.

Blackta's warriors waded in, each clawing for his war club. Keresa had rushed forward, trading blows with a barely seen assailant.

To fight in such a way was madness, slashing at dark forms, trying to dodge and weave flailing clubs.

Keresa! Spirits, where is Keresa? Windwolf ducked a hissing war club that would have missed him by a hand's width anyway.

"Now, Kakala," Blackta grunted. "I've waited too long for this."

Windwolf ducked down, peering, seeing Blackta hunched atop Kakala's prostrate body. *He's only half-recovered from the blow at Headswift Village.* Blackta was choking the life out of him.

Windwolf leapt, slamming his body into Blackta's. A hot rage burst through him, remembering Bramble's naked body: the dart jutting from her chest; the bite marks on her skin; the stains between her thighs . . . and a little eight-summers-old girl lying spread-eagled with tears running down her face.

Windwolf bellowed, raising his war club, smashing it down on the scrambling man beneath him. Time slowed as Windwolf methodically worked his club, hammering away, feeling each satisfying impact as stone crushed flesh, bone, and skin.

He reveled in the droplets of gore spattering his hands and face, and battered away, revisiting each burned camp, each haunted expression. The smell of smoke from burning lodges stung his nose. The shrieks of the dying sounded over and over as he pounded his rage into Blackta's body.

"Windwolf?" a voice asked. *"Windwolf?"*

He turned, ready to lash out, as a hand landed on his shoulder, and pulled him back.

"Windwolf!"

"What?" he gasped.

Kakala, voice hoarse, rasped, "Worried that he might get up again, War Chief?"

Windwolf nodded, panting, staring around at the darkness. "Keresa?"

"Here." He heard her voice. "The rest have fled."

"Not all of us." Tanga's voice came from the dark gap of the gate. "The first man who moves, dies. I swear, I'll drive a dart right through him."

"Put your weapons down, Tanga," Kakala ordered. "It's over."

"Oh, no. The pen's empty. The slaves are gone. So help me,

Kakala, you're going to rot your life out in the cages. But first, Windwolf, stand up. Stand where I can see you."

"Why?" he asked, wondering how much cover Blackta's body would give him.

"Because I'm killing you. Now. Tonight. Your head is my trophy to carry into the Long Dark."

Keresa's calm voice said from the side, "If you hurt him, Tanga, I'll hand you your balls."

"You?" he asked. "Side with Windwolf?" He chuckled. "Oh, Nashat has waited for years to have you for his own. And, you, you cold-blooded camp bitch, will be my gift to him. . . . But then, sharing Nashat's bed is better than dying in the cages."

Windwolf caught the faintest movement in the darkness behind Tanga. Then the warrior stiffened and jerked, taking a half stumble. Tanga glanced down, atlatl and darts clattering to the ground. He weaved, coughed. His knees gone weak, Tanga pitched sideways to the ground, kicking, gasping as he fingered a dart point that protruded from his chest.

A dark form rose behind him, saying, "War Chief Windwolf? I think that's the last one."

"Who are you?" Windwolf stood slowly.

"Sacred Feathers, War Chief." The man stepped over Tanga's body, staring down in the darkness. "I found one of your darts by the gate. Grandfather Drummer is dead." He straightened. "He was right all along." He took a deep breath. "My daughter, Elk Leaf . . . she was in the warriors' tent. . . . They . . ." His voice broke.

"I know," Windwolf said. "The other women have already taken her. She's headed south."

"Which is where we need to go," Kakala said, rising stiffly.

A man screamed in the darkness. Windwolf turned on his heel, lifting his war club.

"It's all right, War Chief," a low voice called. "It's Kishkat and Tapa. I hope we didn't get here too late. But there were two warriors out here that were going to stick you like fish as soon as they had a shot."

"A third one ran," a second voice called. Forms emerged from the darkness. Windwolf could make out three of them.

Keresa said, "Come on, Windwolf, let's get out of here before Nashat sends the whole Nightland world down on us."

A familiar woman's voice said, "Nashat is no longer a concern."

Windwolf cocked his head. "Skimmer? I thought you were dead."

"Oh yes, War Chief. Skimmer died long ago. But we have no time for talk. This world is about to be washed away."

"What about the Guide?" Windwolf asked anxiously.

"Dead," Skimmer told him, "by Nashat's hand."

"Blessed be the name of Wolf Dreamer," Windwolf said softly.

"May he be cursed," Skimmer spat. "But you and I can argue the Spirits later. That third warrior will make fast time back to the Nightland Caves."

"It's dark as pitch," Keresa murmured. "We're not going to make much distance getting away from here."

"I can see fine, Deputy," Skimmer told her. "Just follow my instructions." Then the woman turned, stepping off into the darkness.

"Skimmer?" Kakala asked.

"Call her the Earth," Keresa replied.

Sixty-six

Dawn grayed the skies as Keresa climbed through boulders atop a pile of glacial rubble and looked back. In the faint gray light she could see the Ice Giants rising against the glow. Their sharp peaks seemed to saw at the sky.

On the trail below her a line of women and children, all looking haggard, walked wearily toward the south.

Windwolf climbed up beside her, breathing deeply. He'd spent most of the night encouraging, cajoling, and keeping the freed captives moving. The rest of the time he had devoted to Kakala, who had had trouble of his own keeping up.

"Everyone keeps hitting me in the head," Kakala had muttered once when his balance had deserted him and he'd had to lean on Windwolf's arm.

"It's because it's such a tempting target," Windwolf had replied.

"Why?" Kakala had been foolish enough to ask.

"Because anything that ugly just begs to be hit."

Kishkat had laughed, and then made himself scarce when Kakala turned his hard glare that way.

Keresa glanced at Windwolf, aware that the war chief was staring back the way they'd come, judging the progress they had been making. "What are you thinking?"

"That one of Blackta's warriors got away."

Keresa pinched her lower lip and nodded. "When Karigi hears, he'll be after us."

Windwolf reached down and helped Kakala up the rough boulders to the high spot. The war chief looked gray, his scarred face set against an inner pain that came from more than just a bump to the head.

"Karigi's not going to give up." Kakala looked down at the ragged band of refugees.

"No," Windwolf agreed, eyes on the north. "He's already collecting warriors."

"And how do you know that?" Kakala asked, staring down where Skimmer made her way toward them.

"I've got that same old feeling I used to have when you were chasing me."

Keresa turned thoughtful eyes on Skimmer. The woman was climbing up the trail below them. "Do you really think Nashat's dead, like she claims?"

Kakala shrugged. "That's what Kiskhat and Tapa say. I got the whole story from them last night. Nashat killed the Guide with an antler stiletto. They say they saw it."

"And Nashat?" Windwolf asked.

"That's the curious part. Kishkat and Tapa swear the ghosts of the dead got him. Both of them were shivering when they told the story. They said his screams were awful to hear."

Windwolf exhaled slowly. "Power's loose on the land."

Skimmer stopped on the rocks just below them. "Looking for Karigi?"

"No sign of him yet," Keresa told her.

"Soon, Deputy." Skimmer braced her feet. "Very soon. In the meantime, we must break up this party. Have them scatter."

"And why is that?" Windwolf asked.

She stared up with oddly large eyes that seemed to suck at Keresa's soul. Keresa felt a shiver go down her spine. Windwolf, too, took a sudden breath. Kakala, however, remained undisturbed.

In an eerie voice, Skimmer replied, "You know the answer to that, War Chief."

Keresa glanced at Windwolf, seeing his expression tighten.

Windwolf gave the slightest of nods. "I will send the order."

Kakala was already climbing down. Keresa took a final look down the backtrail, seeing only a couple of their stragglers limping along behind.

"What did she mean?" Keresa asked.

"There will be fewer to kill when Karigi finally catches up with us." Windwolf made a face as the wind buffeted their high rocky point.

Windwolf watched as his little band of people splintered into small groups, each winding its way through the torturous tundra with its piles of rock, holes, and boulders.

Satisfied, he trotted along the trail to where Keresa, Kakala, and his two warriors waited with Skimmer. They crouched in the lee of a boulder pile, out of the worst of the wind.

"That's it," Windwolf told them as he approached. "Karigi should find the trail confusing from here on out."

"Then we should go," Keresa added. "Silvertip was specific about crossing Lake River by the fourth day."

"Silvertip," Skimmer mused, a hardness in her expression, "Wolf Dreamer's tool." Then she sighed. "But he sees clearly. We're in a race with the end of the world."

Kakala ordered, "Kishkat, Tapa, take scouting positions. Ewin might still be out here someplace. We don't want to run right down his throat and have to make uncomfortable conversation with the man."

Windwolf gestured for the others to take the trail ahead of him and then matched his pace to Skimmer's. They hadn't made two tens of paces before she asked, "Questions, War Chief?" and turned her eerie eyes on him. The effect was like cold water dribbling on his soul.

"You haven't asked about Ashes," he said.

She smiled slightly, not even breaking her confident stride. "She is fine."

"You know this for a fact?"

"Raven Hunter told me. Though I am a little disappointed about her attachment to this Silvertip."

"I thought you no longer believed."

An ironic smile bent her lips, and the too-large eyes narrowed. "Let us just say that I serve a different Power now."

The hair at the back of Windwolf's neck prickled. He glanced down at the leather-covered bundle at her waist. The premonition of danger worsened. "I didn't think you had it in you to kill the Prophet."

"He was innocent," she said simply.

"What about the lives you could have saved?"

"Do you question the thunder, War Chief?"

"Of course not."

"Then do not question the ways of Power."

He gave her a thin stare. "But I do question, especially when it involves the lives of my people."

"Then you have your answer, War Chief." She laughed, the sound like something echoing from a deep cavern. "Perhaps, in a way, I did kill Ti-Bish. But it's a complicated give-and-take . . . something in the very balance of the Spiral itself."

He shot a sidelong glance at her, aware of her finely formed face, the skin smooth, her lips full and sensual. Rich black hair hung in long and glossy luster. She walked with a light grace that swung her hips, and the cloak she wore couldn't hide the swell of her high breasts.

Was she this beautiful last time I saw her? He remembered her as an attractive woman, but this magnetic allure puzzled him.

"Yes, War Chief?" she asked, shooting him a knowing glance. Her dark eyes seemed to swell, as if drawing on his very soul.

"Nothing."

"Good. You would hate yourself if your thoughts strayed too far from Keresa."

He frowned. "I don't know you anymore."

"You *never* knew me, War Chief." Then she relented. "I shouldn't be so harsh. You don't know Raven Hunter's Dream; none of us did. Not even poor Ti-Bish."

"And just what is Raven Hunter's Dream? Death and war?"

She smiled slightly, as if in the presence of a naïve boy. "It's life, War Chief. All of it right down to the last spurt of blood in your veins. It's seizing life and savoring it, milking it of every last drop of bliss."

She lifted her hand, watching her slim fingers curl into a fist. "The goal is to struggle and win, and enjoy the fight with every step you take. In the process, we are to love and hate with all of our hearts. Don't you understand? Life is creation, fertility, change, and curiosity. I didn't begin to understand until I was locked away in the bowels of the Ice Giants." She shook her head. "Only then did the terror I'd survived make sense."

"That's what the Nightland Prophet taught you?" He asked skeptically.

"Ti-Bish wasn't a Prophet, Windwolf. He was a Dreamer with only half the Dream. No, he taught me just how deeply rooted love was in the soul. My days with Hookmaker were passionate, and I did love him. But not with the complete dedication of being that Ti-Bish loved. It was elemental to him, as much a part of who he was as the beating of his heart. He gave all of himself in the attempt to save our world, right down to his last dying breath."

"But he couldn't?" Windwolf guessed.

A wistful smile died on her lips. "Ti-Bish lacked the courage. He was only the final step along the trail to save Raven Hunter's Dream."

"And what is that final step?" he asked, unsure if he wanted to hear the answer. "This terrible flood that's supposed to roar down on us?"

"I am," she replied simply, and lightly stroked the leather bundle at her hip. "All of the death, suffering, and anguish—everything hinged on getting me to the ice caves. The terrible things we lived were the means to prepare our world for the end." She gave him a half-lidded look that pierced his soul like a sliver of ice. "Did you really think it was happenstance that brought you to Kakala's camp that night you discovered me in the rocks?"

Windwolf chuckled. "You're saying *you* are Raven Hunter's Dreamer?"

"Power is swelling on the wind, War Chief." She raised her right hand high, clutching it into a fist. "Those with Power can call it at will."

Windwolf heard the rasping of wings on air and ducked instinctively as a great black raven hissed through the space where his head had been. The big bird backed air, and settled on her raised fist to stare at him with a gleaming black eye.

"Blessed Spirits!" Windwolf cried, recovering. He glanced up at the bird that rode so easily on her hand.

"Welcome to the end of our world," Skimmer told him, her eyes on the glistening black raven that clung to her hand. The bird threw its head back; the hoarse cawing seemed to shake the world.

"It is."

Bishka glanced at Rana. "We should be out there, protecting our war chief."

Rana muttered, nodding in agreement.

"What of your duty to the people?"

Bishka gave him a dark shrug. "The people? These same ones who are cursing us because we won't let them go search out the Guide?"

Rana growled. "We've been out dying for them for moons. Now they would as soon split our heads as look at us."

Goodeagle looked back at the crowd. The gazes were hostile, but none of the fishermen, hunters, and women had quite mustered the courage to press the warriors.

"Where's Nashat?"

"No one knows," Bishka whispered. "No one has seen him for three days."

Goodeagle considered leaving, but hated to face the mass of humanity again. "I heard warriors are searching the tunnels. I'll go see if I can learn anything, and I'll let you know."

Either the ruse worked, or Bishka could care less anymore. He allowed Goodeagle to pass.

Winding his way along the gravel-packed floor, Goodeagle marveled at the grandeur of the great ice caves. In his warrior's shirt, no one bothered to ask his business.

He saw the woman first, recognizing her as she hurried down the gavel path. His first instinct was to ignore her; then, screwing up his courage, he turned to intercept her.

Blue Wing carried a pack slung over her back, a desperate expression on her face. She kept peering back over her shoulder, as if expecting a shout at any moment.

"Blue Wing," he greeted as he stepped into her way. She glanced up, startled, and he watched her fear turn to loathing.

"Goodeagle." A resignation filled her voice. "My life is truly cursed."

"What's happening back there?" He indicated the deeper caverns.

"Why should I tell you?"

He gave her a ruthless smile, remembering how soft her body had been against his when he'd taken her during the long march north from Nine Pipes territory. "Because I'm ordering you to."

She narrowed her eyes. "I'm Nashat's now."

"And where is he?"

Sixty-seven

Karigi trotted at the head of his warriors. Looking behind, he could see four tens of his trusted men. At the distance-eating dog trot at which they traveled, they could go all day. Each man carried a handful of long darts in his left hand, his atlatl, war club, and a pack tied to his back.

They had passed several women already. Wounded or dying, they had fallen back, finally succumbing to fatigue. From them, Karigi knew that the others weren't all that far ahead.

"Look, War Chief," Terengi called from behind.

Karigi glanced back and followed his deputy's pointing finger to where a great dire wolf watched them from on high.

"He won't bother us." Karigi chuckled. "If anything, he ought to be grateful. That last woman we killed will fill his gut for a week."

Karigi ignored the animal, concentrating on the rough trail. Here and there, where the silt had blown in, he could see tracks. A lot of moccasined feet had passed this way.

Kakala! You always had a ridiculous soft spot in your soul. I should have known you'd turn against us.

Blackta's warrior's report had been succinct: High War Chief Kakala had helped to release the captives.

My captives!

Karigi reached up to run his hand along his jaw, as if he could still feel the blow Kakala had landed there that day in Walking Seal Village.

I'm coming, Kakala. And this time, you'll wish you were only going to be locked in a cage.

The mountains of packs amazed Goodeagle. Some were piled as high as a man's head. Around them, the Nightland people sat, squatted, or lingered around little fires. Children were everywhere, running, playing, calling happily. Among them he could see Sunpath children, many serving as slaves.

So this is the wreckage of my world? This is what I did? The cramp of grief rose in his belly, swelling the sickness that lurked like a black fog around his heart.

The trail here from Headswift Village had tortured his very soul. For four long days, he'd trotted along at the back of the line, having a full view of Windwolf as he ran side by side with Keresa. At their nightly camps, Windwolf hadn't once looked in Goodeagle's direction.

I am dead to him. He laughed, half-hysterically. *I am dead to myself.*

Every now and then he'd nod to a warrior he knew. Most nodded back, old enmities forgotten in the excitement of the migration into the Long Dark.

He recognized Washani where he stood talking to Klah and Degan. He hesitated, unsure of his welcome, and walked over.

Washani gave him a slight nod, expression tightening.

"Have you heard the rumors?" Goodeagle asked.

"That Karigi is after Kakala and the escaped Sunpath captives?" Degan asked in a low voice.

"The same." Goodeagle glanced around. "People are wondering about it."

"Do you think one of us has talked?" Klah asked.

Off to the side, by a huge pile of hides, an old man cried, "How long are we going to have to wait? It's been days!"

Grumblings of discontent followed as the closest camps picked it up.

"People are getting angry," Degan noted.

"There's been no word from the Council," Washani remar[ked] unlike Nashat to be missing for so long."

"Word is that Councilor Khepa sent a group of warriors i[nto the] caves, searching for the Guide." Klah glanced around u[neasily.] "Something's wrong."

Washani nodded. "I know." He rubbed his jaw, eyes on the pi[les of] loot and the uneasy people who stood by them. "Tensions are ris[ing."]

Degan crossed his arms. "My family wanted to bring a moun[tain] of things. I told them no. It didn't make my wife happy."

Klah shuffled his feet uneasily. "Since I have been home, it is as [I] were a stranger to my family. They have changed, grown fat and laz[y."]

Goodeagle looked around. "Who's going to carry all this?"

Washani smiled uneasily. "With the Sunpath captives gone, I'd sa[y] most of it is going to be left behind."

Klah's expression soured. "Think of how many good friends died to obtain this. And now it's going to be wasted?" He shook his head. "On the war trail I longed to be home. Now, home, I long for the war trail." He lifted a skeptical brow. "Even seeing stinking Goodeagle is a relief."

Goodeagle gave him a weak smile. "Well, I won't bother you with my stink."

He turned, walking toward the great cave. The way threaded through packed people. The odor of their sweat, the smell of urine, and piles of feces almost gagged him. He could see the stewing resentment on the Nightland faces.

"When is the Guide going to *call* us!" kept echoing in his ears.

He wound through the mass, doing his best to ignore the swell of humanity. He raised his eyes, looking up at the thin arch of ice overhead. He could see boulders up there, frozen in place, but ready to fall.

What kinds of lunatics live in a place like this?

It made his skin crawl, and he had a sudden longing to be outside, in the air, where the world was still fresh.

Instead he forced himself through the crowd to where Bishka stood beside Rana, a war club in his hand. The warriors were glaring out at the crowd, who glared back at them.

"Good day," Goodeagle greeted.

"Is it?" Bishka asked. "I've been on my feet keeping the people back since before dawn." He shot Goodeagle a hard look. "Is it true that Karigi's chasing down Kakala?"

She gave a terse jerk of her head toward the rear. But he saw through her bravado, could sense the panic in her.

"Taking the opportunity to run?" he guessed.

The widening of her eyes betrayed her.

"Come, into this side cavern. Let's you and I talk."

She slumped in defeat, gave a nod, and walked slowly into the side tunnel.

Goodeagle lifted a hide flap, finding a storeroom in the ice, and motioned her in. She entered, staring about in the gloom. The place had been emptied in advance of the great journey to the Long Dark.

"What do you want?" she asked wearily.

"Where is Nashat?"

"I don't know."

"And the Guide?"

"I don't know that, either. But Nashat thinks he's a fool. All of this, it's a great trick. There is no hole in the ice. No paradise in the Long Dark. Nashat told me that much." She lifted her eyes. "If you ask me, Nashat's fled."

He reached up, fingering her long black hair. "Then it was all for nothing?"

She looked up at him with wide dark eyes. "What do I have to do? If I lie with you again, will you let me go?"

A slow smile crossed his lips. That might be just what he needed to restore his wounded soul. "I would like that."

She lowered the pack from her shoulders, unrolled a hide, and spread it on the floor. With a flourish, she pulled her dress over her head, and flipped her long black hair back. She stood before him, letting him admire her perfect body.

Whatever Nashat did to her, this new lack of modesty serves her well.

He undid his weapons belt, letting it clatter to the floor. She sighed, stepped back, and lowered herself to the hide, saying, "Your war shirt, too. Take it off. I'm tired of being chafed."

Goodeagle grinned, pulling his war shirt over his head, feeling the cold air prickle on his skin. He turned, selected a stone, and laid the garment there. When he turned back, Blue Wing was lying, ready for him, an odd gleam in her eyes.

Goodeagle stepped over and lowered himself, the tingle of anticipation already rising in his loins.

It annoyed him that she was dry when he forced himself into her.

How long had it been since he'd coupled with a woman who wanted him? What did it say about the quality of the life he'd come to lead?

With that knowledge, the wound in his soul opened. *You are not the only one with a cursed life, Blue Wing.*

She had locked her legs around his hips, her arms clasped at his back. He could feel her fingers, pressing, as if following his ribs.

The moment began to build, the anticipation of release stirring deep in his hips.

She sensed it, tightening herself around him, her arms shifting.

He was lost in the pulsing waves of pleasure. The faint pressure against his skin barely registered. . . . Then a terrible pain lanced deeply into his chest.

In that instant, he stared down into her eyes, feeling the white hot agony drive into the center of his being.

"I have had the pleasure of your shaft," she hissed, "now you have felt mine!"

He rolled off her, reaching around to finger the handle of a bone stiletto where it protruded from between his ribs just below the shoulder blade.

Numb with pain and shock, he barely registered as she grabbed up her dress and fled past the door hanging.

"By Raven Hunter," he whispered. "No."

He got his fingers around the handle, and with one desperate jerk, pulled it free. His scream echoed in the ice. He stared stupidly at the bloody stiletto, the ground and polished bone so familiar. *Mine!* His gaze went to the weapons belt; the stiletto's sheath gaped empty.

When did she . . . ? His war shirt lay folded on the stone. He clamped his eyes shut, remembering how he'd turned his back on her.

He blinked at the pain burning in his center, heart hammering with fear. His chest seemed to scream with searing agony, and an odd tingle began deep in his throat. He stared in disbelief at the bright red blood frothing down his side.

A lung. She punctured a lung.

Goodeagle could hear shouts from beyond his shelter. Had they caught her?

He forced himself to his feet, wincing, hating the fear more than the pain. He staggered past the hanging, wandered down the tunnel, and stopped short, propping himself against the cold ice, heedless of his bare skin.

"Dead!" a warrior called, running toward the front. "The Guide is dead! Murdered!"

More shouts broke out from near the entrance. Goodeagle coughed, feeling warm fluid on his lips.

He forced himself to stagger forward, blinking, feeling as if his soul were already loose in his body.

He slumped to the floor, oddly weak, and watched the milling confusion as Bishka and Rana were overrun by the pressing crowd. In an endless stream, people hurried past, filing into the caverns.

Goodeagle watched them go, coughing blood, gasping for breath. He leaned back against the ice, thankful for the cold on his skin.

No one noticed him, but the Nightland People continued to pass, shouting in fear and confusion. It all grew faint as Goodeagle began to shiver.

The pool of blood around his buttocks spread, frothy and red, as his life drained away.

"Bramble, Windwolf, I'm so sorry. . . ."

He toppled on his side as the world turned gray.

Sixty-eight

The spruce gave way to willows as Kakala led the way down the sloping bank that led to Lake River. He pushed through the greening stems of willows, aware of the first mosquitoes that hummed up from the damp earth.

Summer would be coming, and with it, a plague of insects. Time was close when he'd need to brew a concoction of spruce, sticky geranium, and nightshade leaves to mix with grease. The concoction worked to keep the worst of the mosquitoes, bots, and black flies at bay.

But that was for another day, assuming they all lived that long. By pushing, they had reached the river, and just in time. He had seen the worry on Windwolf's face as the weaker of the captives that dogged their path dropped behind. Now only three women remained with them. All Windwolf had managed to save.

Kakala stepped out onto the gravel shore. Was it his imagination, or was the river running higher? The normally wide channel should have been covered by interlaced snakes of current. When he had crossed no less than a moon past, there had been six distinct channels. Now there were four.

"I don't know," he muttered as the rest of them stepped out onto the rocky beach beside him. "Water's up. Most of the stones in the ford are covered. Think we ought to make camp and try it in the morning?"

Skimmer fixed him with her oddly luminous eyes. "No. Karigi is right behind us."

Kakala looked back at the willows, able to see the tips of the spruce rising above them. "You're sure?"

"Trust her," Windwolf said, as he wearily stretched his tired muscles. "Only a fool argues with a Dreamer. She may serve Raven Hunter, but he also serves his Dreamer."

"We go," Keresa decided, her attention on the river. "But if Karigi's that close, we should take measures."

"Wade up the current? Hide our trail?" Skimmer asked in a hollow voice. "No time."

Kakala took matters into his own hands, picking his way through the rounded stones to the first channel. He splashed into the water, trying to remember where the shallow places were.

Cold leached through his moccasins, biting his tired feet. He stared at the water, reading the ripples of current, winding his way across the slippery bottom. The amount of silt in the water surprised him; it obscured the bottom, hiding the rocks he hoped to use for purchase.

Behind him, Skimmer, Kakala, Windwolf, and the rest followed behind.

"You know what you're doing?" Windwolf called over the purling water.

"Of course," he lied. "This was my main trail south. I had to cross this every time I made a raid."

But the river hadn't been running this high. He looked nervously upstream. Had a storm passed? But when? And why hadn't he seen the distant clouds?

"The end of the world, War Chief," Skimmer chided, her knowing eyes flashing. "We don't have much time. You had best hurry."

Kakala wadded onward, sloshing through the cold water, wincing as the current tried to pull his feet off the rounded rocks.

He was up to his thighs, fighting for purchase, as he studied the rushing water. What gave the current such added strength?

Slogging into shallows, he reached back, giving Skimmer a hand. Her skin was cool against his; her knowing smile as she met his eyes sent a curious calm through him.

What was it about her? He shook his head, making sure the rest climbed, dripping, onto one of the rocky islands. Even as he watched, the water seemed to be rising, creeping in around dry stones.

"Come on," he ordered, almost trotting across the dry rock and wading into the next current.

Then he stopped, staring at the rocks. Yes, that black one. A gravel bank lay just to the west of it. He changed his course, splashing along upriver as he hurried.

"Look!" Windwolf shouted, pointing.

A tree came floating down the next channel, branches broken, roots rotating as the great pine rolled along with the river.

"One of those catches us, we're gone," Keresa reminded.

Kakala led them safely to the next narrow strip of dry riverbed. He thought he heard a faint shout over the sound of the river, and looked back. The willows they had just left remained empty, almost forlorn in appearance.

Kakala watched as one of the Sunpath women stumbled, went down, and scrambled for shore. She emerged wet to the bone, looking cowed and worried.

The great tree had been beached, water breaking around the roots where it had come to rest against a submerged rock.

"No time to waste," Skimmer cried, wading into the next of the braided channels.

"No!" Kakala barked, pointing. "Over here. It's shallower."

He hurried forward, feeling the cold in his feet. Gods, they were already going numb! That's when he noticed the first piece of ice. He took a second glance, seeing a thin band of gravel in it as it floated past. Glacial ice? Here? This river drained Loon Lake, and he could think of no glacial ice anywhere around the perimeter of Loon Lake.

So where did it come from?

With rising unease, he frowned at the silt-choked water, trying to remember the path he'd used to cross last time. The great rock with the white quartz scar was the key. He lurched to the downstream side, where the current split, following a long flat rock that lay just under a U-shaped ripple.

Then he took a step, lost his footing, and sank. Cold washed around him, numbing, shocking his skin. He floundered around, losing his grip on his darts, letting the current take them. He got his feet under him and pushed off the bottom. Orienting himself, he fought the current and climbed up on a submerged gravel bank.

"I don't know another way!" he cried. "We'll just have to cross it."

He watched Skimmer bravely leap, splash, and almost keep her feet as she fought her way across. Then, one by one, they each made the crossing to the shallows.

"Trouble!" Keresa called as she rose dripping from the water. She pointed back to the bank.

Warriors were emerging from the willows they had just left. Kakala squinted across the distance, recognizing Karigi out in front. The river drowned the man's orders as he gestured his men forward.

"Does he know the ford?" Windwolf asked.

"As well as I do." Kakala turned, trotting into the next channel. He knew this one: Take the route that winds between the two gray boulders. Each had a long gravel bar behind it.

He sloshed through the water, stepped in a hole, and went down again. Fighting for purchase, he struggled as the current whirled him around. Frantic, he braced on a stone, and floundered ahead. Behind him, the others were coming, but one of the women was in trouble. The current was carrying her downstream.

"Leave her!" Skimmer ordered. "There's no time."

"But, someone—" Windwolf began.

"No!" Skimmer pinned him with hard eyes. "We make it now, or die!"

Kakala forced his way ahead, taking a quick glance over his shoulder. Karigi's men were splashing through the first channel, war darts in their hands.

"Up there!" Skimmer pointed as she hurried beside him. "That high rocky point!"

Kakala nodded, seeing where shale bedrock rose above the bank. A narrow trail led up the side, a place more fitted to deer than humans.

He splashed into the final channel, wading through water up to his chest. Mercifully, the current was slow here, but it kept dragging him downstream, his progress more swimming than anything else. Then, with each sodden step, he rose higher, finally climbing out on the rocks.

Karigi's warriors were crossing the second channel, just out of dart range.

"Hurry!" He pulled Skimmer up, indicating the trail. "Climb! Help the others up."

He pulled Keresa, and then Windwolf up the steep bank. Kishkat stopped to help, adding his strength as the floundering women, fear bright in their faces, were pulled from the water and started up the nearly vertical trail.

Windwolf stared at the pursuing warriors. "I don't suppose you have any ideas? I lost the last of my darts splashing around in the river."

"We all did," Kakala replied. "Let us hope they lose theirs, too."

Windwolf chuckled grimly, then attacked the steep trail. He made it partway up, moccasins slipping on the mud left by others. Kakala watched him grab a root and muscle himself up.

He barely heard the hissing dart over the growing roar of the river. It missed his shoulder by a finger's width and splintered against the shale.

Kakala scrambled for the now-greasy trail. He leapt, caught Windwolf's root, and prayed it would take his weight. Spruce root was fibrous stuff, good enough for constructing baskets. This one ripped loose, dropping him a couple of hands' length, then held.

Handhold by handhold, Kakala pulled himself up until Windwolf reached down to jerk him the rest of the way.

Gasping, Kakala flopped onto the moss-covered soil and asked, "Now what?"

He looked back at the river. Four lines of Karigi's warriors were tracing their way across the channels.

Keresa took long enough to ensure that Kakala was safe, then looked around. "We need weapons."

Windwolf nodded. "Did we lose all of our darts?"

"Oh, yes," Kakala told him darkly. "Running isn't going to do us much good, either. Not with that many behind us."

"Sticks, rocks, anything. Find them!" Keresa ordered, staring desperately around the shale formation on which they stood.

"It is time." Skimmer's voice had an eerie certainty that stopped Keresa short.

"Time?" she asked.

Skimmer unlaced the leather bundle from her belt and walked to the high lip of the shale formation. She raised the bundle high, a soft Song rising from her lips.

Windwolf started forward to pull her back out of sight but Kakala laid a hand on him, saying, "No, this is Power."

Keresa searched her soul, trying to hear the words that Skimmer Sang. They seemed oddly familiar, but alien, as if from another language. Then an odd prickling sensation began along Keresa's limbs, as though a warm wind was blowing.

A dart hissed through the air above them and vanished among the spruce branches. Keresa ducked, dropped to her belly, and crawled up to the edge. The river below them was washing over the small beach where they'd just passed.

"I wish she'd get down," Windwolf muttered as he slipped up next to Keresa."

"Can't you feel it?" she asked.

"Feel what?"

"The Power."

"No."

Keresa shook her head. "You belong to Wolf Dreamer."

In the river, Karigi's men were having troubles of their own. As she watched, two of the lead warriors waded into one of the channels, fighting the current, searching for footing. Both went under at the same time, bobbing up to be carried away thrashing and splashing. One managed to pull himself out in waist-deep water; the other continued to flounder about as he was carried farther downstream.

The great pine, Keresa noted, was no longer beached, but had been washed away. Two of the small islands they had crossed were no longer visible. A large chunk of ice came bobbing and spinning down the closest channel.

Skimmer's rich voice called, "Come, Raven Hunter! The time is now!"

Keresa watched in horror as the waters rose, sweeping more of Karigi's warriors away, whirling them about, whisking them downstream. Others turned back, desperate to return to the far bank. Some even made it.

"Karigi!" Kakala pointed as he came to kneel beside them.

She could see the war chief where he had climbed up onto a great boulder, wet and bedraggled. He kept looking about him in bewilderment as more and more of his warriors lost their footing and were swept away.

Terengi started to crawl up on the rock, only to have Karigi kick him viciously in the face. The man fell back, splashing into the current, and was carried headlong in the rush of the murky waters.

"Wolf Dreamer's flood," Windwolf said in awe. "This is from the broken ice dam far to the west."

"Here? It's come this far?" Keresa shook her head.

Skimmer bent her head back, shouting to the sky, "Call the thunder, Raven Hunter!"

The quake was unlike anything Keresa had ever felt. A great jolt shook the earth, pitching her body up from the ground.

Her reeling senses recorded a confusion of sights and sounds: the water in the river leaping, vibrating, and rising in spikes of spray; Karigi toppling from his boulder as it rose and fell; trees swaying; and odd spurts of dirt, duff, and twigs rising from the very earth.

Somehow she managed to grasp Windwolf's hand as they bounced like cones on the pitching shale.

Somewhere through the roar, she swore she heard a great mammoth trumpeting in fear.

Sixty-nine

Blue Wing gasped for breath as she climbed to the high point and looked back. She could barely see the Nightland camps where they tucked up under the jagged wall of the Ice Giants. From this distance, the great cavern was little more than a dark spot in the grimy ice.

I am free.

She walked up to one of the erratic boulders that littered the high ridge and leaned against it, looking back, wondering at what she had lost: her husband, a son and daughter, the sanctity of her body.

"And part of my soul," she whispered. She looked down at her hand, remembering the feel of the bone stiletto she'd driven between Goodeagle's ribs.

Did I really do that?

The great quake caught her by surprise. The land leapt, and a rolling thunder filled the air. She barely had time to claw her way to her feet when she pitched sideways. The great stone she had been leaning against rolled on its base and toppled, just missing her.

For too many heartbeats the ground shook, pebbles and gravel leaping as she staggered for balance. Silt rose in a low cloud, only to be carried away by the wind.

And then it was gone. She lay panting, trembling with terror, the thunder fading off to the south.

For a moment, the world was silent, as if holding its breath.

An earsplitting squeal erupted from the Ice Giants, followed by a deep-throated groan.

"Wolf Dreamer, help me." She started, rising to stare back at the Ice Giants.

Blue Wing watched as the first massive slab of ice cracked loose. It seemed to hang, moving slowly, as if lowering tentatively into the Thunder Sea. Where it sank, white water foamed and a stunning wave of water rolled away from it, traveling at unbelievable speed. The floating bergs rose and fell like a ripple of dots.

Blue Wing stared in disbelief as the great wave spread like a huge ring. It raced across the narrow band of water, rushing up the southern shore, covering the tundra. As it engulfed the land, it dislodged the grounded bergs, tossing them high up on the pockmarked land. Then the water seemed to settle for a moment, filling the hollows, swirling around the hillocks and drumlins.

Behind it, the beach remained bare, reefs of rounded rock sticking up like pimples on the naked seafloor. Then the remnants of the wave began to flow back across the denuded shores, and the roar of it came thundering across the land. She felt the power of it by the trembling of the earth beneath her, and the rumble that deafened her ears.

As she watched, a series of cracks shot through the bellies of the Ice Giants, racing away in every direction, and another slab sloughed off. It crashed into the lake. Then another peeled off and fell with what seemed an agonizing slowness. The massive waves that rolled away smashed into the backwash of the first. Giant geysers of white shot high into the air; the mist rainbowed in the sunlight.

Terrified birds fluttered this way and that like disoriented bats. An arctic hare ran past her in panic.

In one gigantic grinding wail, a piece of ice bigger than all of Nightland country broke free. . . .

The lake exploded. A wall of water raced through the pitching waves for the shore.

It came like thunder, the sound growing louder by the instant. The great wave overwhelmed the draining waters of the first, thrusting them back into the rocks and old ice that lined the tundra.

Blue Wing watched in stunned amazement as the edge of it rushed across the land below her, churning, dashing, shooting high as it engulfed the country she had just crossed. The rumble of it shook her, shivering her very bones.

In panicked immobility, she watched wide-eyed as it rolled up almost to her feet, and slowed.

To the south, the Thunder Sea rushed through the hilly moraines, spilling out across the uneven ground in a wild torrent.

The earthquake trembled to a stop, but a new roar filled the air.

As more and more water poured through, the gap widened and sent the icy lake water crashing down what had been the narrow channel of Windigo River. The wave pushed a flood of enormous rocks and chunks of frozen earth before it, scouring the channel.

The water had overflowed the banks of the river and was flooding out like a black sea, washing toward the distant ridge where Headswift Village stood.

Blue Wing climbed uneasily to her feet as the water below her began to drain away. Every hollow was filled; rivulets were being cut into the slopes before her eyes.

Every vestige of the Nightland Caves and villages had been wiped clean. The beach below the camps stretched empty, the water far down the gentle slope. Damp mud glistened in the sunlight with an eerie sheen. Here and there, great rivers of backwash roared back toward the dancing waters of the Thunder Sea.

She had no idea how long she stared, but a distant wall of white caught her eye. It lay along the eastern horizon of the narrow Thunder Sea, a hazy thin band.

She looked at the exposed mud flats where water had once rested, thought about the waves that had washed out of the basin, and looked back at the distant band of white.

Was it bigger now?

"Water always finds its own level," she whispered. And the Thunder Sea ran right into the ocean.

She turned and ran.

Seventy

For two days following the great quake, Silvertip led his people eastward along the ridges. Behind them, the water continued to rise, slipping up valleys, spilling into hollows.

At last he topped a final ridge, following a path between large pines. He stopped, staring, stunned to see with his eyes what his Spirit had known only in Dreams.

Ashes came to stand beside him, her war club resting on her shoulder. He heard her sudden gasp of disbelief. Lookingbill and Dipper walked up on either side, standing in silent awe.

Below them, what had been Lake River Valley had become what at first appeared to be a flat plane that extended almost without relief to the distant peaks of the Ice Giants. To the eye it seemed like flat land at first, until a decided movement became apparent, as if the great expanse of plain moved inexorably to the east.

Looking closer, the observer realized that what passed for matted earth was floating debris consisting of rafts of uprooted trees, icebergs, tangles of wood, sticks, and branches. Most, however, was duff and leaves floated from the forest floor. Occasional clear patches of water, like cracks, gleamed a gray granitic sheen.

Close to the shore Silvertip could see the bloated carcass of a mammoth, the long red hair of its hide clotted with debris. The great cow floated on her side, bobbing slightly, head turned down into the filthy brown water. He spotted other carcasses: a bison, two elk, and the dark hide of short-faced bear. All animals that had no chance to flee the great sprawling mass of water that had rolled out of the west.

In places, high ground stuck up, catching the great rafts of debris, holding it for a time, until the relentless eastern flow spun it one way or another and bore it relentlessly toward the distant ocean.

"So much water!" Lookingbill whispered under his breath. He swallowed hard. "Where . . . where is Headswift Village?"

Silvertip pointed. "There. That little knob in the distance." He turned his eyes on the pinprick amidst the debris-matted water.

"No one who stayed would have lived," Dipper said softly. "That water's up to the highest rocks."

"It's flowing through the passageways," Silvertip told them, "eating away at the base. Even the great rocks are collapsing, sinking down. When the water drains away, it will only be a low mound covered with silt."

"Is that a mammoth?" Dipper pointed to where a single calf stood perched on a shallow island to the east. It kept raising its trunk, as if scenting for its mother. Then it would whirl, splash down into the water where wood had collected. Raising its right foot, it would press anxiously at the floating wood, as if in search of solid footing. Finding none, the calf retreated to the limited sanctuary of the rounded hump of land. Even as they watched, the saturated ground seemed to be sliding under the calf's feet. Panicked, it whirled and dashed about in ever smaller circles, destroying its haven as it went.

Ashes swallowed hard. "When will the flood subside?"

"Our children may see it." Silvertip watched the mammoth calf with a leaden soul. "The trees will slowly wash out into the ocean, carrying the carcasses of dead animals, and those few that survived by clinging to the wood: squirrels, raccoons, some beaver."

"The size of it," Lookingbill cried. "It runs all the way to the Ice Giants. What of the Nightland?"

"Gone," Silvertip told him. "Washed away. Their corpses have already been carried off by the tides of the Thunder Sea."

"Raven Hunter's Dream?" Ashes asked.

"Alive," he said simply, and pointed to the south. "The Raven

W. Michael Gear and Kathleen O'Neal Gear

Bundle is there. I can feel it, like a darkness on the land." He glanced at Ashes. "Your mother lives."

"What now, Dreamer?" Lookingbill asked. "What do we do?"

Silvertip filled his lungs, smelling the odors of wet wood, earth, and water. "We go south. There we will meet up with the remains of the Sunpath People who are fleeing to the Tills. It will not be easy. The forest peoples down there won't be pleased to see us encroach upon them. We will need Silt's warriors."

"More war?" Dipper asked.

"Raven Hunter has rebalanced the Spiral," Silvertip whispered. "Where there is order, there will be conflict."

He bent down, grasping a handful of soil. Then, slowly, he opened his fingers, letting it trickle away through his fingers.

In the distance, the mammoth calf trumpeted in fear as it crumbled its fragile island beneath its feet.

Epilogue

Windwolf sat on a high outcrop of limestone and watched the northern horizon. The band of brown hung low in the sky, like a great distant smoke that ran from horizon to horizon. Wind whipped white strands of hair around his lined face.

He coughed, hating the nagging tickle in his lungs. It had become a constant thing over the summers after the end of the world.

He could never rest on a high place without thinking of the great flood. Memories of the time they'd spent watching Lake River swell into a huge torrent remained, as did their frantic flight to the south as the river washed over the shale bench and pursued them through the forest trails.

He wondered: Was any of that country left?

Below him, the great forest—oak and hickory, walnut and beech—stretched off to the distant north, still and green in the summer. The carpet of forest undulated over distant ridges until it merged with the far brown haze.

In the valley below him, a great river ground away at its limestone banks. So much water, but nothing like he'd seen in the north.

At the soft padding of Keresa's feet, he looked up, smiling as she came to sit beside him. The faint breeze tugged at her graying hair. He envied her for that; his own had gone white years ago.

"Any change?" she asked, pointing at the distant brown cloud. Her hands had hardened with time, the bones knobby under thin and wrinkled skin.

"No." He turned his eyes to it. "The winds are still carrying it east."

When the west or north winds blew across the great empty lake beds of the north, they picked up the loose silt and rock dust, carrying it far and wide to settle on the land in a fine dust. Most of the country up north had been abandoned, unfit for man or beast. In places the wind-blown silt could be seen in cut banks, taller than a man. It had suffocated the land. Where once mammoths had fed on lush grasses, dark silt now piled in rippled dunes that stretched for as far as the eye could see. According to the few hardy individuals that dared journey there, the north had become a dead zone.

Winters had grown colder as well.

When the silt blew south, people tended to stay in, their faces wrapped with cloth. Despite that, most people had developed the common cough after years of enduring the fine dust.

Windwolf grimaced. At those times, the sun was gone for days. People huddled in their lodges, waiting out the long dark days. He wondered if that was what Ti-Bish had meant. If so, it was certainly no paradise.

On the other hand, where the silt fell, and the rains came, the forest seemed to swell with life. Nut crops were plentiful; cattails and goosefoot grew. The deer, elk, and bison thrived.

Keresa said, "Silvertip and Ashes have sent a runner. They are holding a gathering again this summer." She shot him a curious glance. "As usual they have invited Skimmer."

"And again, she will have nothing to do with it." Windwolf reached down, toying with the grass before him. "Did Kakala show any interest in going?"

"No. He's happy to stay with her." Keresa looked out at the distant brown haze. "Now that Black Bird has taken the Raven Bundle, Kakala wishes to concentrate on raising his own sons."

Windwolf shot her a knowing look. "She had the boy less than six moons after Kakala began sharing her robes."

Keresa kept her level eyes fixed on the distant haze. "Black Bird is Ti-Bish's child. No doubt about it. He has that wide-eyed look."

Windwolf pulled the grass up, chewing thoughtfully on the stem. "Kakala doesn't care. He owes his happiness to Skimmer. Only a woman with her Power could have put his ghosts to rest."

"Then I must be full of Power, too." She gave his bony knee a squeeze. "Not only did I cure your ghosts, but I gave you four strong children in return."

He gave her his wary grin. "They tell the other young people that they had two fathers for parents. That you were tougher on them than I was."

She chuckled at that; then her voice turned serious. "Chief Silt sent a message to you. He wanted you to know that Blue Wing died last moon."

Windwolf nodded. She hadn't been doing well. "I owed her. Had she not survived and married Silt, I would never have known what happened to Goodeagle."

"Would it have mattered after all these years?"

"It would have."

She studied him. "Windwolf, so many summers have passed, Kishkat's and Tapa's children have grown and married into Silt's band. No one cares that some of us were once Nightland People. We could join their band, become one with them."

Windwolf shook his head sadly. "Skimmer wouldn't go. She and Silvertip . . . they just wouldn't see eye to eye. War Chief Ashes would side with her husband, even if she follows Raven Hunter's Dream."

"Separate and opposite?" she asked.

He nodded. "Silvertip told me the Spiral is just beginning to regain its balance. Let's give the earth some time before the Wolf and Raven Bundles clash again. Until we are gone, our little band will be the last of the Nightland and of Ti-Bish's Dream."

She wound her fingers into his. "I don't care. As long as I can Dream it with you."

In the forest behind them, a great black wolf watched with glowing yellow eyes. He often followed the man through the forest, watching, studying the man's ways.

The only warning came as the soft whisper of wings. The black wolf ducked nimbly to the side, then leapt and snapped as the big black raven dove low over his head.

The bird cawed, flipped over on its back, and disappeared behind the trees.

The wolf watched it go. There would always be another opportunity. This thing between him and Raven was only beginning.

Afterword

At the time of the cataclysm, PaleoIndians lived near the ice, and made their camps along the borders of the gigantic lakes. In fact, some of the oldest archaeological sites in North America are found close to what was—when the prehistoric peoples lived there—the edge of a melting glacier: the Udora site in Ontario; Debert site in Nova Scotia; Michaud site in Maine; Whipple site in New Hampshire; Meadowcroft Rockshelter, Shawnee-Minisink, and Shoop sites in Pennsylvania; Bull Brook in Massachusetts; the Hiscock and Dutchess Quarry Caves sites in New York; the Hebior–Schaefer in Wisconsin; and in Michigan, the Holcombe, Gainey, Rappuhn, and Barnes sites—all of which reliably date to between 11,000 and 14,000 years ago.

In the area where *People of the Nightland* is set, archaeologists have identified three distinct cultures of PaleoIndian hunters. We call them Gainey, Debert, and Parkhill, after the locations where their distinctive fluted spear points were found. For a general introduction to the archaeology, we recommend Peter L. Storck's excellent *Journey to the Ice Age*. Other resources are contained in the bibliography.

Why would human beings have been drawn to one of the most inhospitable environments on earth? First of all, the area immediately adjacent to the ice was certainly tundra and there is evidence of permafrost, but a short distance to the south, the Pleistocene taiga—which formed a belt along the southern margin of the ice—consisted of spruce, jack pine, and oak. The taiga also had many parklike meadows filled with shrubs. At Meadowcroft Rockshelter in Pennsylvania, the archaeologists discovered nutshells, wood, and charcoal from walnut and hickory trees. We call these places *refugia*, that is, sheltered locations that fostered a more temperate ecology. Probably many such refugia existed around the glacial margins.

This is important because the taiga meadows would have provided big game animals with better grazing and browsing opportunities, and *that's* why prehistoric peoples camped there. Kill a ground squirrel and one person can eat for a night. Kill a mammoth and a village can eat for a month.

Try to imagine a world where extinct animals like mastodons, mammoths, giant ground sloths, tapirs, and camels walked alongside deer, fox squirrels, raccoons, and elk. Each year, huge flocks of ducks, geese, herons, and other migratory birds winged north with the spring. The largest bird in the sky was the California condor; its range extended over all of North America.

The prehistoric peoples were outstanding hunters. Their spear points—fashioned from a variety of stones and propelled by an atlatl, or throwing stick—could penetrate the rib cage of an adult mastodon. In fact, bones from mastodons, and to a lesser extent, mammoths, are among the most common Pleistocene fossils in the Great Lakes region. PaleoIndians were also master traders, exchanging goods across much of eastern North America. As well, we know from the Hiscock site in New York and Meadowcroft Rockshelter in Pennsylvania that they weaved nets and textiles.

So what happened 13,000 years ago?

Global warming peaked. The glaciers collapsed. Ice dams must have partially blocked the Mississippi River drainage and opened a new spillway along the eastern edge of Lake Agassiz, which resulted in catastrophic flooding. Eighty-five percent of the lake's volume rushed into the Nipigon Basin in western Ontario, and from there into the Superior and then the Huron Basins, and finally flooded out into the North Atlantic through what paleoclimatologists call the Champlain Sea. A small remnant of that sea is what we know today as the St. Lawrence River.

The final triggers for this cataclysmic event may have come from three sources. First, when sea levels rose enough to flood the Bering Strait 13,000 years ago, it established the Trans-Polar Current that sent warmer waters flowing into the Arctic Ocean, melted the sea ice there, and flooded the North Atlantic. Second, as the glaciers melted, the land that had been weighed down by the ice began to spring back. This is called isostatic rebound. (Incidentally, this is happening today in the Alps. Recent surveys have demonstrated that the Alps are losing 1.5 billion tons of ice per year to global warming, and as the massive glaciers melt the reduction in weight on the peaks is causing the entire region to gain altitude. Italian glaciologist Claudio Smiraglia and his colleagues reported this in their excellent article in the July 28, 2006, issue of *Geophysical Research Letters*.)

Also, 13,000 years ago, when the land began to spring back, there were strong earthquakes that probably helped to further destabilize the glaciers. Lastly, ice cores taken in Greenland verify that one of the most volcanically active periods in the past 100,000 years was the period from about 8,000 to 15,000 years ago. It's possible that this flurry of volcanic eruptions resulted from the stresses on the earth's crust that accompanied isostatic rebound. But whatever the reasons, these eruptions spewed enormous amounts of dust and sulfuric acid into the atmosphere and dramatically affected the global climate, resulting in decades of "volcanic winters."

Also, keep in mind that glaciers grind up rock and gravel, creating a fine dust. As the glaciers melted, this powdery sediment settled into the meltwater lakes. As the lakes in turn drained, wind scoured the thick layers of fine dust and silt, blowing great clouds of it to carpet eastern North America. Geologists call this wind-deposited dust loess, and in places deposits were sixty and seventy feet thick. We can only imagine the terrible impact those huge dust storms had on the local flora and fauna. Suffice to say that when the dust finally stopped blowing, mammoth, mastodon, dire wolf, short-faced bear, condor, giant beaver, and giant sloth were extinct in eastern North America.

Our goal in writing the *People* books is to allow our readers to see through the eyes of prehistoric cultures, in the hope that we can learn from them. In this regard, we are often helped by historical records. For example, eyewitness accounts of similar volcanic events proved extremely valuable in writing *People of the Nightland*, particularly accounts from the second century AD, when there were a series of explosive eruptions in Alaska. Chinese historians during this time period recorded that "several times the sun rose in the east red as blood and lacking light . . . only when it had risen to an elevation of more than two zhang (24 degrees) was there any brightness. . . ." Perhaps one of the most chilling chronicles of these eruptions was written in AD 186 by the Romans: "The heavens were ablaze . . . stars were seen all the day long . . . hanging in the air which was a token of a cloud . . ."

We are also helped a great deal by the oral histories of the native peoples. There are many stories of terrible floods. After the Yavapai emerged into this world, they failed to close the hole to the underworld and it caused a great flood. Tears of mourning often cause floods, as in the Kathlamet story about Beaver crying for his lost wife, or among the Cherokee when Mother Sun's beloved daughter dies from a rattlesnake bite and her tears cause a flood. The Wiyot story of Above-Old-Man and the Arapaho story of Neshanu tell of how the creator grew unhappy with human beings and flooded the world to cleanse it. The Pawnee creator, Tirawahat, flooded the world to kill the evil giants who lived there. The Cree culture hero, Wesucechak, fought the powerful water lynxes after the great flood to avenge the death of his brother.

These stories may have been inspired by the great flood of 13,000 years ago that brought about a global climatic reversal, rolling the Earth back into an Ice Age we call the Younger Dryas.

Academically oriented readers may question whether people inhabited the ice caves. While the violence of the collapsing glaciers probably erased any such evidence, we know that modern Inuit build houses out of ice and snow for protection from the elements, and the honeycomb of glacial caves would have provided similar shelter from the winter winds, as well as a handy deep-freeze for long-term food storage. Finding evidence for such is a daunting task, but a fertile field for investigation.

Lastly, for those who think the Pleistocene Ice Age ended ten thousand years ago, let us suggest that it may not have. This current warm episode, the Holocene, encompasses only about half a percent of the Quaternary Period. Which means today's climate could be just another in a long line of brief warming periods.

As you listen to the news tonight remember that Ice Ages are almost always heralded by sudden episodes of global warming.

In fact, with atmospheric carbon dioxide at the highest level it's been in the past 750,000 years . . . we're overdue.

Selected Bibliography

Agenbroad, Larry D., et al. *Megafauna and Man: Discovery of America's Heartland.* Northern Arizona University, Flagstaff, and the Mammoth Site of Hot Springs, South Dakota, 1990.

Bonnichsen, Robson, and Karen L. Turnmire. *Clovis: Origins and Adaptations.* Corvallis, Oregon: Center for the Study of First Americans, 1991.

Bradley, Raymond S. *Paleoclimatology: Reconstructing Climates of the Quaternary.* Amsterdam: Elsevier Academic Press, 1999.

Bryant, Vaughn M., and Richard G. Holloway. *Pollen Records of Late Quaternary North American Sediments.* Dallas: The American Association of Stratigraphic Palynologists Foundation, 1985.

Deller, Brian D., and Christopher J. Ellis. *Thedford II: A Paleo-Indian Site in the Ausable River Watershed of Southwestern Ontario.* Memoirs of the Museum of Anthropology. No. 24. University of Michigan, 1992.

Dixon, E. James. *Bones, Boats, and Bison: Archeology and the First Colonization of Western North America.* Albuquerque: University of New Mexico Press, 1999.

Ellis, Christopher, and Jonathan C. Lothrop. *Eastern Paleoindian Lithic Resource Use.* San Francisco: Westview Press, 1989.

Fagan, Brian M. *Ancient North America: The Archaeology of a Continent.* London: Thames and Hudson, 2000.

Guthrie, R. Dale. *Frozen Fauna of the Mammoth Steppe: The Story of Blue Babe.* Chicago: University of Chicago Press, 1990.

Hansel, A. K., D. M. Mickelson, A. F. Schneider, and C. E. Larson. "Late Wisconsinian and Holocene History of the Lake Michigan Basin." *Quaternary Evolution of the Great Lakes.* Eds. P. F. Karrow and P. E. Calken. Geological Association of Canada Special Paper No. 30, 1985: 39–53.

Haynes, Gary. *Mammoths, Mastodons, and Elephants: Biology, Behavior and the Fossil Record.* Cambridge: Cambridge University Press, 1991.

Helm, June, ed. *Handbook of North American Indians.* Vol. 6. Washington, D.C.: Smithsonian Institution, 1981.

Jablonski, Nina, ed. *The First Americans: Pleistocene Colonization of the New World.* Memoirs of the California Academy of the Sciences. No. 27.

Jackson, Lawrence J. *The Sandy Ridge and Halstead Paleo-Indian Sites: Unifacial Tool Use and Gainey Phase Definition in South-Central Ontario.* Memoirs of the Museum of Anthropology. Ann Arbor: University of Michigan, 1998.

Martin, Paul S., and Richard G. Klein. *Quaternary Extinctions: A Prehistoric Revolution.* Tucson: University of Arizona Press, 1989.

Mead, Jim, and David J. Meltzer. *Environments and Extinctions: Man in Late Glacial North America.* Orono, Maine: Center for the Study of Early Man, 1985.

Pearson, James L. *Shamanism and the Ancient Mind: A Cognitive Approach to Archaeology.* New York: Altamira Press, 2002.

Peilou, E. C. *After the Ice Age: The Return of Life to Glaciated North America.* Chicago: University of Chicago Press, 1991.

Roosa, W. B. "Great Lakes Paleo-Indians: The Parkhill Site, Ontario." *Amerinds and Their Paleoenvironments in Northeastern North America.* Eds. Walter S. Newman and Bert Salwin. New York: Annals of the New York Academy of Sciences, 1977. No. 288: 349–354.

Saunders, Jeffery J. "A Model for Man-Mastodon Relationships in Late Pleistocene North America." *Canadian Journal of Anthropology* 1.1, 1981: 87–98.

Storck, Peter L. *The Fisher Site: Archaeological, Geological and Paleobotanical Studies at an Early Paleo-Indian Site in Southern Ontario, Canada.* Memoirs of the Museum of Anthropology. Ann Arbor: University of Michigan, 1997.

Storck, Peter L. *Journey to the Ice Age: Discovering an Ancient World.* Vancouver: UBC Press, 2004.

Straus, Lawrence Guy, et al. *Humans at the End of the Ice Age: The Archaeology of the Pleistocene-Holocene Transition.* New York: Plenum Press, 1996.